EVEN IF
EVERYTHING
ENDS

EVEN IF

EVERYTHING

ENDS

JENS LILJESTRAND

TRANSLATED BY ALICE MENZIES

SCOUT PRESS

NEW YORK   LONDON   TORONTO   SYDNEY   NEW DELHI

Scout Press
An Imprint of Simon & Schuster, Inc.
1230 Avenue of the Americas
New York, NY 10020

First Scout Press hardcover edition May 2023

SCOUT PRESS and colophon are registered trademarks of Simon & Schuster, Inc.

For information about special discounts for bulk purchases, please contact Simon &
Schuster Special Sales at 1-866-506-1949 or business@simonandschuster.com.

The Simon & Schuster Speakers Bureau can bring authors to your live event.
For more information or to book an event, contact the Simon & Schuster Speakers
Bureau at 1-866-248-3049 or visit our website at www.simonspeakers.com.

Interior design by Kathryn A. Kenney-Peterson

Manufactured in the United States of America

10 9 8 7 6 5 4 3 2 1

Library of Congress Control Number: 2022947394

ISBN 978-1-6680-0501-9
ISBN 978-1-6680-0503-3 (ebook)

Hilary Mantel, *Bring Up the Bodies* (Picador, 2013).

Bruno K. Öijer, "Even if Everything Comes to an End" from *While the Poison Acts*
(Wahlstrom & Widstrand, 1990). Translation by Victoria Häggblom.
By permission of Bruno K. Öijer.

Tomas Tranströmer; "Romanesque Arches" from *For the Living and the Dead*
(Albert Bonniers Förlag, 1989). Translation by Robin Fulton.

For Tove

There are no endings. If you think so you are
deceived as to their nature. They are all beginnings.
Here is one.

Hilary Mantel, *Bring Up the Bodies*

1

THE FIRST DAY OF
THE REST OF YOUR LIFE

THE LAST TIME I WAS HAPPY, WE WERE AT A RETAIL PARK. Society had finally opened up again, and we drove out there with the kids, past the roundabouts and the Ikea, the electronics store, another selling appliances, a huge supermarket, to the place she had found: the last physical shop for that kind of thing now that everything had shifted online. We wanted to go there in person, actually see it with our own eyes, allow ourselves to get drunk on longing for our child.

Carola was in the baby carriage section, on her face the blank alienation of someone who has entered a shrine to a religion she's aware of but has never actually belonged to, waddling and heavy as the kids who would soon be getting a younger sibling ran among the shelves, between the teddy bears and blankets in shades of baby blue and flamingo pink, changing tables and cribs and beds, pacifiers and oils and bottles, breast pumps and nursing bras and nursing blouses and nursing armchairs, educational wooden toys and electronic monitors that told you when the baby woke up or let you watch the baby as it slept or gave you temperature and carbon dioxide readings for the air around the baby.

Then the kids stopped dead in the middle of the shop. *Oh my God*, they said. *Oh my God, look.* They pointed at the rows of adorable onesies and hats and unbelievably small socks. There was a vulnerability to those tiny garments that was almost unbearable, and they stroked the fabric, buried their noses in the material, and sniffed it as though it were a baby, as though their little sister had already arrived, and our eyes met over the shelves and we smiled at having made the right decision to come to such a crazy commercial place, at having brought the kids with us to help them understand, so that they could see and feel the flannel-soft wind that would soon blow through our lives, changing them forever, and I heard myself say, *Just grab whatever you want.*

My family stared at me in confusion. We were only supposed to be looking at one of the baby carriages, we wanted a point of reference before we bought secondhand, we always bought secondhand, and Carola said something about our carbon footprint, about a cousin whose daughter was about to outgrow her clothes, but I said, *Please, just this once, please please please just grab whatever you want.*

She froze to the spot, helplessly watching as the children's eyes lit up and, with a series of thrilled hoots, they filled their hands and arms with comforters and slings and a huge baby gym made from gasoline-blue cashmere. But before long she started looking around herself, asking the woman behind the counter about cloth diapers, about organic fabrics and ethical, climate-neutral clothing, whether they had any bath sets that were *slightly* less plasticky, where the cotton in those nice polka-dot cushions came from. Everything she wanted cost twice as much as anything else, but I just laughed and grabbed a cart, and as she was standing with her back to me, I took out my phone and transferred more money.

Once our baskets were full and our love for all things cute and sweet had been sated to a dull satisfaction, she and I walked back over to the baby carriages. Suddenly the only choice was the luxury French model that had won best in test, with a chassis that had taken five years to develop. We chose fabrics for the mattress and the sun hood and the rain cover; we chose phone holders, cup holders, bag holders; we chose everything there was to choose.

The woman behind the register rang up our things and managed, somehow, to find a breezy way to say that we could return the baby carriage for a full refund *if anything did happen*. And despite her carefree, cheery tone—*we'd just need to see a little medical certificate*—it was as though everything ground to a halt and we saw the blood on the toilet seat, the deafening ambulance ride, a tiny coffin, a grizzled old gynecologist polishing his glasses and writing *a little medical certificate*, having to come back here, having to bring the baby carriage with the beautiful designer fabrics and cognac-colored leather accents on the handle back to this grotesque temple to consumerism, and I heard her whisper into the void: *Mommy'll have to do that if so.*

But even that anxiety faded, even that moment passed, and all that was left was the sum total, the numbers on the display, a figure that was slightly larger than the amount I'd paid for my first car.

"Would you like to put it on credit?" the woman asked with a dazzling, inviting smile. I glanced around the shop and noticed the other fathers for the first time—the harried soccer fan in the team shirt, the immigrant in the crumpled suit, the man in the leather jacket and taped-up glasses—and I realized that that was how it worked. People have to borrow for that kind of thing, they take out text loans, pay interest, arrangement fees, late payment fees, they sit in their cramped suburbs and chip away at the bill for their teddy bears and blankets and carriages one monthly paycheck at a time, and the feeling of pride inside me grew.

"No, no," I said, holding out my card. "I'll pay the full amount now."

And Carola stood right beside me; she reached up to my forehead as though I had a fever and mumbled that we could look elsewhere, we might be able to find a nearly new baby carriage online, but all I could feel and hear was her hands in my hair, her fingers on the back of my neck, and *are you sure, are you really sure?* She touched me, she finally touched me, I couldn't remember the last time she had touched me, *it's fine, honey, I've got this*, and the way she looked at me right then, the person I was in her eyes, when everything was forgiven, when everything was perfect and so goddamn well deserved.

MONDAY, AUGUST 25

THERE'S A SPOT BETWEEN THE SMOOTH, TAUT SKIN ON HER FORE-head and her already thick, dark hair. A downy, indeterminate point that occasionally—especially when it's hot and dusky, as it is right now—shifts over to her temple or behind her ear or the fontanelles, even the back of her neck; a spot where I can bury my nose and smell the scent of velvety skin and sweet, dried-on milk, slightly sharper when she hasn't had a bath for a few days, almost like mature cheese. Her weight in my arms is like a sack of warm, freshly ground beef, the consistency of raw sausage, carefully fed into the casing with damp hands to avoid splitting the delicate surface; no tension or swelling, no muscles or calluses, and drowsiness blurs the boundary between her and me and everything comes down to breathing and soft, warm, sticky tissue. She's naked except for her diaper, it's been months since she last slept in pajamas, it's too hot.

Becka has finished her bottle and burped over my shoulder and we've dozed off together when the first sirens echo through my dreams, distant and unimportant at first, like the beeping of a dishwasher or a tumble dryer at the end of its cycle, just part of the never-ending hum, growing clearer thirty seconds or so later, cutting through the filter, through the bubble, right in to us.

"It's probably just a car bomb," Carola mumbles with her back to me, an old joke from our semester in Malmö. A couple we hung out with there lived close to the violence, criminality right on their doorstep. The older girl was from the countryside and she found the whole thing terrifying, but her girlfriend was born and raised in the heart of the city and she radiated that typical slow Malmö calm, the constant shrugging and the thick drawl as she proudly described how she had learned to accept the social problems as *a natural part of the urban landscape*, the only people who complained about the crime and the violence were racists, *it's not necessarily a shooting if you hear a bang at night, y'know*, she continued, her pierced lower lip curled in slight disdain, *often it's just a car bomb*. We laughed at her forced butch attitude once they had gone home, and since then any disruption at night is always *just a car bomb*.

The sirens are getting closer, they must be out here on the country lanes now, maybe they're coming for the lonely old man in the blue house, the one with psoriasis all over his face, he must be well over seventy? But the emergency services wouldn't use sirens for a natural death, would they?

I lower Becka to the mattress. She whimpers and holds her arms in the air, her little body a tense arc, and I swing my feet down to the old wooden floor and walk over to the open window. It's not quite as hot as it was yesterday, probably only around eighty-six degrees, and there's a nice breeze, I can see the top of the big pine swaying and bending in the wind. The heat has broken, the wind has picked up, and the air finally feels a little less suffocating.

"It's going to be a nice day," I say to no one at all.

I can't hear a peep from the kids' room, so I knock and open the door. They're both sprawled on their beds with their screens and their headphones, the air so thick with the smell of dirty clothes and sugar and their languid little bodies that you could cut it with a knife, and I tell them to turn everything off and come downstairs, it's ten thirty. Vilja gives me her usual irritated glare, but Zack's face lights up and he triumphantly grabs the glass jar from his nightstand. Beside the tooth is a glittering gold coin.

"The tooth fairy came and she left ten kronor in my jar!"

"Wow, really? But she didn't take your tooth?"

"No, because she knows I'm collecting them! I'm saving them!"

"That's great."

"Dad?"

He smiles. A sugary, slightly over-the-top smile, one he has only started using since Becka was born and he realized he was no longer the youngest, whenever he's aware of his own childishness, when he knows he's doing something he should be too old for, a piece of theater he performs to make himself feel little again.

"Dad, do you think they have the tooth fairy in Thailand?"

I ruffle his damp hair, play along with the charade, possibly because I need this too.

"Of course they do, sweetheart. She's like Santa, she flies around the world, though she doesn't have any reindeer, she has . . ."

"Tooth trolls!"

"Yes! Tooth trolls that she's . . . caught, using . . . ?"

He doesn't need any more than a second to think.

"Using floss!"

We both smile at the shared fantasy, both equally smitten with the silly idea of the tooth fairy in a sleigh—made of teeth that have fallen out, glued together with toothpaste?—being pulled by a bunch of strong, angry tooth trolls. This is the kind of thing we do, did, we used to improvise stories for hours when he was younger, and I often thought that I should be writing them down, though of course I never did.

Yesterday's dirty dishes are still piled up in the kitchen, all the pots, pans, sticky plates, and wineglasses; we always forget to save water for the washing up. The Monopoly board and the stacks of money remind me that Carola let the kids win, that we argued afterward. I was concerned and started talking about rules and consequences, saying that sure, Zack is only ten, but a fourteen-year-old like Vilja needs to learn that she can't just take a wad of cash from the bank whenever she runs out of money, but Carola just smiled that sad, resigned smile of hers and said *they'll learn how capitalism works soon enough, sadly, that's unavoidable.*

Out of sheer habit, I try the tap. Nothing but a faint rattle, still. It bothers me less than it used to. We've got bottled water, we've got juice for the kids and beer for us. We can piss behind the tree, wash our clothes in the lake, wipe down the plates with a bit of paper towel. The only really unpleasant thing, the one thing I'd gladly pay to avoid, are the turd logs floating in the toilet bowl, which slowly fills up with more shit, more paper, and even more shit. We've been trying to get the kids to let us know so that we can help them with a chamber pot, but Zack always forgets and Vilja simply refuses, and in the end the whole thing inevitably needs cleaning out with a pot and a bucket while I listen to music through my headphones, breathe through my mouth, and put my brain on standby.

Zack is here now, already in his swimming trunks, he hasn't worn anything but swimming trunks for weeks now, and I hand him a glass of milk and watch as he drinks it down. Then we head out, him running ahead of me along the narrow gravel track, almost white with dust, the warm, dry wind caressing our arms and legs like a freshly laundered sheet, these lovely summer mornings, yellowing bushes and stubbly, overgrown lawns, dead flower beds, the silence and the bright blue sky and the silence, nothing but silence, there were sirens not long ago, but now there's nothing.

The old man isn't dead, he's squinting in the sunlight when we reach the jetty, the wind tugging at his gray windbreaker, the reddish crust on his cheeks less prominent than I remember it. The sun helps, of course.

"Are you still here?" He almost sounds annoyed.

"Yup," I say. "We rented our place out over the summer, so we—"

"You're still here," he says, in the same reproachful tone. "Most people left over the weekend."

"It's actually OK." The old guy bothers me, but not as much as my own reaction, the fact that I feel like I need to defend myself, like I'm seeking his approval. "Could be good for the kids to see the impact with their own eyes. It's so abstract if they only ever learn about it in school."

Zack runs straight past him, out onto the little scrap of sand by the jetty, looking for our things. The inflatable dolphin and the blow-up mattress we always play with are beneath the flaking wooden bench, along with a small toiletry bag containing soap and outdoor shampoo. He loves washing while he's splashing about in the water, the foam floating over the waves, *Dad, can we wash our hair?* he hoots, looking out across the empty lake with the proud gaze of a child who recently owned a hotel on Pennsylvania Avenue and three houses on Boardwalk.

The man watches the boy charging around. An imperceptible shake of the head.

"Can't you smell it?"

He raises his hand above his head and points back, toward the lake, his eyes locked on mine.

"Can't you see? It moved several miles overnight."

The lake, the waves, the froth farther out. The forest on the other side, green giving way to yellow and brown. And beyond that, among the tree-tops, a dark haze in the empty sky, like a thundercloud in motion, a sweeping, billowing formation.

The old man sniffs loudly, his nostrils flaring, and I automatically do the same. It makes my nose sting.

Smoke.

Zack is already sitting at the end of the jetty, the inflatable dolphin in his arms. He's talking to it, his nonstop, nasal, childish, introspective babbling. Air has leaked out of the toy, and the dolphin's body almost looks like a V in his arms.

———

For the next hour I feel more alive than I have in a long time. There's a sense of adventure to everything. I take a selfie with Zack down by the jetty, the lake behind us, then upload it and write The forest is on fire over there. Time to get out of here—now we're climate refugees too. Sad but true. #climatechange, and the hearts and emojis and messages asking where are you? and OMG, is there anything we can do? come flooding in. Carola's mother calls to go through the valuables, the things we absolutely need to take with us *just in case*; her sister calls, her friends call, no one calls me. I feel focused, efficient. I tell the big kids that they have exactly thirty minutes to pack their bags, and I task Vilja with helping her little brother and plugging in all the phones and power banks to charge. I ask Carola to get everything for Becka ready—bottles, spare clothes, diapers; it could be hours until we next get to a shop or somewhere with a toilet. My family let me boss them around without a single grumble, as though we're instinctively seeking out our most primitive roles. I go online, memorize the best routes, read the latest information from the emergency services. I turn on the radio and find a local station talking about flames twice the height of a cathedral; it's such a huge event, what's happening is apocalyptic and we're right in the middle of it. Carola comes down with our suitcase and an Ikea bag, nudging my shoulder and giving me a quick kiss, *we can do this, right?* and I notice that she feels the same thing I do, that this is bringing us closer together in a beautiful, new, adrenaline-addled way.

The text messages and likes keep coming. I go out to the car to load everything into the trunk and a radio station calls me, the stressed producer asks if I would be willing to do an interview and suddenly I'm live on air, *Didrik von der Esch, a PR consultant, is with his family in the fire-ravaged area to the north of Lake Siljan. Tell me, Didrik, what's happening there right now?*

Yeah, so, we've been at my mother-in-law's place here in Dalarna for the past few weeks, and it's been getting tougher and tougher because of the drought and the heat, and we've just heard that we need to evacuate the area immediately for reasons of safety.

Didrik, are you satisfied with the information you have been given by the authorities?

I connect my phone to my headset and load things into the trunk as I continue the interview. The movement makes the tempo of my voice go up slightly, giving it more drama, I say *sorry for the background noise but I'm busy packing the car, we need to get out of here as quickly as possible . . . Information, uh, I guess it depends what you mean. We've been given information about leaving the area and that kind of thing, obviously, but from a longer-term perspective this extreme heat is a result of the climate crisis that every government in the Western world has been actively ignoring for decades, so on that front I think they definitely could have INFORMED us better, and I don't just mean now but ten or twenty or thirty years ago, they could at the very least have INFORMED us that they had no intention of*

*fulfilling the state's most basic function, which is protecting the world's peo-
ple from a long line of entirely predictable disasters.*

I enjoy the conversation, relishing every word. Folding the baby carriage
and loading it in on top of everything else, I hear the impressed silence from
the woman in the studio, who leaves a nice pause for effect before she says
Didrik, you seem so calm and composed, despite the gravity of the situation?

*Yeah, well, we'll be absolutely fine, our possessions and property are all
insured, it's not like it is in some of the poorer parts of the world, where the
climate catastrophe claims millions of victims every year—the megacities in
India and Africa that have run out of water, or the western United States
and Canada, where entire regions practically burn to the ground. Maybe
this is exactly the type of wake-up call we need here in Sweden so that we
really understand where we're heading.*

The studio thanks me for taking the time to talk to them, *that was Didrik von der Esch, whose family is in the process of fleeing their summer
house in Dalarna as a result of the widespread wildfires to the north of Lake
Siljan that the emergency services now say are burning out of control. We go
now to,* and I hang up and slam the trunk shut, and after the thud the silence
seems to echo.

No birds. No cars. Just the rustling of the wind in the trees.

I check my phone again. Plenty more likes but no new messages. People probably assume we've already left.

"Is everyone almost ready to go?" I shout into the house, proud of how
relaxed I sound.

Carola and Vilja come out with Becka, and we lower her into the car
seat and clip her in. Zack is in the hallway with his Spider-Man backpack,
and I'm just about to lead him out to the car when I notice that he's crying.
Silent, dogged tears, something he never normally does. I crouch down in
front of him.

"Hey, buddy, what's up? You're not scared, are you? It's OK, we're
leaving now."

"I can't find it."

I take his backpack, weigh it in my hand. It's full of clothes, books, the firm rectangle of his tablet in the front pocket.

"But everything's here, you've done such a good job packing."

Two fat tears roll down his cheeks.

"The gold coin. And the tooth. I've looked everywhere, but Vilja says we can't keep looking or we'll burn to death."

"Oh, Zacharias, no. Nothing's going to burn. We're just going home a bit sooner than planned, but that's not so bad, is it? Come on, let's get into the car. What do you want to listen to? *The Phantom of the Opera*? Or do you want *The Magic Flute* again?"

His face is a steely mask of stubbornness and despair.

"The gold coin. And the tooth. I wanted to keep it."

I hear the car doors open, Carola and Vilja are getting in. I stand up, feel my thighs cramping, my back straining. Why did I have a third child?

"OK, sweetheart, let's think back. It was by the bed when you woke up this morning, wasn't it?"

There is no point trying to be thorough and taking him through the house in his mind; it's too small. The kids' room, our room, the bathroom, the tiny kitchen and living room downstairs, that's it, you could search the place in two minutes flat. And I can see it on his face, he knows, he just doesn't dare say it. He's too scared.

His skinny little body running out onto the jetty, the shampoo and the inflatable dolphin, he was sitting right at the end when he saw the haze and the smoke on the other side of the lake. His neck tensed, he turned back to look at me, seeking comfort or security, and for a brief moment, before I'd managed to take in the scope of what the old man was pointing at and come up with a plan, I wasn't there for him, I was just as lost as he was.

"I wanted to show Flipper the tooth," he sniffs.

"Of course you did."

"And now the tooth's over there and it's going to get burned."

"Of course it's not. It'll be right there in its jar, waiting for you, until we next come back."

Zack looks down at the ground, nods. Walks slowly over to the car with his bag. Carola is in the backseat, the door open to the unbearable heat, and she gives me a questioning look.

"He left his tooth down by the jetty."

Maybe it's because of the hint of fear in her eye, or because of the moment earlier, when she came down with the Ikea bag, when she kissed me, when there was a spark between us, but I say *five minutes, OK?* and without waiting for her to reply, I stride back along the same path I've walked countless times before, looking for strawberries, blueberries, for the newspaper in the mailbox, hand in hand with small children in bathrobes, life jackets, pee-stinking pajamas, with dreams that need to be shared before they fade and disappear.

The old man is still there. He's sitting on the rickety wooden bench, looking out across the lake. The sky above us is almost the same shade of gray as his windbreaker, but on the other side it is more like a dark, fluffy blanket, swelling and billowing. Just an hour ago the smoke was nothing but a hazy plume, but now it looks wide, compact, scary.

And the air. The filth, the way it makes your eyes water.

"Hey," I say. "Time to go."

With some difficulty, he turns around and looks at me.

"It's funny, last time they wanted to force me to stay at home. A year and a half I was shut in. Wasn't allowed to see anyone, not even the neighbors. But now it's the other way around. Now I'm not allowed to be here."

From his tone and his choice of words, it's obvious that he prepared this speech in advance. Maybe I'm not the first person to ask, maybe he's been on the phone to his kids or his grandkids; the rash, pompous stoicism of aged country men like him.

"I'm not going anywhere. This is my home. I've sat by this lake every morning since 1974. I don't have anywhere else to go."

"I really think we—"

"Plus the car isn't roadworthy," he adds with a grin. "Didn't pass its emissions inspection. That'll be my license gone if they catch me."

"Stop it," I say. "Surely there's someone who can come and get you?"

"The police were here not long ago, came right up to the house and banged on the door. But I stayed away. I can look after myself."

The way he proudly nods and turns his back on me to keep staring out across the eerie lake is so pathetic it's almost unbearable, it's like watching a drunk try to get into the bar for the fifth time in one evening, that's how wide the gulf is between what he thinks I'm seeing (the captain of an ocean liner determined to go down with his ship) and what I actually see (a confused old man complicating the rescue effort).

I walk out onto the jetty. The little glass jar is at the very end, right by the ladder. The thermometer is bobbing in the water like always, tied to one of the piles on a length of nylon string, and I feel a sudden urge to check it. Eighty-four degrees. There's no sign of the dolphin, the wind must have taken it.

I peer over to the edge of the forest. The smoke has changed from dark gray to jet black, and I can see flames between the treetops. The sky is a sludge of soot, ash, and streaks of red, quivering in the heat, and I can hear the crackling of burning trees and bushes over the breeze.

I quickly turn around and head back. "Come on," I say to the old geezer. "We can all squeeze into our car, surely you can see that you can't stay here? Do you really want them to waste time and resources, just because you . . ."

He doesn't budge, and I take a step toward the bench, hold out a hand. His old body stiffens, a shift beneath his clothes, something sinewy and gristly tensing. The thought of even getting him up from the bench, never mind leading, coaxing, carrying him back to the house and the car, where there is already a family of four waiting with all their luggage.

I hear a bang. A loud bang, a sound unlike anything I've ever heard before, a deafening, booming blast that echoes across the lake.

"Car tire," the old man says, a hint of a smile playing on his furrowed, scabby face. "That's what it sounds like when they burst in the heat. Carries for miles."

I grip the glass jar in my hand. I run.

———

Becka is crying, the sun is high in the sky, the wind has dropped, and the temperature has risen, not quite as high as yesterday, but almost. Carola is feeding her while she's strapped into the car seat, and that never usually works, the angle is always wrong and she spills and drools and spits up the formula in sour little gulps.

"Here," I tell Zack, trying to smile. He takes the jar in sluggish silence, hunched over on his sticky seat, carefully checking to make sure both the coin and the tooth are inside.

"The old guy is still there," I say to Carola. "He's refusing to leave."

"But he has to. They said on the radio that the entire area has to be evacuated. Everyone is supposed to head for Östbjörka or Ovanmyra."

"He doesn't want to go."

"Did you try to change his mind?"

I give her the look she always used to talk about in therapy, the look that says that I (right now, in this moment) think she is a worthless idiot and that our years together have been the biggest mistake of my life; that cold, empty hatred that has ruined so much, the look that is the only thing that can get her to shut up, and she shuts up and turns her head.

"Yes, Carola," I say, excessively slowly and clearly. "*Obviously* I told him he could come with us. He said no, but you're *very welcome* to go down there and try yourself."

"I'm feeding Becka," she snaps, looking down at the baby in the car seat.

Her perpetual trump card. I sigh, try to think rationally. Get in behind the wheel and fasten my belt.

"OK, let's drive down to the lake. If he's still there, we can both try to convince him. It might be harder for him to say no if he sees the kids, we can use them as leverage somehow. And if he refuses, we'll come up with another plan, OK?"

She nods, stiffly at first, but the stiffness soon eases and she manages to make herself look up at me and whisper *fine, OK*.

"Is he the one who lives in the old house next to where Ella and Hugo used to live?" Vilja suddenly asks. "The really old guy? Is he going to burn to death? Aren't you going to rescue him?"

Yes, we say in unison, and Carola continues by saying *the fire isn't going to reach this far, honey, they just want us to be cautious* and I say *we just don't want the people fighting the fires to have to look for him*, and while we're saying all this I press the start button, but the car doesn't start.

It doesn't start.

I'm so conditioned to it starting, it always starts, that in my mind I'm already driving, gripping the cool, steady wheel, listening to updates on the radio (and saying no in an authoritative tone when Vilja tries to change the station), cool air streaming toward me, the GPS showing the best route to Östbjörka or Ovanmyra, if that's where we're heading, maybe we'll just drive straight down to Rättvik and from there to Stockholm. Maybe I can find the clip from the interview I did earlier, play it for the kids over Bluetooth, let them listen to their dad talking about the fire. I could get Carola to drive for a bit once Becka goes to sleep, upload the clip on my phone, shares, likes, pull over at the gas station in Borlänge, there'll probably be a lot of people wondering, who recognize him from the TV debates, that's him, he's the one who just escaped the forest fires with his family, imagine being evacuated with a baby and still looking so relaxed as he charges his BMW and buys ice cream for his kids, if you ask him about it he just shrugs, *God, yeah, I mean, God, we just had to get out, hesitated for a moment at first but then I heard a tire explode and that was that.*

But the car doesn't start.

I push the button again and again, check that the gearshift is set to park, that I'm pressing the brake, that all the doors are closed, even though none of that makes the slightest bit of difference, but the car won't start, nothing is blinking, beeping, responding; it's completely dead.

I take a deep breath through gritted teeth and am just about to start yelling, at Zack, at Vilja, at whichever of them turned on one of the lights to look for something they'd dropped between the seats and then forgot to turn it off again, whichever of them forgot to close a door, or was playing with the headlights, using the USB charger for one of their fucking phones or tablets or whatever else could have happened, right now my rage knows no bounds, but I feel a hand on my arm and it's Carola saying *sorry. I'm really sorry.*

"It was yesterday, when it got so hot. Becka was screaming. We sat in here, just for a while. With the AC on. She loved the cold air."

Silence fills the car. My hands feel heavy on the wheel.

"I wasn't thinking," she continues, more hesitant now. "I didn't think the battery . . . sorry. Sorry sorry sorry, please Didrik, I'm so sorry."

———————

I would never want to live with another man's child. It's not something I've ever really thought about before, but that's how it is. Sure, if he was dead, or maybe if he was missing, if I felt like I was stepping into his shoes (and I don't mean *missing* in the sense of doing time or spiraling into drug abuse or mental illness, a loser who calls asking for money in the middle of the night, but really *missing*, gone). But if he was someone who was actually *there*, who longed for them, who wanted them . . . taking them away from him, stealing half their lives from him, making him into an every-other-week dad, an every-other-birthday and every-other-Easter and every-other-Christmas dad, I'd never be able to do that, and hand on heart it's not out of compassion for some bitter old ex but because *I* don't want anyone's kids but my own, because I'd never be able to deal with the knowledge that they had another dad but me.

But she wanted my kids. As we lay there, limbs entwined, she would start talking about how she'd been looking at pictures of the kids on Facebook and dreamed of taking care of them. She thought Vilja would hate her at first, that she'd see her as the enemy, take Carola's side. That Zack would be shy and cautious. But that with time.

That was probably when things first started going downhill, because until that point I'd thought of us as just her and me. Our conversations about art, politics, and philosophy in small back-street tourist restaurants where no one we knew ever ate, the longing glances, the interlinked fingers beneath the table. The marathon—yet much too short—afternoons in hotel rooms where, having fucked for hours like we were possessed, our wildest, most desperate desires sated, we hit pause and ordered room service, washing it down with champagne and then taking a shower before *really* getting down to some proper sex, on a completely different level this time, systematically realizing games and fantasies we'd never even known we had. The long message threads in which we took control of each other's thoughts and turned them in a direction we'd never dared before.

In my world, it was just her and me. I started looking at one-bedroom apartments, two-bedroom apartments, absentmindedly thinking about stashing the kids' stuff in boxes under the bed every other week; and for a month or so, when things were at their very best or worst, I even started looking at studio apartments, because was the whole every-other-week thing really that important, wasn't it just a middle-class convention? Shared custody, sure, but did it really have to be quite so regimented?

When I was at my most infatuated, I dreamed of long breakfasts in white bathrobes, sticky sex orgies on a sun-drenched terrace, walks along the beach, art galleries, theater premieres, nights out in hip neighborhoods, intellectual boxing matches, and three-ways with hot strangers. That was my most taboo fantasy: abandoning my kids and devoting myself to a life with her.

She had started saving up for driving lessons, she whispered, pressing her lithe, naked body against mine. So that she could do the *pickups and drop-offs.* She didn't know much about what life as a parent entailed, but she knew that a large part of it revolved around *pickups and drop-offs,* and she wanted to be able to do that.

I glance back at Carola, sitting in the seat beside Becka, quiet, timid, lips trembling and tears in her eyes.

She wanted your kids. I was willing to do anything with her, anything but give her your kids. So I stayed.

And had a third.

"It'll be OK, honey," I hear myself say. "It'll be OK, we can fix this, right? *It's just a car bomb.*"

For a few seconds I sit perfectly still, doing nothing at all, just pausing for a moment in the smell of the car, the compartment in the door with the ice scrapers and candy wrappers, the glove compartment with its owner's manual and a load of receipts, a red pouch of CDs we never play, the feeling of the wheel beneath my palms and fingers, the slightly bumped surface for improved grip, the cup holder where I usually put my coffee, the dark dashboard that used to show the mileage, the speed, the battery level minute by minute, the luxury of knowing—never actually saying it out loud, but knowing—that at one point in my life I could afford a near-new electric BMW.

Then I get out, the heat now oppressive, almost no breeze at all. I take a deep, searching breath and feel my throat burn. The closest charging point is miles away. You're supposed to be able to start the battery using cables, but I have no idea how to do that kind of thing, I've never even popped the hood, I always just drop the car off at the garage. What I do know is that you need another car with the engine running, and we're all alone out here.

Carola has calmly explained what is happening to the kids, and they react differently of course, with Vilja alternating between crying, comforting, and pointing the finger and Zack talking about superpowers, about helicopters and hot-air balloons that could come and rescue us, and I have time to think *if only I had the kind of gifted son who was interested in chemistry, physics, and mechanics, who could come up with a plan to run a cable to the power supply in the house and get the car going that way, who knew where there was an abandoned rusty old Saab 900 that he could hot-wire, the kind of son who won prizes and got to meet the queen and knew things that were smart and useful instead of a load of Harry Potter crap* before I see a plane thundering overhead, close to the ground, one of those big yellow ones.

"Here!" I shout, waving so hard that my arm feels like it might pop out of its socket. "Here!" But it's stupid and futile, I'm just scaring the kids.

They have both leaped out of the car and are standing beside me, looking up at the sky, wanting to know what I saw.

"A plane. One of the ones that picks up water and drops it onto the fire."

They stare at me, searching my face for answers. Is it a good sign that the plane is here, does this mean we can go home, how close is the fire?

How close *is* the fire?

Becka is screaming. I move around the car, open the back door, and lift her out of the seat, hold her sweaty little body to mine.

"Come on," I say. "We'll have to walk."

"But what about the old man?" Vilja's distrustful eyes are on me, on her mother. "We were supposed to be going to get the old man."

Carola pushes a lock of damp hair back from her forehead.

"Grab your things, kids," she says, opening the trunk.

Carola has the blue Ikea bag and the bright red changing bag we bought to take on vacation. Vilja is pulling the big suitcase containing most of our clothes. Zack has his Spider-Man backpack and is still crying because I forced him to leave his books behind, three of them were library books that we've already received repeat reminders about, and now he's worried he'll never be allowed to borrow another book again, he's crying and whining and complaining that his feet hurt. I have our valuables in a Fjällräven backpack, and I'm carrying a bag of food and water in one hand and pushing

Becka in her baby carriage with the other. We're all wearing face coverings, fresh new masks made from hypoallergenic neoprene that we bought for Thailand and brought out here "just in case." Becka is whimpering and trying to push hers off, and I have to keep stopping to tug it back into place.

According to my phone it's seven miles to Östbjörka. We never go over there, but judging by the satellite image it's a gravel track followed by a swing to the left, a straight stretch that gradually curves off to the right, over a crossroads and then along another long, straight stretch to the houses. *Ten minutes in a car, fifteen max*, says Carola, she used to go there when she visited the area as a child, there was a shop back then. *I went with Dad to get cigarettes once, it took no time at all.*

The heat has settled like a saucepan lid over the forest, and we're trying to stay in the shade, Zack in swimming trunks and flip-flops, Becka in nothing but her diaper in the baby carriage, me in cut-off jeans and a faded Lacoste T-shirt. We can hear the sirens in the distance, see several planes roar across the hazy sky, but we don't see another soul.

A stack of wood, an anthill, a hand-painted sign warning of *WILD CHILDREN AND SENIORS AT PLAY*. I often come past here when I'm out jogging, and during particularly hot summers there are blackflies everywhere, swarming around me, if I take off my shirt they land all over my stomach and armpits and back, everywhere I'm sweating, it's unbearable, they follow me for miles.

But today the air is empty, the forest silent. All we can hear is the monotonous rumbling of the suitcase and the baby carriage.

"Ella used to take his dog for walks," says Vilja, looking down at the tarmac, two pale eyes above her black mask. "Ajax, a black Labrador. I got to go with them sometimes."

Vague memories of a shaggy, unkempt pooch, a red leash, the summer it poured nonstop, Vilja wearing rubber boots in the rain, walking alongside the neighbors' girl in a red rain poncho. Christ, that must be ten years ago now? An old hunting dog he'd had since he used to traipse through the woods with his rifle, hunting wild boar, he must've had it put down not long after we started coming out here every summer, it's incredible she still remembers it.

"One time he came down to the lake with us and we went in the water with him and it was like we'd made friends with Ajax, he swam for sticks and—"

"Surely you didn't go in the water," I interrupt her, I'm not sure why. "You can't have been much more than five, you'd never have been allowed to go in without an adult. Maybe you just splashed around on the shore?"

The mask makes it hard to tell, but I think she might be smiling at the memory, her eyes are smiling. This is almost the only way to get through to her these days, talking about her as a child. Whenever we're snuggling with Becka I tell her what she was like as a baby, that she also spent most of her time throwing up and shitting and sleeping. I tell her about her first words, take out the old clothes we kept as vintage pieces for our future grandkids, things that will now do for our surprise baby, and the incomprehensible cuteness of the fact that *she* once wore those tiny dresses and bibs and cardigans brings a sense of calm to her chaotic teenage brain and somewhere, deep down, is the vulnerability and tenderness that is now Becka's but was once hers.

"I'll let the firemen know he's still at home the minute we get there," I tell Vilja.

She nods.

"Once, when we went over, he said that Ajax was the best dog he'd ever had. He'd had several, like a whole *gang* of dogs, but Ajax was the only one left, and he was getting old."

She pushes her damp bangs back from her forehead, moves the handle of the suitcase over to her other hand. I should suggest swapping, but I want to put it off, wait another thirty minutes at least; the minute you start shifting the burden your body realizes just how tired it is.

"He said it was his last dog," she adds. "And then he'd really be on his own."

We walk a few hundred yards. The forest is thicker here, which means more shade, and there is a breeze coming from the other direction, dispersing the smoke a little. I manage to take a few deep breaths through my mask without my throat stinging. Becka is asleep in her baby carriage, and if you forget about everything else, we're absolutely fine, we're just a family out for a walk in the woods, the kind of thing we're always saying we should do more often.

"How much farther is it?" she asks, as though she can read my mind. "I want to be there now."

"A bit. A few miles."

"A few *miles*?"

"That's what you said when we were in New York. Do you remember when we walked from Times Square to the Meatpacking District? It was hot then too, but it was all fine in the end. We just had to tick off one block at a time and we were there before you knew it."

She frowns.

"If they let me I'll go with them in their . . . fire engines, or whatever they've got, I'll show them where he lives," I say. "I'll help them rescue him, OK?"

"What if they don't want to go?"

"Then I'll talk to their boss," I quickly reply.

"Will you?"

"Yes, of course. If the firemen say no, I'll say I want to talk to their boss, otherwise I'll call the people in charge in Stockholm, or the papers. I won't just let this go."

She nods, changes hands again, takes out her phone and checks the screen. I come close to asking her to save the battery, but decide that it's more important she feels like everything is normal, like there's no reason to panic.

We walk for an hour. We take turns with the baby carriage, the backpack, the Ikea bag. We reach a clearing at the top of a hill and get a better view of the countryside; behind us the air is gray and hazy, but we can't see any flames, no more planes. We pause by a large pile of logs to drink water—Carola ran back into the house to fill a couple of large plastic bottles before we left the car—and eat biscuits, raisins, and salted peanuts.

When we get up to leave, Zack refuses. He doesn't say anything, doesn't whine, just stays sitting on his log.

"Come on, buddy, we've got to go."

He shakes his head, eyes on the ground. I crouch down in front of him, run a hand over the skinny, bony legs sticking out of his swimming trunks.

"Buddy?"

One of his feet is dirty, something blackish brown on his little toes, and when I reach out to wipe off the soil or sap or whatever it is he flinches and jerks his foot away.

"Sweetheart?" Carola's voice is shrill behind me. "Sweetheart, what is it? What's wrong with your foot?"

"Isbeeng," Zack mumbles, in the babyish language he reverts to sometimes, and I force myself to keep my voice cool and calm when I ask him again, *could you speak up, buddy, we can't hear you with the mask on, what do you mean, isbeeng?*

"It's bleeding."

Carola is already in front of him, by the foot no one is allowed to touch. He wails as she pulls off the flip-flop, his wail rising to a drawn-out, catlike mew when she touches his toes.

"It's the strap," she says, her voice taut. "It's cut into his toe."

"Zack . . . honey, why didn't you say anything?"

Zack shakes his head, two fat tears cutting a path across his dirty face mask. I bend down and see the blood that has oozed out between his big toe and the one beside it, dirt and gravel and flapping skin.

"Zack? Sweetheart?"

His eyes refuse to meet mine.

"Are you going to leave me now?"

There must be something wrong with him, no, don't think that, *yes, because there must be something wrong with him, ADHD autism Asperger's, some sort of diagnosis must fit, that's just not fucking normal, that needs investigating.*

"We'd never leave you," says Carola, stroking his hair.

"Never," I say. "Never ever ever."

"That's what Vilja said," he sniffs. "That if I whined about my foot, you'd go without me."

"Did *not!*" His sister laughs, that cutting, sarcastic laugh she has started deploying to assert her innocence. "I just said it would be good if you didn't say anything to Mom and Dad because they already have to look after Becka and can't drag you along too, and you might have to go back to the house to wait for the fire engines there instead."

"You said the fire engines would come and get me!"

She laughs again. A hollow, cold sound through her mask.

"Shut up, you retard, I *did not.*"

She's ashamed, I can tell, it's the shame that's making her vulgar and mean. She off-loads her anxiety onto her little brother, and when he calls her out on it she says the worst things she can think of, throwing it out there like stun grenades to distract us. I know all this, we've discussed it in family therapy, but that doesn't stop it from working. I feel a sense of rage wash over me and I get up and roar a few choice words I didn't know I had in me, Carola tries to move in between us, *no, Didrik, calm down*, but we're screaming at each other as Becka cries into her mask and Zack clamps his hands over his ears and smoke swirls through the empty sky above us.

———

The uncomplicated, joyous love I once felt for my daughter has transformed into something else, something much more difficult. Her snottiness, her selfishness, the numbing lack of gratitude that seems to flow through her veins, all of that has settled like a dirty, greasy film over the happiness that once swept me away every time I looked into her bright blue eyes.

We try to blame it on her addiction to screens, to social media, on the long nights of endless chat threads, all the things that got worse during the pandemic. We blame it on mindless consumption, on the fact that it is now seen as perfectly normal for a child to walk around with a pocket full of technology worth as much as an average schoolteacher makes in a month, the fact that any child who doesn't have the latest mobile phone, headphones, GoPro, jacket, or shoes is a *loser* or a *newb*; we blame the neoliberal system, Carola always sighs and says something like *we've built a society where teenage girls don't bat an eyelid at asking for a Prada bag.*

This is where we are now, she says, *in the post-postmodern decadence of late capitalism, a perverted world in which the southern hemisphere is ravaged by famine, war, and chaos while the global elite in the north accumulates a degree of wealth that makes the average Westerner expect a lifestyle that would require twenty planet Earths to sustain everyone.*

But there is no political analysis, no Marxist lecture that can free me from the shame of our fourteen-year-old daughter behaving like an escort girl, of having learned to soften her voice, occasionally putting a hand on my shoulder, whenever she wants the latest merch from the latest band, whenever she wants money for sushi, whenever she wants new *mods* and *skins* for whatever mind-numbing computer game she's playing right now. Or of knowing that the only time, literally the only time, my daughter ever shows me anything resembling love or respect is when I have my credit card in hand, ready to click order on the next new thing. That the only time she ever calls or texts is to ask for the flow of money, the steady stream of cash she must imagine our finances to be, to be redirected toward her.

We've tried talking to her about empathy, about what it means to be part of a family where everyone has to pitch in and take care of one another. We've tried to tell her that money doesn't grow on trees, to encourage her to tidy up, fold the laundry, take the trash out, mow the lawn, anything to somehow earn the money she wants us to give her. And that did help, sometimes, for a week, maybe two. But then she got bored and returned to her nagging, demanding, manipulating ways.

Then the pandemic slowly passed and Becka came along and everything suddenly felt a little easier. Board games made a reappearance, evenings around the dinner table, playing cards, guessing games. And Vilja has even started playing the piano again. It's been a long time since she stopped taking lessons, of course, but she still sits down with music she finds online, singing along with the simple minor chords, sad ballads. She has a beautiful voice, slightly wistful and one-note, and she sings in completely the wrong key, as though she can't hear the piano at all, hour after hour of melancholic, off-key tunes. But every once in a while, on a verse or chorus, she manages to find the right note and follow the tune, it happens by sheer coincidence, she doesn't even seem to notice, but if Carola and I are in the same room we always stop what we're doing and look at each other, like we're amazed to find ourselves in a state of perfect harmony, a glimpse of how it could be, how it should have been, our family.

We finish our argument and spend a while searching for a Band-Aid before realizing that we left the first aid kit in the car. Becka is hungry again, so I take out the thermos of hot water and the tub of powder and mix up a bottle of formula, feeding her as best I can under her mask while Carola grabs some wet wipes from the changing bag and manages to clean the wound between Zack's toes; we dig a sock out of the suitcase and pull it on so that he can keep walking, a flip-flop on his good foot and just the sock on his bad one, but he's limping, crying, it hurts.

He leans against his mother, against the baby carriage, against me, but we get slower and slower. He tries walking on his heel, but the tarmac is hot and it burns his skin through the sock. In the end he asks to sit on my shoulders, and I lift him above the backpack I'm already carrying, him still wearing his Spider-Man. It must be several years since I last carried a child on my shoulders, and it's nice for a few minutes before I begin to feel his weight on my collarbone and neck, his sweat trickling down my skin, mixing with mine in the baking sun; my shoulders start aching, his sweaty thighs rubbing against my neck, a jolt of pain every time his clammy little hands press on my Adam's apple or pull on my hair and the constant *are we there yet are we there yet are we there yet?*

The road sign is nothing but a blue speck at first, a half-hearted promise of voices, of taciturn men in yellow hi-vis jackets and a first aid kit for Zack's foot, a toilet and maybe even a cup of coffee, Christ, I hope they have coffee, huge pump thermoses of the stuff and maybe even some buns that a local Scout troop or church group have baked. The speck gets bigger, and for a brief, unbearable moment I think it says *8*, but then I realize that it's really true, that it says *ÖSTBJÖRKA 2*, that we'll soon be in the mythical Östbjörka, and just as we reach the sign we see the car driving toward us, a white station wagon speeding in the opposite direction.

It's the first car we've seen since we set off, and we all stop. I carefully lower Zack to the ground and start waving, Carola starts waving. It shows no sign of slowing down, so I step out into the road and for a bitter, suffocating moment it feels like they haven't seen me at all, but then it brakes suddenly without really coming to a complete halt and the window winds down a few inches. The man is around my age, with a handlebar mustache, graying blond hair tied up in a ponytail, a bare chest, and a big sleeve tattoo on one arm. I catch a glimpse of a younger woman in the seat beside him, dark-haired, with dreads and trendy sunglasses. The radio is on, the tense and dry yet somehow *hungry* tone of a national broadcaster reporting on a major news event, saying *the authorities warn* and *out of control* and *anyone in the vicinity.*

"Been driving since last night," the man says in a weak voice, a hand clamped over his nose and mouth. "From Jämtland. What a fucking mess."

The car keeps rolling. I'm half running alongside the driver and pointing to Östbjörka.

"How does it look back there?"

"Didn't see a soul. The water bombers are probably the only ones around here now. It's a fucking scandal Sweden doesn't have its own planes. We're heading for Rättvik, that's the only place to go."

"Our car wouldn't start," I say, the helplessness in my voice making me want to curl up in shame. "We've got a baby."

He just shakes his head.

"Get to Rättvik as fast as you fucking can."

I hear the woman beside him whisper *Micke* and then the window rolls up and the car accelerates and speeds away.

A white Toyota. I remember looking at one just like it before I chose the BMW. It felt more . . . I don't know, grown-up somehow. *What did they say?* Carola shouts over to me as I jog back, her face a tense question mark beneath her mask.

"They were going to Rättvik, it was . . ."

"But what about Östbjörka? Was there any help there?"

"I don't know . . . he said he *didn't see a soul* . . ."

I'm getting closer, can see that she is on the verge of tears. Her voice is shrill and Zack is clinging on to her, or maybe it's her clinging on to Zack, Vilja is standing off to one side with the baby carriage.

"But were there any fire engines? Was there any information?"

"I don't know."

"Didn't you ask?"

That disappointed, accusing face again.

"Look, they're coming back," says Vilja, pointing.

The white Toyota has done a U-turn and is racing toward us again. It brakes hard and stops, the engine still running. The woman gets out and I see that she's pregnant, a floral maternity dress, rubber boots on her feet.

"Listen, we can take the baby," she says. She has wrapped a shawl around her face and has pushed her trendy sunglasses up onto her head, her eyes are shining with magnanimity. "It's OK, we'll take the baby."

No one speaks.

Carola seems to have frozen to the spot.

"We can take the baby," the woman repeats. "Micke? Right, Micke?"

He winds down the window again, glares at me, barks out their offer.

"Yeah, sure. We can take the baby if you want."

"But we're . . ." Carola gestures lamely in the direction of Östbjörka. "There's supposed to be . . ."

"Everything's on fire over there," says Micke. "The whole area's gone up. You can't stay here."

I don't think, I just walk over to the baby carriage and pick up Becka, her soft body against my skin, her smooth little sleeping face. I pass her to

Carola and whisper *you go, just to be on the safe side, we'll be fine*, and she has already started making her way toward the car when Micke says *hang on a sec, just the baby*, and she tenses.

The sky is getting grayer. The grayness is coming from every direction, a dull, swirling haze slowly settling over us. The air is dry, dirty; it stings through the mask.

"I can hold her on my lap," says the woman. She's crying, has grazed knees, I realize, trickles of dried blood on her calves, and she holds out her hands for Becka. "Please, for God's sake," her voice rises, cutting through the shawl. "You can trust me, I can't leave a baby out here on the road, that's what I told Micke, we just can't fucking do that, no one can, we wouldn't be human if we did."

Carola clutches Becka to her chest, rocking her gently as she shakes her head, tears streaming down her cheeks, and it's so hot, she shouts something, the woman shouts something, she shouts something back.

"Listen, man," I say to Micke, moving closer to his window, looking down at him. He has a wad of tobacco under his lip, hidden beneath his hipster mustache, you can only see it once you get up close. "I'm sure we can work something out, can't we all just squeeze together in the trunk?"

He doesn't reply, just glares at me again. I lean forward, peer into the car, and see two blond boys in swimming trunks in the backseat, each with wide eyes and a tablet in his lap.

"Hey, kids, thanks for letting us hitch a ride with you," I say in a voice I hope sounds open and friendly.

"There was another family, a while back," says Micke, sounding slightly more authoritative now. "Flat tire. He said the same thing, unbelievable that we don't have our own water bombers."

The woman starts gesturing, shouting something about the smoke and pointing to the trees. Carola shakes her head again.

"But they didn't have a baby," the man continues. "You've got a baby. So we turned around and came back. But not so we could stand here *arguing* with you."

His grip tightens on the wheel. A glimpse of something ugly on his filthy face, eyes already tearing up because of the smoke.

The woman gets back into the front seat, stares angrily ahead.

"Please," I say. "The trunk."

Micke glances at the woman.

"We've got all our stuff in there."

"Please, I'm begging you. Be nice."

"We *are* being nice," she hisses, drying her tears with her wrist, she has made the switch from generosity to rage. "We're being *really* fucking nice."

Micke scratches the strawberry-blond hair in his armpit, eyes wandering. This must be how they work as a couple, I realize: she's temperamental and impulsive, he's calm and indecisive, they complement each other.

"Anna, another option is that we—"

"We *turned around* and came back and now you're just standing here bickering with us. It's fucking nuts that you could be so selfish!"

They complement each other, but in the end it's her who makes the decisions, and she has now made up her mind.

A hand on my waist. A voice behind me.

Dad.

Vilja is holding Zack's hand. He's crying, coughing through his mask, *don't think, just do it*, and I pick him up in my arms like a big, warm seal, his forehead is red and sweaty, I turn toward the car.

"My son has asthma!" I shout to the boys in the backseat, in a tone I hope they won't question. "He can't handle this air for much longer!" They huddle together and glance at their parents, then one of them opens the door out of sheer reflex—*Assar!* the woman hisses, but it's too late—I fling it wide and bundle Zack into the back, throw him in among the other children's bodies, lean into the vehicle and feel the coolness, the clean air, and I kiss his forehead, the smell of smoke, dirt, and lemon shampoo and all the dark years in this very moment; he shouts *Dad* and I slam the door, *go on then* I mumble to Micke, who nods, a flicker of brotherly understanding in his eyes as he says *Rättvik* and turns the wheel and shoots backward, almost into a bush; he turns the wheel again and shouts *Rättvik*, his voice relieved, as though the name of a small community in Dalarna will make all our worries disappear, and the wheels screech and the car races away.

Carola is still standing with Becka in her arms. She closes her eyes, burrows her nose in the baby's neck, mumbles *they seemed nice didn't they they seemed nice didn't they love they seemed nice oh my little love my love my love.*

Less than five minutes have passed since we first spotted the car. Spider-Man is lying on the ground beside the road sign. *ÖSTBJÖRKA 2.*

"Lana Del Rey," Vilja mutters into the hot air, adjusting the straps before she puts on her little brother's backpack. "Lana Del Rey."

═══════

The house in Thailand. That was how it all started. A house with a widescreen TV and a gym with a treadmill and an exercise bike and its own turquoise pool.

We're walking toward Östbjörka but in my head the explanations have already begun, because I know I'm going to have to explain this, how it was that an intelligent, well-adjusted person like me got into this situation, whatever happens now you're going to wonder how the hell I wound up staying in an empty house to the north of Lake Siljan the summer when Dalarna, Jämtland, and Härjedalen burned.

Becka had arrived, I'll tell my wife's best friend at the funeral. *We were so happy, she was our third and final child and we wanted to do something extra special to celebrate that, so we decided to spend Carola's maternity leave abroad, and Thailand is so great for kids.* A simple Italian buffet with Tuscan red wine, a church with white lime-washed walls, Österlen, Gotland, somewhere like that, *Carola was really looking forward to it, she was so happy,* her friend is tall and pretty and accusatory in her black dress and waterproof eyeliner, *six months on the beach, that was her dream, I just wanted to make it happen for her.*

It takes us an hour to walk the two miles to Östbjörka. Carola's back starts aching from carrying the diaper bag and the Ikea bag, and we have to keep stopping to hold Becka, who doesn't want to lie in the baby carriage anymore. She's screaming, trying to push off her mask. We should give her a bottle, but that might mean sitting down at the edge of the road for an eternity.

The wheel on the suitcase breaks just as we reach the first house, a simple stone wall, a playhouse in the yard, a broken goal, a trampoline almost entirely obscured by the weeds growing in its shadow. A sign with red paint that has darkened in the sun: *FLEA MARKET NEW POTATOES.*

Vilja swears and I pick up the suitcase and study it. The plastic is cracked, it wasn't made for long walks along uneven tarmac. *Cheap junk,* I hiss, and in a rage I lug the bag into the deserted yard, tear open the door to the playhouse—like a sauna inside, the smell of untreated wood, twigs and leaves, pastel-colored toy crockery, a pack of condoms, a crate of water-damaged picture books—and toss it in.

"We can pick it up later," I say. "Once everything has calmed down."

Because Thailand isn't exactly cheap anymore, I'll tell the insurance company. *And what with the flights, the kids' school fees, all the vaccinations, the money just disappeared. Plus, we wanted a house with decent rooms for both kids, with its own pool, a good kitchen, recently renovated and clean and close to the beach; it's the Chinese doing all the building work down there now that everything has opened up again, and they really know how to charge, Airbnb is basically a license to print money for those damn oligarchs.*

Östbjörka is a bus stop, two forks in the road, a few deserted houses and a scrap of grass with a withered maypole in the middle. My eyes desperately scan the large noticeboard by the turning circle, but it's all *Hosepipe ban Cabin Owners' Association AGM Quadbike For Sale Price Negotiable Call Kåre on 070-85 58 23 45 Tree Felling Fiber Broadband from DalaEnergi Prima Birch Logs.*

There are tire tracks from all-terrain vehicles, an abandoned trailer with some blankets in one corner, beside two dirty pairs of overalls and a shopping bag containing a couple of bottles of water and a pack of cookies. We take the water but leave the cookies.

It just made sense to rent out our house for the autumn, I'll tell the neighbors. *That's what everyone does when they go abroad, surely almost no one can afford two places these days. And then we thought we may as well rent it out over the summer too, to sweeten the deal.*

We find some shade beneath a pine tree and change Becka's diaper. It's full of sticky, brownish-yellow, foul-smelling shit, and it takes a whole wad of wet wipes to get her clean. Vilja deftly bundles it all up and heads off among the houses to look for a garbage can. I come close to telling her not to bother, just to dump it somewhere, but I change my mind and keep quiet.

Besides, it's never a problem to go away for the summer, I'll tell my friends. *The plan was to head to my sister's place in Bohuslän for Midsummer,* then *down to Båstad, where Niklas and Petra's house was standing empty, seriously luxurious that one,* then *we'd all jet over to Cannes because work had rented an entire house for the duration of the film festival and there was plenty of room for everyone,* then *Carola's cousin was supposed to be getting married on a vineyard in Oregon, so we'd all fly over there, the mother-in-law had booked us into a cute B and B by the beach, so we'd stay there for two weeks, all very nice, and* then *we were actually planning to go camping in Norway, because that's something we've always wanted to do but never quite managed to get around to before.*

Carola is feeding Becka with one hand and holding the phone to her ear with the other; I've decided we should save the phones and only use one at a time, and she's been on hold for the past half hour. I step into a yard, not quite as overgrown as the one with the playhouse, someone has weeded it recently, there's a stepladder beneath a tree with a pair of pruning shears on the top step, some fraying denim shorts on the washing line, and for some reason I walk over to feel whether they're dry and that's when I hear her, her voice taut and shrill.

"Hello? Hello? Can you hear me?"

I race out of the yard and back over to the tree. She has put Becka down on the ground and is standing to attention, her free hand clamped over her other ear, her face creased as though to block out anything that could disrupt this incredibly important call; she has even pulled her mask down to make her voice clearer.

"Can you hear . . . yes, hello, my name is Carola von der Esch, I'm in Östbjörka with my family, we've got a baby with us and our car won't start, we're in *Östbjörka*, hello? You told us to come to *Östbjörka* but there's no one here?"

I sit down in the sharp, dry grass, pick up Becka and hold her to my chest. The tears and drool have left pale streaks in the dirt on her temples and eyelids, and I kiss her soft, plump cheek and taste soot.

The voice seeping out of the phone is a woman's, she sounds friendly, I can't hear her words but the melody seems questioning.

"Yes . . . no?" Carola coughs, rubs her watery eyes. "I mean, we've only seen one, there was a family in it, they took our son with them, but otherwise . . . Where? Outside of Ovanmyra? But that's three miles away?"

The voice on the other end explains something and Carola laughs, a mean, grating laugh that, during our twenty years together, I've only heard maybe four times.

"Do you mind me asking who you *are* prioritizing, then? If you're not . . . We've got a four-month-old baby here."

The voice on the phone changes, growing faster, more formal, wanting to wrap things up.

"Please, for God's sake," Carola pleads, turning to look at Becka. I have to resist the urge to nip the girl hard on the thigh to make her scream, that could work, if the woman on the other end heard a child crying in the background, but Becka isn't crying, she just coughs softly and looks up at me with her red eyes and Carola begs and pleads some more, but the voice is going and then it's gone.

She stares down at the screen as though it has just bitten her.

"She said we'll have to make our own way out of here," she mutters. "That we should have been here yesterday when they were evacuating everyone. That fire and rescue is prioritizing people who are injured or can't take care of themselves, people with *extenuating circumstances*."

She makes a face, looks away.

"And then she asked why we didn't get in the car, why we couldn't all squeeze in."

She doesn't say it, possibly because I haven't blamed her for the whole AC thing, possibly because it's more powerful if it remains unsaid:

You should have convinced them. You should have figured this out. You should have protected your family.

"Sorry," I say to her mask and averted gaze.

Though most of that never happened, I'll tell the woman I want to be with. *Niklas and Petra had promised their house to someone else and there was some weird misunderstanding with the villa in Cannes and we didn't make it to the States because we did some math and realized that we couldn't actually afford the accommodation and the car rental and the bachelor and bachelorette parties and the rehearsal dinner, the cousin had hired some wedding planner who seemed to think the guests were just one big cash cow, it was impossible, we didn't know what we'd been thinking, we'd already paid for the carbon offset plane tickets, so we just had to give up the lot. Well, you understand*, and she'll give me an understanding nod, we're lying in a hotel bed somewhere, talking about our exes and all the crazy things we got up to because of them, *it was the whole middle-class life we were living, a facade we had to keep up whatever the cost. So we bundled the kids into the car and drove to Norway instead, but that was no good with Becka, the tent was like an oven by six in the morning, and do you have any idea how much a latte costs over there?*

Vilja comes back, subconsciously rubbing her hand on her shorts to get rid of any trace of the shitty diaper.

"I saw a dining table," she says, sounding jittery. "Set for a dinner on a deck. Plates, bottles of wine, everything."

I nod.

"I know, sweetheart."

She frowns, looks all around.

"People have just dropped everything and run as fast as they can."

"Yeah."

"And now we're the only ones here."

"Yeah."

The summer house was your idea, I'll say to my mother-in-law. We're at Carola's funeral again, out on Lidingö this time. *You said why don't you just take the house for the rest of the summer, I can go back to town, it was your idea and we thought it sounded like a good solution*, it's a lovely funeral, coffee in the fancy china, Janis Joplin and Amy Winehouse on the stereo, *even though it was so hot and dry and the water was turned off between ten in the evening and six in the morning.*

You put out warnings about fires every year, I'll say to the leader of the rescue operation when he meets us in Rättvik in a few hours' time, once this is all over. *You put out the same warnings every year, so we stopped paying attention to them, we thought you had things under control, and sure, we smelled the smoke from the fires to the north, but you get used to it, you people have cried wolf so many times now.*

And we were having such a nice time together, I'll tell Zack, years from now, once he's older. *You and I went to the lake every day, we splashed around for hours, you got really good at swimming that summer, you learned to dive from the jetty, we read books and played games every evening, and the smoke wasn't actually so bad, some days you could hardly smell it at all.*

Because you get used to it, I'll tell the journalists when they ask, *that's the really bad thing about climate change, that we're learning to live with the forest fires, the heat, the homeless people cooking to death in Paris, Berlin, Madrid; millions dead in India when the monsoon rains fail to arrive, Greek society has virtually collapsed, the agricultural sector in the western*

U.S. is withering and dying, there are downpours in Europe that wash entire communities away, but we just turn on the AC and fire up the barbecue. Mankind's survival has always been based on our unique ability to adapt, and now it's leading us to our downfall and we're just trotting along obediently, and when all the cattle is taken for emergency slaughter that'll just mean that organic steaks are cheaper.

Vilja reads in a chat thread online that the emergency services are still hanging around the church in Ovanmyra. We leave the Ikea bag on the trailer and, after a bit of back-and-forth, grab the pack of cookies and set off in that direction. It's almost four in the afternoon and the heat and the smoke are unbearable. Becka is squirming and twitching as though she's convulsing in the baby carriage, she screams herself hoarse, and I put on the baby carrier and lift her into it, but she keeps on screaming, we just walk through her screams.

Because we were ashamed, I'll tell my therapist. *We were ashamed that we'd poured so much goddamn money into the flashy house in Thailand that we'd made ourselves and our kids homeless that summer, two highly paid careerists blowing their life savings on something as banal as plane tickets and six months in a luxury villa costing three hundred dollars a night, and all so that we could sit on the beach and eat fried rice one last time.* The therapist will glance up from her notes and give me a questioning look and I'll nod and say *sure, there were alternatives, we should've asked our friends if we could camp in their yard, we could've moved into Carola's mother's guest room, but instead we stayed behind even after the authorities warned us to leave, after everyone else had gone home, we were so ashamed of everything, of having bought plane tickets to the U.S. that we never actually used, of our electric BMW that we bought on a down payment, of all the milk and cheese and meat.*

We've been walking for an hour and the straps of the baby carrier are cutting into my shoulders when we hear them in the distance, first the sirens, then the rumbling of the engines. There are several vehicles, all coming from the direction in which we're walking: three, four, five fire engines and a red car with the fire and rescue service logo on the side and blue lights on the roof. They emerge from the edge of the forest and drive parallel to our road, and we shout, we jump, we wave, Carola runs toward them waving Becka's red flannel blanket like a flag as they turn off onto a forest track.

This is just one of those things you think will never happen to you, I'll say to Micke in half an hour's time, once we track him down in Rättvik, and then I'll hug Zack, whose foot has already been patched up and who, naturally, has already become firm friends with the two boys and is playing on their tablets and wondering what the grown-ups are making such a fuss about, *we thought they had it under control; this is Sweden, after all, it really is a scandal that we don't have any planes of our own.*

The vehicles don't see us, or maybe they see us but don't care; they disappear into the forest as suddenly as they appeared, and I realize that they're not on their way to put something out at all, they're fleeing the fire, because when I glance up toward Ovanmyra I see the flames dancing above the treetops. There's a fire where we're heading, there's a fire where we've come from, we stop, we stand still.

It was for you, I don't say to Carola as she crouches down by a decorative old bike cart painted a shade of pale blue. There is an equally decorative old-fashioned milk bottle to one side of it, various objects made from wood and glass, a flat rock with the words *JANZON FAMILY* painted in round, bright red letters and a white sign offering *Fiber Broadband from DalaEnergi*. We've unclipped Becka from the carrier and Carola is sitting with her in her arms, crying in long, awful sobs as the smoke from the forest swirls all around us, Vilja is trying to find more information on her phone, and I'm on hold in some sort of line for the emergency services, the screen feels prickly against my cheek; we've been doing this for a while now, Carola's phone is dead and mine is down to its last red sliver of power, the heat and the bright sunlight really do eat up the battery, we had power banks but they're in the suitcase, the one that broke, the one I left behind.

It was for you that I got us up to our eyeballs in debt. It was for you that I had a third child. And now she wants me again, it's started again, we're like two secret agents at war. She sent me a picture yesterday, one that I took that summer, we were lying naked in the sun in the cockpit of a sailboat and I took a selfie of us from above with her phone, and it's not about how she looks naked, she's obviously so beautiful that I feel sick, but it's not about that, it's about how I looked when I was happy.

And beneath the image, she wrote: Don't be ashamed to be human, be proud.

"Didrik, please, get us out of here," Carola says in a gravelly voice. "Get me and the kids out of here now."

I don't say: *I wanted to stay out here for as long as possible because I'd decided that once we got back to Stockholm, I'd leave you. This was our last summer together. I stayed for you.*

Becka is screaming again, and I sit down on the ground beside them, rummage through the diaper bag for her bottles, the thermos, the powder. Something about the sign from DalaEnergi is bothering me. Broadband. I remember when we had it installed at the summer house five years ago, Carola's mother had to pay a fortune, as she frequently likes to remind us; they dug up the whole yard and we've had reliable, lightning-fast Wi-Fi ever since, we've been kept up to date on the fire, the fires, hour by hour, with flashes and push notifications on our phones and tablets, and I've *still* managed to get us into this mess, it's completely incredible, it's utterly, sensationally idiotic that we, two smart, modern, educated people with money, phones, computers, and fiber broadband, ended up here.

Broadband. Something about it keeps niggling away, irritating me, something I should have thought of.

Broadband. You can have broadband installed. You can buy wood. You can pay someone to cut down a tree. Broadband. Right.

You can get fiber broadband from DalaEnergi.

I jump to my feet, tell Carola:

"Don't worry, honey, I'll fix this. Wait here."

I kiss Becka on her clammy brow and start running back toward Östbjörka.

The smoke is thicker than it was earlier, no longer just a harsh, dirty scent in the air. I can actually see it now, swirling, billowing, winding between the trees all around me. I try not to get carried away, to keep jogging calmly, methodically, at a pace I can manage for several miles without getting my heart rate too high.

The noticeboard is still there, and I was right: between DalaEnergi and the Cabin Owners' Association AGM is a plastic pouch, stapled to the board, a printed sheet of paper with the words *Quadbike For Sale Price Negotiable Call Kåre on 070-85 58 23 45* above an image of a shimmering orange beetle with huge, rugged tires and two slanting, evil eyes.

I try to keep my breathing steady, to ignore the smoke. *Forget that you ran, forget that you left Zack with two strangers and didn't even bother taking their number, forget that Becka is screaming through her mask back there. This is smart, you're finally about to do something really smart, just keep going.*

I move into the shade and take out my phone, wipe down the screen on my thigh, automatically check for likes before entering the first few digits, 0708558, then stop, delete it. No. I open the directory map, zoom in on Östbjörka, type *KÅRE*.

The only name that comes up is *Levander, Kåre Ingmar*. The house is fifteen hundred feet away, and when I try to enlarge the image to get a better view of the road the display freezes and dies, but by then I've already started running, a blue sign with the words *PRIVATE PROPERTY*, followed by a gravel track leading straight into the woods.

The minute I see the house peeping out from between the burnt orange leaves, I know I'm in the right place. This isn't some pokey little cabin for summer guests, it's a full-size home, two stories of shining white wood with blue corners, solar panels on the roof. As I come closer I see a new-looking terrace and a couple of deep, flashy sofas by an oval-shaped pool with a spotless cover over the top, the kind that rolls back at the push of a button; in the corner by the wall is a large outdoor kitchen with a gas-powered barbecue the size of a spaceship. This is the kind of place I've always wanted, the kind of house my dad would call *a show home* with barely concealed contempt. I walk around the corner and come out into a large, manicured yard with a newly planted apple tree, a greenhouse, two hammocks on frames in the shade of a neatly pruned plum tree. A robotic lawn mower trundles like a sleepwalker over the dry, sun-bleached grass.

I keep going. There is a parking area on the other side of the house, a trailer for a motorboat, a tarpaulin, but no vehicles. A toolshed built in the same style as the house, white with blue trim. I run over to the door, wide enough for a car and secured with a huge silver padlock that I weigh in my hand, studying the hot lump of metal for a moment.

The hammocks, I quickly decide, running back over and unhooking the big, inviting hammock and studying the frame. I've seen this kind of hammock before, by the pool at a luxury hotel, I saw the staff setting them up; it's just a couple of metal tubes that slot together, taking it apart takes no time at all. The hollow metal tube feels warm and smooth in my hand, and I run back over to the terrace by the pool where there are a number of big, beautiful panoramic windows.

A moment of hesitation, thoughts of insurance companies and money and having to sell off pension funds, then the image of Becka coughing away in her baby carriage comes back to me, her naked body, her chubby little thighs sticking out of her diaper, eyes wide and red above her mask, and I swing the metal pole like a heavy, rigid golf club, straight through the window.

The clatter of broken glass is immediately followed by the blaring of an alarm, a deafening sound that must be audible for miles, and I manage to paint a futile, hopeless picture of a security firm showing up, a car with some sort of reassuring company name on the side, a stocky, uneducated man in a cheap uniform, and I quickly clear away a few shards of glass with the edge of the tube and then run over to the poolside sofa to grab a couple of cushions, all blue and white and red, elegant New England Classic style, placing them on the bare window ledge before carefully climbing in.

The house is just as luxurious on the inside, a mix of modern designer furniture and older pieces that might have been inherited or won at auction. There's a Mora grandfather clock, an incredibly old hand-painted wardrobe, a wall hanging, an enormous open fireplace. On the wall in the living room is a huge panoramic photograph of the Manhattan skyline against a colorful dusk or dawn sky. The colors are very sixties or seventies, and despite the expensive frame it feels wrong in a home like this. I decide it must have hung somewhere else at some point in time, only ending up here for sentimental reasons, the Chrysler Building, the Empire State Building, the World Trade Center, beacons from another world.

I take off my mask and breathe in the cool, clean air. Feel a sense of weariness, of having come home; I shiver in the delicious chill and realize that the AC is running. The alarm is still blaring, but I ignore it and go through to the kitchen, gleaming stainless steel everywhere. I open the fridge and see plastic trays of smoked salmon and marinated lamb cutlets, bottles of sparkling rosé wine, blue cheese, jars of herring, meatballs, a large bowl of salad, they were clearly expecting guests. *Welcome*, the fridge whispers to me, *have a seat, just for a minute, you've barely eaten anything other than a few cookies all day, why not find a cable and plug in your phone and catch your breath for half an hour or so?*

I grab a can of beer from the shelf and press the cool metal to my cheek, reaching for a plastic bottle of sparkling water with my free hand. I use my teeth to unscrew the lid and pour the fizzing, gurgling water over my head, just letting it run, pooling on the floor around me as the chill makes me shiver. I rummage for a plastic bag from beneath the sink and fill it with anything that looks easy to eat: containers of fruit yogurt, a pack of sliced salami, grapes, a cucumber. I open the pantry door and grab crackers, raisins, nuts, peer around the kitchen and spot another few bottles of sparkling water. I carry everything over to the back door, to the pretty carved key cabinet, and I open it, two key rings and a handful of loose keys of varying shapes and sizes inside, they could be for absolutely anything. I throw the lot into the plastic bag and then unlock the door, there are three postcards stuck to the back of it, one featuring a heart and the words *The Best We Have Is Each Other*, another *CARPE DIEM* and a white cloud against a clear blue sky, the third a close-up of a child's smiling, open, innocent face and *Today Is the First Day of the Rest of Your Life*. I put my mask back on and step outside into the heat and the smoke.

The third key fits the padlock, and there it is, just like in the picture: an orange bug, surprisingly small, like a large motorbike on four tractor tires. There is some sort of cargo rack behind the seat, and I stash the plastic bag there, peer around the toolshed, see a chain saw, a pressure washer, a leaf blower, an old kettle barbecue, a brand-new racing bike. It's all neat and tidy, shelves and boxes everywhere, but I quickly find what I'm looking for: an axe, a pair of work gloves, and a jerrican of something that smells like gas.

Right. One of the key rings has a big plastic key with a logo and the number *ATV200CC* on it. I get onto the quad bike and study the handlebars. The key fits. I take a deep breath and turn the ignition. The soft, muted rumbling makes me want to sob and cry with joy.

Other than very briefly at a company event, I've never been on an all-terrain vehicle before, and definitely never a quad bike, but you see them everywhere out here in the countryside. I once saw three girls in swimsuits come rolling in on one that was only slightly smaller than this down by the lake, they couldn't have been much older than Vilja, fifteen or sixteen tops, laughing and hooting as though they were on a pool float. Gently, cautiously, I turn the right handlebar and immediately feel its power, the way it jolts and vibrates beneath me, through my thighs, under my feet, the vehicle roars and I shout again as I roll out of the shed—stupidly easily, as though I've never done anything else—and across the parking area, down onto the forest track, and away from the screeching house. If only she could see me now.

The winter when Vilja was three, before we got pregnant with Zack, we went up to Åre with William and Lisa the weekend before Christmas. It was a spur-of-the-moment decision, they'd just bought a new ski-in/ski-out condo on the slopes and they wanted to christen it with us, get a few runs in, do a bit of Christmas shopping, nothing special.

But then it started snowing. That was becoming increasingly rare at Christmas, but it was really coming down heavy. We enjoyed one beautiful, shimmering day after another, repeatedly telling each other how lucky we were with the snow-covered spruce trees and the rim frost on the windows, Vilja tumbling around in the area by the slopes, building a snowman in a pair of red overalls and going for long, magical runs through the fresh snow on my new snowboard; it looked like the entire country would see a white Christmas that year, the kind of Christmas we vaguely remembered from childhood but never thought we'd get to see again.

The only problem was that it didn't stop, it just kept falling and falling, wet, heavy snow, and when the time came for us to head home everything had ground to a halt, the planes couldn't take off and there were pileups on the roads, reports of cars that had driven up there without winter tires skidding into ditches; it could take up to ten hours for the tow truck rescue vehicle to arrive, and one physically disabled person actually froze to death in their car.

We'd taken the sleeper train north, this was back when we still tried to take the train everywhere—the train to London, the train to Berlin, the summer we first fell in love we took the train down to Greece, four days and eighteen transfers. But when we tried to head home from Åre that Christmas, there were no trains, there was snow on the tracks, frozen exchanges, signaling problems, broken-down engines, chaos at the station, desperate families who had booked accommodation for one week and now had nowhere to stay and no way to get home. The authorities arranged buses down from the mountains so that people could get to Sundsvall or at least Östersund, but they quickly filled up and then several of them got caught in one of the traffic jams after all. We had a three-year-old and just didn't want to take that risk.

So we stayed put with our friends in their new condo, day after day. We let our employers know that they would have to cope without us, and it wasn't actually so bad, we both had our laptops with us and could manage quite a bit of work from there, our bosses and colleagues almost seemed to find it charming that we were stuck in the mountains, trapped in the middle of what the papers were calling the *SNOWMAGEDDON*, an exciting story that they could follow from a distance, cheery messages and smileys, how's it going in the SNOWMAGEDDON and we've got our fingers crossed and go you guys!

But as the days passed we started to realize that we'd have to celebrate Christmas in Åre, stuck in an apartment that was starting to feel pretty cramped and sad. Wille and Lisa were child-free for environmental reasons, and they made it crystal clear that they wanted to spend that magical Christmas alone in their eye-wateringly expensive Jacuzzi and bedroom with a mirror on the ceiling. We were supposed to be celebrating with Carola's mother at the summer house in Dalarna, she was recently widowed and kept sending us videos of flickering red candles on white tablecloths, roaring fires, a pile of presents for Vilja beneath the tree, and on the twenty-third Carola started crying and said *please, Didrik, isn't there some way, is it really impossible?*

So I pulled my coat on and walked to the center of town. All the car rental companies had closed for the holiday, and the rideshares were, of course, long gone, but I'd seen something else over by the slopes. They were busy setting up for the Alpine Ski World Cup on New Year's Day, and there were barriers, construction huts, and diggers all over the place, the entire area had been fenced off, but I found a dark corner where the snow had drifted so high that it was easy to climb over, and I wandered into the deserted arena, saw the sponsors' banners, the big grandstand, snow groomers crawling up and down the steep slope on Caterpillar treads, the snow still coming down heavy.

And over by the finish line, at exactly the right angle to be visible in the background when the camera zoomed in on the competitors as they skidded to a halt and squinted up at their times, smiling and waving to the crowd, there was a huge glass box containing a deep-blue Range Rover.

I took out my phone and made a few calls.

Two hours later, at some time around midnight, I rolled through the three-foot-high snowdrifts and out onto the streets of Åre. It had finally stopped snowing and the stars were twinkling down on me through the panoramic sunroof, and I realized right there and then that it was true, that what the older guys at the agency muttered about during dinner parties or late at night at hotel conferences, when the push notifications came through about hurricanes in Mozambique, flash floods in the United States, famines in Yemen, or the suicide epidemic among farmers in South America, North Africa, Australia. They always said *there'll be lifeboats*, and they said it without pride, without arrogance, nothing but a dry statement, and I realized that if you just pulled the right strings, if you played the game right, if you simply made up your mind that when it comes to you and your family's safety and freedom, there's no limit to what you'd be willing to do, there would always be a way out, a lifeboat.

I pulled up outside the condo and marched inside and woke Carola and told her to pack our things, not that we had much, we'd only been planning to stay for the weekend. I tossed everything into the cavernous trunk and she came out with our sleeping daughter wrapped in a blanket. She saw the enormous SUV with its fat new winter tires, and that was when it happened, when she saw the performance, the comfort, the four-wheel drive of the car I'd found for us and she didn't kiss me, didn't tell me that she loved me, didn't even look me in the eye as she asked *where's the car seat?*

At first I didn't understand the question, blurting out something about how Vilja could maybe just sit on a few cushions.

She needs a rear-facing car seat. You know that, don't you?

"I completely lost it," I said many years later, in therapy. "I was just so disappointed. I'd expected . . . I don't know. Something more."

"What, did you want a *medal* or something?" Carola forced out the words between sobs, snot running down both sides of her mouth; I had to look away to avoid showing my disgust.

"That you'd think I was *good*," I said lamely. "That you'd say something *nice*."

"Didrik," the therapist spoke up, looking genuinely interested. "What is it that makes you seek affirmation from Carola?"

"Not affirmation," I muttered. "But maybe, just once in a damn while, a bit of . . ."

"Gratitude?" She managed to get the sarcasm out between sniffs.

"Yes, actually." I gave her a cold smile. The therapist jotted something down. "For a change. A bit of fucking gratitude."

She can't face forward until she's four, I thought you knew that, she said, and I thrust the keys into her hand and said *do whatever you fucking want I'm going to bed Merry Christmas*, but before long, of course, we were cruising south toward Dalarna, her half dozing with Vilja in her arms, and we didn't say a word to each other for the rest of the night or for most of Christmas.

But not even our fight and the silence that followed it could ruin those hours as I sped down the country lanes toward Dalarna in the dawn, the snow thick and white like vanilla ice cream, Östanvik, Sunnanhed, the snow-covered church, the smoke from the chimneys, my sleeping family in the huge backseat; not even my anxiety over the humiliation, the string-pulling, the scruples I'd had to throw out the window to be able to borrow that obscenely expensive sponsor car for three days while some event person cooked up a story about it needing an extra tuning in Stockholm, none of that could cloud my triumph at having *worked it out*, at having refused to be the little man, someone who just sat around, mouth open like a baby bird, waiting for Daddy State or Mommy Bank to step in and solve all my problems, at having rolled up my sleeves and just *worked it out* instead.

I feel that same sweet feeling now, multiplied by a hundred, as I cruise down the forest road toward Östbjörka on the back of the quad bike, and when I turn past the noticeboard and stop to grab the Ikea bag we left in the back of the trailer, then have a sudden brain wave and start backing up and fiddling and adjusting and after a few minutes' sweaty work actually *manage* to attach the trailer to the tow hook, the smoke and the heat are all that stop me from breaking out in song.

I tell myself it won't be so undignified this time, that even if she doesn't immediately drop to her knees and show me her gratitude for saving us from this hell and instead starts whining about where Becka is going to sit, or where I got hold of the vehicle, or why it took me so long, I won't be annoyed, I won't snap or argue, I'll just calmly tell her that this is as good as it gets, that we can use this to get to Rättvik, *I've done my best here, so let's go.*

Stop hoping for praise. Stop expecting applause. Be a grown-up.

You asked me to get us out of here and that's what I'm doing. Something like that.

And Becka's little arms around my neck.

———————

The baby carriage is abandoned in the ditch.

The haze is now so thick, the road and the forest and the sky so murky, that I almost drive straight past it. It's standing with the handle toward the road, as though someone was about to push it straight into the woods before changing their mind. The canopy is unfolded, I recognize the material, can see all the details: the cognac-colored leather on the handle, the little white cushion with the zip in the basket underneath, the one that turns into a rain cover that can be quickly and easily pulled out and draped over this particular model.

That's all.

The white sign from DalaEnergi, the shiny gold wrapper from the pack of cookies on the blue bicycle cart, pushed between the milk bottle and the flat stone with *JANZON FAMILY* painted on it. This was where I left them forty-five minutes ago. An hour, tops.

I pull in, switch off the engine, jump down. Shout *CAROLA* and then *CAROLA, VILJA*, and then just *HELLO*, I shout *HELLO* quite a few times.

The only response is the soft rustling of the trees, the distant sirens, and beneath it all, a faint, persistent note: The roar. The noise. The fire.

I shout again. Scream, bellow. I stand by the baby carriage, reach into it, feel the soft, hypoallergenic material of the mattress. The comforter and the blankets are gone, but I do find a little yellow rag doll. It was Zack who picked it out in the shop that day, she often buries her nose in it when she sleeps, we call it Snuggly; I take it out and hold it to my face and breathe in the scent of old milk and sleep before I yell again. *HELLO.*

I told you to wait.

But I don't feel any anger, no disappointment that she—they—have left me alone here. All I feel is shame. Because it was me who left them, after all, I just ran off. I should have told them my plan for the quad bike, but I was afraid she would say no or argue or pick a fight, that we'd end up in all that difficult stuff again. It was easier just to act.

They kept going. We were on our way to Ovanmyra and they kept going, maybe they saw something, or maybe they got scared and ran.

A flake of soot comes sailing down from the sky.

I put Snuggly back in the baby carriage, detach the mattress, and fold up the chassis, then lift everything into the trailer and climb back up onto the quad bike and set off in the direction they must have gone.

After a few minutes the landscape opens up and I see houses through the haze, a church, a soccer field, the whole lot ominously quiet and deserted. I must have missed the sign, this must be Ovanmyra, and I shout *CAROLA* again, though I can barely hear myself over the roar of the engine, *CAROLA* and then *HELLO*, and there is a bus parked outside the church.

Really.

A good old-fashioned coach, engine ticking over. The sign at the front says *NOT IN SERVICE* and there is a pimpled twentysomething standing beside it, wearing overalls and a cap with a logo on it, no face mask, smoking a cigarette as though it was the most natural thing on earth, muttering into a walkie-talkie. He gives me a stressed, irritated glance as I pull in, then gestures to the burning forest on the horizon.

"You seen anyone else?" he shouts over the din of the two vehicles. I shake my head.

"Have you seen a woman?" I ask. "Blond, with a baby?"

But he doesn't hear me, he just keeps talking into his walkie-talkie. I can see a handful of people inside the bus, can hear a dog barking, a child crying, and I yell *CAROLA* again but the child is older than Becka, Becka can't talk and this one is shouting *daddy* over and over again. An older man, probably somewhere around sixty, appears in the doorway. His face is black with soot beneath his white hair, a pale ring from his mask, he is clutching a laptop to his chest and has a bag from the liquor store in one hand, and he shouts *have you seen a black dog? A Bernese mountain dog?* and I shake my head but he just repeats the same question, *a black dog? A Bernese mountain dog?* and the screaming child appears in the window, a chubby red-haired girl in a T-shirt with a unicorn and a rainbow on it, her face a pink ball of howling and tears, she shouts *daddy* at me through the glass and I just stare blankly at her.

"A woman, blond?" I repeat. "With a baby? And a teenage girl?"

The kid in the cap shrugs. "We can't keep track of everyone. There were two buses, the first one left half an hour ago."

"But surely you must know who you've got on board?" I point to his walkie-talkie. "Who are you talking to on that? Can you ask if they know?"

He shakes his head with the all-important expression of a boy promoted to God.

"Command is evacuating over by Mora now. They want me to head up there."

The older man is still lingering in the doorway, paying close attention to our conversation.

"Have you checked down in Östbjörka?" he asks.

"We were there earlier," I snap. "There's not a soul there."

"Did you see a dog?" he continues eagerly. "A black dog, a Bernese mountain dog?"

"It's my wife," I say, hating the sound of my voice. "My wife and two daughters. Someone gave our son a lift to Rättvik."

"See, you got lucky there," says the kid in the cap, he seems slightly happier now. "I'm leaving for Rättvik in seven minutes."

"We have a baby," I say, my tone flat. "A four-month-old baby. She's still here somewhere."

"Or maybe she's in Rättvik too," the kid sighs, nonchalantly stamping out his cigarette on the gravel. "People get there in all sorts of ways. I saw a guy arrive with a bunch of people in a motorboat this morning. He had his kids and whatever in the car, but he was towing a motorboat on a trailer and there were, like, three families inside, it looked insane."

"My phone is dead. You need to put out an alert. Helicopters. Something."

"We can't keep track of everyone," says the kid. "Command has told us to take anyone who wants to go to Rättvik, so you can either get in or stay here. Five minutes." He holds up a hand, his fingers splayed, and uses the other to fish out another cigarette.

I'll stop watching porn.

I've passed Östbjörka and am on my way back, the sign says *FLEA MARKET NEW POTATOES* and I think *I'll call Mom and Dad more often, stop losing my temper with Vilja, pay more attention to Zack's babbling, read more picture books to Becka, be a better son and father, be there for them, really there*. The road slopes up and bends off to the right, a clear-cutting, an abandoned residential study center, *I'll eat vegan three days a week*.

She wouldn't do something like this. The idea of her and Vilja dumping the baby carriage and carrying Becka all the way to Ovanmyra, getting on a bus, and traveling to Rättvik without leaving a message with anyone by the church, it's unthinkable. *I'll set up a monthly donation to Greenpeace Amnesty Save the Children.*

She would never leave me here.

Our paths first crossed through work, a few emails back and forth, and on a complete whim I asked her if she'd like to go swimming one day, it was going to be hot that weekend, up to eighty-six degrees. So we lay down on a rock in the archipelago and spent a long, magical Saturday baking in the sun, Carola reading a feminist journal and me various research summaries on methane gases in Siberia. We dozed for a while and when we woke I took her hand and, with a level of confidence that surprised me, led her into the woods. She didn't say a word, just seemed amused and surprised and flicked a few ants off her thigh afterward, and once we were back on the rock she smiled calmly and said *maybe I should take a quick dip.*

We had a barbecue that evening, in the yard outside the small house she still shared with the man she had decided to leave, and after we ate we fucked again on the kitchen floor and then I took the bus home and I don't think either of us thought we'd meet up again.

But we kept running into each other at bars and pubs that summer, and she came back to my pokey little studio flat one evening, and as I lay naked with her horny young body on top of mine I experienced, for the first time in Sweden, the feeling of sweat dripping down my body in the middle of the night, of literally lying in a pool of my own sweat, a close, oppressive heat even with all the windows wide open onto the August night. This was back when the papers still ran headlines like *SUPER SUMMER CONTINUES!* and *MEDITERRANEAN HEAT TO RETURN!* as though heat waves were something to welcome and enjoy, sandy beaches and outdoor seating areas, balmy nights at music festivals, happy children playing in sprinklers, a time when the Mediterranean heat was all tan lines and cocktails with umbrellas.

But heat is death, I think as I sit on the back of the quad bike, watching the flames dance in the treetops all around me. It means dying, withering, shriveling, fading away and becoming ash. Heat makes us slow, lazy, passive, and indifferent. And then there's the fire, and with it, annihilation.

Becka. Her gummy little mouth. The rasping, babbling sound she has started making more often these past few weeks. *If I can just hold her one more time, I'll cut my working hours and make us a foster family for unaccompanied refugee minors.*

There's the other sign, WILD CHILDREN AND SENIORS AT PLAY, a woodpile, a bike tossed into a ditch.

They've walked the whole way back to the house. The thought comes slowly, swirling up through my consciousness, *they've worked out a way to start the car, they're probably waiting for me there now,* but surely that can't be right, I stop the quad bike, panic pumping through me in heavy, nauseating spasms.

Something makes the dry leaves rustle, a swishing, clip-clopping sound, and I see three deer, one big and two small, bolt out of the forest and across the road, disappearing on the other side.

They're fleeing. Just like those fire engines we saw earlier.

I put the quad bike in reverse, the whole thing lurching when the trailer tips at the edge of the road; I turn back.

WILD CHILDREN AND SENIORS AT PLAY

ÖSTBJÖRKA 2

FLEA MARKET NEW POTATOES

The sign from DalaEnergi. The bike cart.

This was where we stopped, where we saw them coming toward us, they turned off the road to the right here. I slow down and keep going. There are no signs, no road markings, just a bumpy forest track leading straight in among the pines. It slopes down gently, and the air feels slightly less unbearable, more greenery left on the bushes, more shade. I spot a pair of swimming trunks hanging from a branch, something glittering between the trees, through the haze. A swimming spot. A lake.

I saw a plane that morning, one of those water bombers. Where did it get its water from? Where do the fire engines get theirs?

They followed them. They made their way down to the lake, to the planes.

The road is bumpy and the quad bike tilts, the trail becomes steeper, narrower, there's barely enough space to drive here. I see a jetty, a figure standing at the very end, arms wrapped around a child, and I yell *CAROLA* again, *HELLO* again, *I'm not going to leave you, I'll never leave you again never fly again never eat meat again never regret my life with you again*, and the trailer bounces along behind the quad bike as I reach the little bathing area, but there's nothing here.

There's nothing here.

The figure on the jetty is a post holding an orange life buoy. And all around the dark, empty lake, the forest is on fire. A huge burning pine tilts toward the calm surface of the water on the other side. It falls slowly, roaring, crashing, hissing. Sparks and flakes of soot swirl through the air like swarms of insects, and it burns, an evil stinging sensation when the tiny glowing particles hit my bare arms, shoulders, chest. I'm wearing workman's gloves and I'm awkwardly trying to brush myself down when I see a strange light from the corner of one eye, feel a disgusting little beast clawing at the back of my neck, nipping my skin, the pain hits me a moment later and I scream and start beating my hair, beating the fire, howling, yelling in agony and reaching for a bottle of water from the cargo rack, desperately unscrewing the lid and emptying it over my head.

Still sobbing and groaning in pain I try to turn the quad bike around, but the track is too narrow with the trailer attached, the bathing area flanked by large rocks, I'll have to reverse up the trail, try to make my way back up the steep slope. The smoke mixes with the sparkling water in my eyes, and I find the right gear and lurch backward, away from the lake and the swirling fire; the quad bike jolts, it tips, teeters, the trailer swings the other way and into a bush, I swear and pull forward before trying to reverse again, it goes better this time, I'm back in the forest now, the trees protecting me from the worst of the smoke.

Out of here. You need to get out of here.

CAROLA, I yell again.

She's probably drinking a latte macchiato outside a café in Rättvik right now. Becka is dozing on a blanket in the shade. Vilja is on her phone. Zack is reading his book.

The shock has subsided, and I reach up and touch my hair, whimper when the rough finger of my glove touches the raw, burned spot on my scalp.

My hair caught fire. I stole a quad bike and a trailer and spent hours driving around the place, looking for you, but then my hair caught fire and that's when I gave up.

I keep reversing up the slope, glancing back over my shoulder; the ground levels out and the road gets wider just up ahead.

No, I didn't give up. Rättvik. You were waiting for me here in Rättvik. I worked it out in the end, that you'd made your way here.

I'm back on the forest road, off the narrow trail, and I start angling the handlebars to turn around when something catches, a root, a rock, something that stops the wheel. A gust of wind blows a billowing gray veil of smoke and ash through the trees, blinding me, and I accelerate to push past whatever it is, but something back there really is stuck, so I put the quad bike in reverse and accelerate again, feel it loosen, feel something lightening, lifting, I glance up at the trees to see which way I'm going but everything is just a big gray haze, and when I accelerate again I hear rather than feel that the wheels have left the ground, and it's the whipping branches against my face and torso, rather than the loss of balance, that make me realize that both the quad bike and the trailer are about to roll over and then everything is upside down and there's a rasping, creaking sound, a metallic thud, a sledgehammer, a safe falling on top of me, pushing me down into the hard, dry ground, my shoulder against a tree trunk, the rough bark mute, indifferent, and merciless.

———

Because nature doesn't give a damn about us.

That's the key thing here, the thing we need to try to grasp.

Nature doesn't care.

It's not going to thank you for buying an electric car. It won't play nice just because you've put a solar panel on the roof. It definitely doesn't think it's OK for you to treat yourself to that flight to see your dying sister if you promise to avoid flying for the rest of your life. It's not going to give you any extra rain just because you decided to stop at two kids, or one, or none. It won't absorb any more or less carbon dioxide just because you've gone to vote. It won't spare the coral reefs, the glaciers, or the rain forests because you've convinced your kids to at least try the Impossible Burger. Nothing you do will have any impact on what we're experiencing right now; this is a consequence of decisions that were made—or, more importantly, not made—ten or thirty or fifty years ago.

Nature doesn't negotiate. It can't be talked round, appeased, or threatened. We're a natural disaster that has been escalating for the past ten thousand years; we're the sixth mass extinction, a super-predator, killer bacteria, an invasive species, but to nature we're nothing but a ripple on the surface. A minor detail, a slight cough, a nightmare you barely remember you've forgotten.

She looks out at the room, pauses for effect, takes a sip of water.

When we say that we are "destroying the planet" or "harming nature," it's nothing but a self-centered lie. We aren't destroying the planet. We're simply destroying our own ability to live on it.

Those of you involved in shaping public opinion probably have clients who want to come across as good and moral and responsible, and they probably want your help developing initiatives to become greener, less energy intensive, and more sustainable. And all of that is great, of course, don't get me wrong, it's not a bad thing to want to be good.

She lowers her voice half an octave.

But don't forget the other aspect. The fact that more and more of today's consumers are aware not just of climate change but of the ultimate truth: that it's already too late. That it's over. That our civilization is coming to an end, and with it, of course, the entire species. Most people think that hu-

mans will still be here a hundred years from now, and three to five hundred years' time is probably also possible in some shape or form, at least in certain regions, but what about a thousand years? Ten thousand? That's just ridiculous; why would we still be here then?

She flashes her dazzlingly white teeth.

If you ask me, there's a certain freedom in that. A comfort. There are no environmental problems, no climate crisis, no end of the earth. What there is—or was—is a species of mammals that has multiplied to such an extent that it ultimately crashed the ecosystems on which it depends, committing collective suicide. And of course it's sad if you happen to belong to that particular species, but seen from the perspective of a few million years, from a cosmic or evolutionary perspective, it's utterly irrelevant. It doesn't matter at all.

She looks out at her audience. A few people are making notes, but most of us are just sitting quietly, listening to her.

So what does matter?

Her eyes scan the rows. She passes me with a teasing wink, focusing instead on a young man in a pink designer sweater and expensive English leather shoes, a new recruit to one of the big firms.

What matters is good red wine. Dark chocolate. Juicy steaks. And beautiful clothes. Dream holidays to exotic places. Nice cars. And smart new technology.

Her smile grows wider.

And maybe . . . just maybe, a bit of great sex.

The audience titters. She pushes back a lock of long black hair.

What matters is that you get your clients and their customers to understand that there is no reason to be ashamed. Don't be ashamed to be human, be proud.

Her eyes drift back to me. Into me. Her face turns serious, her voice soft.

That last part was Tomas Tranströmer. He knew. We aren't bad people. We're just people.

"It's just the handlebars."

A hoarse, muffled voice through the smoke.

The weight shifts, a mountain of knuckles being slowly dragged over my ribs. Everything becomes hazy in the smoke and I don't even know if my eyes are open, but I can hear or feel the creaking and the pain and suddenly the force gives way and there is a thud that ripples down my spine as the quad bike lands on the ground beside me but not on me, and my body is free, as light and as dead as a sack full of ash.

The hand drags me up, I help with a hand against a tree, can make out the overturned quad bike, its engine still ticking over. The voice wheezes, spits, *can you walk?* and I don't answer, just lean against a hand or shoulder and limp forward. Something in my left foot is screaming or shouting but otherwise my legs seem to be moving, though no, I stumble and collapse like a rag doll and the voice barks *up with you now*, a gruff old rasping voice, and there is that hard, pinching hand again, so I get up, stagger forward, try to breathe, and despite the mask my lungs fill with burning, poisonous filth.

Then we're out of the woods and it gets slightly brighter. I glance over to the man and see gray hair above a blue-and-white scarf wound around a face. There is a burgundy Volvo on the road, one of the blocky models from the mid-eighties, a good old *social democrat wagon*.

The rear door opens and Carola comes rushing out, shouting, Vilja right behind her, both are crying and shouting, *Didrik* and *honey* and *Dad*, and I must have fallen again because they help me to my feet and I cling on to their shoulders and drag myself over to the Volvo, tumble into the roasting-hot backseat, and there she is, naked on a blanket, she's dead, I just know that she's dead, the gunk around her mouth and her glassy, lifeless eyes, *oh God, no no no*, and I kiss her filthy little cheeks, her shoulders, her forehead, and she coughs and starts crying, a shrill, trembling sound, her eyes open in blind, sobbing cracks.

Carola gets in behind me and quickly closes the door, shrieking again when she sees my burned head. She glances down at my crotch with a look of horror and disgust, and I don't want to do it, but I have to lower my hand and feel. My thighs are covered in a damp, claggy goo, and I raise my hand to my face and see that it's piss shit blood, no, it's a dirty white mess, that sour smell.

Yogurt. Fruit yogurt. The containers I took from the house must have popped against me when I overturned.

The gray windbreaker is in the driver's seat. The old man has tugged down the scarf, and his face is sooty and his eyes are twitching, but his back is straight, his hands steady on the wheel, focused up ahead.

"Right, then," he says, coughing uncomfortably. "Anyone else need picking up?"

The baby carriage, my sluggish brain thinks. *The baby carriage is still in the trailer, it cost a fortune*, but I don't say anything, the car starts with a jolt and my ears are ringing, the car rocks and I slip, fall down from the seat into the gap behind Vilja, the dirty old rubber mat against my face, it feels so good to give in at last, to let go, to subordinate myself, to finally be able to throw up.

———

there   *hello*   *please, we need to*

is he breathing?   *my son*   *prioritize*

get to the emergency room   *can't you see that*

several hours out there and

hello   *for God's sake*

OK, but if you don't   a four-month-old baby

to the left   the left

it's a fucking outrage that you

hello   our taxes

The world is a body of water, a swamp of despair, and I'm at the very bottom. I hear voices that sound like they belong to dark, ancient fish up at the surface, sometimes Vilja, sometimes Carola, cars starting and stopping, doors slamming, engines spluttering and rumbling; there is shouting and crying and strangers' voices, shrill or gruff or just indifferent, sirens and howling children and barking dogs, and we come to a halt and the doors open and cool, clean air floods in over me, I cough, spit, gasp, and then there are hands on my shoulders and legs, *get him out*, and I'm floating through the air for a moment before the blanket, the ground, the bottom, the voices are back, cold, cold water on my face, it runs over my chin and forehead and down onto my throat, the wound on my head stirs to life and I take a stinging, prickling breath and scream and throw up again.

where did you go?

Carola's voice, her hands on my face, she is kneeling over me with a piece of material in one hand, carefully dabbing around my eyes, a red plastic bucket, a greenish-yellow lawn, red cabins.

where did you go we were looking for you?

Everything goes blurry again and I sink back into the sludge. *Becka,* I think, *Becka,* and Carola can clearly hear what I'm thinking because she quickly says something reassuring about *medics*, and the shame of lying flat out here rather than being with my children is so unbearable that I try to sit up and feel a stab of pain in my ribs, and I whimper and groan and slump back onto my elbows.

Through aching, squinting eyes I see a large lake opening out onto an empty horizon, reflecting the summer evening light. A sandy beach, a group of people standing in the distance, green tents, vans; I turn my head and see a row of identical small red buildings with decks and white corner panels, a sign welcoming me to *SILJANBADET CAMPSITE—DALARNA'S RIVIERA*.

"We're in Rättvik," she says. "Just lie down."

"Zack." My voice is listless, pathetic, barely a whisper.

"We're going to go and ask around later, apparently there's someone who . . . some sort of information, over there in the tents."

I slump back and close my eyes but she keeps asking *where did you go.* or maybe she doesn't say anything at all, maybe the Carola tape deck in my head has switched itself on and is telling me things I've already worked out, that the old man showed up in his Volvo a few minutes after I ran off, that they drove around looking for me, *back and forth all over the place* and *we couldn't understand* and *really weird* and *Becka almost stopped breathing* and *thought we saw you on one of those weird motorbike things and we shouted but you just rode off* and *we could've been here hours ago.*

"I was coming to get you," I say, my voice no more than a whimper. "You were meant to wait for me."

She grabs her rag again, I recognize it now, one of Becka's tiny pastel-pink socks, the thick, soft fabric on my eyelids, *don't think about that now, we're all here together.*

A few minutes pass, possibly an hour, and we see Vilja coming toward us, striding back from the tents with her baby sister in her arms. I feel a pang of anxiety and pride when I see the dark shadow of adulthood on her face. Behind her are a man with a gray beard and a woman with short hair, both in green military gear. Vilja steps around my half-sprawled body as though I were a beggar outside the supermarket and carefully hands Becka to Carola.

"Are these your parents?" the stressed-sounding woman asks, going on without waiting for an answer. "So, this little one seems to be breathing normally now, it's lucky you had the mask and kept her in the car." Her eyes drift down to me. "She'll probably be cranky for a few days because her eyes-nose-throat sting, but it should pass." She has some kind of tic when she talks, a twitch at the corner of one eye. "So, it's important she has a chest X-ray as soon as possible once you get back to Stockholm, just to be on the safe side."

"Why can't you X-ray her here?" asks Carola, and I see now that the woman is wearing a white armband with a red cross on top of her green uniform.

"So, we're from the Home Guard, we only provide emergency care," the woman quickly replies.

"OK, but there must be a hospital somewhere nearby where we can take her?"

The woman glances at the man standing quietly by her side.

"Stockholm is better," he says in a kind, almost singsong tone.

"We've been out in the smoke all day." Carola's voice has grown shrill. "Are you telling me we need to—"

"There are fires all the way from Östersund to Mora, hundreds of miles," he says in the same soft, polite tone, his dialect as broad and comforting as an old tapestry. "A million acres, they say. He's up in the mountains too, the fire. Reached the Sylan range this morning. The tourists made their way up to the mountain station because they thought . . . But the vegetation round about was so dry that . . ."

He squints toward the sunset over the lake. The piercing sound of an engine, two men in colorful swimming trunks on a Jet Ski, fizzing over the calm surface of the water, hooting with laughter.

"No roads up there. Families with young children and that. A helicopter crashed, so the hospitals up here are . . ."

He looks down at Becka with a kind smile, holds out a stubby index finger and strokes her cheek. "Better for this little lass to get to Stockholm. Mmm."

Becka lets out a shriek and rubs her red, damaged eyes, a pattern of movement she probably wasn't even capable of a few days ago. The huge complexity of becoming a person, all the muscles, nerves, synapses, proteins, neurons, and whatever else that have to learn to work in harmony in order to first grip, then reach for something, then carry out such a simple act as to ease the stinging in your eyes.

"What about Martin?" Vilja sounds tense. "What's happening with him?"

"So, Martin is on oxygen in the tent," says the woman. "I'm going over there now. You can come with."

Martin?

Carola starts asking about Zack, whether they've heard anything about a boy arriving with another family in a white car, but the woman just sighs and shakes her head and turns around and Vilja follows her.

The man with the beard seems slightly relieved that the woman is gone. He scratches a mosquito bite on his throat, stretches his back, and crouches down over me with a quiet sigh. A gnarled paw on my face, carefully turning my head to study the wound, softly humming an old tune I vaguely recognize. He takes out a red medical bag and digs out a tube and a bandage.

"Clean the wound and apply this, then just bandage it up. You'll have to get it checked later, once you're back in Stockholm."

Carola seems to be on the verge of saying something, but she changes her mind and simply nods and takes the things from him.

"What happened to you, then?" he asks in his gentle voice.

"He was driving around on one of those quad bikes in the forest," she says before I have time to open my mouth. "Seems like he got confused in all the smoke."

"I was going to save you." My voice quivers like jelly. "It tipped."

"A quad bike?" The man gives me a curious smile. "You had a quad bike?"

"I found it."

A glimmer in his tired, icy blue eyes.

"Found it? Just standing there, was he? With the keys in?"

"No, it . . . I went into a house to get the keys."

Carola groans and I see something tense on her face, the same distant look she gave me when I told her about the affair, her shock and distress hidden behind a thick layer of indifference, as though none of this really affects her, a car accident she simply happens to have driven past.

The man, on the other hand, studies me with something bordering on infatuation. He has been longing for something like this, I realize, possibly for years, all those weekends camping in the snow and the mud instead of cozy Sundays at home, canned ravioli instead of baking muffins with the kids, shitting into holes instead of drinking beers and betting on the soccer with his pals on the sofa in front of the TV; this is what he has been hoping for, this day, someone like me.

"You went into a house?"

Something about his calm tone makes me want to talk. If my throat wasn't so damn sore I would tell him my entire life story, but as it is I can only manage three words.

"Through the window."

He nods slowly. "Incredible, really. How fine the line is. Afghanistan, Congo. Stuff you only read about."

The ground feels hard beneath me, and I wonder when they'll give me a bed. Or are we going to be transported to Stockholm straightaway? Is Zack on his way here?

Who is *Martin*?

I hear a shout from the tents, an angry male voice yelling something about *insurance* and *you fucking bitch*, a nondescript murmur in response.

"Easy for people to lose their patience," he says apologetically. "Like I said, such a fine line, when it really comes down to it. And so close. Varies from person to person, of course."

He pats me on the shoulder and gets up with a sigh.

"The police will probably be in touch, so . . ."

He nods politely to Carola and gives Becka one last flirty smile before trudging off toward the tents.

"Martin," I say.

But she isn't listening, too busy fiddling with something on Becka. I remember our things, the Fjällräven backpack containing our valuables, the Ikea bag, the clothes, the diapers, where did everything go?

"Martin?"

"Yes?" There is something stern about her mouth. "Seriously, Didrik, whose house did you break into? Do you know who they are? Maybe you should get in touch with them now and . . ."

I shake my head.

"The place probably went up in flames anyway, it makes no difference. Vilja went to see someone called Martin?"

"Yes, the old man."

"The old man?"

She sighs and studies the tube and the roll of bandage the man gave her with a look of resignation.

"You know, the one who drove us here."

Everything seems to come to a standstill before I manage to put the name to the furrowed, psoriasis-riddled face. For some reason I've always thought he would be called something . . . well, *old*. Torkel. Sixten. Gösta. Not Martin.

"Oh, him."

———

I'm a good parent. I've been there for my children growing up. I've changed their dirty diapers, played with them, wiped their snotty, running noses, looked after them when they were ill, dropped them off at daycare and at school, gone to their parent-teacher meetings and piano recitals and sports days and Christmas pageants and end-of-term celebrations, taught them to cycle, swim, and read. I've also listened to them, respected them, and repeatedly told them that I love them. I've never raised a hand to any of them. I think I've probably fulfilled most of the requirements of a modern Swedish father.

But on the few occasions when I have failed as a parent, it's always been because of the rage I feel toward Vilja. My daughter's ability to make me feel like my life is nothing but a long, worthless series of weak and poor decisions sometimes feels almost unhealthy. And unsurprisingly it's that same feeling that greets me as I limp into the medical tent. The Home Guard soldiers move to stop me, but the huge bandage around my head and the general look of me are enough to make them hold back. Everything is calm and quiet in here, removed from the noise and anxiety outside. There are four beds lined up along one side, two of them empty. A young man in a hi-vis vest and a sturdy pair of boots is lying in one, his face covered in blood and soot, and as he coughs and gasps for air I notice that even his tongue and gums are black. There are two nurses at his bedside, exchanging short, robotic bursts of medical jargon, and I push past them and the empty beds. He's right at the very end, they've draped an orange blanket over him, put an oxygen mask on his wrinkled, dirty face, and she is sitting in the seat by his side.

"It's all your fault," she says, her voice flat.

"I know it's natural to want to point the finger in situations like this, honey, but . . ."

"He had a car," she says. "Our car wouldn't start but he had a car, we could've just walked over to his house and asked if we could drive with him."

Not roadworthy. He said his car wasn't roadworthy. That it hadn't passed its emissions inspection.

Which obviously isn't the same thing as it not starting. Stubborn old bastard.

"He saw that our car was still there, so he drove around looking for us, but by the time he found us you'd run off. And then we spent, like, hours trying to find you."

His gray windbreaker is hanging neatly by the bed, along with his blue-and-white scarf, the one he had wound around his face. I see now that it's a hockey scarf, it says *Leksands IF* and has the team logo on it, some kind of circle with strange symbols inside.

"If you and Mom had just gone down to get him, or if you hadn't disappeared like that, forcing him to run around after you in the smoke."

The oxygen mask is making a hissing, whistling, pumping sound, and his chest rises and falls almost imperceptibly in time with it beneath the blanket.

"I. Was. Trying. To. Help. You." I speak slowly, overemphasizing every word. "I. Was. Trying. To. Take. Care. Of. You."

"Where's Zack?" she asks, as though she hasn't heard me, as though I was talking to someone else. "Have you found him yet?"

"Your mom is asking around."

"Asking around?" She sounds more sad than snide. "Did you take their phone number, the people he went off with? Or get the registration number?"

I sigh.

"We were in a hurry, sweetheart. Zack's foot was bleeding. Your mom and I, we panicked. They said they would drop him off in Rättvik."

She shakes her head.

"You're both so fucking dumb. You're the world's worst parents."

I shrug.

"Well, we're the only ones you've got. Come on, let's go. We've been given a cabin for the night."

One of the nurses steps forward, a harried look on her face.

"Sorry, who are you? Are you a relative too?"

I give her a confused look. "I . . . no, I'm just here to get my daughter."

The nurse—a thin woman, nicotine-stained teeth, short gray hair—seems confused, and points at the old man.

"But she claims this is her grandfather?"

I glance at Vilja, who looks away, suddenly a child again, caught in a lie, and I finally get to be the adult as I wink at the nurse and give her a reassuring smile and place a hand on my daughter's slim shoulder.

"Martin here was with us when we escaped the fire, so I guess she must've had a slight . . . reaction somehow, but that's surely only natural? It's easy to get confused when things like this happen, you know?"

She gives me a warm smile in return.

"Oh, of course. That's actually what we're most worried about with these fires, not people burning to death, that almost never happens, only every once in a while if someone from the emergency services gets stuck somehow . . ." She nods solemnly at her own words. "The confusion is the really dangerous thing, people getting stressed and making bad decisions that lead them to take all sorts of unnecessary risks."

I have no idea what she's talking about, it's as though she is hinting at something else, and she notices my uncertainty and smiles again, points to the bandage around my head as she lowers her voice.

"You're the one who borrowed the quad bike, aren't you? And flipped it?"

They talk. They talk to each other. Possibly to others. The papers. Online. Is there no such thing as confidentiality these days?

"What's going to happen to Martin?" Vilja asks suddenly.

"We only really deal with emergencies here, so he'll be moved first thing in the morning. To the general hospital, they've cleared an entire ward for all the people coming in with smoke inhalation. We've got that emergency preparedness, that's one carryover from the pandemic. Plus all the spare oxygen."

"So he'll be OK there?" Her lower lip trembles and I desperately want to hug her, to let her crawl into my arms, to rub my nose against her cheek, hush her, kiss her, comfort her, call her *Vilja-vanilla* the way we used to when she was younger, but I can't, I've lost her, mislaid her somewhere in the heat and the smoke and the hopelessness.

The Home Guard woman looks tired, glances at me.

"It would be better if we could send him to Gothenburg or Stockholm, but there aren't enough transports and they're prioritizing children and young people. Do you know if he has any relatives? I mean, it's great you're both here, but—"

"No," I interrupt her. "He doesn't have anyone. Not that we know of." My hand is still on Vilja's shoulder. She shakes it off.

"Come on, sweetie. Let's leave them to work in peace. We're done here."

I put my hand on her shoulder again. Not too hard, just enough for her to understand.

———

The cabin we've been given is small and cramped, and we're sharing it with a family from Germany, a father and two boys around Zack's age. Vilja is on the top bunk of one of the beds, listening to music through her headphones. Carola and Becka are below her, and the two German boys are on the other bunk bed. The German father and I have each been given a sleeping mat and are lying on the vinyl floor.

The room smells like old wood and damp mattresses and, of course, like smoke, the smoke from our clothes, hair, bags, and bodies. I tried to wash in the lake earlier, but the pain in my chest meant I mostly just splashed myself by the shore; what I really wanted was to take a nice long shower, but there are only three of them and the lines are long. I asked whether there was anywhere else I could go, showers you could pay to use, but those three are all there is, and everyone has to wait their turn.

The Germans seem happy and carefree, wearing identical burgundy tracksuits and playing what I eventually work out must be some kind of soccer history quiz on their phones. They keep shouting things like *Hansa Rostock!* and *Jupp Heynckes!* and *Bökelberg!* as they pass a bag of chips up and down between the bunks. Maybe this is all just an adventure to them, a story to tell once they get home, tales of their dramatic escape from the Great Arctic Blaze that will while away many a cold winter's night back in Hamburg or Cologne. *Rudi Völler?* the father grunts beside me, making his stomach jiggle, and I'm envious of the laughter in the boys' eyes when they boo him for being wrong as they munch on their chips. I should have taken Zack to soccer, even though I hate being just one in the crowd, hate the very thought of standing among all those drunk, pubescent men hurling abuse from some cold, damp stand in the suburbs, I should have done it for his sake, and I think for probably the hundredth time today that if I ever get out of here, if I ever get him back, everything will be better, everything will be different, everything will be how it should have been, *Gladbach zwei zu null!*

I've been given some pills to help with the pain from my burned scalp, the kind of pills you're supposed to take every six hours, but only if it becomes unbearable; I've taken two and they haven't helped in the slightest. I've also charged my phone a little—an hour-long wait for ten minutes at the plug—and uploaded a picture of the Home Guard men in silhouette by the lake: After a chaotic day (if you know, you know) we're now being well looked after by these heroes, followed by hearts and the Swedish flag and tensed biceps and #climatechange. I took a few selfies first, but on second thought decided to save them until later, I look too awful with my blood-shot eyes, sooty marks that won't wash off, the bandage, and my singed hair. Mom might get worried and confused, and the haters and the climate skeptics would accuse me of faking and posing; that's why I went with the Swedish flag and the praise for the Home Guard instead, it means they can't get at me. I don't write anything about Zack, of course, Carola has sent messages to her mother and sister asking if they've heard anything, he might have made it back to Stockholm, tried to reach the house, he could be with the American family we rented it out to, or maybe he's in the neighbors' kitchen, playing with Filip like usual, the one with the red hair, the skateboard, and the mild ADHD.

I scroll through likes, comments, hearts, and emojis that are anxious, sad, and angry. I read the messages, friends asking if we know when we'll be back in town, if we need any help once we get home, if we have enough clothes, toiletries, stuff. One of the partners at the agency wants to know whether I would be willing to take part in a breakfast seminar this week about the consequences of the climate crisis, got time to squeeze it in before you head off to Thailand? A newspaper is offering me a column or a debate piece about our escape from the fire, and the organizers of the *Fossil Free Future* demonstration on Friday have asked if I'd like to say a few words, just a couple of minutes, we need to accelerate the introduction of a complete ban on fossil fuels.

Carola seems to have fallen asleep beside Becka on her bunk, so I log in to my secret account to see whether she has written anything, whether she is worried about me, she might have heard me on the radio, might have sent a picture and some hearts, she often just sends a picture, but there's nothing there, only the latest message, the one with the image from the boat. I check her profile instead, but it's just the usual selfies and ad lines. I used to find it cute but I'm starting to get sick of the plasticky nature of her pictures, the filters that make her skin look as smooth and pink as a baby's, the glittering doe eyes and glistening lips, all the dirty comments from men she doesn't know.

Instead I methodically work my way through the pictures she sent me last spring and summer. The image of her sitting outside a bar on the waterfront, a glass of red wine in one hand, model beautiful in a pair of dark sunglasses and a mysterious smile, lightly made up with natural reddish-pink lips. The image from the bathroom, a selfie taken from an angle in the Jacuzzi bath, the one in the luxurious hotel suite, the room I booked the very first time; she's standing with her back to the huge bathroom mirror so that I can see her damp, bare face in the foreground and the reflection of her naked, soapy back and bottom in the background. She must have taken it in secret, during the brief window when I went to the door to collect the pizza and champagne we'd ordered. She didn't mention it at the time, didn't send it to me until this spring. *I've been saving this for you*, she wrote, *I knew it would be like this, I knew there would be a time when all we had were our memories and our longing, I knew it, here, take it.*

I study the images for a while, trying to feel something down there, something other than the aching and throbbing and niggling, but it doesn't work, so I pop another two pills and swallow them dry. The Germans are sleeping peacefully, Vilja is still listening to her music with the little bedside lamp switched on. I should probably tell her to turn it off, apparently we have to leave early in the morning.

I reread the message from my boss and decide that this breakfast seminar could be a good idea, the debate piece and the climate demonstration, too. A way to up my contribution, to show that it's no longer just a question of rain forests, glaciers, cocoa plantations, coral reefs, or slightly more expensive food; it's about an acute risk to our lives, a catastrophe worse than ten Hitlers and twenty Stalins combined, we need to start a third world war against stupidity, cowardice, greed.

And I'll tell the truth about myself, I decide as I try to find a comfortable position on the sleeping mat, about how I ended up like this. I was an activist once, a radical, and I lived an alternative and sustainable lifestyle; all my clothes were secondhand, I ate according to the seasons, and I used a canvas tote bag whenever I went shopping. I was in the process of completing my PhD when I met Carola, and we moved in together at record speed, just a few months after that strange first date in the archipelago. Her father died and she had the opportunity to take over his apartment, but the bank said no to a mortgage, so rather than finishing my thesis I started doing the comms for various environmental organizations, followed by a period as an adviser with the Ministry for the Environment, and before I knew it I'd been headhunted to a PR company specializing in shaping public opinion. That job came hand in hand with benefits and networks and money and apartments where the kitchen needed renovating, the bathrooms needed renovating, and then we bought the house and took out yet more loans and then Vilja and Zack came along, they both wore cloth diapers and used secondhand baby carriages, of course, we bathed them in lukewarm water with organic cooking oil, their parties were toy-swapping parties, we saved the coffee grounds and tried to grow mushrooms one summer, and we took the train everywhere, of course, always the train, but then a few of the guys from the agency wanted me as a partner in a new start-up and that meant a new house and a new bathroom to renovate and a car and even more loans and a third child and suddenly my life had taken a turn that I'd never wanted.

The fire and everything that happened around it really opened my eyes, I'll say. *It made me look back at the path I'd taken. We were supposed to be going to Thailand. To be "treating ourselves." And it wasn't until I stood there, surrounded by chaos and panic, that I really realized what I was doing. What I had been doing.*

Because the truth is that I wasn't running that day in Dalarna. Anything but. I'd been running for years. It was the fire that finally made me stop.

That sounds good, I think, suddenly overcome by tiredness. My hands feel like kettlebells when I pick up my phone to write that a breakfast seminar should be doable, opening the chat thread to see that he sent me another message just five minutes ago, no greeting this time, no niceties, just a single sentence that flickers before my eyes.

Didrik, seeing claims on social media that you broke into a summer house, probably pure nonsense but give me a call to discuss strategy ASAP when you see this.

I feel more weary than surprised. I knew this was coming, just maybe not quite so soon. I scroll around on social media and the gossip sites, a couple of emails arrive a few minutes later, one of the tabloids wants a comment about the rumors of me breaking into a house and stealing private property. I check their home page and see that they're running with the headline *FAMOUS PR CONSULTANT ACCUSED OF LOOTING DURING WILDFIRE CHAOS*, but when I click on the article my phone freezes and dies and I'm left alone in the darkness.

———

And then nothing matters anymore, because Zack is right here by my side. I want to get up and find a socket to charge my phone, but my body feels heavy and I decide that it's probably best not to get carried away, to think through the situation in peace and quiet before I—yet again—act with an impulsiveness that was, of course, an understandable and natural consequence of the life-threatening, traumatizing situation I found myself in, so instead I lie flat on my back and take a few deep breaths and suddenly Zack is here, fragile and beautiful, he's holding in his hand the little glass jar containing his tooth and the coin, and I don't want to bother him, don't want to get him mixed up in my worries, I just whisper *sorry* into the darkness, I think it must be a dream but it really is him, he's sitting right beside me in the darkness with a blanket pulled up over his knees, his face softly illuminated by the moonlight outside.

Forgive me, my love, we'll soon be snorkeling off a tiny island in Thailand, a motorboat will take us out to sea and I'll teach him how to rub saliva onto the inside of his mask, I'll teach him how to use fins to swim out into the calm ocean beneath the baking-hot sun, and somewhere out there we'll find a section of coral reef that's still alive, I'll show my boy the colors, the fish, you just want to go deeper and deeper in the crystal clear water, swimming through a magical world so beautiful that it makes your eyes ache, we'll chase shoals of tiger-striped blue-white-pink emerald-green fish through tunnels and beneath arches and over a landscape of shimmering, sparkling colors, maybe as soon as next week if we can just get out of here.

I close my eyes for a moment and when I wake Zack is still here, he's lying beside me in a sleeping bag and I bury my nose in the long hair at the back of his neck, it's like a fine smoke-infused yarn, we'd been planning to wait until Thailand to get it cut, there's something exotic and comforting about doing that kind of thing abroad, I remember train journeys through India when I was younger, stopping off at barber's shops, often little more than a hole in the wall, their razor-sharp blades and thick foams and soft fingers, voices calling me *mister*, my face has never been so smooth as it was then, imagine drinking a cold beer in the sun on the beach while two or three giggling Thai women fuss over my son's hair, and we doze off again and Zack rolls over in his sleep and drapes his little arm over my back, an unexpected but instinctive movement that fills me with a tenderness that is almost too much to bear, *I'm so sorry, my love, sorry for losing you.*

I'll have to tell Carola about this when I wake up, I think, tell her that I dreamed we were running, that there was a huge forest fire and I tried to save you all, I dreamed that everything came crashing down around us, I dreamed that everything came to an end, I stretch out beside my boy and close my eyes for a moment, when I open them again everything will be back to normal and I won't be lying on the floor of a cabin somewhere, when I open my eyes everything that has been aching and stinking and itching will be gone but the memory has to remain so that I can tell her what I dreamed, so I can warn her, ask her for help, and I open my eyes and Zack has moved his arm and I can see his expensive German multisport watch, the kind with GPS and maps and altimeters and barometers and pulsometers, the red digits tell me that it's 11:48, casting a pale pink glow over his smooth, pale face, a stranger.

TUESDAY, AUGUST 26

A LOUD KNOCKING DRAGS THE DAWN LIGHT IN. I HEAR VOICES, Carola talking to someone in the doorway, and I think *please please please say that you've found him*, but I can tell from her back and her weary posture that it's something else, and she closes the door and stares down at me.

"We have to go."

She is holding Becka, the girl's small face tucked in beneath her chin, one of her hands cupping Becka's sweaty neck, the other mechanically rocking her small body.

"Can you get up? We need to leave in fifteen minutes."

"What time is it?"

My voice is the hoarse, powerless whimper of an old man.

"Six thirty. There's a train to Stockholm in an hour. They need the cabins. Everyone has to leave."

The German family and their things are already gone, I see them sitting around a camping table when I stagger outside to take a piss. It's early morning but there isn't a hint of moisture in the air, no birds, nothing but dry, stifling muteness. They have their breakfast laid out on the table in front of them, an alcohol lamp bubbling and spitting on the ground, the boys are wrapped in blankets, eating sandwiches, and the father gives me a relaxed nod in greeting when he spots me.

"Are you heading to Stockholm too?" I ask in English.

"No. Kebnekaise." He sounds so German when he says it. *Kebnekaizzzer.*

"But . . . the fire?"

His face cracks into a clean-shaven grin and he gestures to the two boys, to their nice new tracksuits, their walking boots, the backpacks on the ground, the tent, the sleeping bags.

"This has been their wish for several years," he says. "It may be their last chance to see a glacier. And the fires up here are the biggest in Europe. They learn about polar amplification in school, but it's different to actually see it with your own eyes."

He gives his sons a proud look as he says those last few words, *wizz your own eyz*, and they raise their blond heads. The younger one smiles shyly, the older one purses his lips in embarrassment.

Back in the cabin, Carola and Vilja have packed our things. Without the suitcase and the Ikea bag and the baby carriage, we don't have much. I take the Fjällräven backpack and the diaper bag, Carola her purse and Becka in the carrier, Vilja puts on the Spider-Man backpack, and we set off. I'm wearing the same ripped, filthy shorts and Lacoste T-shirt as yesterday. Other than Becka, who had a clean set in the changing bag, we're all wearing the same clothes as yesterday.

We walk down a street I assume must lead to the train station. No one has told us where to go, but we're following a thin stream of people, not quite a crowd, more a few scattered families trudging along in the morning sun. Up ahead of us, a big bearded man is carrying a baby and pulling a handcart in which a young child is sitting among cushions and bags, the mother walking behind them with a backpack and a bag of food. I drowsily wonder what Becka is going to eat during the journey but assume Carola must have thought about that already, that she has prepared the water and bottles in the tiny kitchen in the cabin, she's usually the one to do that kind of thing, and the shame of no longer being in charge of any of my children mixes with the shame of not walking at the head of the line, not like yesterday, I'm two steps behind her and she's two steps behind Vilja; I feel like a burden, a hanger-on, I want to say something, do something to make her look me in the eye, something, anything.

"Zack," I say lamely. "What are we going to do about Zack?"

"I've been up since four," she says without turning around. "No one knows anything. We should probably call the police again. Can you do it from your phone?"

"It's dead," I say, feeling ashamed of that, too. "The battery."

She doesn't react, just keeps walking, says something calming to Becka, who is crying again, she could have been crying all morning, or whining at least.

The parking lot outside the train station is full of people, some sleeping on camping mats, some on the bare ground, others sitting and standing, alone or in groups. Something about them feels different, I can't quite put my finger on it at first, but they don't look like people on their way somewhere, not like people usually do while they're waiting on a platform with suitcases and backpacks and briefcases, no thermoses or small tubs of food. A man in a crumpled gray suit is sitting on the edge of the pavement with his phone, an old woman in a coat is lying flat out in the shade with her arm over her face, five children with the words CHERRY ORCHARD scrawled in Magic Marker on both sides of their reflective yellow vests are sitting in the grass, staring at us with wide eyes. There are plastic bags everywhere around them, black garbage bags, suitcases, a TV set, a bicycle, a girl in her twenties with a gym bag under one arm and a shopping bag that seems to be holding a potted plant in the other hand; the volunteers have set up a table, and a pimpled boy in a pink hi-vis jacket is tossing bottles of water to people and pumping coffee from airpots. Behind the table, in a quiet corner, four disabled adolescents are sitting in their wheelchairs, accompanied by a single carer.

And what I initially thought was a few dozen people multiplies as we get closer. I see that they're sitting on the steps by the white station building, that there is a long line snaking away from the newsstand even though it seems to be closed, others sitting and lying on the floor inside the station. There are people everywhere. We turn the corner and see them crowding the platform, taking shelter in the shade of the building. Someone has laid out blankets and mattresses, and a teenage memory comes back to me, a rainy music festival in the countryside, the way the small community was suddenly overrun by noisy teenagers with crates of beer and broken tents and guitar cases, a thronging chaos of damp, sweaty bodies materializing out of nowhere, but this is different. Vilja turns to Carola and me, suddenly a child again, anxiously whispering *are all these people going home to Stockholm?*

Carola shakes her head, and I would like to say something, we have to step over bodies, wade through a sea of people, a silver-haired woman in a pink woollen sweater and a silk scarf and white sneakers, a girl in a soccer uniform, more wheelchairs, strollers, walkers, Carola mutters *now I see why they needed the cabins*, and I'd like to tell our daughter that everything will be OK, that these people just got unlucky, that they ended up in the wrong place while out traveling.

"They're not going home," I say instead. "They don't have one."

———

There is no train. Becka is screaming, and we manage to find an empty scrap of platform, I mix her formula in a bottle and sit down with her in my lap. I still have this, the satisfaction of seeing my child eat, her tiny lips closing around the nipple, eyes intensely focused on nothing at all, driven by a primitive instinct to survive, nothing but survive, whatever the cost. The sun is beating down on the back of my neck, it's going to be a nice day.

"What's happening with Zack?" Vilja asks.

"We'll track him down once we get home," says Carola. She tries to smile. "He might already be back, sitting with his nose in a book somewhere."

She makes a face, mimicking Zack. That's something we used to do when the kids were younger, mimic one another, we took it in turns, I mimicked her, she mimicked me, the kids mimicked each other, *who am I now?*, it was our favorite thing to do. Carola's Zack has a silly, almost joyful smile, reading a book and singing to himself, and Vilja laughs at her, the laugh of someone who hasn't made enough butter-sugar-cinnamon filling for their cinnamon buns and has to use every trick they can think of to make it stretch to the corners.

"Maybe we could go to that sushi place tonight, he likes it there, doesn't he?" she says, and her mother takes the bait and starts talking about how we should book a slot at the climbing wall, the one we all enjoyed so much, Zack was so scared at first but during the last fifteen minutes he started climbing *like a chimpanzee on steroids*, her hands scratch at the air like little claws and Vilja laughs again and says that we should get a climbing wall at home, we could build one in the backyard or buy one of those machines where the wall sort of rolls down as you climb it, meaning you can have it in an ordinary house, Tyra has one and it's sweet because you don't have to bother with all the safety lines and Carola says what a fun idea, why don't we have one of those, we'll have to look into it once we get home and suddenly I can't stand it anymore, I can't stand hearing about meaningless luxury products on a station platform full of climate refugees, the skin beneath my bandage is itching and stinging and I say *what do you mean, get home?*

They stare at me.

"Home?" says Carola. "As in . . . home."

"But we've rented out our house, honey. We're supposed to be going to Thailand next week. We've plowed every last krona we have into a holiday that's never going to happen. And our son is missing."

"We'll just have to . . ." She gives me a hesitant glance. ". . . we'll have to check with friends. I've already messaged Lisa and Calle, Henny and Staffan, and they—"

"Seriously, what are you talking about?" I keep my voice low to avoid disturbing Becka, who has maybe half a bottle left. "Are we going to move in with your friends from your moms' group, is *that* the plan?"

Clearly this is a conversation we should have had yesterday. In some respects it's a conversation we should have had a long time ago, way before all the fires and the chaos, but we definitely shouldn't be having it in front of Vilja, and definitely not right here, I can hardly believe what I'm saying.

"People step up at times like this," Carola says lamely. "They help each other."

"And who have we helped, honey? Honestly? We've been going through this crap for a day now, but have we helped a single other person?"

Perhaps I'm looking for a crack, a way to get through to her, a second of honesty.

Her blond face crumples.

"I helped you," she says. "I made Martin drive around for hours, looking for you. All because you wanted to play the hero on someone else's motorbike."

"Quad bike," I correct her. "It was a quad bike."

She laughs. A short, hoarse laugh.

"A quad bike. Honestly, it's fucking ridiculous, what the hell did you think you were doing?"

Suddenly it's no longer the pain on my scalp that is bothering me, or the shame, it's the fact that Carola is trying to take that last shred of dignity away from me, the brief moment in the toolshed as I climbed onto the shiny new machine and turned the key and felt the vibrations shudder through my crotch, the way it purred and quivered beneath me, the sense of being on my way, of action, of freedom, God, I honestly don't know when I last felt so free and I remember shouting, involuntarily, ecstatically, my voice didn't sound like me, it sounded like it did when I was with her, when I roared with pleasure, it sounded like it did when I came inside her, screaming her name, the muscles in her arms, the scent of her sweat, I want everything to break, I really do.

I smile at my wife.

"Riding it felt really fucking good, I'll have you know."

She stares at me, her eyes dark with rage, and everything grinds to a halt. It starts as a twitch at the corner of her mouth, a crease disappearing from her forehead, then a single tear rolls slowly down her right cheek. I hate it when she cries, I can't stand it, if I wasn't sitting here with Becka in my arms I would try to hug her, hold her, rub her shoulders, and say *sorry*, but right now all I can do is smile apologetically and shake my head at the situation.

"I'm tired, Carola. I'm in pain. Sorry. Let's drop this for now."

"When were you going to tell me?" she mumbles.

The platform has slowly started to empty out, people wandering back down to the parking lot. A bus has pulled in and a boy in a hi-vis vest is holding up a handwritten sign, felt-tip letters, too small for me to read from here.

"Not in the middle of all this shit, in any case," I reply, surprised by how calm I sound. I press my cheek to the downy back of Becka's head. "Maybe later."

Vilja moves closer to her mother, her eyes bright and scared.

"What are you talking about?"

"Your father and I have a few things we need to discuss," says Carola. She sounds calm too, almost indifferent. "We just need a bit of time to ourselves."

Vilja's eyes dart between us and the platform, the people, the bags, the overflowing garbage cans, the bloody sanitary napkin someone has thrown onto the tracks, the old man in a pair of filthy Bermuda shorts, some kind of sticky, cottage cheese–like gunk in the corners of his mouth, sitting alone on the platform, muttering something about the idiots, the cunts, the fags, the refugees, the politicians, and *all my things*.

"To *yourselves*?" Vilja coughs out a joyless laugh. "You want some *privacy*?"

I point over to the parking lot and the volunteers. "Look, they're handing out bottles of water over there. Would you go and grab us a few? They'd be good to have for the train."

She shrugs, takes out her phone, scrolls.

"Why don't you go and get them yourself?"

I sigh.

"I'm feeding your sister."

"That's not my problem, is it?"

She is wearing the snotty, obstinate expression that always makes me flip and start shouting like a madman, and that's obviously what she wants, to bring the situation back onto home turf, to a place where she feels comfortable, where everything is familiar, but things are different this time.

"Vilja," Carola sighs. "Do as your dad says. Go and get some water."

She stands very still, looks down at her phone again. Looks up at us.

"Lana Del Rey," she says. There is something about her tone of voice as she says it that reminds me of those long evenings at the piano, the hours of piercing off-key singing, and then, as though by chance, the moment when she found the right note and followed the tune, the sudden instant of purity, like when a dead phone screen comes to life and buzzes in your hand.

"The car that drove off with Zack. Lana Del Rey."

Carola stares at her daughter in confusion.

"What do you mean, honey, what does the car . . ." She trails off, doesn't finish her sentence.

"The letters on the license plate," she says. "LDR. Lana Del Rey. I tried to memorize the numbers too, I think it was 386, but it could've been 368 and there might have been a four too, or a seven, I tried to remember it, Mom, but it drove off so fast and I didn't have anything to write it down with, but I remembered the letters because of the name."

Carola takes a step toward her, and Vilja backs away but then stops, lets her mother catch up with her. They both hesitate for a moment and then Carola wraps her arms around her, I hear her crying, hear her whisper *Vilja-vanilla*, and I want to be up there with them but Becka has fallen asleep in my arms and I don't know how to get up from the platform without waking her, I want to be with them but instead I just sit here as they embrace for several minutes.

In the end Vilja pulls away, wipes her face on her wrist, smooths her hair.

"I'll go so you can talk in peace," she says in a kind, adult voice, turning around and striding away along the platform, pushing through the crowd, her supple young body moving with the determination of an adult's, hopping and circling around the upright and horizontal bodies, the outstretched legs, the sleeping children, the bags, the blankets, the fragments of former lives.

Carola slumps down beside me.

"Is she asleep?"

I nod.

"She took almost the whole thing," I say, holding up the bottle, shaking it, formula sloshing against the plastic.

"That's good. She must've been hungry."

"How much water do we have left?"

She picks up the thermos, deftly weighs it in her hand.

"Two bottles, if we're careful. And we've only got enough powder for two more. We'll have to change her later. There's one diaper left. For the train."

"If there are any trains," I say.

"Mmm. I'm sure there will be."

We talk that way for a while, simple, everyday phrases about Becka's clothes and my wound, whether there is any point in running over to one of the shops to try to buy some lunch, whether there might be any toilets nearby. We do it robotically, without looking each other in the eye, taking refuge in the tangible, in the things that keep us alive, but before long we run out of words and we stop tiptoeing around our broken marriage and we fall silent and I turn to her and say *sorry* and she simply nods.

"How did we end up here?" she asks, taking Becka from me, gently rubbing her back. Suddenly I remember the ultrasound, the alien images of the fetus where all you could see was a skull and a spine like a string of silver pearls, I remember the smell of the hospital room, I remember her hand was cool and slightly damp as I held it, she had used hand gel after going to the toilet for her urine sample; I remember the tears, I remember everything, and then the other one: the black-and-white image like a vague sense of unease, an indefinable, hangover-like mix of anxiety and nausea, *not even a fetus, it's still just an embryo* said the midwife, *two centimeters*, the one thing I'll never be able to tell her.

"Everything just felt so . . . small," I say with a sigh. I get up, tired of sitting in the dirt on the platform, push the bottle into the pocket of my shorts. "The house, the kids. You. Surely there must be more to life than candy and TV shows and trying to lose weight and planning the next holiday and looking forward to the weekend and scrolling on our phones and experimenting with Asian cookery or wine tasting once every five years, fantasizing about houses we can't afford, cars we can't afford, gardens we can't afford; there must be more to life than pancakes with jam and pasta and vegetarian stews and moaning about the cleaning company and the handymen and the kids' schools. It's not enough just to fill the fridge, fill the freezer, fill the pantry, or try to watch porn together after you've had a few glasses of wine, you always think it's too rough and gross and would rather try massages and candles and checking whether any fucking spa hotels have midweek discounts. It's just not enough for me."

I pause to catch my breath. She sits quietly, presses her face to Becka's cheek, her nose to her skin, closes her eyes. I can't really see her and assume she must be crying, sobbing, sniffing, but when she turns back toward me I see that she's smiling.

She's smiling.

"Surely not even you can be this banal, Didrik. We have three children together, we've been married for fifteen years, and you want to leave me because you're . . . *bored*? I mean, excuse me?"

My head is spinning, the bandage itching. The sun is high in the sky and the heat on the platform is starting to become unbearable. I need water, Vilja should be back with the water soon, here I am opening my heart to her and she treats me like an idiot.

"Carola, please. I know my feelings might not mean much to you, but—"

She laughs.

"Stop. Just stop. Yes, we're middle-aged. Yes, we have a boring middle-class life, we live in a house in the suburbs, you snore, I have cellulite, what the hell did you expect?"

"More," I say lamely. "I don't know. Just . . . more."

A couple around our age appear at the far end of the platform, the man carrying a heavy bag in his arms, the woman pushing a small stroller. The baby inside is screaming, making a shrill, piercing sound, its face is red and its tiny body is shaking as though in spasms; this isn't the usual unhappy howling, it's something else, something ill or injured. The father is going between people, asking for something, crouching down, speaking in a low, stubborn voice. He has good posture for someone so gangly, looks strong when he gets up to move on, crouching down again a few feet later, something vaguely familiar about him.

"I guess it's all this crap, too," I say, gesturing to the chaos on the platform. "Life is running away from us, and it would be one thing if we had something to look forward to, if you and I could enjoy a bit of luxury once we're fifty or sixty, but that's never going to happen, is it? This is what life is like now, and it's only going to get worse. All of it. The best we can hope for is that we die before it becomes completely unbearable. With the heat, the water, the food. That we can keep society functioning for a few more years, until the next pandemic shuts everything down again. That we don't have to eat insects. That the racists and lunatics don't take over even more of the world. That there's still coffee in the rest home."

The couple with the infant are moving along the platform toward us. They must be at least fifty yards away, but the baby is screaming so loudly that I can barely hear myself speak.

"And ultimately it doesn't really matter all that much, the fact that humanity is collapsing isn't a problem, not from a cosmic or evolutionary perspective, the planet will still be here, life will go on, for millions of years I'm sure, it's just us that doesn't have a future."

I look down at Becka, at her blank, sleeping face. Her eyelids are twitching, she's dreaming. I've read that babies dream a lot, more than adults, though of course no one knows what they dream about, it's not like you can ask them when they wake up, we'll never know, it's one of life's great mysteries.

"So I want to enjoy myself. I want to live life to the max. I want to burn through every last krona. I don't want to waste a single day on a life I'm not happy with. There's no point waiting for things to get better, because nothing is going to get better. This is the world we live in now. Don't be ashamed to be human, be proud."

She shakes her head.

"This isn't you, Didrik. This is someone else talking."

"Yeah, it's Tomas Tranströmer."

"You know what I mean."

I'm just about to deliver a cutting reply when we hear the singing, squeaking sound from the tracks, a vague rumble in the distance, and then we see the train rolling toward us from the north. It isn't one of the shiny new snub-nosed ones, it's one of the old-style trains, big, black, and square, and it thunders into the station like a dark memory, the last ash cloud from a dormant volcano.

"Vilja," she says, and we both turn toward the parking lot, to the table where the volunteers are standing.

She isn't there.

I get up, scan the route she took, the platform, the few steps down, past the station building, out into the parking lot. Nothing.

She isn't there.

The train comes to a halt in front of us with a screeching, hissing din. It smells like junk, dirt, old rubber. I can make out figures through the window, crowding, it looks like the children are sitting on the adults' laps, a few people seem to be standing in the aisles. The doors don't open.

"Vilja!" Carola screams, but her voice is drowned out by the sound of hundreds of people suddenly moving toward the train, the howling child, a barking dog, shuffling, rolling, dragging.

I'm already on my way, slaloming in the wrong direction through the crowd. As I pass the couple with the howling baby the gangly man I vaguely recognize lights up and says *hi Didrik!* but I don't slow down, I just keep going into the parking lot, through a wall of dirty bodies moving toward the train, over to the table where the water was, but there is no one here, my eyes dart around, I jump to get a better view, shout *Vilja!* over and over again, a handful of passersby give me an absentminded glance but the majority barely even seem to notice me yelling my daughter's name. A few steps down the left-hand street, I quickly turn back and run over to the right, over the little crossing, *Vilja!* I must have missed her, she must have gone around somehow. I rush back toward the platform, and it's much slower going moving the same way as everyone else, anyone running in the opposite direction forges their own path but this time I have to jostle, take someone else's place, physically force myself past their knees, elbows, shoulders, back up onto the platform and into the pocket of space that opens up on the other side as everyone crowds toward the doors, a breath of air. I run back, past the couple again, *hi Didrik, do you remember me?* and Carola is standing with Becka in her arms, her phone in one hand, *she's not picking up*, she cries, *she's not picking up, did you see her?* and I shake my head, out of breath, she's gone, she's gone.

"Didrik!"

It's the man again, the bag heavy in his hand, the woman with the stroller and the baby behind him. It seems to have settled down now, though its tiny face is still bright red, the woman's eyes bloodshot from crying. The man is wearing a threadbare T-shirt with Bruce Springsteen and the American flag on the front, the colors faded from red and blue to pink and gray.

"Didrik, it's me, Emil." He gives me a warm smile and holds out his free hand. His palm is broad, a wiry, powerful grip. "William's cousin. We met before the wedding."

Wille's wedding? That must be three years ago at least, maybe five? The cousin who organized the bachelor party earlier that summer, he did a great job with a summer house by a small lake in the Dalarna forests, saunas and whiskey until dawn, no strippers or throwing up into buckets like we used to when we were thirty; it was all very nice, mature, atmospheric, a good guy, he was the headmaster of a school up there, wasn't he? Wille got drunk and called him the *headmasturbator*, and it was childish but also kind of funny, we were sitting around the campfire, roasting an entire wild boar, feasting like Stone Age men, dipping hunks of meat into huge tubs of béarnaise sauce with our bare hands, *headmasturbator*, but the cousin just laughed and took out a guitar (*strum your instrument, headmasturbator!*)

and played songs by Bob Dylan, the Rolling Stones, and U2, and we sang along as we passed the bottle around the fire. *Dead white men*, that was what Carola said, pulling a face when I got home stinking of booze and smoke on the Sunday, *dead white men*, but then he was the toastmaster at the wedding and I remember that she liked him, we both agreed in the car on the way home that the cousin had done a good job, he was funny and easygoing without taking too much attention for himself, the kind of person who *knows how to talk to people, nice in an old-school way*, Carola said, *you forget they still exist.*

"Hi, Emil. How's it going?"

The last part sounds almost ironic, and he smirks and rolls his eyes.

"Not bad. You? Got a lot on at work?"

I find myself laughing, feel a stab of pain in my ribs. He nods to my wife. "Carola, right? Christ. You two seem stressed?"

"Our eldest has wandered off somewhere," I say. Putting it into words makes me relax a little, suddenly it doesn't sound so bad after all; a vague sense of relief flickers by. "She went to get water, but now we can't find her."

Emil rolls his eyes. "Probably just that age. Are you OK, you need any help?"

He and the woman—what was her name, Irma, Inez?—have parked their stroller right beside us, in the middle of the stream of people flooding around the train, despite the fact that the doors are still closed. Someone shouts *open up* and we hear something clattering, but nothing is happening.

"I don't know where she can have gone," says Carola, lips trembling and eyes wandering, searching for reassurance. "Didrik and I were . . . having a chat and she went off and . . . now . . ."

"Oh, honey," says the woman—Ida?—putting an arm around her. "It's chaos everywhere. We were evacuated from Orsa last night. It's crazy."

Emil glances at my bandage.

"What happened to you, you OK?"

"Yeah, yeah."

"The fire?"

I nod.

"Damn."

A wave passes through the crowd, a shudder, and the voices die down. I crane my neck and see that one of the train doors has opened. A big, thickset woman in a dark blue uniform comes out, stands on the top step, and leans out to make herself visible.

Anyone for STOCKHOLM.

A powerful, piercing voice with lots of diaphragm support. The patient, indifferent voice of someone used to providing too little information.

Anyone for STOCKHOLM, this train is for those traveling with YOUNG CHILDREN ONLY.

She is immediately drowned out by a tidal wave of questions, protests, and general unhappiness. It's the men who are shouting and screaming, but the woman just smiles and repeats the same message three or four times.

"OK, what's she wearing?" Emil is calm, efficient.

"Who?"

"Your daughter. Tell us what she looks like and we'll go and look for her, you and me, the girls can wait here with the kids, OK?"

We're going to open the doors now, and we'd really appreciate it if ONLY those of you traveling with YOUNG CHILDREN would board the train.

The doors open and I lean forward to get a better look. The train car is full, even the cramped, dark space just inside the door, by the bathrooms and the bags. I see a woman sitting with a crying boy on her lap, feel a waft of hot air. The boy's chest is bare, sweat glistening on his skin, and the woman is staring out at the platform with dull eyes. She has a spoon and a jar of jam in one hand, she's feeding her child jam. I look away.

"That would be so great, Emil, but aren't you going to try to get on the train too?"

He smiles and shrugs.

"It's cool. We'd like to help."

The woman—Irene?—sighs, her eyes wandering. It almost looks like she is staring at my crotch.

"We won't be getting any train," she says stiffly. "We're staying at some campsite, apparently."

"Over by the lake?" Carola asks, her voice encouraging. "We were there last night, it actually wasn't too bad."

A strange silence follows. Carola doesn't say anything, I don't say anything, we both give them a questioning look. The baby has started wailing again, and she lifts him from the stroller.

"He's only three months," she says, her voice slightly louder to overpower his howling. "I'm not breastfeeding. And we don't have any formula left. At the campsite they say they're only giving it to the babies who come in without their parents."

Emil smiles apologetically.

"We tried to explain that Isa had breast cancer and everything, but they're just *so* damn bureaucratic. And the shop is closed too, apparently. Someone tried to loot it last night."

The woman looks down at my crotch again, and I reflexively tug on my shorts, check the fly.

No. She isn't looking at my crotch.

She's looking at my pocket. At the bottle.

"You don't happen to have any to spare, do you?" Emil's voice is still relaxed, as though he were asking for a napkin. "They told us to come down to the station and ask around, *you might find someone you can borrow some from there*, they said." He chuckles and shakes his head, as though he can hardly believe what he is saying. "And I was like, *what the hell, is this lord of the fucking flies or something*, and they just said they were sure people would be nice." He cackles, rolling his eyes. "So, here we are. What a ball ache, you know?"

Carola hugs Becka to her chest.

"We only have enough powder for two bottles," she says. "And that has to last until we get back to Stockholm."

The woman looks at her with mute, glassy eyes.

"Yours isn't even crying," she says. "Wilmer has been crying since yesterday evening. We tried ordinary milk, but he just throws it up."

The child in her arms is screaming, bawling, his little body unmoving, nothing but a blotchy red face with glazed eyes, no tears, mouth wide open, a piercing animal cry. That's all a baby is when it really comes down to it, sheer instinct in cute packaging.

"It's cool, right, Didrik?" says Emil, cocking his head and reaching out to squeeze my shoulder. I think back to the way I saw him just a few minutes ago, begging his way along the platform, walking around in a place like this, begging strangers for food for his baby, and I think about the diaper bag, the way four spoonfuls of powder mixed into hot water produces five ounces of formula.

I take a deep breath.

"If we give you half of what we have left—"

"Are you serious, Didrik? Oh my God, that's so kind, Isa can stay here and feed Wilmer and we can go and look for your daughter, right? That's perfect." He blurts the words out, trying to sprint through them, but I can see it now, the hint of desperation in his eyes, the slight shrillness that has crept into his voice, like a guitar string slowly being tightened. There are impatient people all around us, jostling and pushing to get onto the crowded train, and I shake my head.

"Listen. If we give you half of what we have left, you'll be able to feed your child now, but he'll be hungry again in four hours. And we'll be stuck on that train, and in four hours we won't have any food either."

Emil stares at me, still smiling.

"OK, so what you're saying is that it's better for your child to have a full belly on the train to Stockholm, where you can go straight to the nearest shop and buy more formula, while mine is stuck here, screaming with hunger? Is that your logic?"

I sigh.

"You'll just have to try to work something out. It's not like he's going to starve to death."

Carola is standing right by the woman's side, trying to comfort the child in her arms. She has taken out one of Becka's toys, a pink-and-orange thing made from biodegradable plastic that chirps and mews, and she's waving it in front of his sobbing face. The mother gives her a dark look.

"Do you want money? Something else?" Emil reaches into his trouser pocket and pulls out a watch, a black leather armband, silvery face. I don't know a thing about watches—it could be worth a fortune, it could be junk—and I shake my head again.

"I'm really sorry, Emil, but Jesus Christ, everyone has to take responsibility for their own kids, that's how it works."

He takes a step closer. He's tall, at least four inches taller than me, his face tired behind his pearly white smile, dirty, harried. He takes the sobbing baby into his arms and holds him up to me.

"For fuck's sake, Didrik." The words catch in his throat. "I mean, for fuck's sake, just look. Christ, come on. You can hear him screaming."

"You should've planned ahead," I say dumbly.

"Come on, Emil, let's go," says the woman, but he doesn't seem to hear her, he leans in to me, the child's foot touches my stomach.

"You know what people are saying about you online, don't you?" His voice is dripping with contempt. "That you've been going around looting people's summer houses. Good job you *planned ahead*. Congrats, seriously."

My wound is itching, my feet are aching, and I try to ignore him, to focus on the platform behind him. Suddenly I see her slim body, her fair hair, the Spider-Man backpack; she's standing with her back to us, can't see us in the crush, she's trying to make her way forward, maybe she thinks we've boarded the train without her, that we've left her on her own in this shit, *oh honey*, and as I open my mouth to call her name she turns around and is a teenage boy with a downy upper lip, shouting something at his dad by his side, and I fall apart again.

"Shut your mouth," I snap, fighting to hold back the tears. "You come over here pretending to want to help us, but all you really want is our baby's food. You're fucking pathetic."

"Emil," the woman says again, starting to move off along the platform. The baby is still screaming, hoarse, piercing. "It's OK, Emil, we'll find someone else."

He gets right up in my face. His breath stinks of smoke and energy drinks.

"I hope your fucking daughter gets raped."

He walks off with the hysterical baby in his arms without waiting for a reply.

Carola shouts something after him, I don't hear what, maybe it's nothing but a howl, a noise. I reach out for her, she's still holding Becka, turns toward me, *did you hear what he said, my God, did you hear what he said about Vilja?* and I nod and say *shh, he's gone now, just ignore them* but she is shaking with shock, her eyes scanning the strangers all around us, looking for Vilja, for Zack; I hold her to me, *ignore him he's lost his mind these things happen they've gone now*, and we stand like that, with Becka between us, her sleeping body, the soft sound of her breathing, and Carola sobs *please Didrik why is everything so fucking awful Didrik get us out of here now Didrik shit shit shit I don't want to do this anymore I can't do this anymore please Didrik what the fuck should we do?*

"We should get on the train," I say awkwardly. "Becka has to get out of here."

"But what about Zack and Vilja?"

"They're still out there. We'll find them. But Becka can't survive without us."

She is now in floods of tears, snotty and silent. Her lips brush Becka's cheek, kiss the top of her ear, the soft cartilage.

"I can't," she says, her voice faltering. "I can't leave my children."

I nod.

"We have a license plate for Zack. Or half of one, anyway. And Vilja can't be too far away. If you get on the train with Becka I'll stay here and round up the big kids. I'm sure we can catch another train this afternoon, and we'll all be back home this evening. We'll pack some clothes for Thailand somehow, or just buy stuff when we get there."

She makes a face, sniffs.

"Now you're doing it."

"Doing what?"

"Acting like everything is normal. Saying we'll be home soon. The sushi place. The climbing wall. Thailand."

I sigh.

"Well, we have to try. To hope, I mean. Tell ourselves it'll be OK."

"Or maybe we don't," she says, suddenly calm. "Our children are missing. You've ruined everything for us. You broke into a house and you're going to be arrested. We don't have anywhere to stay and we're not going to fucking Thailand. Everything is a mess."

The crowd on the platform has started to thin out, most people without young children have given up trying to get on the train, and those with them seem to have already crammed into the cars. We can talk without having to raise our voices, and as the noise dies down I realize just how tired I am, so unbelievably tired of all this. I nod toward the train.

"Becka," I say. "We need to take care of Becka."

"Yes," she says. "You're right. We do."

"Do you want me to come on board with you, help you find a space?"

She slowly shakes her head.

"No, Didrik."

"OK, but remember, it could be cramped as hell in there, try to talk to someone and see if Becka can—"

"No," she says again. "Listen to me, Didrik. I'm not going."

I stare at her, but she doesn't meet my eye, focused on a point behind me, unsure of how to go on.

"I can't leave Vilja and Zack here. And you . . . I think it would be better if . . ."

Her words are left hanging in the air as what she is saying sinks in. Somewhere nearby I hear a dog barking, is it the same one as earlier, or is there another one?

"You can't do it," she continues. "You get that, right? You can't handle this. Not this crap."

I want to argue. Open my mouth, close it again, think back to our walk yesterday, all those hours in the blazing sun on the way to Östbjörka or Ovanmyra or nowhere at all. I think about the quad bike, the shiny orange beetle, and I think about the smoke, the panic, the fear in Zack's eyes as I threw him into the backseat with two strange boys and let them drive off, *Jesus Christ, how could I let them take my son, what the hell was I thinking, why didn't anyone stop me?*

"No," I say. "No, I guess not."

Everything happens very quickly after that. She repacks our bags, takes my Fjällräven, and shoves all of Becka's things back into the diaper bag, showing me where the last diaper is, the wipes, the ointment she rubs between her legs, the spare clothes, the yellow sheet of paper detailing her height and weight charts and vaccination record. As ever I'm amazed by just how little I know, how little involvement I really have; this is my child and I like to think of myself as an equal partner, but the nitty-gritty of actually taking care of a baby is her domain, always has been. I thought things would be different third time around but of course they weren't, and I suppose I must have accepted that, it is what it is, we are who we are.

She hugs Becka, pressing her cheek to hers, our daughter squirms, starting to wake, and Carola quickly passes her over to me. She says her usual hushing, comforting words, tells me that she'll be in touch as soon as she knows more.

Then she hangs the diaper bag over my shoulder, gives me a stiff smile, and runs a quick hand over my bandage. I wait for a kiss that never comes and realize that this is how it is now, that we're no longer together, that this is it. She says goodbye and turns and walks off along the platform with her head held high, determined, resolute, and I've never admired her as much as I do right now, never been as proud that she is mine as I am in the moment when I know that she no longer is mine, and I shout *just a car bomb* after her but she doesn't turn around, maybe she didn't hear me, I hope that's the case, that it's because she didn't hear me.

I'm alone on a station platform in Rättvik. It's still morning, but I can feel the heat rising from the dry gravel, the concrete, the metal all around us. I put on the carrier and clip Becka to my chest, her soft body wriggling and moaning against my shoulder, a bare foot kicking my stomach. *It's just us now, sweetheart*, I whisper, climbing on board, into the throng, the stench, the heat, her tiny clawlike hand pulling my hair, a spot where the bandage doesn't quite cover the burn, *it's just you and me now*.

———

In terms of sustainability, the worst thing a person can do—worse than throwing food out two days after its best-before date, worse than flying to Australia three times a year, worse than shopping for clothes out of sheer vanity and boredom—is have children. Every single one of us represents a huge burden: a body that must be fed, kept warm, transported, repaired, and entertained for ninety years. You could argue that kids are necessary for the survival of the human race, but the planet is already overpopulated as it is, and for those who feel the urge, there is no shortage of children to adopt, take care of, or spend time with.

As an inhabitant of Sweden, reproducing and spawning your own biological offspring entails a carbon footprint that simply can't be justified outside of some kind of sentimental family norm.

Having two children? That's just plain selfish.

Having three? Grotesque. Madness. Pure climate sadism. Babies drown in the Mediterranean every single week as their desperate, panic-stricken parents try to escape the punishing heat in the desert hell of North Africa, babies grow up in refugee camps in Greece, Italy, and Turkey, babies are buried alive in the barbarism of the Middle East, babies are slowly suffocated by the smog of Beijing and New Delhi, babies are cut down with machetes by drug-addled child soldiers in Congo, and all so that coltan continues to be cheap enough for the car manufacturers to keep down the costs of their electric SUVs—and you want *three* children of your own?

But I loved it. Unreservedly, shamelessly. And after the drudgery of the early years with Vilja and Zack, the faltering economy, the degrading mortgages, the wage slavery, and the constant guilt over not being the person I wanted to be, after our marriage had died, after the pandemic, after everything we had made it through, we found ourselves facing a pregnancy we weren't sure we wanted, a child neither of us had expected, in a world full of precipices and darkness, a world in which evil, stupidity, and ugliness smile their cloying smiles everywhere, and how much does a pack of diapers even cost nowadays?

So we said *yes*. We said *yes* to a third child, what did we have to lose? Sure, it would be a child who, according to all established science, would grow old in an apocalyptic, nightmarish world of chaos on a level we can't even imagine, but people have always had babies, despite war and famine and disease. People are middle-aged when they hit thirty-five in Zimbabwe, but they still have babies; there are island groups off the coast of New Guinea that are on the verge of being swallowed up by the ocean, and they still have kids. Her generation will be the fossil-free generation, the one armed with the right knowledge from the get-go, the one that doesn't try to shirk its responsibilities, whose entire lives will be one long struggle to protect our civilization as best they can, and we could equip her for that, we genuinely told ourselves that, we could raise her to be a smart, sensible, responsible, and compassionate citizen.

It's just that we thought she might have a bit more time first.

I'm huddled on the cramped floor of the train, between the rows of seats. There are people everywhere, two or three to every seat, and the toilets are overflowing, piss seeping out beneath the door. I've got Becka on my lap and I'm trying to play a singing game with her, it's the only thing I can think of, *itsy bitsy spider*, *Humpty Dumpty*, and I can feel the old train moving forward, slowly, jerkily; if I look up I can see a sliver of sky through the window, no more than that, but it's a huge relief to finally be on the move.

The air around us is thick with the sound of whining, crying children. A toddler is waddling around with a diaper sagging almost to their knees. Beside me an immigrant woman with terrified eyes is trying to cover herself with her headscarf as she feeds her baby, and the equally nervous man in thick glasses by her side is fiddling with something in a plastic bag. A group of five- or six-year-olds are playing together, clambering over the backs of the seats and using the luggage rack as a handrail as though the train were an obstacle course, an adventure playground. The grown-ups protest half-heartedly and in vain but the kids just keep chasing one another, hooting and shouting whenever the train tilts on the bends. I think that if Zack were here, he'd be one of them, pretending that the train was on its way to heaven, to the underworld, to Hogwarts.

I consider getting up to go to the restaurant car, but a grumpy old man, probably someone's grandfather, announces to the entire carriage that there's no *damned* food or drink left on this *godforsaken* train, he's going to write to the government, he's going to report the government to the police, he's going to write a letter to the editor, *just you goddamn wait.*

And in the crush of bodies on the dirty gray carpet, I try to smile at my child. I blow on her naked body in an attempt to cool her down, I rock her in my lap as I sing to her, making the spider climb up and down my fingers, my right thumb against my left index finger and vice versa, over and over again, down comes the rain and washes the spider out, out comes the sun, the spider climbs the spout again, the same thing over and over. It's funny that I've never realized that before, that the song is all about optimism, about never giving up, about being washed out and climbing back up again, washed out and climbing back up again, in a never-ending cycle of death and resurrection. The rocking motion of the train has caused the pool of excrement to run out into the car, and I hear the adults' disgusted whispers behind me and imagine the carpet soaking up inch after inch of piss. *I'll be in the shit soon*, I think, tittering to myself, *I'll really be in the shit soon, but that doesn't matter, out came the sun and dried up all the rain.*

"Hey, you."

I look up.

"You."

How long have I been asleep?

"Hello. You, with the baby."

The voice belongs to a lanky man with graying hair at the temples. Clean-shaven, glasses, a yellow hi-vis vest and a walkie-talkie beeping and crackling at his hip. He's leaning over me and jabbing my shoulder with a stubby finger. The sounds are different now, the traffic sharper, more voices in the murmur, the train must have stopped.

"You need to get off."

"Are we in Stockholm already?"

He gives a friendly shake of the head.

"No, but you need to change trains here. That's how we're doing things now, anyone with very young children, it's meant to be under threes only, but that's a bit fluid, we need to get you onto another train."

A faint scent of aftershave from the man, his voice is soft but used to being obeyed. I want to ask why, but all around us the others with babies have gotten up: a tall man with an infant dozing in a sling, a dirty woman with a screaming baby wrapped in a striped pillowcase. The immigrant woman gives her husband an anxious glance, he gives me an anxious glance, and I try to smile and murmur something reassuring. We get up, follow the aftershave, push our way out of the sweaty, noisy carriage toward the platform. The air smells different here, more like tarmac, gravel, dirt, more like a city. I sway as I'm about to step down, try to steady myself with one shoulder, Becka squirms in my arms and I come close to losing my balance but the tall man holds out an arm and now I'm standing here, blinking in the daylight.

"Hello! Could I ask you a few questions?"

She's a Midsummer's dream with her blond braids and pretty face, dress, heavy makeup, high heels, and she holds out a microphone with the logo of a media company on one side, a cameraman behind her.

"You've just come from Rättvik, is that correct?" A warm, empathic smile. "How would you describe the *mood* among those who have escaped the fires?"

I stare at her. The platform is crowded and chaotic, journalists and TV cameras, one or two I recognize but also a few ordinary people filming on their phones, crying children, adults holding up handwritten signs, *PERNILLA SVENSSON, JUANITA KANDINSKY, HAMPUS HJORT, Have you seen 7 y/o MARSTON???* Their eyes bore into me, searching for something to cling on to, some sort of foothold, and the Midsummer woman smiles invitingly, I don't recognize her, probably a summer temp.

"I'm wondering how it *feels*, how you're *doing* after coming so close to these fires that . . ." Her tone changes here, from intimate to solemn. ". . . that are being described as *the worst EVER wildfire catastrophe in Northern Europe*."

"Uh . . ." I clear my throat. "I mean, it's really awful."

Becka looks up at her, babbles, the temp smiles back with excited eyes and gently brushes a knuckle across her cheek.

"What's her name?"

"Becka."

"God, she's so cute."

"Where the hell am I?" My voice sounds like someone else's.

"Borlänge," she says. "Borlänge. Haven't you been given any information?"

I shake my head.

"They just said we had to get off."

"The government has stepped in and ordered some trains from Germany to handle the evacuation, what do you make of that?"

"I just want to get home."

"They got involved after a train came to a halt outside of Östersund for four hours yesterday. Three children were taken to the hospital because of the heat, and we've just heard that two of them have since passed away. Your reaction?"

My left arm is aching, I shift Becka over to the right.

"Uh, what can I say. Terrible."

She nods eagerly but I don't go on. A vague lack of interest flickers across her pretty young face, the skin around her painted lips creasing in a soft frown of disappointment.

"Yes, and over two hundred people are now confirmed to have died in these terrible fires. Your thoughts on those affected, on what society should do?"

"Do?"

"Yes? How can we better protect ourselves?" She is starting to get bored of me, bristling with impatience, scanning the platform for someone else to talk to. "I mean, you must feel incredibly disappointed."

I laugh, cocking my head so that the bandage is more visible, clutching Becka to my chest—this is good TV.

"Disappointed? Why, because my car has gone up in flames and I've lost my family and half my hair and . . . seriously, *disappointed*? Yeah, gosh almighty, you can't help but feel a bit *annoyed*, honestly, it's a bit of a *bummer* that half of Sweden is on fire, is that what you mean? Nah, it's *really not OK*, lots of us are very *unhappy* that the entire world is one big fucking nightmare, is that what you're getting at?"

She studies me, her eyes glittering again. This is what I want, I want her interest, I want to give value for money, to deliver content, *to create cutthrough*, as my first boss used to say; I just can't resist the pull, the rush, the hunger.

Hello? Didrik? A voice breaks through the murmur. She's short, with dark, cropped hair, khaki shorts, and a simple black top, we worked at the same agency a few years back. *Didrik? God, it* is *you, isn't it*, a thin little body, the tang of sweat, *shit, how are you?*

"Jossan. It's been a while."

"I'm with TV4 News now. Climate Desk." She completely ignores the summer temp, moves right in front of her. "Shit, you know your name is all over the place, right?"

"Excuse me," says the reporter, sounding irritated. "I was here first."

"Didrik and I are old friends, we were colleagues."

"Didrik?" The temp frowns.

I nod.

"Yes."

Jossan holds her phone out to me, talking fast, trying to overpower everything else.

"Didrik, do you want to take me through what happened, I think a lot of people are wondering how it feels, we used to work together and have the same perspective on many of these issues, so if we—"

"Oh my God, Didrik?" The temp stands tall in her heels, towering over the shorter, older woman.

"Yes?"

"So it's you?"

She holds her hand to her ear, raises an eyebrow, takes a deep breath. "OK, OK . . ." I can tell from her tone that she's talking to someone else, and she quickly turns away and glances at the cameraman, who gives her a thumbs-up.

"OK. Right, Didrik. I'm here with Didrik von der Esch, who has just arrived in Borlänge with his daughter Rebecka. Didrik, could I ask you, how do you respond to the accusations of having broken into and looted a private property?"

Jossan has waved over another cameraman, who is standing only a few inches from their rival, and she asks a question I don't catch, they're talking over each other now, several other reporters hold out their microphones, cameras turn toward me, mobile phones like small, dark windows onto another world. I hold Becka out to them, feel a pang of guilt at using her like this, but my anger outweighs anything else.

"Do you see this child? She was out on the road, in the smoke. We'd been walking for hours, surrounded by fire. I broke in to save her. What fucking *accusations*? Of trying to take care of my family, of just wanting to survive a crisis that society has been actively trying to deny for decades? One that you parasites only care about when people are dying, when things are on fire, when there's a gripping story to tell? A week from now you'll have forgotten all about this and you'll be reporting on some shooting in Gothenburg or a bunch of Afghans taking over some hole of a town in Blekinge, and this, this utter collapse, it'll just be a . . . a . . . ." My voice breaks and I cough, a shooting pain across my ribs.

Her eyes light up, a new focus, something sharp and poisonous that was likely there all along, hiding beneath the makeup, beneath her summer dress, it's hot, I see a bead of sweat glistening on her downy temple.

"But, Didrik," she raises her voice slightly, the others have stopped talking and the stage is all hers, despite her youth and inexperience or possibly because of it, she's in complete control of the situation. Jossan holds out her phone in silence, now just following along. "We're still talking about criminal acts here, not just in your case but across the region. There are reports of looting and theft and criminal damage, what would you say to all the private individuals affected?"

I shrug.

"Fucking live with it."

My response hangs in the air for a moment or two. I'm on the verge of saying something else but I can feel another coughing fit coming on and the platform sways beneath me, I meant for it to sound sarcastic but no one is laughing, maybe I went in too hard?

"Didrik," says Jossan, a pained look on her face, "wouldn't it be better if we—"

"I have to get back to Stockholm now," I say. "We can talk more there. Ciao." I wink at her, press my dirty fingers to my lips and wave, that's something we used to do on Zoom calls during the pandemic, and once we got back to the office we just kept on doing it, blowing kisses instead, it became a funny thing, a kind of in-joke. I smile and wait for a flicker of recognition on her face but there's nothing there, just an absent, questioning emptiness, so I turn around and push through the people on the platform.

The lanky man in the hi-vis vest is standing by what looks like a fighter jet, a futuristic dream in gleaming white with a bright red line running along the carriages and nose. He is surrounded by people with backpacks and suitcases and plastic bags, and there are children everywhere, teenage girls carrying younger siblings, tearful boys with black snot running from their noses, a girl around Zack's age screaming *MOMMY MOMMY MOMMY* though no one is paying any attention to her. *Only those of you with very young children* the man says calmly, *very young, children who can't walk on their own.* He takes a step forward when he spots me, parting the muddle of people with his hand and waving me over, a squinting smile in the sun.

"Time to head home now, Didrik," he says, pressing a button.

Two doors glide open with a hiss and I step into paradise. The contrast to the pile of junk I was sitting in just a few minutes ago is so stark that it makes my teeth ache. Clean new plastic in shades of buttery yellow and nougat brown, no smells other than the subtle aroma of sterility—like the soft, barely audible bassline of a pleasant pop song—everything dazzlingly clean and new, signs telling passengers they can leave their bikes and buggies in the huge open spaces where people have spread out blankets and sleeping bags, letting their babies crawl on the floor. Other than them there is no one sitting or standing in the aisles, the seats aren't even full, perhaps only every third seat is taken up by parents and babies; several have even pushed back the middle armrest in order to lie down.

And the air. It takes me a moment or two, once the doors glide shut behind me, to really feel it. The sudden, frosty chill. I've been hot and sweaty for so long that I can barely remember what it feels like to be cold. It's like walking down a humid street in Bangkok or Madrid and then nipping into a Starbucks, like jumping into a hole in the ice, like being at your place in the country where the kids are screaming and your wife is in a mood and then getting into the hot, stuffy car and turning the AC down as far as it will go, cranking the fans up high, and leaning back in the imitation leather seats, an erotic shiver when you close your eyes and think about her.

I sit down with Becka, wrap a blanket around her, glance at the others, relief on all our faces, one person gives me an encouraging grin, the immigrant father from the previous train recognizes me and raises his thumb with a shy smile, the same discreet, satisfied smile everywhere; we're here, we are the chosen ones. Two girls in Scout uniforms walk through the train handing out bottles of water and fruit and neatly wrapped sandwiches, we can choose between hummus and some sort of roasted pepper spread. And then the train starts moving, without a single jolt or shake, it's like being slowly sucked through a straw, leaving the others behind on the platform, crying, screaming, and waving their signs, we zoom away from them, faster and faster, and the TV monitor at the end of the carriage is showing images of burning houses, smoldering forests, the prime minister at a press conference, a demonstration somewhere. The clock beside the news feed reads 10:22 a.m. and I wonder what Carola is doing right now, I want to call her and tell her just how well things worked out for Becka and me, but to do that I'll need to charge my phone and that will mean having to see all the rest of it, the emails from journalists, the messages from work, the comments on social media, and why should I call her anyway, it's over between us, we're not a couple anymore; I feel a tingle in my crotch when I remember where I'm heading, the adventure awaiting me.

Maybe I would rather just sit here for a while as the high-speed German train accelerates without a sound, feeling pride over everything I've achieved. *I got my child out of there*, I'll say, *it was chaos, worse than you could ever imagine, people were dying all around us but I got her out of there. I have no idea how I did it but I guess something inside me just clicked, you become a kind of caveman again, it wasn't me that got Becka home safely, it was my DNA.* That last part sounds good, I can work with that.

There's a spot on your head that I love to kiss, between the smooth skin on your cheek and ear and the crown of your head where your hair is already thick and dark. A downy, indeterminate point that occasionally shifts to your temple or behind your ear or your fontanelles—the spot on the back of your neck has already started to fuse, but in my head it's still a thin, soft film—somewhere I can bury my nose and breathe in the scent of velvety skin and sweet, dried-on milk; it's my comfort, my incantation.

In the future, when you ask, I'll tell you that this was what happened. I changed your diaper, gave you a bottle, burped you and talked to you, looked out through the window and told you about the world we could see racing by outside.

I charged my phone and tried not to read everything that came flooding in, but several people from work had sent a link to a film they wanted me to see. There were security cameras in the house and the files had leaked and now the whole world could watch as I climbed in through the broken window, as I stood in the kitchen and took a mineral water shower and then helped myself to the food in the fridge. Someone had also taken my interview from the platform and edited it together with the footage from the break-in, making it into a mock cowboy film, my voice saying *fucking live with it* over the soundtrack of a classic western, *fucking live with it* followed by me blowing a kiss and giving a warped smile into someone's phone camera. A security camera on the driveway had caught me driving off on the quad bike, my name in some garish orange Wild West–style typeface, *DIRTY DIDRIK—OUTLAW FOR LIFE*.

It was almost funny, I snorted to myself and then switched it off.

We rode the train, we looked out the window, just me and you, my daughter, and I thought that no matter what the outside world thought of me, they would never be able to take that moment away from us, those hours when I was taking you home.

The train stopped in Hedemora and then again, for almost half an hour this time, in Avesta. More people got on board, more babies. They were afraid the fires might spread south, apparently, and everyone wanted to get to Stockholm. Before long the train was full, the new passengers hungry and thirsty, but there were no more Scouts with water and sandwiches. There were long lines for the toilets and the restaurant car and then, just after we'd sat for an hour in Uppsala, someone announced that there was no more water or food on the train, that beer was all that was left.

We were twelve or so miles from Stockholm, with maybe fifteen minutes left to go, when the train came to a halt. By this point we had been traveling for five hours and the train was in the middle of a littered, sunbleached stretch of grass. We could see the motorway several hundred feet away, a gas station, a McDonald's, a shopping center in the distance, taxis, gridlocked traffic on the roads leading into central Stockholm, and the train fell silent. Until that point I hadn't even noticed the noise inside the car, the extremely faint buzz of electricity that had now disappeared.

The heat came creeping up on us, only a few degrees at first, a comfortable room temperature, then increasingly fast. And the sweat. The thirst. The stench.

The screens on our phones were still showing images of fires and politicians, helicopters, ambulances, the demonstration that had now grown larger, it looked like hundreds of thousands of people; riots had broken out and there were people with blood on their faces, police on horseback or firing water cannons, and it took me a moment to realize that they were in Stockholm, that it wasn't a big city in some shithole country somewhere, it was my hometown. I heard the others around me whispering that the protest had spiraled out of control and somehow the electricity had been knocked out across the city, which meant that no trains could get in or out of Central Station.

After two hours of various voices and explanations and apologies over the PA system, they announced that the train would be turning back, and we started moving in the opposite direction, north toward Uppsala again, back into the scorched forests and the wilderness. We came to a standstill in a dusty field somewhere and then started trundling down toward Västerås and Enköping. The hours passed and the temperature rose. I dozed off for a while in the stifling heat and woke to the sound of you screaming; you had diarrhea and it had leaked out of your diaper and smeared across your body and onto your clothes and blanket and the train seat where I had laid you down.

Södertälje.

I peeled off my sweaty T-shirt and wiped off the shit using the damp cotton. We were slowly rolling toward Stockholm and the heat was now unbearable, someone started shouting for help, it was 140 in there, like a sauna; we'd run out of everything, and I saw a mother trying to cool her baby's forehead using beer, the golden bubbles fizzing and running down its swollen, tear-streaked face. We came to a halt again in Flemingsberg, we shouted for them to open a window but there was some sort of code missing, the German trains were configured to a different operating system, or maybe it was a different signaling system, or maybe they needed a special key that no one could find because the person in charge of it had left the train and been sent by car to another train standing outside Ludvika or Fagersta or somewhere.

I blew on you as you lay naked and howling on the seat. We were out of diapers and it felt wrong to be blowing between your chubby thighs, your buttocks, the folds between your legs, but I didn't even stop to think about it, I wasn't scared, wasn't angry, I'd made up my mind and everything stunk of shit and sweat and beer, the mothers were crying, the fathers shouting, you threw up mucus and formula and I took off my shorts and wiped you down.

It was seven in the evening by the time we rolled into Stockholm, from the south this time, over the Liljeholm Bridge, through Tantolunden and down into the tunnels, and on the bridge over Riddarholmen the train stopped again, all the lights went out. In the city around us the billboards and streetlamps also went dark and the air became difficult to breathe, a tingling sensation in my head. We saw Stockholmers sitting outside bars, beautiful young people laughing on the waterfront, we saw others out jogging in the bright summer's evening, a motorboat with a party on the deck, girls in swimsuits dancing with bottles of champagne as the men dived into the water, protesters walking with signs on their shoulders, some limping, others still shouting slogans, *WHAT DO WE WANT?—TO SAVE THE PLANET!—WHEN DO WE WANT IT?—NOW!—WHEN?—NOW!— WHEN WHEN WHEN?—NOW NOW NOW!*

We weren't moving. We heard frightened cries and shouts from one of the train cars behind us, a baby had fainted and *is there a doctor on board*, two drunk men started fighting over the last apple from the Scouts, a voice over the loudspeaker told us to calm down *or we will take legal action*, and we shouted and bellowed and raised our middle fingers and someone threw an empty beer bottle at the TV screen, which cracked and sparked and went out. Everyone fell silent then, as though they were afraid of what we were capable of.

That was when I got up. I was wearing nothing but my underpants, with you naked in the carrier and the diaper bag slung over my shoulder.

"Enough," I said calmly. "This is unacceptable."

I saw the recognition in their eyes, heard the whispering, the muttered agreement, the frightened protests, and without waiting for a reply I walked over to the wall. The signage was in German, *ACHTUNG!* and *VERBO-TEN!* and I broke the glass with my elbow and took out the fire axe.

"Out of the way," I told the people sitting by the window.

They grabbed their children and backed away and I swung the axe against the window with the stubby end first. The glass was surprisingly tough and it was awkward with you in the carrier, it made no more than a small crack. Harder next time, right in the middle of the crack, it widened and I felt you against my bare chest as I hit it again and again, I heard someone shout, several others joined in, a gravelly, guttural sound, something like *YEAAH* or *WOOO* or maybe just *EHHH*, but it spurred me on and I hit it again and again until the window bent outward and a few pieces came loose. I barely even noticed I was bleeding from a couple of scrapes on my elbow; I could smell Stockholm and the late summer's evening.

"Didrik."

It was the lanky man, he had rushed through the carriages and his face was sweaty and red. I could see the huge damp spots on his shirt beneath his hi-vis vest, the scent of aftershave now diluted, mixed with a hint of bitterness.

"Put that down right now."

I shook my head.

"This is unacceptable," I said again. "People can't breathe."

"What you're doing now means the train can't go any farther," he panted, reaching for the axe. "It forces an emergency stop. We'll never get to the damn station."

I raised the axe, felt its reassuring weight in my hand.

"You've had thirty years to plan for this catastrophe and we don't even have trains that work," I said. "Why the hell should anyone care what you say?"

He pulled his walkie-talkie from his belt but a hand reached out and snatched it from him, the immigrant father with the glasses, shouting something in his language. Another man grabbed his arm and dragged him away from me, more hands and arms appeared, sweaty, half-naked bodies, and the man in the hi-vis vest shouted as a hand with cherry red nails and gold rings tugged on his graying hair. I turned back to the window and knocked out the rest of the glass with the blade of the axe, felt the damp weight of your body against mine.

There were murmurs about live tracks, but a few brave young fathers climbed out first. They lowered themselves down to the ground and stood looking at the rails, and when nothing happened after one of them cautiously nudged one with the tip of his sneaker, we all climbed out. We helped one another, held other people's children while we evacuated ourselves onto the bridge, an ambulance turned up to help the unconscious baby and there were police cars and security people all around us. At first it looked like they were going to intervene, but there were just too many of us and there were TV cameras and protesters, a helicopter hovering overhead.

The journalists shouted questions, someone wrapped a blanket around us, and I heard a voice calling my name, but it was starting to get dark and in the blinking blue lights and the sirens and the camera flashes and the tumult of screaming children and crying mothers, we slipped away.

We just slipped away.

And I walked out into the city with you.

We used to dream about the future when I was a child. At preschool we boasted that we would become policemen and firefighters, on the playground we claimed we would cure diseases or invent things or construct bridges and roads and buildings, that we'd just become rich, that we'd be able to afford trips to Thailand. So many endless opportunities, so many paths out into the world.

But that's all over now.

"You're going to escape," I whispered to you in the carrier. "I'll teach you. You'll be someone who escapes."

We walked past people sitting at candlelit tables outside bars, lovers making out in stairwells, others illuminating the way using their mobile phones as flashlights, and I remembered running around there with her one night. We'd had a romantic dinner in a dark corner of some tourist joint and afterward we snuck down the alleyways together, slipping in and out of the shadows, laughing and kissing, whispering dirty words like caresses, and as I walked with you there a thousand years later I felt a sting of jealousy toward everyone who seemed so carefree, so weightless, as though the nightmare didn't affect them, as though they were living on a planet it was still possible to live on.

Then I forgot the future existed. There was only the now, the moment.

I carried you like a shield, the ancient cobblestones beneath my bare feet, you in the carrier with the blanket around your legs, me walking through the dusk in nothing but my underwear, the diaper bag thudding against my back, the axe hanging from my left hand. Everything was good, just as it should be.

To most people I passed, I was just yet another body, but a few really saw me and I continued to stare at them long after they looked away. I wanted them to see me, to recognize me, welcome me; I was waiting for a reward but there was no reward.

2

THE CHINESE WORD
FOR CRISIS

OUTSIDE THE BIG DEPARTMENT STORE, THERE'S A PRETTY park with an avenue of Japanese cherry trees, and when they're in bloom the entire walk is like a cloud of amazing pale pink flowers. It usually happens in April, but the winter I moved to Stockholm they started blooming in January. I guess it was probably just a bit warmer than average and the trees miscalculated, thought it was spring. I was early for my shift at the coffee shop, so I walked around the park enjoying the pink, almost cerise miracle of nature in the middle of the dull, damp winter grayness; it didn't look like Sweden, they were like bougainvillea or frangipani or one of those other flowers you see people posting about when they're on holiday in the Caribbean or Zanzibar. I took a few pictures, thought I'd probably want to remember that moment, my first few months in the big city, and then I treated myself to a latte—painfully expensive even with the staff discount—mostly to warm up my hands, which were freezing despite the mild weather. I wanted to be a part of the spectacle, I wanted to belong.

Once I'd finished my shift and set the dishwasher running, cleaned and locked up and gone home to my sofa bed on the fringe of the city, I spent a long time looking through the pictures before I uploaded the nicest one. This was before I'd started posting regularly, back when I took them just for my own enjoyment, but the flowers were so nice that I wanted to share that moment.

People reacted immediately.

Damn, that's messed up.

Crying emojis, angry faces.

R.I.P. Swedish winter, gonna miss you.

Green, puking emojis.

That's not fucking normal.

My photographs weren't beautiful, they were an omen of the end of the earth. The cherry trees weren't a sign of nature offering up its dazzling beauty, they were proof that nature was stressed, warped, ruined.

I felt so stupid. I hadn't realized I was supposed to be sad.

But then I got angry. Why did these people think they had the right to decide how I should feel? What good did it do the climate if people were puking over a picture of some pink flowers? They bloom for a week or two every year, sometimes only a few days; how are we supposed to go on living if we can't find joy in things that are beautiful, exquisite, delicate, fleeting? Why would we even *want* to go on living if we're just going to insist on seeing death and destruction in absolutely fucking everything?

I went back to the park during my lunch break the next day and took more pictures, experimented with different filters, tried a few hashtags, uploaded them. The angry comments and puking emojis just kept on coming. The same thing happened the next day, and by the weekend it had almost become a thing with everyone who was triggered by them, people taking screenshots and sharing and reposting the pictures of me smiling and looking happy beneath the bubble gum–pink clouds. Under one of the pictures I'd written 1.5 degrees Celsius feels great after all! with a heart and a sunshine. Someone replied stupid fucking denier whore, u think ur so hot and I almost felt scared then. Sure, I'd wanted to annoy people a bit, but there was something about their anger, the sheer depth of their humorless, almost fundamentalist hatred, that frightened me.

On the Saturday morning, I got an email from a guy called Vitas. He said he was a professional photographer and that he wanted to do a photo shoot with me, so I traveled back into town and met up with him and his hot—but super gay—stylist. He took pictures and filmed until the daylight faded, didn't want to be paid, said he just wanted them for his portfolio. He wasn't actually a professional, but he wanted to be, and he said I could use his pictures however much I wanted.

On the Sunday morning, I uploaded the pictures with a short film I'd edited together, captioning it #choosejoy. I'd been into town every day that week, so I was planning just to stay home on my sofa bed, watching TV, but then work called and I knew that no one lasted long if they had a *bad attitude*, so even though I was exhausted I went back into town to serve the hungover weekend shoppers who wanted extra shots in their lattes, screaming kids who wanted muffins and cheesecake and fudge cake. The other girl who was meant to be working never showed up, so I was all alone behind the counter for ten hours straight, I had to stand with my legs crossed as I frothed their milk. In the end, I couldn't hold it in any longer, I put up the *BACK SOON* sign on the counter, which I'd been told was basically only for use in a terrorist attack or something, and I staggered through to the staff bathroom. I checked my phone as I emptied my bowels, and I got such a shock that I actually dropped it. It came so close to literally falling in the shit, but it bounced off my kneecap and landed on the filthy floor.

The best thing wasn't the likes or the comments or the shares, it wasn't the requests to take part in podcasts or appear on regular radio, it wasn't even the Japanese YouTuber with eight million subscribers who wanted to fly to Stockholm just to meet me or the inquiry from a luxury hotel up in Lapland that said they'd pay for my travel and board if I went up there for a photo shoot.

The best thing was the man who wanted to send me money. Not some gross old perv, no sleazy remarks about my looks or questions about underwear, nothing like that. Just an ordinary middle-aged man, his profile full of pictures of his wife and kids, asking if there was any way he could sponsor me.

It just makes me so happy to see someone actually dare to find joy amid all this doomsday prophesizing. Being happy is one of the most radical things a person can do these days; it's more extreme than being a damn Nazi or a Communist or what have you. Good for you! Could I send you a hundred bucks as thanks?

I washed my hands and went back out to the espresso machines and the line of angry, impatient, ungrateful people all staring down at their phones, and I've never felt more proud than I did as I took off my sour-smelling apron and dropped it into the sink, walking straight out without looking back, without saying a word to anyone, without a single thought other than wanting to see the cherry blossoms again, one last time before they fell from the branches and blew away and vanished.

TUESDAY, AUGUST 26

FIRST, I JUST NEED TO MAKE IT THROUGH THE NIGHT.

The heat has eased off a little and I breathe slowly, feel my body getting heavier, lighter, sinking, and floating, everything around me becomes soft, sumptuous, soothing, and the sense of finally finally finally drifting away takes over.

My roof terrace is a tropical paradise full of plants: a palm, a lemon tree, dog roses, another tree with big, round fruit on its branches, papayas or mangoes, maybe both, it could be both, surely not? The power is out again, but it's cozy up here; I've lit some candles, and I found a few cute little oil lamps in one of the cupboards. I'm half sprawled on the super-soft outdoor sofa in my workout pants and sports bra, a glass of chilled rosé on the coffee table in front of me. I like using rosé to wash them down, it feels kind of glamorous somehow. Everything is just perfect right now. I love my life, I've won the lottery, I've met the love of my life, and he wants me *as I am*.

My fingers dance over the keys, trying out a sentence just for fun:

All my life, I've been ashamed.

Six words on the screen, a blinking cursor after the full stop, pecking like a hungry bird that wants more.

More. One more.

No. No more.

Back to the text.

Of the air I'm breathing. Of the food I'm eating. Of the space I take up.

A sip of rosé as reward.

The shame of existing has always been with me, from my childhood in the sticks, through my years as an influencer and a public speaker, making my cheeks blush even now, as I write these words.

I push a damp lock of hair back from my forehead, change position on the sofa. There are sirens on the street down below, probably something to do with the power outage, yet more chaos.

A sip of wine. Right. Let it flow through your fingers.

This book is about my journey away from shame. About growing up in poverty in modern-day Sweden and about my pride at belonging to the working class who built this country. About my path through life, a path that has been winding and bumpy and far from clear-cut. And about my views of society today, a society in which intolerance and cancel culture are spreading and the killjoys are stealing all the oxygen.

I put my laptop to one side, lean back on the sofa, sip my wine. Skim through what I've written so far. There's a tone to it I don't like, a superficiality I want to move past. *The killjoys are stealing all the oxygen*, does that really sound good? I want it to feel elegant. Extraordinary, ecstatic, delivering an endorphin kick.

I read through it again. Ah, it's actually perfect.

Above all, this book is for you. For those of you who might have seen me on social media or heard one of my talks and want to find out more about the woman behind the ballsy attitude—and maybe even get a few tips for your own life journey.

This book is for anyone who is tired of being told that you can't do this, that you shouldn't do that, that you'll never manage. Tired of everyone telling you that humans are weak.

Because the truth is that we're survivors, starting from our very first breath. We are never so strong as when we are born.

I check the time. It's taken me three hours, but I'm finally on a roll. If I can keep this up, I'll have a book in three months. Talk about a goddamn work ethic!

I check my phone, which has been facedown, on silent, all evening. I can't focus otherwise. A dazzling flood of pushes and notifications, messages, threads, suggestions, requests, and missed calls. It pings and buzzes and vibrates, a digital sugar rush, but I'm a good girl and I ignore it all; it's time to work now, which means delivering content, no mindless browsing.

The display lights up, an unknown number. I reject the call, but it immediately starts ringing again. I reject it. Weird, they usually only try once.

The phone starts ringing again, I block the number. Fuck you.

I go inside to grab the carton of milk from the fridge, plus a nice glass. I fill it and put it down beside my computer and the lamp, play around with the angles to get the right light and vibe; the cushion on the sofa has a cute orange cat on it, and I'd like that in the background. Anders told me it was the official mascot of the 1988 Seoul Olympics, the first time tennis was included since Paris 1924.

My phone is ringing again, from a different number this time. I block that one, too. Thirty minutes later, I'm finally happy with the shot. I edit the picture a little so that the white milk and the logo on the carton and the cozy colors on the sofa all come through better in the glow of the lamp, then I write:

BIG NEWS! On a magical night like this in Stockholm, you just want to smash the solar system and start over with something brand-new. First: do you know how good it feels to drink a glass of milk that has none of the fat but all the amazing natural taste?!? Try it for yourself— order direct from #zerofatmilk and get a 10% discount, just click on OFFER and enter the code MELLIMILK! And second: I'm partnering with publishers Döbeln & Rehn to bring you my autobiography— seriously, The Story Of My Fucking Life! It'll be an honest, crazy book in which I lay myself bare and gather my thoughts about where we're heading and how we can maximize our one life on this earth—and now, at midnight on this epic summer night, I've written my first chapter! Thanks to everyone who has made this amazing opportunity possible—it's a dream come true. If the blackouts continue I'll just have to dig out a quill, because nothing can stop me now! HERE I COME. #dobeln&rehn #zerofatmilk #choosejoy

I add a heart and stars and the number people can use to send me money. It's taken me an hour, but surely that's OK?

Share.

And there it is. I put down my phone and lean back on the sofa. Feel a warm sense of satisfaction flood through me. It's so great, everything turned out just how I wanted it, as I imagined it. A summer night of luxury and writing. When I was a kid, this was how I imagined adult life. A place like this, high above Stockholm, miles away from my tiny hometown and my tiny apartment and Mom.

Daisy and I got jobs at the conference hotel down by the lake one summer, me cleaning rooms and her washing dishes. It was a pretty easy gig, because the place had almost no guests and was probably going to shut down soon, and we spent our free time partying or watching TV at one of our boyfriends' houses. One warm night, the gang met down by the lake to barbecue and swim until late, and Daisy got high on something and started waving her key in the air and saying that we should have an after-party at the hotel. Before I knew it, we'd trudged over there and let ourselves into one of the many empty rooms, there were people smoking hash in bed, someone else throwing up in the bathroom, and two of the guys tried to impress us, sneaking down to the bar to get vodka and banana liqueur. But then everything went to shit, Daisy was being a real downer, crying and going on and on about how it didn't matter if she lost her job, she was going to start studying after the summer anyway, and besides all guys were pigs and I was her only friend, this time she was serious, nothing could stop us because we were *better than this.*

In the end I couldn't take it anymore. I was freezing in my bikini and I pulled on one of the robes from the bathroom and went down to the garden by the lake. It was a cool, clear, sunny summer's morning, and I slumped down onto a bench and lit my last cigarette and tried to think about nothing at all. A pretty blond woman, somewhere around forty with full red lips and a lightly tanned face, came toward me from the hotel. She was carrying a tray with a glass of juice and a plate of grapes on it, a newspaper beneath the plate, and she sat down at the table beside me and smiled but didn't speak, just ate her grapes, one at a time, as she gazed out over the calm surface of the water. Then she opened the paper and slowly flicked through the first few pages.

I was out running earlier, she said absentmindedly, pointing down to the beach. *There's a really nice loop around the lake.* I jumped. Was she talking to me? As though I didn't know about the running track down there, after years of excursions and school field days and embarrassing attempts to start jogging. She got up and walked back toward the restaurant, *just going to grab a coffee, would you like one?* I was starting to realize that she thought I was someone else—not surprising, really, given I was barefaced, my hair messy from swimming the night before, wearing the same white terry cloth robe as her—so I just said *yes*, and before I knew it she was back with two cups and a plate of mini muffins. She served them to me and gave me a teasing, almost girlish smile, the tip of her tongue poking out between her teeth. *Late night, huh?* she asked as she sat down with a sheet of paper—I glanced over and saw it was some sort of schedule—and then she smiled again and said *the guy who runs the afternoon class is insanely hot*, and I mumbled *not really my type* and she laughed and said *no, I know* that, *a cupcake like you.*

And then we just sort of sat there with our coffees, the lake and the warm morning to ourselves, and the feeling of being someone who lived like that filled my entire body: a woman who stays at conference hotels over the weekend, who can sit in the garden in her bathrobe, enjoying a quiet cup of coffee and flicking through the newspaper rather than scrubbing someone else's toilet or rinsing yogurt or cream sauce or ketchup from someone else's plate. The woman got up and said *well, see you inside later* as she walked away, and I went home and Daisy and I were both fired that same day, not that it mattered, because I'm sorry, but what a shitty job.

Being free. Creative. Independent.

She was who I wanted to be.

And now I am.

I check my phone. Seven hundred and eighty-two likes. Not bad, considering it's the middle of the night, especially with the power cut and everything. It'll blow up in the morning. Over ten thousand likes, easy.

There are a whole load of messages in my in-box, but I don't open them, only the one from DrSverre74. He's as sweet as ever, writes So glad you're having a good night, my lovely Melissa, followed by a heart. I don't have the energy to write back, but I film myself for a few seconds, smiling flirtatiously and moving one hand down to my crotch and then back up to my lips. I blow him a kiss, whisper *It'd be even better if you were here, baby*, and hit send. That's enough for now, they always want more.

Always. More.

No. No more.

I just need to make it through the night.

ding-dong-ding-dong-ding-dong-ding-dong

The sound makes me think of church bells, only cleaner, more delicate than here in Sweden, like a mountain village in Switzerland. I've never been to Switzerland, but that's how I imagine it: brown-and-white cows and snow-covered mountaintops, a girl called Helga with blond Nazi braids. Except it doesn't stop, and there's no reverb, just *ding-dong-ding-dong-ding-dong-ding-dong*, and my mind turns to danger, to evacuation, an emergency situation. A warning. One last chance to escape.

But I'm in the middle of Stockholm. It's a warm summer night, the power is clearly back on, and there's nowhere safer than this roof terrace.

ding-dong-ding-dong-ding-dong-ding-dong

I turn toward the apartment and hear the sharp electronic sound, *ding-dong-ding*, over and over again, cutting through the rosé and the morphine and the dusk. I wander inside and hope it's just some sort of gadget gone wrong, *dong-ding-dong*, an alarm clock someone has forgotten to turn off, but that's just wishful thinking. Deeper into the darkness, past the kitchen and the other cavernous rooms, the hallway, the front door. *Ding-dong-ding.* It's there, it's on the other side.

ding-dong-ding-dong-ding-dong-ding-dong

Someone is ringing my doorbell at two in the morning.

I open my mouth to shout *who is it* but quickly change my mind. As long as I don't say anything, no one will know I'm here. As long as I keep quiet, I'm safe. The door has two locks and a safety chain, there are security cameras and a high-tech alarm system I can control from an app on my phone, help will be here in ten minutes.

It's probably not even for me, why would he tell the world that he's letting me stay in his apartment? One of his friends must have been out drinking and decided to come over here for an after-party, either that or one of his women feels like a bit of dick slash drink slash drugs and wants to see what's up; he's been hanging around the nightclubs in town for the past thirty years, half the celebrity elite must know the code to the front entrance.

Ignore it. Block it out.

ding-dong-ding-dong-ding-dong-ding-dong

But I'm not a child anymore, I'm not a little girl who needs to hide, I'm not a dirty secret who has to wear her mother's wedding ring when she checks in somewhere; I'm a professional woman housesitting a good friend's apartment for a few weeks over the summer, and I have every right in the world to be here. No excuses, no sneaking around, no more faking.

So I make my voice a little sterner, more annoyed than afraid: a forty-year-old woman with rollers in her hair, night cream on her face, comfortable slippers, a negligee that looks more like a robe. Worldly, wealthy, wise.

"Who is it?"

The bell stops ringing. Thank God.

Breathing on the other side. A low voice. A man's voice.

"Hello? Who is it?" I shout, my voice echoing down the empty hallway.

His voice again. Louder, closer to the door:

Melissa? Are you there?

First relief, then a shiver down my spine.

A sinking feeling.

Shit.

"Didrik?"

Melissa? Melissa Stannervik?

This would be the perfect moment to hit pause, to stop mid-sentence and think about what is going to happen next. I could ask questions through the door, demand explanations, straighten out old debts; I could go back out to my terrace, put on some chilled club music, and pour myself more rosé, pop another OxyContin and watch the dawn paint its glow over the church spires and Stockholm's pathetically few skyscrapers as I calmly analyze and pick the situation apart.

Melissa? Please, open the door.

I'm not an impulsive person, that's the most common misconception about me. It's the way I look that does it. But the truth is that I'm deliberate, introverted, philosophical. The kind of person who wants to sit alone, thinking, writing, moving commas around. I was good at school. No one ever believes that either, but I was, always got everything right.

Melissa?

With every second that passes without me opening the door, it's as though something becomes even uglier and more broken, and as my hands fumble with the lock and the chain I remember the beach, the one Mom and I used to go to during the summer holidays, a big plastic jug of lemonade, sliced white bread, and a jar of strawberry jam, maybe even a package of cookies or crackers. And she sighed and said the heat was so nice, why bother going to see family when you could have such a nice time in Sweden, her stomach was so doughy and wrinkly, the illness had already made her stiff and inflexible and you could no longer read the tattoo on her back, but

I knew it was my name, written in an elaborate script, and the families with young kids spread their blankets in the parched meadow beside the lake, the fathers with rounded bellies and collapsible chairs, the mothers running around and keeping an eye on the kids with sunscreen and sand-beaten plastic toys, and she turned to me, a moment before she lowered her body into the warm water with a groan of pleasure, and in Serbian, she said *don't get stuck with any man, Milica. Men just take; you give and give and they take, take, take.*

WEDNESDAY, AUGUST 27

DIDRIK IS SITTING ON THE SOFA WITH HIS FEET ON THE COFFEE table, drinking a cold beer, an IPA I found in the fridge. The baby is sleeping under a designer blanket beside him. I'm still in shock at seeing him, both the fact that he's here and the state he's in: the cuts on his face and his upper body, his bloodshot eyes, the disgusting wound on his head (I quickly gave him a damp towel to cover it so I wouldn't have to look at it), and the sheer chaos radiating like a Wi-Fi signal from his stinking, sweaty body.

"They said you were here," he says. "I managed to get hold of Matilda, no, Hanna, I eventually managed to get one of them to tell me where you were, and then I stood outside until someone showed up, I had Becka with me, told them it was an emergency—diabetes." He grins to himself. "Can you believe it, I came up with the diabetes thing and then they just let me in, and then I was standing by your door, ringing the bell for so long, my God it feels so good, honey, finally, finally finally, Christ, what a nightmare, but at least we're together now."

I sip my rosé and scroll on my phone. He keeps talking about video clips, films, all these rumors about him and what he calls *the escape*, but I can't find anything in particular, most of it seems to have been uploaded hours ago and the news tonight is all about other things, the fire has spread to central parts of Åre and Duved and a conference center is in flames, the Norwegian mountain regiment has come over the border to help out, but there are several areas in Norway at risk of fire, plus landslides because the glacier on the Hardanger Plateau has melted so much over the summer. A landslip near Geilo has destroyed a road and a bus has overturned, forty-two tourists are feared dead, at least eight of them Swedes. Dirty Didrik is kind of yesterday's news, and to be perfectly honest he's more a joke than anything.

"So . . . what are you planning to do now?"

He takes another sip of beer, wipes his mouth on the back of his hand, and tries to stifle a burp. Looks around the terrace.

"What a place. How come you're living with him?"

I shrug.

"I don't really know Anders, we just met at a mingle thing and he asked if I wanted to borrow his apartment over the summer."

"So he's just letting you stay here?"

His voice is gruff and surly from tiredness, and I can hear that he's trying to keep it neutral, no insinuations, but it still irritates me somehow. Just come out and ask, you wimp.

"He said he was going to Paris and London for the tennis, and then he was going sailing, I think. I don't know, I guess he just wanted to be nice."

Didrik nods but doesn't say anything, and even that drives me crazy. It's as though I need to explain myself, as though I should have been *saving myself* for him, as though I don't have the right to a boyfriend or a lover or to have live-streamed orgies with a bunch of random guys if I feel like it, and what irritates me *most of all* is that this irritation is niggling and burrowing and chipping away at the great feeling I had earlier, that thick blanket of calmness, emptiness, expectation, like a child who knows that the biggest present under the tree is hers.

"You didn't answer my question," I say, aware that I'm slurring slightly. "What are you going to do now? Do you want to tell me what's going on?"

"Don't worry," he says stiffly. "I'll clear off in the morning, just need to get my bearings a little."

I sigh.

"Didrik, please. Don't get annoyed. I just need to know what's what."

The baby—Becka is her name, I've seen pictures of her before but hadn't quite realized she was already so big, somehow I thought she was still a tiny pink thing that just lay there and cried; when he first uploaded the pictures I told myself it was really over for good, he's had a third kid with the woman he said he didn't love anymore, the woman he was about to leave, it's finally over—is squirming, whimpering, sleeping the way only a baby can: flat on her back, with her little arms and legs outstretched in a cross. She's naked aside from the towel Didrik has wrapped around her like a diaper.

"I've left Carola," he says calmly, practically sighing with relief. "It's done. It took me a while to get back, but now I'm here."

He sighs again and bends down, fumbling with a bag, struggling with the zip. He takes out a box of pills and pops two from the blister pack.

Tramadol.

"They gave me these for my head," he mutters. "It's so fucking painful."

He throws them into his mouth and washes them down with a swig of beer, grimaces.

I don't speak, no words will come out, but Didrik keeps talking, seems to have rehearsed a little speech, whispering about how he has lost everything, his kids are missing, his career is in ruins, he is coming to me *empty-handed, all I have is my love for you, this violent passion, this desperate longing for you, Melissa. All I have is the hope that you still want to be with me.*

This was what I liked about him, the way he showed his vulnerability, the fact that an older man with money and power and status would turn into a trembling schoolboy in front of me, a needy bitch on his knees, begging for my affection. That he dared be so pathetic, so lost. His cocker spaniel eyes and those fine lines.

"It was complete fucking chaos up there," he sobs. "I still can't take it in. Zack and Vilja are both missing and now I can't get hold of Carola either, and it's all just too much, please just let me and Becka get our bearings here, I know you want to throw us out but just let us . . . I mean, it's . . . I can't . . . just for tonight, if that's OK, please, please, I know I've . . ."

"It's been two and a half years," I say. "Two and a half years since you said you wanted to be with me. Two and a half years since you left me."

"But I never left you."

I stare blankly at him.

"And I'm ashamed of that," he adds. "I'm ashamed because I still follow everything you do, because I google you all the time, listen to every single podcast. Because I know what music you listen to when you go running, which cafés you go to and what you order there, which apps you use, which TV shows you watch when you can't sleep. I'm ashamed because I know your mom's MS is slowly getting worse, that you visit her less and less, and when you do go to see her you just sit by her bed and help her with her crosswords and Sudokus and puzzles, the easiest ones, the ones meant for kids."

His voice is getting thicker.

"I'm ashamed because I've never been able to let you go, because not a day goes by without me fantasizing about what it would be like if we were together. I'm ashamed for grieving, because the grief never goes away, I'm ashamed of all the times I thought I'd be willing to sacrifice anything—my family, Becka, everything I own—just so I could wake up next to you, that's probably all I really want: to wake up one morning and be with you."

A bubble of snot swells from his nostril.

"To fall asleep and . . . wake up and . . . you're still there."

His lips are trembling. The situation is so dreamlike and longed-for and beautiful and ugly and absurd that I want to scroll past it, log out of it, turn the screen away, as though it were happening to someone else.

Oh, Didrik.

"I'm ashamed because I'm still so in love with you, Melissa. I guess that's it. I'm ashamed of love."

"Honey," I whisper, tasting the word on my lips, letting it into my body. "Oh, honey."

I get up from the armchair and sit down beside him. He smells like dirt and smoke and a hint of beer. His upper body muscles have shrunk since I last saw him, he now has a belly and man boobs where you could previously at least *visualize* washboard abs with the help of a sugar detox and a sixteen-week training program; he's crying, and I dry the tears on his cheeks. He's beautiful when he cries, I think. It's beautiful when I dry his tears.

———

How is my lovely Melissa Stannervik today? DrSverre74 asks, attaching a picture from his jetty, the sunlight glittering on the waves, the old wooden boat he's so proud of—he calls it a *Pettersson*—the Swedish flag flapping in the background, his fat dick, pale against his tanned stomach. Thinking about you, beautiful.

I snort and close the message. Whatever happened to "good morning," you know?

It's nine a.m. Cappuccino, croissant. Me and my laptop, the tall bar counter by the window in the corner, my favorite seat; it's tucked away, but I can still see everything going on out there. Soft music over the speakers, two half-hot hipsters hunched over their computer screens, an elderly American couple, him with a potbelly, her with duck lips, they're studying their tourist map and talking loudly about castles and churches and museums. Outside, people walk by, giving the city its pulse. The workers sweeping up garbage and broken glass from the demonstration yesterday, the morning joggers zigzagging between piles of paving slabs and ripped-up tarmac, the electric bikes, e-scooters, and electric cars silently zooming by; the sweet preschool children walking in a line, blond, brown, black, hand in hand. It's just like the sign above the bar says, written in big, bright letters: *WE ARE BLACK, WHITE, LATINX, ASIAN, MUSLIM, JEW-ISH, HINDU, BUDDHIST, CHRISTIAN, ATHEIST, GAY, LESBIAN, TRANS, AND STRAIGHT. IT WORKS REALLY WELL!*

Not a perfect society, by any means, but a society worth protecting. Maybe that's why I love police officers? Because, when it really comes down to it, they're all that stands between us and barbarism?

My coffee is cold. I've barely touched it, can't stop thinking about Didrik and his baby in the bed upstairs. We got a few hours' sleep on the sofa on the terrace, but woke when the first rays of sunlight broke through. He suddenly got stressed, borrowed some clothes from the wardrobe—a white shirt and a pair of designer jeans he could barely do up—and then went out. The baby woke up and started screaming the minute he left, screaming and howling and tensing her entire little body, and I tried to hush her, to soothe her, hug her, show her some videos on my phone, but it was like she couldn't even see I was there. I've never taken care of such a young child before, and I started shouting at her, started crying myself, then the diarrhea hit like it always does and I had to stagger through to the bathroom with the kid in my arms, letting it run out of me as she screamed and screamed and screamed. It was like the time I had a summer job at a home for people with dementia, like Vitas when he had one of his hash psychoses, and I remembered reading that you could dip the infant in ice-cold water and had just turned on the taps when Didrik came back with his arms full of baby food and diapers, and only then did I realize that I was drenched in sweat and I tried to say something cutting, but all that came out was sobbing. He looked surprised, said *I've only been gone twenty minutes.*

After being bottle fed and shitting and puking everywhere, she fell asleep like a clubbed seal and he lay down beside her on the big double bed in the primary bedroom and I tiptoed over to his bag and quickly popped the last two tramadol. It serves him right for dumping his baby on me.

Other than milk, yogurt, and butter, there is no food in the fridge. I thought he might get something nice for breakfast while he was out, but he didn't buy anything for us, just a load of things for her, so I decided to come down here for a coffee at my favorite place instead.

I've always liked mornings, the crystal clear thoughts before the day's noise manages to eat into my brain. Sometimes I wonder what might have happened if I'd followed my teachers' advice and studied law or something, I could have been a high-powered prosecutor or a star lawyer by now. I would have loved getting to work at five thirty and having the entire case ready by the time the others came strolling in at nine, wearing a pinstriped suit and glasses, my hair in a bun, the whole bitchy teacher look. Early morning is my favorite time of day. No one believes that, either.

The sound of a screaming child makes me look up. A girl in her late teens is standing just outside the window. She is wearing a black hijab and a ripped dress in some nondescript shade of brown, and she's sitting by a shopping cart stuffed with plastic bags and empty bottles, plus a howling, naked baby on a grubby sleeping bag. She struggles onto her knees and pulls a piece of filthy cardboard from the cart, a couple of laminated photos, and an empty jar that once contained prawn mayonnaise, for dropping coins into. There are two older children huddled by her side, the boy with dirty black hair, the girl in a hijab the same color as her mother's. She glances up at the window and a pair of frightened brown eyes meet mine.

"God," I whisper, looking away. I want my gaze to land somewhere else, and I close my eyes for a moment.

But why?

The thought comes to me like a burst of fresh mint, and I immediately write it down.

You see a mother and her children begging on the street and you think, "my God, how unfair." But why?

I turn back to the window, look down at her hunched back, head bowed in shame over the scrap of cardboard with its misspelled message in greenish-black felt tip.

How do you know she doesn't like begging? What did she do before she came to Sweden? Maybe she was a sex slave in an Islamic terror sect? Or maybe she was married to a ninety-year-old man who abused her every day? She and her children might have lived in ruins, surrounded by war and famine like everyone else. How do you know this isn't sheer heaven for her, being in a country where she is free to beg on the streets and dig through other people's garbage?

The waitress comes over with a plate, setting it down in front of me. It's some sort of super salad, with avocado, passion fruit, feta cheese, fat-free prosciutto, and tiny leaves, probably Thai basil.

Would I want to trade places with her? Absolutely not. But since when is that an argument? I do plenty of things that many women around the world would detest: I eat bacon, I drink alcohol, I have sex with complete strangers I chat up on my phone while I'm sitting on the toilet.

I try a piece of avocado. It's perfectly ripe, verging on creamy, a slight hint of sea salt and lemon juice.

Why do we always assume that everyone wants to live like us? It could just as easily be the case that the refugees you see love this town, that they love sitting outside in the morning, breathing in the crisp Scandinavian air; this could be the adventure she's been dreaming of all her life. Perhaps, right now, she is happier than you or I have ever been.

The point is that we don't know. Neither you nor I know.

I lift my hands from the keyboard and wrap them around my coffee cup, gaze out through the window, trying to be one of those women who are completely focused, no fiddling with my phone, no mindless surfing or searching for an affirmation kick; just being here, in the moment.

I write:

To a large extent, this book will be about me and how I have been affected by the things I see around me. My lovely mother lives in a rest home, and there have been all sorts of restrictions in place since the start of the pandemic, face coverings and gloves everywhere. She loves cats, but she isn't allowed a cat. She loves Coca-Cola, but she isn't allowed carbonated drinks. And she is only allowed to eat vegan food—if you ask the government why, they'll refer you to their climate policy. After a long working life, surely our old people deserve a good steak from time to time!

It's been over six months since I last saw Mom, I realize. When I went home at Christmas, I paid for a nice meal at the conference hotel, but she refused to eat it. Ham, sausages, meatballs. Nothing. "I've got to do my bit for the planet," she said, hunched over her walker. Even though the food was already right in front of her. Even though the animals had already been reared and slaughtered.

I write:

The best thing we can do to help other people is to stop feeling empathy, because with empathy comes resentment. The sense that you're living a life that's worse than mine, that you're helpless, defenseless, a victim.

A sip of coffee as reward.

This was what I dreamed of. Being able to sit somewhere like this in the morning, all alone, letting my mind wander. Philosophizing. Dreaming. Creating. And now I am.

Outside, the mother has picked up her baby and started breastfeeding it, eyes closed in the morning sun. The boy has taken out a mobile phone and is scrolling and scrolling, his dirty fingers dancing over the pictures on the spiderweb cracks on the screen.

———

I'm in my girl cave, that's what I call this room, the smaller (though still huge) of the two living rooms. It's the only room in the apartment that doesn't have a window, making it cool and dark. There's a comfy old leather sofa, a well-stocked bar cabinet, and a big flat-screen TV, and with all the soft yet cool cashmere blankets and the cushions and duvets, it's really cozy, my very own writing room, insulated from the noise out on the terrace. I'm not used to having so much space to myself, and for the most part it's incredibly nice, but sometimes it's almost like I get agoraphobia, a sense of impending danger. One evening I actually had to run around turning on the lights in every room just to make sure I really was alone.

But this is my cubbyhole. In here, I'm the queen.

I don't know why I was invited to that party. I often get invites, but mostly to openings, events, premieres, not to big things like that, enormous boats with onboard staff, fresh orchids flown in by helicopter, oysters and lobsters on huge mounds of ice, bottles of champagne—but no glasses, because they were there to be sprayed, not drunk. I guess I just ended up on some list, filling a quota of some kind. I found a few girls I vaguely knew and we swam and sunbathed on the rocks. It was only early June, but the water was amazingly warm.

No, I didn't actually know who he was. I'd heard of him, but I couldn't have put a face to the name, and he really wasn't anything special, just another tanned, fit old man with bushy gray hair. Some men like to show off their status with watches, shoes, and sunglasses, others through their gestures, their posture, the way they speak, the way they look at you. But he was the opposite, quiet and softly spoken; he didn't even glance in my direction. His clothes were simple but stylish, white jeans and a white shirt, white sandals, white everything. His status was in the vacuum that arose around him, in his aura, in the models with designer dresses and huge lips, the men who were his age but had slightly bigger bellies, slightly snazzier clothes, slightly hungrier eyes. He was just another reasonably handsome, somewhat slender man in his sixties, and I had no idea what was going on when one of the girls whispered *shit, he's coming this way, I'm gonna die, he's a legend.*

At first I thought he was coming on to me, but then I realized that he just wanted to talk. He'd listened to a podcast I was on, talking about consumption, about the *three Ls—luxury, liberalism, and lifestyle—*and he seemed really impressed by my ideas. Then nothing else happened, he got drunk or high and went off with a couple of Russians, and one of the girls had some tramadol, so I got into a motorboat and headed back into town with her.

But the next day, a woman who introduced herself as his assistant got in touch and asked if I would be interested in joining Anders for lunch. When I found out we were meeting up here, on his roof terrace, I was convinced he was coming on to me, it was almost insulting that he thought it would be so easy, so I put on my ugliest underwear in protest: a turquoise thong with slack elastic. But again, he was perfectly nice. We sat out on the terrace, yet another early summer's day without a cloud in the sky, and he just seemed to want to talk. The food was simple but delicious, a tuna-and-egg salad he'd discovered while he lived in Monaco. And just like at the party, he said he thought I had exciting ideas, but it was all starting to feel a bit forced by then, like he was trying to charm me, badly, half-heartedly, the charm of someone who has never needed to charm anyone before.

So I started fiddling with my phone, said we had to take a selfie because my boyfriend watched all his matches on TV and would never believe that

I'd been to his place if I didn't have photographic evidence, *pics or it didn't happen*. He laughed and said he felt sorry for me for having such an old boyfriend, because he'd played his last competitive match against Andre Agassi in 1992. He was quiet for a moment after that, then he asked whether I liked his apartment. Without waiting for me to reply, he asked where I lived and I told him the truth: nowhere. He nodded compassionately and then asked, just like that, whether I'd like to stay in his apartment for the rest of the summer. Eight, ten weeks, while he was out of town. Water the plants on the terrace, stack his mail. *Free, of course*, he hurried to add when he saw the horrified look on my face.

Then he showed me around, the two living rooms, the guest bedroom, his son's room, the bathrooms, and the kitchen, all stainless steel and tiles so clean that you could tell it was the kind of kitchen no one had ever cooked a meal in. He pointed to the pantry and the fridge and said they were fully stocked with food and beer and wine, that I could help myself to whatever I wanted. Last of all we went through to the primary bedroom, a bright, wonderful space. There was an enormous dark-wood bed in the middle of the room, a mirrored wardrobe, a balcony, and windows in three directions— even one in the roof. But he seemed embarrassed, almost shamefaced, and I thought, *what the fuck, sugar daddy, are you going to act all shy now?*

I only have one condition, Anders began, and I forced myself not to look away, to hold his gaze. No matter what came next, no matter what he wanted, I was planning to say no, and if I did say yes then I wasn't going to be ashamed of it.

What he then told me was so unexpected that I almost started laughing, it sounded like some sort of weird prank. But he was deadly serious and I said yes, of course I did, the apartment is a dream, and it was only after I told Hanna and Matilda and saw their reactions that I really understood just how gross his condition actually was, but by then I'd already moved in, it all happened so quickly. When Hanna and Matilda came over for my housewarming party, they just screamed. For at least half an hour, they just walked around the place screaming.

I never sleep in there, though. The first thing I did after his assistant gave me the keys and the alarm codes, once I was all alone in my 2,200 square feet of penthouse, was to check the other rooms for blankets and pillows and ready my girl cave.

The second was to search the bathroom cabinet, and when I saw the OxyContin my knees gave way beneath me and I lay flat out on the floor and cried and thought about how much I loved my life.

I check my phone. How's it going, beautiful? Fancy coming over to cool off? All alone out here on Dalarö this week, and the water is soooo nice.

The tramadol has started to wear off, it never lasts long, and I'm *this* close to taking a naked selfie and hitting send, just to keep him hot, but I really do need to try to phase it out, plus I think I have a 40 mg reserve in the purse I was using on Saturday, I'm almost certain I do, and it's not like I'm going to need that, so I just grip my phone tight and close my eyes and try to breathe through the nausea.

A bit of toothache, that was all. One slightly painful tooth.

Fuck me, I'm pathetic.

"So this is where you've been hiding."

Didrik is standing in the doorway, a cup of coffee in his hand. Becka is awake and is staring blankly at me, clutching a yellow rag. It's called Snuggly, apparently, and I can smell it from here. She's sitting or hanging in some sort of carrier that was probably pale gray at one point in time, but is now black with soot and covered in what looks like—and judging by the stench, may well actually be—feces.

"Been looking for you. Christ, this place is big."

He scratches his stomach. He has borrowed a polo shirt, one of those white ones with a little collar, and it's too tight for him, his belly poking out of the gap between the top of his underwear and the edge of the carrier.

"It feels surreal, doesn't it? That we're here together. Of all places, I mean."

I nod.

"Yeah, for sure. I definitely wasn't expecting you."

I can tell he was hoping for more, I don't know, enthusiasm, energy, euphoria. I grip my phone as though I am trying to strangle a kitten.

"Good news from Carola," he says in his adult voice. "Vilja is back and they've found Zack, he'd ended up down in Hedemora somehow . . . So now we need to talk through how things are going to work going forward, with the kids and the house and everything, it's still complete chaos up in Dalarna, but things will calm down sooner or later and we'll get back to normal life, I'll have to speak to my financial adviser." I zone out as he starts talking about a future in which we have an apartment together, a rented two-bedroom, a one-bedroom at the very least, his kids can keep their things in a box under the bed every other week, and every other week it'll just be me and him, long breakfasts, museums and theater trips, things might be a bit tricky at work after his *escape*, but he has emailed his union and besides, we have each other—who needs middle-class climate-wrecking comforts when you can live on love alone? I don't have 40 mg in my bag, I remember, I've got 80 mg, maybe even 160, that's it, I'd been saving it for an emergency like this. He keeps droning on and on, and after a while I realize that this feels familiar, I've heard it somewhere before, and eventually it comes to me: it's just like that Strindberg play, *Miss Julie*, the monologue at the end when Julie shares her hopeless fantasy about her and Jean and Christine running away together, managing a hotel by Lake Como, the same heartrending attempt at optimism in a hopeless situation. Only, halfway through her monologue she starts to realize exactly what a naive and needy bitch she is, and there are a whole load of dot dot dots between the words. I wrote an essay on *Miss Julie* in school, and that was my favorite scene. My teacher loved that I was so precocious and arranged for me to take the bus to Stockholm to watch it being performed at the Royal Dramatic Theatre, she paid for it out of her own pocket, I think; they saw me as a real talent, destined for higher education. No one ever believes that, either.

I feel an urge to tell Didrik all about it, about how sad it is when love gets watered down and loses steam, becoming a lame, clichéd daydream, but my stomach and my body are starting to ache and I can feel my sweaty scalp prickling, plus he'll only get annoyed if I interrupt him, he'll probably tell me that the scene reflects Strindberg's crazy, woman-hating, dick-swinging antisemitism, and by the way, have I ever been to Lake Como—or Italy, for that matter—because he has.

Instead I mumble: "How long are you staying?"

He is midway through an explanation of his pension fund, telling me about *the option to start withdrawing some of the capital early*, and he pretends not to hear me, so I ask again, my voice a little sharper this time.

Becka whimpers and rubs her eye with her tiny hand.

"She needs to sleep," Didrik says softly. "Will you join us in the bedroom?"

So I close my laptop and we walk through the huge apartment together, right to the other side, to the primary bedroom with its warm light and sense of space created by the open skylight, the air flooding in from the balcony. Now that she isn't red and teary and screaming, now that she's a warm, tired little creature who smells sweet like the fake milk she drinks, there's something both cute and a little disturbing about seeing him fuss over her, taking out a pacifier and quickly changing her, his fingers moving over her naked body, stroking and patting and bouncing her diaper-clad bottom until her tiny, panting body relaxes.

I knew I was dating a father, but the kids were nothing but pictures on social media, imaginary figures. He hardly ever talked about them, and though I knew—hoped—that one day I would be their stepmother or bonus mother or extra mother or whatever you want to call it, it was like looking at a postcard and thinking that's a beach I'd like to relax on compared to actually saving money and booking flights and a hotel and crowding onto a plane and then arriving and feeling the sand between your butt cheeks.

But here she is, sleeping on the luxurious Egyptian cotton sheets in the old tennis legend's enormous bed. Didrik presses a button on a remote control and the blinds roll down, the skylight closes, another remote control sets the AC running, and the room is soon cool and dark and comfortable. He lies down beside her little half-naked body, his lips on her fuzzy head, nuzzling and whispering and humming a song I vaguely recognize from one of the Astrid Lindgren DVDs Mom used to borrow from the library.

Then we go out onto the balcony off of the bedroom. It's smaller than the roof terrace, of course, but that just makes it more intimate: a cute little metal table and chairs in a florid French design, it's like something from one of those old black-and-white films set in Paris or Rome, a secret tryst in a cozy little bistro, splashing in a fountain, doves flying over a piazza at dusk. Down on the street, two police cars and a fire engine drive by. There's another demonstration, according to the push notifications on my phone, a spontaneous gathering heading for the American embassy, or maybe it was the Chinese one, the reports aren't clear, maybe it's both, they're on the same street, after all. Several riot vans and more fire engines race by, an ambulance, but up here among the rooftops, the howling sirens and flashing lights just mix with the background hum of the city, the music from the bars and restaurants, the glittering water, the church spires, the palace, a garish tourist bus with a blaring sound system, the people, there are people everywhere, walking along the pavements and crossing roads. Sometimes, quite often in fact, I wish I lived in a skyscraper—a proper one, the kind you see in New York or Dubai—though this is nice too. The cool air from the bedroom wafts out toward us through thin white curtains.

"They should march to the TV studios instead," says Didrik. "The media's betrayal overshadows everything else. Why doesn't the climate get its own segment on every single news program—with the weather, for example? Why hasn't climate change been the main focus of every political debate broadcast on TV since the eighties?"

"How long are you staying?"

"The Swedish public has so much faith in state TV and radio," he continues, nodding slowly as he speaks. "If they'd taken their responsibility and kept the population informed, our energy supply might have looked completely different today. This is definitely a point people should be making."

"Didrik? How long are you staying here?"

His mouth hardens.

"We can go as soon as she wakes up, if you want. It's not a problem."

I sigh, hold my tongue, try to repress the urge to run inside and grab my handbag.

"It's been over two years. You haven't even asked how I've been, you just barge in here with a baby and all sorts of chaos when I'm trying—"

"Fine," he snaps. "Fine. Tell me how you've been, Melissa."

The sun has moved, and the first few rays are shining through his thin hair, straight down onto his wounded scalp, as though he were translucent. We sit in silence.

"I've missed you," I eventually say. "A lot. And . . . I've been thinking."

Those puppy dog eyes again. Damn it.

I have to tell him, I think. *Have to. Maybe he can help me.*

"I had a toothache," I continue, my voice low.

He raises an eyebrow.

"Toothache? Damn, that kind of thing can be painful. Becka's teeth will start coming in soon, that's basically the hardest thing with babies. Vilja screamed and refused to sleep for weeks, we felt like we were losing our minds, and . . ." He glances over to me and smiles. ". . . anyway, you had a toothache. Too much sugar?"

I shake my head.

"No, I didn't have any cavities or anything like that. It was a fracture, a crack, you know?" I try to point to the side of my mouth. "It was fine at first, but after a few months I started to feel it whenever I ate ice cream or drank coffee, a shooting pain, and then I started feeling it all the time, and in the end it hurt so much." I'm speaking quickly, can feel the tears coming, the sweat, know that the diarrhea is on its way, goddamn it. "It was awful," I continue. "Worse than you could ever imagine. I went to the dentist, but she wanted to extract the tooth and that would've ruined my appearance, plus I had a whole load of debts at the time, I couldn't afford the money for a new tooth, but the pain was like one long fucking nightmare, I couldn't eat or drink or sleep or anything."

Didrik looks sympathetic.

"That sounds really awful, Melli. You can't go around feeling like that. You should have called."

He is about to say something else when a hacking, whining sound cuts through the fluttering curtain and he leaps up and heads inside; she can't have slept for much more than half an hour, and he has already explained that this afternoon nap needs to last at least an hour and a half *if we're going to get her back into a daily routine*. I hear him hushing and babbling to her and think to myself that what's going on in there is love. Out here is something else entirely, I don't know what it is.

My handbag is empty. I shake it, rifle through it, throw it at the wall, and slump to the floor. I'm out of Oxy. The stash in the bathroom ran out weeks ago.

I grab my phone. DrSverre74 has written again, almost as though he knows, of course he does, it's his job to keep on top of these things.

Hi lovely Melissa, stuck here without any breeze—though something else is stiff (hehe)—thinking about you, beautiful! Would be so good to swim naked with you here. How're you doing? Need a new prescription soon? Will be at my computer this afternoon, happy to issue one.

I write a quick reply but delete it when I see that he's off-line, that he hasn't been active for the past hour. It's Didrik's fault for distracting me with all his bullshit, I missed his message and now it might be hours before he logs on again. I sob, it's so awful, like suffocating, don't want to don't want to don't want to.

I fiddle with my phone, desperate for a rush. My latest post has 32,459 likes, and I stare at the screen, practically paralyzed by the number. Last night's post hasn't exploded—it's *erupted*. Sure, I had expectations, I was curious to see how the news of my book project would go down, but *over* 30K likes? Plus comments and messages, media requests, companies approaching me for new collaborations, an agent from a streaming service wanting to bounce ideas for a TV format, and I just can't help myself, my fingers take on a life of their own, I have to check my account. *Abracadabra*, the money has been flooding in all night and morning, more money than I usually bring in from my fans in a month.

My eyes well up, I'm so proud. There is nothing more beautiful than ordinary people—people I've never met—opening their wallets to support *me* and my ideas and projects. My dreams. The cold turkey eases off a little and I go out onto the terrace, lie down on the sofa, start sketching ideas for a new post talking about just how grateful I am, but I delete it after just a few words, it's like my gratitude is just too big to express, plus some people might not have had time to transfer anything yet. Better to hold off for a few days.

Didrik comes out, eyes bloodshot, Becka on his arm. He's eating a small container of blueberry yogurt, which is pretty much the only edible thing in the fridge right now. It's been an hour, he must have fallen asleep in there.

"We need to . . ." He studies me. "Or, I'm wondering . . . There's some new video out there."

I've already seen it, Matilda sent me a link, it's from the security camera on the train. There isn't any sound, but you can see him standing half naked, an axe in one hand and the baby strapped to his chest, making a threatening move toward the conductor. The newspaper that published it has blurred Becka's face, but Didrik's is crystal clear.

"So what happens now?" I ask, amazed by how calm I sound.

"I guess it'll be . . . maybe a police report or something, I don't know. Or maybe it'll just fade away, there's so much other stuff going on—have you heard about Malung? All the people at the conference center there? It's insane."

"Yeah," I say. "Totally insane."

"It was one of those fire axes," he mutters, squinting in the sun. "Break glass in case of emergency. People were dying on that train, it was just a tool; it's not as though I was running around with an axe like someone in a fucking horror film. You could argue that there are worse things to be worried about than someone breaking a train window."

"Or maybe that's precisely the kind of thing people should be worried about," I hear myself say.

"What?"

"I just mean . . . Well, all these fires and floods and storms or whatever, they're nature's way of testing society. Testing us, to see if we work. If we can stick to the rules, the ones we came up with together. Law and order. Keep calm and carry on."

Didrik scratches the wound on his head, looks like he's on the verge of saying something else, makes a face.

"It really fucking hurts now. Have you seen my painkillers? I feel like they were out here somewhere."

I shrug.

"No idea."

"I've got a prescription for more, obviously." He yawns. "It's just such a bother to have to go to the pharmacy to get them, especially since people might recognize me and everything."

"Weren't the two of you leaving, by the way?" I ask, forcing myself to relax. "Or what's going on?"

"So, I was thinking . . . a hotel or something, it's just . . ." He is dragging this out. "I checked my account, and it seems like . . ."

"No problem," I blurt out. "You can stay here, both of you. It's fine. Nice to have company."

Becka seems more alert now, and she gives me a cautious smile, her chubby little arm reaching up and trying to grab his chin. Right then, her jaw seems to clench, her entire body tensing like a coiled spring in his arms. Her face turns red, focused, a mix of surprise and superhuman effort, it's almost scary looking.

And then the smell. The smell.

"We need to buy more diapers," he says, running his fingertips down her spine as she grunts and strains in his arms. "The ones I bought this morning were too small, she must've gone up a size over the summer, it's so damn hard to keep track."

"I'll go shopping," I say. Then, almost off the cuff, I add: "If you give me your ID I can pick up your prescription, too."

"Ah, thanks, that's great," he says, yawning as he searches the red diaper bag for his driver's license. "Can I have another one of those yogurts, by the way? It was great."

"Help yourself. What's mine is yours."

———

I walk through the park with the cherry trees on my way to the big department store, smiling at the memory of that winter when I first moved to Stockholm, the frothing pink blossom. It really is a fantastic story, I used to tell it during my talks and it got better every time. My old friends are as beautiful as ever, their branches forming a roof over my head. Their leaves are golden and rusty red today; autumn will be here any day now.

The blister pack in the pocket of my jeans represents wealth, the thin, crackling layers of plastic and foil pure happiness. Just pushing a finger in from time to time to feel that it's still there makes me calm and happy. They kicked up a fuss at the pharmacy, wanted to give Didrik the smallest pack possible, sixteen pills, but I can always collect more. Besides, I have DrSverre74 as a backup, everything is fine, I only took two, there are plenty left.

The children's department on the top floor is practically deserted. It's the first time I've ever been up here, probably the first time ever I've bought kids' clothing, too. I didn't even realize you could get designer clothing for kids, super-sweet pink blouses from Ralph Lauren, dresses from Gucci, an amazing French brand called Petit Bateau that I've never heard of before, tiny white silk socks. I almost start giggling over how cute it all is. Having kids just so seems so damn cozy.

"Hello, can I help you with anything?"

A pretty, dark-skinned girl, smart in her white shirt and black jeans, red lips and subtle highlighter on her cheekbones and forehead.

"No, I'm just looking . . . actually, I need to buy some clothes, for a four-month-old girl."

A big smile, beautiful white teeth.

"Great, are they for your daughter?"

I give her an uncertain nod, slightly disappointed that she doesn't recognize me.

"Exactly."

"Were you looking for anything in particular? Because we've *just* got some *amazing*—"

"No, it's more . . . a few things, you know? Enough to wear for three or four days."

"Are you off to somewhere nice?"

I squirm.

"Nowhere. She just needs clothes."

The girl is silent for a few seconds, her pretty eyes and fake lashes suddenly looking lost. I thought she was older, but beneath the makeup I realize she's actually around my age. She's used to charming rich old women who have just become grandparents, flirting with middle-aged couples who have been invited to christenings, and I don't fit in here, in my flip-flops, ripped jeans, and faded black tank top.

"We only really carry the more exclusive lines here," she says hesitantly. "If you need basics, it would be better to try . . ." Her dark fingers, nails painted a silvery color, gesture vaguely down and away. ". . . somewhere else."

"There was a fire," I say without pausing to think. "We got caught up in the fires in Dalarna, we lost everything. She's with her grandmother right now, and I need some new clothes."

Her face lights up like I've just flicked a switch, a sisterly look of horrified compassion. Her slender hand covers her mouth, the way the upper classes do when they're laughing or in shock.

"Oh wow. Wow! How are you, sweetie, are you OK? Where are you staying now?"

"I'm fine," I say. "We're staying in a hotel. Everyone is fine. Like I said, we just need some clothes."

"I guess your insurance will pay out, in any case? I saw on the news that they're not sure whether everyone will be covered for everything—there are over half a million homes affected now. One of the bosses said that they can't pay out that much, that the state will have to step in like it did during the pandemic."

I don't reply, just move past her between the rails. She follows me through the empty department, grabs a few hangers on the way. I pause by the Burberry section and study the beautiful little checked skirts and dresses—they even have soft toys and blankets. I want to touch everything, I want everything.

"It's crazy what's happening right now," she says in a half whisper. "My dad runs a fish export firm in Nigeria, but he's going to sell up and move over here because there are practically no fish left. The sardines are half the size they used to be, and people think they're going to die out completely soon because there's no plankton left."

I shrug.

"Lucky I don't eat sardines. Or plankton."

She gives me a confused look.

"But it affects everything else. If there are no sardines, that has an impact on the bigger fish, the gulls, and . . ."

"I don't eat gulls either." My fingertips stroke a soft Burberry blanket. "Do you know what kind of wool this is?"

"What . . . wool?"

I quite liked her at first, but she's annoying me now. Beautiful idiots are some of the worst people: that concerned face, those pouting lips, the unnaturally straight, silky-smooth hair.

"Wool. She likes snuggling with blankets like these, but the material has to be right."

For a strange moment, it's as though she sees straight through me, but then the creases smooth out, like a balloon filling with air.

"Merino, I think. Or cashmere." She says the latter with an English accent. "One of the two. Merino wool is more durable and it's easier to wash, but cashmere is obviously warmer and softer." She gives me a sweet smile. "But they're heavenly, both of them."

Walking around with two full bags with the brand's logo on the side looks so good that I decide to swing by the perfumes and lacy lingerie, not to buy anything, more as a way to keep surfing the feeling of luxury. I nip down to the little supermarket to buy diapers, wet wipes, formula, pacifiers, everything on the list he gave me, then through to the smart little café where one wall is covered in jars full of different teas and coffees. The café is right next to the kitchen department, with its Japanese knives, Danish glass, Portuguese porcelain, thick chopping boards made from teak, oak, and acacia, espresso machines that look like spaceships. Working in the coffee shop often felt like being in the middle of a noisy, steamy factory, but the machines here are amazing, it's more like an art gallery full of gleaming surfaces in chrome and steel, the promise of cozy weekend mornings in the countryside, wrapped up in a bathrobe with some kind of interesting, educational show on the radio, croissants in the oven—everything my life with Didrik was supposed to be, everything he promised me.

The truth is that I kept checking his photos too. More often at first, in the year after he tossed me aside like a broken sex doll. They were mostly of Zacharias and Vilja, of their birthdays and summer holidays, occasionally his goddamn wife in a swimsuit and that *smug* smile on her face. He posted a picture of a morning like that once, from their place in the country, a hand-painted wooden chair, two mugs of latte with hearts in the froth, just like I'd taught him, a bowl of freshly baked croissants, and I felt a sense of disgust and grief that practically paralyzed me, thinking *Christ, he's trying so hard*.

I head down to the food hall, sail across the glittering marble and the creamy tiles, past the little deli sections where the prices and offers are written in chalk like in old films. There are barstools everywhere, people drinking and chatting while white-clad beefcakes with tattoos and bushy beards slice sausages and fillet fish a couple inches away, slapping down huge hunks of meat—I see *wagyu* on one of the chalkboards, *iberico*, *ayam cemani* on another—and big, slimy fish onto slabs of ice; the air smells like seafood, blue cheese, raw meat, and freshly baked bread, and I elbow my way past a group of old men in pastel-colored shirts talking loudly about the price of different types of lobster. It's like being in Barcelona or Milan, I hadn't realized this kind of place still existed, that they've existed here all along.

Over by one of the bar counters, a gay-looking waiter with long side-burns is smiling at me, I vaguely recognize him from some event.

"Melli? Do you remember me?" There is something puppyish about his softly kohl-lined eyes, his admiring smile, almost as though he is wag-ging his tail. "I always comment on your stories, I'm a superfan! Can I get you something?"

I nod happily and sit down at an empty table. This is just what I need right now: a nice glass of something, a bit of chitchat, avoid having to go home. I let him pour me a glass of champagne.

"Looks like you've been power shopping," he coos. "Great work!" He peers down into my bags. "But you don't have a baby, do you? Is it for a baby shower or something?"

I give a mysterious shake of the head.

He winks at me.

"New guy?"

I nod.

"Kind of. I don't know."

"Ahh, I love this kind of thing," he purrs. "Who is he and what's his name and when where how?"

I sip the fizzing drink, giggle, it makes my nose tickle.

"We met years ago. He wanted someone to have an affair with, and I guess I just needed to get away."

I don't know why I'm being so open with him, I don't even know the guy, but something about the champagne and the feeling of tiredness that comes with shopping is making me chatty.

"It was never meant to last this long, but he fell in love and I guess I did too, right at the very end. He said we'd move in together but then Covid came along and everything went wrong and he stayed with his wife and kids. I ended up single and everything turned to shit."

"You just disappeared after the pandemic," says the waiter, cocking his head. "I never really understood why. You had the pictures, the podcast. The collabs. I always wondered what happened."

I nod.

"He happened."

I take a few more sips and remember that Didrik always used to bring champagne in the beginning, that he would go over to the minibar in the hotel room and take out all the tiny bottles of spirits and mixers to put his own bottle inside. I thought it was cute that he'd made such an effort, with flavored condoms and lube and red roses and bubble baths; he even asked what kind of candy I liked. And then we would lie there naked, each with a glass of champagne, and he was so nervous that he wolfed down the entire box of chocolates (lemon licorice truffles) and the champagne went up my nose and I started laughing because it was all so wonderful, it was so great, his wife was out at some girls' lunch, Vitas was working, and we were locked in a junior suite that he'd booked using his loyalty points, having marathon sex sessions, our phones switched off, completely present in the moment. After just three weeks of chats and a few quick meetings in backstreet cafés, we'd managed to whittle down the distance between us until neither had a facade to keep up any longer, until we were in a free zone where nothing— nothing at all—could be ugly or gross or too intimate; everything we did was forbidden, and the best thing we'd ever experienced.

Walking down the corridor on my way here, it felt like I was heading to my own execution, he said quietly, and I replied, *at your age there's definitely a risk of heart attack if we carry on like this.*

Melissa, he continued, giving me a serious look. *Whatever happens, I'll always respect you. I'm never going to apologize for how I feel when I'm with you, I'll never regret these magical moments.*

Then he drank the rest of the bottle and asked if we could try anal before he left to pick up Vilja from gymnastics.

"*He* happened," I repeat, slightly louder and slightly firmer this time.

"And now?"

I shrug.

"Now he's left everything and is holed up in my apartment and it's just like it used to be, only not quite, but I can't throw him out."

"Why not?"

"Because he's got a four-month-old baby with him."

"But what do you want?"

The waiter's questions come quickly, calmly, almost mechanically. Like everyone else, he's probably been in therapy. Once you've spent a few years on that couch, sniffing and answering question after question, it probably just becomes the natural way of having a conversation like this.

"I want to be happy," I say, well aware of how lame it sounds but unable to express it any better. "To have a good life. To work, create, travel, meet cool people. To earn money, spend it. Just be happy. To stop feeling so fucking sorry for myself that I can't even get out of bed in the morning, to stop feeling like my life is never actually going to start, to stop constantly, constantly, constantly being—"

"In pain," he says, his voice flat, topping up my glass and then turning to a group of people with two bottles and saying, *listen, I've actually got a great South African red, a 2017 Swartland, super-limited run, and I really want you to . . .* before the rest is drowned out by the background noise.

That empty feeling inside me is back again, and I dig out the blister pack and pop two more tramadol, washing them down with a mouthful of champagne, and just as I put the glass down

I hear

a crash

it's like a falling tree, branches slowly breaking, dry leaves rustling in the wind

and shouting

It's strange, I think, that no matter how much noise or chatter there is in a place like this, so loud that you can barely hear yourself speak, you can still immediately tell when someone has really raised their voice, made it into a weapon rather than a means of communication, like a junkie yelling on the metro.

out of here

you fucking pigs, sitting here and

I said GET OUT OF HERE, FOR FUCK'S SAKE

and you, shut your GODDAMN mouth

Gruff male voices, a shrill young woman, more voices, they're coming from outside, making their way in, scared, angry, triumphant, chanting.

WHAT DO WE WANT?   *TO SAVE THE PLANET*

WHEN DO WE WANT IT?   *NOW*

WHEN WHEN WHEN?   *NOW NOW NOW*

The waiter is suddenly nowhere to be seen. I don't even stop to think, I just get up and dig out my phone in one fluid motion, swipe to open the camera app and watch through its rectangular eye as the figures move between the bar counters, full of people enjoying an afternoon out just a moment ago, but now empty. They're pulling carts of some sort, shaking and rattling over the stone floor, waving signs and fabric banners, a human slurry of beards, braids, and sweaty pits.

I back up against the wall and film the tables around me: a woman's dumbstruck, frozen grimace. A man's ashen face, hands gripping his wallet. The flirty waiter is standing in front of one of the tables like a goalkeeper, taking small, anxious steps back and forth, his hands raised in front of his face, knees bent.

what the hell is
that fucking protest
do you think they're planning to

One of the bearded men behind the charcuterie counter has raised his meat cleaver, wielding it like a heavy, gleaming sword from some fantasy series, glaring at the intruders with uncertainty.

get out of here, for fuck's sake, why are you here, don't you realize everyone is

A short, stocky guy with dreadlocks and a bare chest pauses in front of the charcuterie counter, his hands on his hips.

what the hell are you doing here yourself, what planet are you living on, standing here selling meat as though

I hear a scream, even louder this time. It cuts through the room, through the police sirens, which I've only just noticed somewhere nearby. I drag my empty chair over and climb up on it to get a better view of the food hall, filming the people who are crouching down, hiding beneath tables and chairs. The activists have jumped up onto one of the counters and started yelling, holding one of their banners upside down, and there is that scream again. I hadn't noticed it until now, but there is a fish section on the other side of the room, with what looks like a huge tank, and a teenage girl is holding a barstool that she *CLANG* swings against the glass *STOP* someone shouts and a man in uniform runs over and tries to grab her, but he slips or is knocked down and the girl runs off to one side and then comes back with the chair, charging like a bull with the legs of the stool to the glass, and there is another

CLANG, followed by the clatter of broken glass and the sound of running water hitting the tiled floor. It isn't spurting out through the crack like it does in films, it's gurgling out, running like water from a broken bucket, and the girl whoops, she jumps up and down, splashing in the flowing water, hands raised in triumph, *STOP* shouts another voice and then

the pop, like a whipcrack

the lights flicker

and everything goes dark, a brief moment of silence

someone shoves the chair I'm standing on and I fumble in the air before

the floor, cold and hard

the scream

and the hand, gently pulling me up onto my knees, my feet, crouching in the darkness

can you walk?

He takes me by the hand and a searing pain in my wrist makes me cry out and pull back, he hisses *shhh* and takes my other hand, gently pulling me down, away, he wants us to be quiet, to crawl, we're playing hide-and-seek, angry voices clattering and thudding above us, flashes of mobile phones like cold stars, I can see the outline of a bar counter, quickly over the wet floor, which smells sour like wine and musty like fish, in behind another dark shadow, *wait* says the voice and someone stumbles over me, shouts *shit*, and now I can hear that the police are here, their authoritative, commanding voices by one of the exits; I can feel people moving in that direction, toward safety and the beams of their flashlights, but the hand, *come on*, grabs me again and we start crawling, crouching, creeping toward the darkest part of the room, *here*, I hear a door open and we get up and run down a pitch-black tunnel, through another door, the dry stench of rubbish and dirt.

"Hi," the waiter says as I look around the parking garage.

He straightens his little black bow tie and gently strokes my arm. It hurts.

"I must have sprained it when I fell," I say. "I was standing on a chair to get better pictures."

It's only then that I realize I'm still holding my shopping bags. They feel heavier, twice as heavy as they did earlier, and I go over to one of the elevators and press the button, feel a flash of pain shoot down my right arm.

Take some more.

His voice is soft, a caress in my ear.

You can take another two, in any case. You're in pain. You shouldn't have to be in pain.

———

I often heard Didrik claim he was a good cook during our first few months together, *our early days*, as he now calls them, but I never really believed it. I never saw him in a kitchen, only in restaurants, where he always—after hesitating for a long time, *I should probably get something vegetarian, but OK, just this once, you've got to, really, it's not like I eat meat during the week*—ordered the second most expensive main, always. He had a theory that the dry-aged beef or the veal was a vulgar, show-off meal for Russians or Americans, that the rack of lamb or the boiled cod with horseradish beurre blanc, the liver with capers and bacon, was actually the best dish on the menu. He liked to come across as a gourmet, passionately arguing that only an idiot would order their fillet of beef *bien cuit* when everyone knows it should be *saignant* or, at most, *à point*, not just because the meat obviously tastes better when it's cooked at a low temperature—and definitely not above 131 degrees—but also because the restaurants skimp on costs by saving the worst, most sinewy bits of beef, pieces that might have passed their best-before date or even fallen onto the floor, heating them up to 175 degrees and serving them to idiot tourists who know nothing about food and obediently munch away on their tasteless, gray, *très bien cuit* beef.

He would sit in those little backstreet restaurants, crammed into a corner with his back to the room, grinning as he eavesdropped on the people behind him talking to the waiter, listening to how clueless they were over the wine list, having to ask what an emulsion was, ordering entrecôte and pronouncing it *ontraycoat* instead of *ontrecott* like you're supposed to. In all honesty, it was the least appealing side of him, and definitely the least sexy, because that could have been my mom sitting there; if she hadn't been too ill to travel to Stockholm for so long I would have loved to take her out to a restaurant so that she could squirt ketchup all over her frazzled fillet of beef, washing it down with a rum and Coke if she wanted to.

Elitism, that was his worst trait. It was the same thing when he tried to go down on me in the back of an Uber. I told him to stop and he was all *what?* and I said *come on* and pointed to the driver, and he looked up from the floor and laughed *what, it's just a cabbie* and I felt about as aroused as an Alaska pollock in the deep freeze, because that could have been Vitas driving, or my uncle, or me.

But this is different. This is cozy. I'm sitting at the kitchen table with my laptop, writing again. He has Becka strapped to his chest in the carrier (which he scrubbed clean in one of the sinks), and he looks so cute as he stands by the huge kitchen island in his too-tight clothes, messing about with a big chunk of marbled beef. He found some herbs growing on the roof terrace and is busy rubbing them into the meat. He also grabbed a few bottles of a particular red wine he says is an *absolute killer* from the bar cabinet in my girl cave, and he's whistling, seems happy.

"Just yesterday, we were stuck on the train from hell, but now we're here with you," he says, kissing Becka on the forehead, stroking her chubby little legs. He gives me a long, loving glance and sips his red wine. "Seriously, Melissa. Thank you. You have no idea how good it was to come here and find our feet."

He'll be leaving tomorrow, he tells me. His darling wife—*my ex*, as he calls her—was on the phone while I was out, and everything seems to have worked out up there in Dalarna. They'll have Zack back from Hedemora soon, and then they're going to try to make their way back to Stockholm. His friend William has also been in touch to ask if he and Becka want to spend a few nights there, *until things calm down*, and though I quickly told him it was OK, that they could stay here for as long as they want, he seems eager to get away. He has a meeting with work in the morning, they need to come up with a *strategy*, and as far as I can tell I'm not a part of that.

"This is our night, so let's enjoy it," he says. "And then we can work out what to do going forward. Did you pick up my pills, by the way?"

"No. Shit, sorry, I forgot. But I can get them tomorrow?"

He shrugs.

"Eh, doesn't matter. I should probably try to avoid that crap anyway. They gave some to Carola after she had Becka, but she only took a few and then got scared and stopped."

"Was she . . . in pain?"

"There was something about a rupture in her womb after Zack's C-section, and when we got home with Becka she had a lot of pain in that old scar. It was awful, I had to take care of Becka for the whole first week."

My voice sounds completely alien, like it's coming from another planet: "What did they give her?"

"Oxycodone, I think it's called. Hard-core stuff, that kind of thing is so scary."

"So what, did she just flush it?"

He shakes his head.

"Throwing medicine away like that is really bad for the environment, you're meant to hand it in to a pharmacy. But I think she just shoved it in a drawer."

I'm sitting with my computer, writing while he cooks. My bandage keeps rubbing against the keyboard, and it hurts a little, but not so bad that it's bothering me. I have a sudden inspiration and try taking a picture of it from one side. It's tricky using my left hand, but after a few attempts I manage a nice shot of my right hand, the bandage around my wrist, the glowing screen, the text visible but too blurry to read. Pretty nails, burgundy red, they look good next to the plate of blueberry yogurt.

UPDATE: A nice afternoon with friends at the food hall turned into a nightmare when a group of so-called "friends of the earth" decided I was the Enemy.

The result is what you see here. I'm OK and I'm not planning to let hate win, but I have become more convinced than ever that these prophets of doom will never be able to save mankind. My poor broken wrist and I will keep writing—don't think for a second that the mob or a bunch of terrorists will ever be able to stop me! HERE I COME. And remember: yogurt is good for both your gut and your nerves! Order direct from #zerofatmilk and get a 10% discount, just click on OFFER and enter the code MELLIMILK! #choosejoy #zerofatmilk

I upload the picture of my wrist with one of the video clips I took during the attack, the one where the fatty with the dreads and the bare chest is standing by the charcuterie counter. I debated blurring him for a while, but it'll have more impact if you can see his roaring, chanting face; his wide eyes, the sweat glistening on his forehead, something that almost looks like saliva around his bearded mouth. And in the background: chaos, banners, security guards, people running and crawling. It looks like a war zone.

I add all the usual hearts, happy emojis, clenched fists, champagne bottles, and sunshines, plus the number people can use to send money.

Share.

"Seriously, darling, this is *good* stuff!"

I look up from my phone. Didrik is holding a bottle of champagne, studying the label with a big grin. It's the first time I've ever heard him call me *darling* before.

"I didn't realize you knew so much about bubbly. You don't see this stuff much these days."

"Well, you always used to bring champagne, so I guess I thought it was my turn."

He doesn't speak, looks away for a moment, seems troubled by the memory.

"I was . . . I didn't really know what I was doing back then. All I knew was that I had to have you. Again and again."

"It feels like a lifetime ago," I say quietly.

"Surely it wasn't that long?"

"March 2020, Didrik."

He looks at me with a frown. A frown that spans a quarter of a decade, that covers record-breaking heat and terrorist attacks and people drowning in the Mediterranean, coups and political crises and pandemics and genocidal war; one that covers my separation and burnout and depression, his management job and freshly baked croissants and the kid strapped to his chest and the pills in my pocket.

"Shit," he says, pulling a face. "Shit."

"What?"

"Sauce."

He quickly turns back to the fridge.

"We can't have a roast fillet of beef and a red wine like this without a great sauce too, that's practically sacrilege. You didn't grab any jalapeño béarnaise, did you?"

"Jalapeño béarnaise?"

Didrik smiles and smacks his lips.

"Ordinary béarnaise, with jalapeño. Just enough to give it a bit of heat. You've never tried it?"

I shake my head.

"I didn't buy anything else. Just some clothes for Becka and . . . the beef. And the champagne."

His face lights up.

"Right! I haven't even had time to look at those, you'll have to tell me how much they were!" The bag is on the floor by the fridge, and he reaches into it and pulls out a small pink blouse, *ohh*, and a pair of pajamas with purple elephants on them, *these are perfect*, and a Burberry blanket, *seriously, darling, you didn't have to get all this*. And then he pulls out a long, thin parcel, like a rolled up newspaper, only much longer, and he looks up at me and laughs, *what do we have here, then?*

"I thought . . ." I say, but that's as far as I get, because I honestly have no idea, I thought the meat and the bottle were all the waiter slipped in. Whatever it is must have been at the very edge of the bag.

Didrik puts the parcel down on the counter and tears off the tape. He unrolls it and *Jesus fucking Christ* backs up, practically jumps, and then it's like he is frozen to the floor, staring down at the sausage.

Or whatever it is. Black, stinking, long. He moves his shoulder so a little more light hits it, and I see its head. A snake?

"What the hell, Melissa?"

He turns around and stares at me like I've just done something illegal, something sick and cynical and *low*, somehow, like selling drugs to schoolkids or torturing kittens.

"What is it?"

"*What is it?* You bought the bloody thing. It's a fucking *eel*."

Eel? The word means nothing to me. Right, of course, some kind of slimy fish thing that used to exist, out in the countryside somewhere, in Norrland or something? Wasn't there one in some short story by Strindberg? Or was it Astrid Lindgren?

"I thought it looked . . . tasty . . ." I say, fighting back the urge to hold my nose to block out the sharp, rotten, fishy stench spreading through the kitchen.

"*Tasty?* These things are fucking endangered, or practically anyway."

And maybe that's just as well, I think, though I bite my tongue in time.

"Come on, sweetie, how can it be endangered if I just bought one?"

But he just shakes his head angrily.

"OK, maybe not endangered, but there's definitely a Europe-wide fishing ban on them."

"This one is farmed," I say, my voice calm. "Responsible fishing. In line with WWF and EU sustainability programs, all that stuff."

"How do you know that?" He snatches up the piece of paper the eel was wrapped in. "I can't see any markings."

I could keep lying, but sometimes it's more convincing just to tell the truth.

"I honestly have no idea, but they would hardly be selling them if it wasn't OK, would they? And either way, it was already dead, it was lying behind a counter when I bought it."

Didrik glares at the fish as though it were the last of its species.

"Do you even like it?" he asks. "Do you even know what it tastes like?"

"What, do you?"

He moves over to the sink and holds the eel by its backside, its tail, whatever it's called, lifts it up, lets it hang in front of his face.

"I think I had it a few times when I was a kid," he mutters. "At my grandpa's place. Smoked eel—rye-smoked eel, I think. He used to have these eel banquets. Really unusual taste, takes a bit of getting used to."

"Well, it's never too late," I say, crinkling my nose at the smell, which is stronger now. "You only live once. We have two options, as I see it: eat it or throw it in the garbage. For me, the choice is easy."

Didrik turns toward me, adjusts his grip on the eel, uses it to point at me. It's stiff but springy, a stinking black wand.

"Now I recognize you," he says softly. "Now I remember."

"What?"

He smiles.

"You. The woman I fell in love with. The one who told us to choose joy. To enjoy ourselves while we can."

The eel is getting closer. I could wave it away, but one part of me doesn't want to touch it and one part knows that there's something in this moment that I need, that we both need.

"I recognize you too," I say calmly, without moving an inch. "The man I fell in love with. The suburban dad I stole away. The nice boy with no limits."

He grins and holds out the eel, lets it nudge my cheek. It feels cold, damp, leathery, like a condom pulled over the feathers of a white-tailed eagle.

"You have to drink spirits with these," he says. "They're so fatty it's inedible otherwise."

I stick out my tongue. Lick, kiss its little head. It tastes like seaweed, salt, smoke.

"I think I saw a bottle of vodka in the freezer somewhere," I whisper. "That should do."

———

I swallow two pills in the bathroom and tell myself I can stop tomorrow instead, I want to be in top form right now, I need to make the most of this. This evening, this feeling. Sitting on the roof terrace with Didrik, getting tipsy on champagne, eating smoked eel, toasting with ice-cold Russian vodka, the cute little oil lamps glowing, singing, laughing, getting drunker and drunker. *There's nothing more romantic than slowly getting drunk with someone you love*, Daisy once told me. She'd probably read it on some relationship site after things went to shit with Neo, and in her case it probably meant that she started dating a whole load of boxed-wine guys, but I thought it sounded nice, because when you really think about it, that's all love is: allowing yourself to lose all control, all responsibility, all judgment, bit by bit, until you find yourself falling headfirst into a spiral of cotton candy and helplessness.

The eel tastes both weird and incredible, as though the flavor of fish could be concentrated and matured and seasoned with salt, burned butter. And just like Didrik said, it coats the inside of my mouth and throat with a thick layer of grease that only the sharp, icy taste of alcohol can shift. We eat, we toast, he tries to remember some of the drinking songs he knew at university. I tell him how close I came to studying law and he says a load of nice things about how cool and amazing and incredibly sexy that would have been, and we slip into it seamlessly, fluidly, the way we always used to during *our early days*, a role-play in which he is the angry environmentalist and I'm the cold, stony-faced, unattainable star lawyer hired by the government or an oil company or a nuclear power plant, locked in a conference room in a skyscraper somewhere with a bottle of sparkling water and two clementines. And we take turns sharing dirty fantasies about everything we'd do in that room; no one is allowed to interrupt or start talking about anything else, but nor can they get emotional or bring up the practicalities. That's the rule: nothing but pure, raw sex. First him, then me, then him again, a pornographic tennis match in which we keep the ball bouncing back and forth over the net from increasingly impossible angles, our imaginations running wild, pulsing in time with our blood, and no one can let go, that's another rule, my eyes locked on to his as he slowly explains what he wants to do to my body and how he wants to do it, and then it's my turn and his eyes are glassy with horniness, the cushion beneath me is damp and my voice is raspy and shaking, my enjoyment teetering on the brink of disgust as I describe acts I can barely even picture, never mind imagine how they'd taste, smell, or feel.

But then the stream stops, and we're both left panting on either side of the table, scraps of skin and tiny pieces of bone on our plates, the stench of oily fish hanging in the summer air.

"Jesus Christ, sweetie," he eventually groans. "Jesus Christ, I've missed you."

"I like it," I say with a smile.

"You *like* it?"

"The eel, I mean. Tasted great."

He shakes his head.

"Seriously, they're *incredibly* endangered," he says, his voice glum.

"Exactly." I laugh, feel the burn of the vodka. "Dirty fantasies and the world's last fucking eel. Doesn't get any better than this."

The fillet of beef is exactly how he wanted it, he says: slightly burned and crisp on the outside, pale pink at the edges when we cut into it, bloody in the middle. I think about how rare it is to really *taste* meat, it's usually the salt, the pepper, the garlic, or the ketchup that sets the tone of the meal, with the meat itself just kind of tagging along for the ride, but this time the seasoning is only on the very outside, and as I sink my teeth into it I can't feel anything but the animal, its muscles, its body, its life juices running down my throat. *I'm a cavewoman*, I think, hearing myself grunt with pleasure, *a hungry predator*. I bite down on the soft tissue, grinding it between my teeth. The taste is slightly acidic, bland, the flesh so tender that it melts into a gooey, meaty pulp in my mouth.

"Cheers, honey," says Didrik, emptying his wineglass. He gets up and comes over to give me a top-up, but stumbles and steadies himself on the edge of the table, laughing and dropping to his knees by my chair.

"What do you want, Melli?" he asks me, suddenly childishly formal. "If you got to choose. What would you want more than anything else?"

I squint, try to focus on him. He looks blurry this close up.

"You," I say with a smile.

He takes my hand and kisses it, sucks on my little finger, my middle finger, his lips a soft ring of muscle moving all the way up to my knuckles, sending shivers down to my crotch.

"More," he whispers. "What else? You've already got me."

"OK, you . . ." I giggle. This is another of our games, I've just remembered it. ". . . and a week in Barbados. A five-star hotel, we've got a huge terrace with ocean views, no one can see in, and we're sitting there at sunset, watching the sky turn pink and red and purple, and you slowly start to stroke my foot and . . ."

"Melli," Didrik mumbles, his tongue curving around my thumb.

"And we order cocktails with umbrellas in them, and . . . and the woman who brings them is a beautiful Black girl, tall and muscular, her skin is so dark it's almost blue, and she has amazing big lips and white teeth, she's disappointed when we don't tip her and asks whether we're unhappy with the service at the hotel and you say we're perfectly happy, we just don't have any cash, and she says that she needs money to . . . buy a beachside bar, and then she sees the way you're looking at her and asks whether there's anything else she can do for us, because she really, really needs—"

"Melli, no," he says, pulling back from my hand. "I'm serious. I want to know."

"Know what?"

He looks up at me.

"What you want."

I close my eyes and try, but my thoughts just keep bouncing around in my head, like one of those pinball machines from an old American film. All the scents around us, the noises from down on the street. The music from the apartment below. The sirens in the distance. A child crying.

For Mom to get better.

For Dad to come back.

An apartment. It doesn't have to be one like this, just a place of my own. A three-bedroom with a balcony and a laundry room and a walk-in closet.

Enough money to go traveling for at least a year.

It's all so boring. So ordinary.

"A book club," I eventually tell him, opening my eyes.

But he isn't there. I look around the dusky terrace, but it's just me and a table of dirty dishes and empty glasses and bottles and the flickering, lonely glow from the oil lamp.

The fingers he was sucking feel cold and wet, I dry them off on my jeans.

Those days of emptiness. Getting up, trying to work out at home, the same old TV shows and podcasts. Tidying up Vitas's crap, throwing it away.

Surfing mindlessly, no longer registering the news about the latest number of deaths, the mutations, the second wave, third wave, the never-ending nightmare, the vaccine that seemed to take forever and ever, the debt collection letters piling up on the mat in the hallway. Knowing that Didrik was safely holed up in his house with his wife and kids, bringing in the same fat wage as ever while he worked from home in his sweatpants. Speaking to Daisy on the phone from time to time, the only person who ever bothered to reach out, she used to call at quarter to three in the afternoon while she was waiting to punch out from work, "just gonna smoke out the time clock," she always said, laughing to herself and then asking if I wasn't going to move back home soon, rather than living on my own and doing nothing in Stockholm.

Showering, maybe taking a bath, doing my nails, making myself look good for no reason at all, just to feel that feeling. Uploading a picture, maybe, purely for the hearts and to feel like I wasn't dead. A close-up of my lips while I did my makeup. Toes peeping out of the bubbles in the bath. A picture in the mirror while I worked out with my resistance bands.

Always the same comments, of course. Hottie alert and JEEEESUS you're sexy and What a tasty bit of ass or just a load of hearts. I got more comments and likes the more skin I showed, and it became a kind of sport, seeing how high I could get. Wearing a new pair of panties would get me five hundred likes. A sweaty workout shot of me doing a plank in a bra, making my cleavage look perfect, would get almost two thousand. And then there were the messages, with their pathetic dick pics and videos of themselves jacking off, married men, lonely men, famous men, and nobodies. If they wrote anything, it was usually something along the lines of do you like it rough, baby? or 8 inches right here, yrs if u ask nice. Only a handful began by writing something that felt honest, that came from within, that revealed more than just a wayward dick. I checked those ones out, and two or three of them actually looked pretty good, so I wrote hi.

And that was when a different type of game began: trying to get them to write how beautiful I was, how much I turned them on, what they wanted to do to me. I dropped subtle hints to let them know that it wasn't their dirty talk I wanted, it was their admiration, their adoration. If they wrote something really nice and deep I might send back a picture of my own, I had a nice good-morning picture, taken from above, me lying naked in bed, my breasts looked great against the white sheets; I'd let them have that, plus an ass shot in a pink thong. It might be weeks before I replied, but then I'd record a short shower film for them as a reward, just to see the impact. Nude shots are like fucking heroin for guys.

A few got bored of my games and dropped away, others popped up in their place, and before long I had a steady group of maybe five men, all working from home. It was like they were him, different versions of him, and I got them to tell me their deepest, darkest secrets. They wanted someone to lick their asshole, to whip them; they wanted golden showers and to have sex with me and another man at the same time. In our fantasies he was big, dark, and silent, and with a few hearts and words and images I got them to grovel to him, I got them to suck his dick, to be penetrated, left sticky and degraded, becoming everything they wanted to do with me, everything he'd done to me.

And then, in the end, there was only one left. DrSverre74, with his summer house on Dalarö and his two adult children. His sexting had none of the desperation or passion of the others, the fantasies he described were hot and vibrant, don't get me wrong, but he never lost control, never overstepped the mark. There was something comforting about the way he started the day with a Morning, lovely Melissa or Hello, beautiful, how are you today? and sure enough, we started talking about other things. I told him about how lonely I was in my apartment; he worked in intensive care and wrote that our fantasies were all that was keeping him going during the endless hours of intubations, respirators, and dying patients. He sent me a picture of himself in a visor and a face mask, gloves, and a plastic apron over his white coat, his serious blue eyes were all you could see. Send a picture, my goddess, he wrote. Something beautiful that you don't show anyone else, five more dead last night, send me something that'll help me through the rest of this awful shift. So I did as he asked, I filmed myself, and I felt a certain pride in doing it, like my body was useful in the crisis; I was contributing to society by shifting my boundaries for his sake.

And eventually, a few months later, once the numbers were trending downward, he asked whether there was anything I needed. Anything he could do for me.

I've got such a bad toothache, I wrote. You don't know a good dentist, do you?

No, he wrote. But are you taking anything for the pain?

Just over-the-counter stuff.

A few hours passed, then he wrote:

You helped me through hell, so let me help you. Please, beautiful Melissa, let me help you.

I look up and see Didrik standing in front of me again, his thinning hair on end, his shirt crumpled, Becka in his arms.

"Damn it," he mutters. "I don't get it, it seems like she's been bitten by a mosquito or something, look here." He pushes back her diaper and shows me her buttock, a pearl necklace of angry red dots on her creamy white skin. "I've never seen anything like it."

"Uff," I say. "Weird. Maybe it's eczema or something?"

The girl whimpers, rubbing her face on his shoulder. He pulls out a chair and sinks down into it, holding the girl close.

The bites. I can't bear to look at them.

"A book club," I say again, focusing on keeping my breathing calm. "With four or five friends. People could come and go as they please, we might meet once or twice a month to talk about what we've been reading. New books, classics, maybe a bit of exciting new research. We'd eat long dinners together and talk about art, about intellectual things, about what it means to exist."

Didrik is staring at me, his face blank, one hand mechanically stroking the half-sleeping child.

"That would be amazing," I continue. "I think I've always dreamed of something like that. Like a kind of university, I guess, only it's full of love. Or a family, but for the brain."

"What are you talking about?" He seems slightly confused, almost as though he just drifted off.

"What I really want. The question you asked me."

I catch a vague glimmer in his eye and he nods in agreement, smacks his lips, they're blotchy from the wine.

"Great. That's a great answer, Melli. A book club."

Becka whimpers, he yawns.

"I should read more."

"Are you reading anything right now?" I ask.

He squints up at me as though he doesn't understand the question.

"Reading?"

"Yeah?"

He grins, coughs.

"Come on, Melli, I'm a climate refugee. Does it look like I have time to read a bunch of books?"

I shrug.

"There are audiobooks, aren't there?"

He sullenly shakes his head. Just a short time ago he was on his knees, sucking my fingers. I make a real effort to remember how that felt. I need to try to remember.

"I was just wondering," I say. "Always nice to get new recommendations."

He stands up, unsteady on his feet.

"I should go and put her down, I think. You coming?"

I nod.

"In a minute."

"See you in bed, then."

He reaches out and touches my cheek. I can see in his eyes that he's searching for me, searching for the feeling we had earlier, the intimacy; it's so strange the way it comes and goes, from being completely raw and

self-surrendering and uninhibited to this, suddenly he feels about as exciting as some random guy sliding into my DMs.

"A book club," he says with a smile. "So goddamn grown-up. You're
the adult here, Melli, I've always thought that. You're the one who's
grown-up and smart."

I kiss his palm.

"And you're my needy little bitch."

He nods and gently strokes my forehead before turning and carrying
his daughter back into the bedroom. I pour myself another glass of red
wine, check my phone.

119K likes.

I check my account. The figures are incomprehensible. I can't believe
what I'm seeing.

I sip my wine and swallow the last few pills. I'm thinking about Becka's
bottom, those horrible bites. I should have a plan, a strategy, but it's like
everything is just happening, a catastrophe or a terrorist attack someplace
else, a whole bunch of hashtags you just scroll by, and I know it's big and
awful and important but I'm not a part of it, I'm stuck here, it's just like
those days when I couldn't get out of bed, the TV shows droning on and
on and the sky darkening to night outside my little apartment, like being
submerged in deep water, in a cave, a mine, a grave.

THURSDAY, AUGUST 28

SHE'S BEGGING AGAIN TODAY. THE SAME FILTHY OLD CLOTHES, the same junk in her cart. The little girl in the hijab lights up when she spots me, shyly raising her hand in greeting. I smile and nod, my lips mouthing a silent *hello*. The boy has something in his hand, it flashes silver as he raises it to his mouth, something long and metallic. The word *knife* automatically races through my mind and I freeze, but then I hear the squeaky, shrill notes. A harmonica. He moves it across his lips, breathing through the instrument, tasting its notes. His sister—she must be his sister, right?—looks up at me and rolls her eyes. A brother. I would have liked a brother too.

My favorite café is practically deserted, people have started staying at home. It sounds like things got rowdy again last night, twenty-three dead following clashes between the police and the protesters out in the suburbs, according to the news flashes—or maybe it was twenty-three injured, arrested, I'm not sure, I just scrolled past the headlines. The streets are as empty as they were during the pandemic, but I didn't understand the hysteria then, either. Every day locked up was one less day to live. Adapt or do something constructive, but stop whining, stop hiding, stop ruining things for everyone else. Wash your fucking hands and take charge of your life, it's the only one you're going to get.

I was angrier back then. And then I got depressed. But now I'm just tired.

The guy behind the counter takes my order and I sit down at my favorite table and stare at the screen.

The climate

The word hangs on the screen, a blinking black cursor before a bright white nothing.

has always changed and always caused chaos

Delete.

has practically become a religion for some people

Delete.

is mysterious. Despite everything we know and all the advanced tech-nology we have access to, no one can even say what the weather will be like tomorrow, so how are we supposed to be able to predict what it'll be like a hundred years from now?

Delete.

The waiter brings my salad, a few green leaves, a couple of rolls of prosciutto, some sad little chunks of avocado and feta, and half a withered passion fruit. I absentmindedly poke at the leaves. The avocado feels hard against my fork, I spear it and try it against my teeth. It's nowhere near as creamy and rich as it was yesterday, I can barely even taste it; it's like a lump of cold, damp plastic. What the hell? I sigh and push the plate away.

doesn't give a shit about us, so why should we give a shit about it?

Delete.

I check the time on the screen. It's been an hour, I'll have to head back up to Didrik and Becka soon. She slept badly last night, because of the bites, and he asked whether I could watch her while he *catches up*. I told him I was just coming down here to grab a coffee.

I want to think happy thoughts, smart thoughts, want my creative juices to start flowing, but it's been hours since I last took anything and all I have is this boring, empty screen and a plate of food that tastes like crap. The beggar has finished feeding her baby outside and has put it back in the cart. She slowly pushes it back and forth on the pavement, as though it were a buggy, then says something to the boy—barely audible through the window, but it sounds like she's hushing him—and he gets up and walks off with his har-monica, the shrill notes fading into the periphery.

I need to get out of this, I write. *The pills, Didrik, everything. I can't live like this.*

The mother leans back on her black garbage bag and pile of blankets, resting in the morning sun. She lifts her face toward the light. Maybe she's making the most of it, maybe she knows that autumn is coming, the Swedish winter, the rain, the sleet, the slush, or maybe she doesn't know a thing, maybe she doesn't want to know, maybe she just wants to live, to make it through one day at a time.

Delete.

———

Didrik cleans when he's angry. The few times we fell out, he would always make the hotel bed and tidy away any wineglasses or condom wrappers, throwing the dirty towels into the bathroom, into the corner beneath the sink. I'd forgotten all about it, but now I remember. When I left this morning, our dirty glasses, still streaked with vodka and wine, were on the kitchen counter, and the gulls were screeching over the scraps of eel we'd left on the table outside. Becka was screaming in what I've increasingly started to think of as *their* part of the apartment, with the big living room and bathroom and the primary bedroom. I mostly stick to my girl cave and the kitchen.

But the place is now quiet and the floor and everything else in the stainless steel kitchen is gleaming. There is a sharp smell of bleach and freshly brewed coffee in the air, the sun is flooding in from the roof terrace, and he has some sort of news broadcast playing over the sound system. When he spots me he jumps, sitting at the bar counter in a pair of too-small tennis shorts, a white towel over his shoulders, his eyes blank and furious.

following an emergency cabinet meeting, the attorney general announced that anyone found guilty of breaking the nationwide ban on fires and barbecues faces a sentence of up to five years in prison. The ban will continue to apply to designated barbecue sites in the countryside and in parks, as well as on private property and balconies

"They're starting to get things under control in Dalarna," he mutters, suddenly getting up. "Finally. The wind dropped overnight, so they managed to put it out, at least there. Still seems to be complete fucking chaos farther north, though. There's another blaze up in Norrland now."

"But there have always been fires up there, haven't there?"

He drops some baby food thing into the sink.

"What the hell are you talking about?"

on the line now, we have Katarina Bergström, who has called in from Ytterhogdal, one of the areas that

"I just mean that it's not the first time a forest has ever caught fire," I say. I can hear how tired and unsteady my voice sounds. "The forests have always burned at regular intervals. The whole of Sweden burned, from river to river. They can tell, by analyzing pollen and that kind of thing."

He sighs and shakes his head.

"They've just released the latest figures, two hundred dead or missing *just since yesterday*."

"People have to die of something, don't they?"

The look he gives me isn't new, it's the same look he gave me that very first time, a mix of infatuation and disbelief, as though I'm some sort of long-extinct mammal. The audience around him laughed and grimaced, they were amused or offended or both, but he just stared up at me with naked, bewitched eyes, and after the talk he came over and said *according to the latest estimates, Switzerland will have lost all its glaciers within the next hundred years* and I just shrugged and said *I think the Swiss will get over it* and then he smiled and asked *do you really mean all that stuff or do you just like the attention?* and I smiled back and said *depends who's asking* and it was an unbelievably lame reply, of course, but that was precisely why it worked. Afterward, we agreed that it was my nervous retort that made him relax, that if I'd said something snide or cocky or sexy and intellectual, like some hot girl in a random American TV drama, he never would have dared ask if I'd like a drink at the bar.

That look, before it fades and the pissed-off face returns. He coughs, the same dry cough he always deploys whenever he wants me to feel sorry for him.

"Melissa, this isn't funny. I was there. The trees weren't burning, they were *exploding*."

the opposition is now calling for a clear plan of action from the govern-

ment, demanding that it take more decisive measures—though it may well prove risky to try to score political points at a moment when many would rather see cooperation and cohesion and politicians standing up for Sweden

"Carola called earlier," he continues. "Zack still hasn't turned up. And they can't get down here, there are no trains, apparently. So they have to stay in the camp."

"Where?"

"Rättvik."

"Is it, like, a camp for . . . climate refugees?"

I try to say the last word without sounding sarcastic, but it doesn't work, he glares at me and then looks away, listening to the radio, the head of some authority is now talking about *emergency preparedness* and *in the long term* and *we're heading toward a future in which.* It feels like the same guy has been pushing this exact message every time I've turned the radio on over the past decade, how the hell can a press conference last ten years, how the hell can anyone bear to listen to it anymore?

"The house didn't burn down," Didrik mutters. "The one I took the quad bike from."

My stomach has started churning, the diarrhea will be here soon, and the contempt I feel for him is like a wave of hot disgust in my gut when I realize that he's actually disappointed, that he thought—hoped—the house would be destroyed in the fire, not just because it would make his idiotic decisions seem more legitimate somehow, but also because deep down, destruction is what he longs for, people like him who live their lives waiting for catastrophe, for ruins and mass graves, anything at all providing it gives them a chance to say, *what did I tell you?*

"That's good," I say, my voice flat. "It's good it wasn't so bad after all."

"The owner has been trying to reach me through work, apparently," says Didrik. "The smoke got in through the window and . . . well, the furniture and the rugs and the chipboard and the insulation . . . He's going way over the goddamn top, of course, probably smells an opportunity to have his flashy fucking show home renovated on my buck."

with large groups of people fleeing the fire-ravaged regions, often being transported or taking shelter in cramped spaces, the authorities are now warning of an increased risk of the mutated virus spreading

His head is bowed, his neck bent so low that his wound is visible. I keep forgetting about it, but it really does look awful, I wonder how long it'll be before it goes away, maybe his hair will have to grow back first, or maybe it'll never grow back, maybe it'll always look like that. I glance over his shoulder to the clock, the one on the microwave. Whenever we were in a hotel room together, I never checked the time, not once; time no longer mattered. But now I'm doing it constantly. It's like I'm waiting for something, anything, for something to happen, for someone who'll never come.

"It must hurt," I hear myself say, more to break the silence than anything. "Your wound. We'll have to get you more pills."

But he isn't listening, just staring down at the table, his lips pursed.

"She'd seen the film from the train, too."

Her and everyone else with an internet connection, I'm about to say, though I manage to stop myself in time, mumbling "OK" and letting him go on.

"She thinks I've completely lost my mind because I was holding that . . . axe. While Becka was with me. I tried to explain that the train had stopped, that we'd been stopped all day, that a slightly younger baby had passed out and almost died, but she just doesn't get it."

His voice has become shriller, almost fraying at the edges; he's about to lose control of it.

"No one who wasn't there can ever understand. It was like being in a war zone. I took care of my baby, our baby. What the hell is wrong with people? Don't they realize this is a global emergency?

the question is what lessons we, as a society, should draw from this kind of

Everything starts spinning, and I have to grip the edge of the table.

"So . . . did you decide anything, or?"

"She says she's going to call the police. And . . . social services. If I don't . . . take Becka to her mother's place."

He glares at me.

"Carola wants to take my kid away from me, can you believe it? She wants me to hand her over to her mother until I've *got everything in order*." He makes small, angry air quotes with both hands. "She wants me to *get everything in order*."

The sound of crying cuts through the apartment, and he sighs deeply and gets up. I'm starting to get used to it, babies cry when they wake up, that's just how it is. Everything is so calm and quiet for the first few hours after they doze off that you almost manage to forget that your real life revolves around a greedy, squirming, howling, demanding little machine. Congrats.

He comes back from his room with Becka against his chest, the good side, the one that doesn't hurt, and suddenly I feel sorry for him again.

"What can we . . . what can I do?"

"If we had . . ." He shakes his head. "Maybe it's just as well. Maybe I'm just selfish for trying, after all the fucking chaos . . ." His eyes well up, and he looks down at the tiny bundle in his arms. ". . . because she needs a chest X-ray, too . . . maybe it would be best for her if . . ."

Oh, Didrik.

"Weren't you meant to be moving in with your friend today?"

He doesn't answer, just buries his face in the back of her neck, scratches a new bite.

"Didrik?"

"I mean, shit . . . Carola doesn't know I'm living here, so she can't . . ."

"Hold on. You *live* here now?"

"I . . . what I mean is that the police and social services and whoever the fuck else won't have time to start looking for Becka if we don't turn up, so maybe it would be best to just . . . lay low for a while."

His lower lip is trembling. He'll probably start coughing again soon.

"Sure," I blurt out.

"Could you collect my prescription?"

"Right," I say, as though I'd forgotten. "Of course, you poor thing. I'll go right now."

He makes a gesture around him, tries to smile. His watery eyes glitter in the sun from the terrace, the glare of all the stainless steel.

"At least I cleaned up."

————————

"Hello?" says a boyish voice I don't recognize on the other end of the line.

The sun is high in the sky and it's baking hot on the tarmac. I've been in line outside the pharmacy for hours now; they're only letting a few people inside at a time.

"Hello? Is that Melissa?"

"Yeah," I say. "Yeah, it's me. Who is this?"

I'm in the parking lot outside some shopping center, I'm not sure where, the taxi driver just dropped me off here. A stressed Somali who kept driving down bike lanes and on sidewalks in order to get past the traffic. At first it was double the usual price, then triple, but then his card reader stopped working and he wanted to go to an ATM so I could withdraw the cash, but they aren't working either and he asked if I was wearing any jewelry, but I'd already sold everything like that when I was broke. People started gathering around the cab, wanting to be taken into town, away from town, anywhere else, waving banknotes and banging on the windows, and in the end he just threw me out, picked up a group of people who wanted to go to the airport, and sped off.

The metro is no longer running, they're afraid of power outages. The roads into town are chaos, with closures because of all the people who've been evacuated from the fires, and in one of the suburbs where all the immigrants live they've been burning cars and throwing rocks at the fire service, and the police are asking everyone to stay at home and avoid even short journeys unless absolutely necessary.

"It's André, I live in the apartment. Have you watered the plants?"

Everything grinds to a halt. André who? The guy I'm borrowing the apartment from is called Anders, isn't he?

"You must have the wrong number," I hiss, ending the call. I don't have the energy to talk to anyone right now.

According to what I've read online, they've closed all the pharmacies in central Stockholm because they're worried the looting might get worse. Pharmacies are always one of the first places people target, apparently. They started boarding up the jewelry and watch and designer clothing shops yesterday, they're used to this kind of thing and already had security staff in place, but the pharmacies don't have anything like that and the police are too busy to stand around guarding condoms and toothbrushes. There are only a few *units* still open, and they're all miles from the center of town.

The man in front of me looks like a builder, his khaki shorts baggy and flecked with paint, his sneakers worn and old, his checked shirt crumpled. He stares at me through his cheap sunglasses and mutters *fuck me, they're taking their time* and *what kind of backward, third world country is this, anyway?*

It's been twelve hours since I took the last of Didrik's tramadol, and my head is now pounding—that always comes hand in hand with the sweating and the feverishness. A feeling of desolation, of barrenness and emptiness, I don't want to do this anymore, I refuse to accept this, I feel like I'm about to throw up and I go over to an abandoned shopping cart and lean against it, clear my throat, spit and groan, but nothing will come out. The wheels move, rattling against the rough tarmac, and I rock slowly back and forth, hanging over my creaking cart, thinking that this can't be my life, not my real life, I just need to make it through the day and the man in the khaki shorts and cheap sunglasses is staring at me with a grin.

An eternity passes, possibly half an hour, each minute unbearable, but suddenly I'm at the counter, holding out Didrik's driver's license, saying that he asked me to collect more tramadol for him, and the woman behind the register has the worst dye job I've ever seen, her roots are yellow and the highlights have gone greenish and gray, she doesn't even look up at me, she just stares at her screen and says *I see you collected medication yesterday, using the same prescription.*

"We're going away," I say, trying to smile. "To the countryside. Our place in Dalarö."

"The prescription you collected yesterday should be enough for a week."

"Yes, but like I said, we're going out to the country."

The woman sighs.

"There are pharmacies in Dalarö."

"But we're going out in the boat. We've got one of those Petterssons. Is he supposed to be in pain out there?"

She looks tired, the corners of her mouth drooping like two broken blinds on her slack, wrinkled face. If it was a hairdresser who did this to her, they should be sent to Guantánamo, but I'm guessing she was trying to save money and used some cheap boxed crap at home.

"In order to prevent stockpiling, the Medical Products Agency has issued guidelines on limiting the amount of prescription medication we dispense," she says stiffly, as though she were reading instructions. "Given how uncertain things are at the moment," she adds in her normal voice, attempting a half smile.

I squirm, rocking from one foot to the other, barely able to process what she is saying. All I can work out is that she has no intention of turning around and going over to the shelf that's only about six feet away from her, grabbing the box that could bring this nightmare to an end.

"Come on," I whisper.

"Maybe he can talk to his doctor and get another prescription. Or try again after the weekend."

"But you don't understand." I can hear my voice getting shriller. "He's just come down from Dalarna with serious burns, he's in so much pain, this really is an emergency."

She looks up from the screen.

"If it's that serious, he probably shouldn't be going out to the archipelago?"

I stare at her. Try to bring my breathing under control.

"Check whether I have any prescriptions, then. Melissa Stannervik."

I reel off my ID number and the old hag types away.

"I can't find anyone by that name."

Her eyes harden. She's fucking with me now.

"Milica, I mean." My voice is no more than a whisper. "Milica Stankovic."

She doesn't even type anything, already knows, just scrolls down the list. Dolatramyl, Nobligan, Tradolan, Gemadol, Tiparol. I'm used to this part, the young guys are always best, they get something tender in their eye and scurry away to grab my pills; it's always trickier with girls, like they're ashamed, averting their gaze and trying to pretend I'm not standing right in front of them. But the know-it-alls like this one are by far the worst, the slight shift around her mouth, the subtle contempt, thinking *pull yourself together, you whining kid.*

"All your prescriptions have expired, I'm afraid. You'll need to renew them before I can dispense anything."

She lowers her voice slightly.

"But I'm sure that won't be a problem for you, Milica."

Time was already moving sluggishly, but it freezes like a lump of cold, gross sauce on an unwashed plate. I glance around the pharmacy. Has the world stopped, is everyone staring at me? Mr. Khaki Shorts is standing at another counter nearby, doing something on his phone. Is he filming me now?

The woman peers over my shoulder.

"Was there anything else? Otherwise I need to see to the next person in line."

I snatch back Didrik's driver's license, wheel around, and storm out into the blazing sun, staggering over the hot tarmac like an extra in a zombie film. I shove the shopping cart, which rolls away with a deafening screech, then slump down in the shade outside the superstore to check my phone, the likes, the comments, the money streaming in, but it's all meaningless and worthless because DrSverre74 isn't online, he hasn't been online since early this morning, if I'd just asked him to prescribe me something yesterday then everything would be fine, everything would be perfect and I'd be having a great time somewhere, drinking champagne and writing my incredible book, if it wasn't for Didrik's bullshit and his burns and his baby and everything else he dragged into my life, it's all Didrik's fault, and suddenly my phone starts ringing again and I answer *Hello?* and hear a stressed woman's voice introducing herself and asking whether this is Melissa Stannervik, and I barely have time to reply before she starts blabbering something about the Fossil Free Future rally being held in town tomorrow, they need someone to say a few words at short notice, it doesn't need to be much, the key thing is to have a presence there. I try to compose myself and ask her to call back later before hanging up. Two seconds later, it starts ringing again, and I think it must be her and answer angrily, but it's the kid again.

"Hi, this is André Hell," he says, trying to sound authoritative. "You're staying in the flat I share with my dad, Anders Hell."

I mumble something in reply.

"You've been watering the plants, haven't you? Out on the roof terrace. They'll die if they don't get water in this heat."

There must be something in my handbag, must be. Sobbing, I rummage through the coins, cards, dry cleaning receipts.

"It's really important that they're watered, especially the rhododendron—it's only just been planted."

I feel something cool, thin, light, take my hand out and tip everything onto the ground, but it's nothing, just an old key that clatters onto one of the paving stones, and I'm so cold, so cold that I'm shaking.

"But not the dog roses," his nagging, breaking voice continues. "They can survive even in extreme heat."

"Do you seriously think I care about a bunch of fucking *plants*," I bellow down the line. "Is there really nothing more important than what the fucking *weather* is like, do you think life is all about fawning over fucking *nature*, are we seriously supposed to go around pretending that we're, what, some kind of fucking *gardener* or something? It's completely insane, don't you realize that there are people who are just trying to survive, who might have *other* problems than your fucking weeds?"

But he's gone, the call has dropped. I wipe away a few tears and call him back, need to apologize, promise to water his plants, ask him if he knows where I can find more OxyContin, but the call goes straight to voicemail.

"No signal?"

Sitting opposite me is one of those people you always see in places like this: small, dark, and filthy, a laminated sign full of grainy pictures of little kids with leukemia or HIV or needing an eye operation.

"No signal," she says again, pointing to her own phone. "Everyone lose just now. Signal disappear."

She nods to me and bares her dirty brown teeth in a smile.

"Need help? Somewhere to go? Sleep?"

A roar has started building inside me, and I crawl over to the little silver key and snatch it up, close my fist around it. That's the way it'll have to be, it's only right.

———

He called it his KGB key, we both thought that was funny. The house where Didrik lived—where he still lives—has a code lock, and he explained at length that it was connected to an app that sent a notification every time someone used the code to open it. If his darling wife took the kids to her mother's place in the country over the weekend, for example, and he wanted to have a bit of discreet hotel fun and sneak home the next day, he knew she would be suspicious if the app pinged on a Sunday afternoon.

But, he went on, triumphantly holding up the key, there was a garage door that still had an ordinary lock, they hadn't bothered to invest in a code lock for it, so if he used that entrance instead, the code lock was transformed from damning evidence into the perfect alibi. *I was working on the pitch at home all weekend*, he'd say with a big grin, pouring more champagne. *Didn't set foot outside.* He liked that part, the sneaking around, living like a secret agent with coded messages and chats on fake accounts with two-factor authentication enabled; all of it became part of his Great

Adventure. Personally, I wasn't so interested. Whenever Vitas wasn't driving his taxi he was smoking, and if I told him I was going off to give a talk at some conference, he barely even looked up from his computer games. It had been months since his last photography job.

One morning, one of the last, as I was getting ready to go down to breakfast on my own—I was the one paying by that point, and hotel breakfasts are one of my favorite things—I heard something clatter when I bent down to pick up my panties, and there it was, silver and shimmering. At first I thought it was a coin, maybe even a ring, he sometimes felt so guilty that he took his wedding ring off, but it was the key, it must have fallen out of his trouser pocket. Without thinking about what I was doing, I dropped it into my handbag and then forgot to give it back. He never mentioned losing it, possibly because the KGB chapter was over by that point; he no longer went to the bathroom to answer when she called, no longer chose the most discreet table in the restaurant, no longer sat with his back to the window—just as he'd stopped bringing flavored condoms and lube and red roses, started buying cava instead of champagne, *it tastes just as good*. We had started talking about an apartment he might be able to borrow from a friend, and I had a bag beneath my bed, one full of clean, folded clothing, the things I knew he liked seeing me in, simultaneously trashy and elegant, the ones I'd wear later, once we were really together.

So I dropped the key into my bag and forgot all about it. I felt the slim piece of metal at the bottom of the handbag every now and again, remembered how pathetic I was and how awful the whole thing had been; I came close to throwing it away several times, but always stopped myself and put it back.

Possibly because it was the only thing I had left.

Possibly because the toothache was so fucking bad.

I have no idea where I am, but according to the map on my phone it isn't actually that far, only a couple miles. From the shopping center, I make my way down onto the cycle lane that runs beneath a bridge and past a few sad high-rises, a DIY store, a playground with no children in it, a shuttered

McDonald's. It strikes me that this is the first time I've ever seen a closed McDonald's, and it's as though it shimmers in the air, or maybe that's all in my head, a kind of dull, stifled, vibrating sound; I try to find some shade, walk to one side of the cycle path, in the rustling, parched grass. A couple of teenagers race by on skateboards, their shouting and hooting like a knife to the brain.

A filthy set of steps lead up onto a bridge. My feet are aching, the heat pressing down on me like the lid of a cast-iron pot. It's too far to walk, it looked close on the map but in reality it's a tangle of snaking roads cutting this way and that across the area, the suburbs weren't made for walking, and I stumble and fall to my knees, crawl up the last few steps. From here I can see across the expressway, and I gasp.

Everything is at a standstill. Stationary cars stretching out into the distance, so little movement that at first I don't associate what I'm seeing with traffic; they're tin cans littering the ground by an overflowing recycling station. There are open doors, people sitting in the ditch, people chatting and waving or just hanging out; some seem to have left their vehicles and started wandering between the cars, men with backpacks and women pushing baby carriages. A bus sounds its horn and tries to get the cars to make room, an ambulance zigzags its way forward on the side of the road, where cars have been abandoned in the gravel and the disgusting grass.

I cling on to the railing, look out across the gridlock, trying to make sense of it. The traffic is coming from the north, from the places that are on fire. People want to get into the city, but the city is closed.

I make my way over the road and down a new set of stairs on unsteady legs, then crawl beneath the barrier and down a dusty slope covered in litter and weeds, over another railing and then I'm right there with them, among the people, wandering in the opposite direction between the gleaming cars. The road is flat and surprisingly wide, a river of smooth, even tarmac cutting between the yellowing trees, the retail parks, the dead concrete corpses.

A woman is carrying a screaming baby, trailed by a boy who looks around ten or eleven, playing on his phone. An elderly couple wander

forward, their hands full of heavy plastic bags; a young girl walks behind
her parents with a black-and-purple *Star Wars* bag, Darth Vader and one
of those lightsaber things on the front, asking how much farther it is to
Granny's house. A few hold up their phones and film while they walk,
talking into the camera, describing what they can see. There's a certain solemnity to some of them, as though they are crossing an ocean, colonizing
a new planet, an adventurer's pride at being first to set foot somewhere that
previously wasn't just unknown, it was unthinkable.

I cut over the verge, there isn't much room between the lanes and
there are hundreds, thousands of people making their way toward the city,
snaking up ahead as far as the eye can see. A few of the people I pass look
like they've been walking for hours, days. The air is thick with dirt and
exhaust fumes, a shimmer on the horizon where the sun is beating down
on the cars. Some still have their engines running, and through filthy windows I see terrified, exhausted faces, all surrounded by the quivering,
dusty heat.

Once you're on the expressway it takes no time at all, he used to tell
me, so proud of himself. *Ten minutes and you're in the center of town—
providing it's not rush hour.* According to the map it's only about a mile
until I need to turn off. I grit my teeth and ignore my feelings of disgust,
amble on in the heat, trying to pretend I'm not here, that I'm sitting by the
side of a pool in Vegas, drinking a cocktail with an umbrella in it; I'm on
the beach in Rio, I'm anywhere at all, but it doesn't work, it's too hot, the
air is too hard to breathe, so I start pretending it's a traffic jam in Calcutta,
Nairobi, a flying visit to some godforsaken shithole of a place, an exotic
adventure, a story to tell people once I get home.

Thailand, I think. Didrik told me they were supposed to be going to
Thailand. His darling wife was supposed to be sunbathing on a beach, having massages with flowers in her hair and coconut oil between her buttocks
as their sweet little baby dozed in the shade on a pink sarong. I imagine her
face, how fucking *satisfied* she would look while I'm running around here
like a junkie, and even though their journey has been called off and his dar-

ling wife is stuck in some forest somewhere, the injustice of it all is just so crazy and bizarre that I lose my breath, the fact that it can even be like this. And to top it all, his darling wife also got some pills she didn't even take because she's too much of a darling wife to do anything as stupid as popping painkillers, I hate her, hate, hate, hate her, I look up and see a huge sign pointing to the right. There is a pile of traffic cones and red-and-white plastic tape in the ditch, all that's left of a blockade, possibly from this morning, possibly last week. A couple of abandoned cars are blocking the turnoff, one with broken windows and another a burned-out shell. All those angry thoughts have perked me up a little, and I have a sudden inspiration, take a picture of the charred wreck. It looks cool, its sooty metal skeleton splayed against a pink sky, no need for a filter.

TO ALL THE HATERS. This is how things look right now, just outside of Stockholm. Chaos, destruction, a country paralyzed by fear. Right now there are only two types of people: those who want to rebuild the country and those who want to tear it down with their victimhood, their doomsday rhetoric, and their hysterical alarmism, which only helps those who want to sow division and create a more polarized society. Which side are you on?

I add a few emojis, the Swedish flag and some sad faces, and the picture of the burned-out car with a short film I took of the traffic jam earlier, blurry and messy but with a great live feeling: kids playing in the ditch, a sobbing old woman with a walker. I consider adding something about the milk brand, but there's a risk it wouldn't go over well. Share.

I move past the wrecked car and turn off the expressway, over another bridge, past a car dealership with broken windows, a stinking patch of gravel where a couple of overflowing recycling bins are glittering in the sun, past a wooded area, and up onto Kryddgatan, which weaves through the neighborhood. Stubby lawns, dead flower beds, a few children listlessly jumping on a trampoline. A half-built roof, scaffolding, a big green container, and a stack of roof tiles, a renovation project that has either ground to a halt or been abandoned completely. Faces peeping out from behind curtains. On the streetlamps, big handwritten signs announcing *NO PARKING* and *NEIGHBORHOOD WATCH* and *CAUTION: DOG!*

Up a hill, right onto Saffransgatan, then left onto Currygatan. There is a car from a security firm parked outside one of the bigger houses, and a young man with cropped hair gives me a suspicious glance through the windshield. He's holding a walkie-talkie to his mouth and his lips are moving. I fish the key out of my bag and grip it in my palm again. I belong here, I have access. In the yard to my right, a scrawny deer is drinking from a swimming pool, the water milky and green with algae. I turn off onto Chilistigen, count the numbers on the mailboxes, 8, 12, 18. This is it.

It's like I've been turned inside out, I'm on the verge of tears and my feet feel like they might start bleeding. I must have made a mistake, something must have gone wrong, this can't be it, not this house. Whenever he talked about his property, he always sounded so proud, so pleased with himself, that I imagined something . . . I don't know, nothing grand, obviously, not some marble palace or flashy American-style mansion with fake columns and a plastic fountain. Somewhere with a bit more charm, like something out of an Astrid Lindgren book, a nice yard with an overgrown plum tree, a cozy porch with creaky planks of wood, a shabby old greenhouse—some lilac bushes, at the very least. Anything, so long as it had character. But the redbrick house I'm standing in front of is low and square, with a tin roof, a flat lawn, and a white wooden garage. A few pieces of rattan furniture in the yard. A small balcony with a blue awning. It's not super ugly, not so bad that it stands out—it looks like everything else around here—it's more that it's so . . . ordinary. Anonymous. The kind of place where any old person could live. There is no sign of anyone around.

I make my way over to the garage door, mumbling one of Mom's Serbian prayers. I barely know what it means, but the words represent safety and courage to me, *you can do this, just get inside, quickly*, and then the key is in the lock, which turns smoothly and silently and the door swings open.

I dart into the darkness and pull it shut behind me, there, good, *now then, darling wife, where do you keep your pills?*

A concrete floor, no car. Tools and other junk, the smell of oil and rubber. Another door, just as quiet, the scent of cleaning products and tax-deductible cleaning services and disgusting, self-righteous, middle-class lives; two doors that I know belong to the children's rooms, they sleep down here, then up a set of stairs. I briefly wonder why there aren't any photographs, none of Zack and Vilja, just boring art prints and pictures of the archipelago.

A small, old-fashioned kitchen with white tiles and black plastic countertops, a red-and-white checked tablecloth on the table, beside a window that looks out onto the house next door. He often used to sit there, *sitting by the kitchen window, thinking about you*, he wrote, *waiting for the bread to finish baking. Dreaming about what it would be like if you were here, fresh from the shower in a bathrobe; imagine eating breakfast with you instead.* I try to place Didrik at the table, the aroma of toasted bread and coffee, a bowl of lemons, but my mind just keeps wandering. There is no more of him here than anywhere else.

A living room with a sofa and a TV. And then the door to their bedroom, they've got their own bathroom in there, I know. My legs are shaking now, I'm so close. I run in, see a double bed, textured wallpaper, two bedside tables in pale wood; a door, a soft glow from the spotlights overhead, sleek white porcelain, gleaming chrome. There is so much to take in that I feel dizzy, dropping to my knees in front of the painted white vanity and pulling out the drawers. Toothbrushes, razors. I try the next one, sanitary towels and cotton pads, the next one, some makeup and oils and sunscreen, damn it, I dig out an empty toiletry bag, nail scissors, an electric razor, where the hell has she hidden my pills?

Are there more bedrooms? A primary bathroom, or whatever it's called? There aren't any diapers here, Becka wears diapers but there isn't even a changing table, the medicine must be in the same place they change Becka; I hurry down the stairs and into another bathroom, a shower cubicle, a small vanity, still no diapers.

There is a handbag on the floor in the hallway. I don't recognize the brand but it looks expensive, and I tear open the zip and turn it upside down: keys, loyalty cards, and *YES*, a small white box. I stare down at it, squinting to read the tiny letters, it says something about allergies, the name *Pesha Horowitz* and a whole load of numbers? I check one of the plastic cards, the same foreign name, none of this makes sense, am I even in the right house?

Then it hits me, like a bitter aftertaste: his darling wife isn't staying here right now, Didrik told me that. They've rented the place out, and if you rent out your house you get rid of any personal items, no family portraits on the walls, no underwear in the drawers, nothing intimate in any of the bathrooms, like dildos or diapers or morphine. I'm rummaging through someone else's things instead of his darling wife's, Christ, I'm such an idiot, they must have locked their things in another room somewhere! I start trying all the doors to see whether any of them are locked, running into each of the rooms and checking the wardrobes, the kitchen cabinets, a cleaning cupboard, back down to the garage to look for anything that might be locked. They must have hidden their things somewhere, but I'll find them, if I just use my head, if I can just get my shit together. I try to think, sluggishness lingering in my brain like vomit refusing to drain from a sink, you run the tap but it doesn't make any difference, you have to get your hand right in there and pick out any lumps of food and gunk with your fingers. I don't know why I've come up with such a gross mental image, I haven't thrown up in a sink since a school dance when I was fourteen.

Suddenly I'm back in the primary bedroom, slumping onto the bed. I curl up in the fetal position, close my eyes, rack my memory. The long, boozy lunches. The chat threads. The sex.

My stomach turns, it feels like I'm going to throw up again.

The sex.

He brought things for sex.

We're lying naked in bed, just about to fuck. He takes out lube and flavored condoms.

Do you buy new stuff every time?

He gives me an embarrassed smile.

No, I've got a filing cabinet in the office, she never looks in there.

I leap up from the double bed like a rocket. The office is at the very end of the hallway, I think, I must have missed it earlier. I almost stumble over the mess I've made on the floor around the handbag, tear the door open, there's a guest bed, a desk and a computer screen, a big gray filing cabinet and a pink Post-it note with the word *PRIVATE* written on it. I let out a sob of joy and pull the handle.

Folders.

Nothing but a few shelves of ring binders, neatly marked with *TAX RETURNS* and *INSURANCE* and *CERTIFICATES* and *PENSION*, some plastic folders, a couple of old phones, I pull everything out onto the floor, cry *no no no* and open the ring binders, just to be on the safe side, tearing out papers, receipts, bank statements, doctor's notes, old ID cards, an entire life sorted into a gray metal cabinet. I grope around the empty space, there must be a small box, a pack of pills, even a single Oxy that can take me away from here.

But there's nothing.

Wait.

Something.

A plastic bag, pushed in behind the shelves. Almost invisible, despite the fact that the folders that were hiding it are now gone. Nothing but a sliver of white plastic, I tug on it, manage to coax the thin, slippery material out. It's an ordinary plastic bag from a supermarket, and I bring it out into the light, tip everything onto the floor in front of me.

Oh, Didrik.

Half a pack of licorice-flavor condoms.

Thick wads of printer paper. He has printed out our chats, all our emails, printed out the pictures I took, in color.

Receipts from hotels and restaurants.

Free soap from a hotel bathroom.

The cork from a bottle of champagne.

A piece of toilet paper I left a lipstick kiss on.

The program from the conference where we first met, *Don't Be Ashamed to Be Human—An Inspirational Session with Melissa Stannervik.* Beside it, he has written "NOT PRIORITY?" in ballpoint.

My business card, Jesus Christ, why did I ever have business cards printed? It was Mom who talked me into it, *all important people have business cards.*

A black metal bobby pin.

My pink knitted hat, the one I wore all that winter, the one I was sure I'd lost. The thought of him sitting here beside this tragic cabinet, sniffing the scent of my hair, is just too pathetic to take in.

And last of all, a glossy sheet of paper, smooth beneath my fingers. At first I think it's one of those passport photos people take in a booth, but we never did that. Or maybe a polaroid, but I don't remember any of those, either.

No.

Please, Didrik, no.

We agreed.

A black-and-white image, square. A gray shadow. A big, dark bubble and inside it, a white mark.

I open my mouth to let out the tears or the howl or whatever madness is trying to escape, but nothing will come. I just stare down at the picture, at the strange numbers around the edge, the grayness, the darkness, the white spot she said was the heart.

We agreed we'd forget all about it.

The betrayal is so big, the grief so incomprehensible, palpitations, a sense of panic, I need to get out need to get away need need need, I leap up and rush out of the room, into the kitchen, tear open the cabinets, a bottle of something clear, I let it swill down my throat, forcing myself to swallow even though it burns, just keep it coming, don't think don't think, a few more sips and then I toss the bottle away and stagger over to the sofa, curl up among the cushions and the blankets.

You took that picture from me and said you were going to get rid of it, not even a fetus, just an embryo, that's what the midwife said, two centimeters long.

The living room is quivering with heat, the walls spinning.

You saved it. You saved us.

In the distance, sirens cut through the suffocating silence.

You hid our treasure in a plastic bag.

The sofa sways beneath me, my stomach cramps, and I prop myself up on my elbows, the feeling of being a dirty, sweaty, stinking animal, of transforming into muscle and fat and meat. It's like sex, like having an orgasm, a wave inside me that can't be stopped, and the beef and the eel and the red wine all make a reappearance in a stringy, shimmering slime, that wonderful feeling of finally being empty, free, I wipe my mouth on a sand-colored mohair blanket and crawl into myself and that's where I stay.

―――――

Someone's been eating my porridge.

The voice sounds frightened and angry, shrill and squeaky and high-pitched. I'm tucked up in bed and Mom is telling me the story, reading in halting Swedish, but that just makes it funny, exaggerating in all the right places.

Someone's been sitting in my chair.

Flashing lights, angry voices, just let me sleep.

Rough hands shaking my shoulder. OK, OK, I will, I just need to rest my eyes for a few seconds, a power nap, you'll barely even notice I'm here.

This is disgusting. How did she get in?

Heavy footsteps. A figure leaning over me. I squeeze my eyes shut. *It was the toothache*, I want to say, but my lips won't play ball. *It can happen to the best of us.*

Mom makes her voice dark and booming.

Someone's been sleeping in my bed.

The bear cocks its head, pushes back the hair from my face.

Are you OK? You can't be here.

"Do you have anything?" I hear myself whisper, my voice raspy and dry. "I need something."

How did you get in?

"I had a key. I . . . I thought . . ."

Can you try sitting up?

The hands tug at me and I slowly sit up on the sofa, closing my eyes in the bright light, someone is shining a flashlight at me, it's dark.

The man has short hair and is wearing a uniform, a baton and other things hanging from his belt. I can see a woman standing a couple feet behind him, she has her arms folded and she's glaring at me, *darling wife*, I think, feeling a shiver of panic pass down my spine. She's standing in the dark with her bike, *sorry sorry sorry just leave me alone*, but then I realize this woman is at least ten years older than her, with short gray hair and a little dog in her arms, *ask her if she's alone* she snarls in English, and the man translates.

"Yeah," I mumble. "I'm a friend of the family. Of Didrik and . . . Carola. Sorry, I didn't realize they'd rented it out."

"You can't be here," he repeats. His voice is firm but his eyes are sweet, he grips my shoulders and gets me up onto my feet. "Come on, let's get you out to the car."

"Who's gonna clean up this mess?" the woman hisses as we stagger out into the hallway.

"Call your insurance company," the security guard tells her.

"Stupid junkie."

"Welcome to Sweden," I tell her, on the verge of laughter. The door swings shut behind us and his flashlight sweeps over the security firm's car, the same one I saw parked outside another house earlier, he opens the door and pushes me into the backseat.

"Was that true, about the key?" he asks, turning back to me. It's dark out, but none of the streetlamps are on. I see from the clock on the dashboard that it's late evening.

"Yeah," I say. "I was looking for something. Then I felt sick. Couldn't help it."

"Where do you live?"

"In town."

He nods and starts the engine and we slowly start rolling through the neighborhood.

When things were at their worst with Didrik, I thought about taking my driving test. I'd be living a different kind of life soon, one in which I'd need to be able to drive, not because we'd be living in a boring suburb like this, obviously, but because I wanted to be able to give Zacharias and Vilja a ride sometimes, do the pickups and drop-offs; they'd struggle with it at first but they'd eventually get used to me, and maybe it would be easier if we had to spend time together in the car, listening to music, the radio. Mom never had her own car, of course, but my friends' parents did, and they went on holiday in them, the kids in the backseat and their moms and dads up front, a folder of old CDs and bags of candy, driving to the mountains, to Granny's house, driving over to Denmark and seeing where we end up, Mom just sighed and packed her basket and mixed her lemonade.

The traffic is still gridlocked out on the expressway, it's never-ending, it's unbelievable, there's a fire at a shopping center a couple miles away and the sound of sirens fills the night sky. They're going on and on about the chaos on the roads on the radio, *turn back if you can and choose another route*, so why are they still going? It strikes me that this is just what you do, it's like everything else on earth: if you're heading in one direction and someone tells you you'll come to a grinding halt up ahead, you just keep going, because what's the alternative, it's not like you can stop or back up, and then you tell yourself it can't be *that* bad, everything will probably be fine by the time I arrive, it's easiest just to go with the flow and let what happens happen, and if the worst does happen and I find myself in the shit, then at least I'm not alone.

"How long have you . . . been like this?" the guard asks quietly from the front seat as we cruise down the expressway. He has a blue light on the roof, and most people get out of our way as we approach, he keeps zig-zagging across the road, driving on the shoulder, honking at anyone who jumps out in front of us, seems used to ignoring the chaos.

"A year or two," I mumble. "But just stuff I can get from the pharmacy."

"When did you last take anything?"

"Last night. Almost twenty-four hours ago."

He nods.

"It takes four or five days," he says, his voice a drawl. "And then you're over the worst of it."

At first the noise is just noise, but then the high notes break through, the howling of police sirens or whatever they are, ambulances or fire engines or all three combined. After another minute or two, it's almost like some sort of dark bassline has started pulsing beneath the rest of the noise: the compact roar of thousands of people gathered in one place, engines growling, metal clattering, dogs barking, angry voices shouting screaming chanting; the traffic jam has grown into a city, illuminated by floodlights.

"My girl," he says without looking at me, "she had this weird pain in her belly. They tried proctoscopies, colonoscopies, all sorts, but in the end they just gave her the pills and she was hooked within a few weeks. The system treated her like an addict, no help from anyone. But she managed to kick it."

They've built some sort of ramp lined with plastic tape and orange cones to lead the traffic away from the expressway, and there are police officers with helmets and shields standing on it, more beneath it, several on horseback. They're surrounded by a sea of people and stationary cars spread across both sides of the expressway, on the grass verges, in the ditches, standing among the sun-bleached trees; they've blocked off the entire area down to the water, and the rescue workers are standing with red blankets and bottles of water, men with yellow hi-vis jackets and walkie-talkies, a woman lying on the ground, surrounded by medics, blood streaming out of her ears.

"How did she kick it?"

"My girl?"

I nod.

"We had a kid," he replies, smiling softly in the rearview mirror. "I think you need something like that to motivate you. Otherwise it's impossible."

A young police officer saunters over. He's wearing a mouth covering, and a lock of his long hair has fallen out from beneath his cap, onto his forehead. The security guard flashes his ID and the officer waves us forward, and we drive on, through, to the other side, where another kind of chaos reigns: police cars, ambulances, a roaring mass of people holding signs and banners. They're shouting *WHAT DO WE WANT? TO SAVE THE PLANET!* and there are broken shop windows everywhere, upturned paving stones. From the corner of my eye I can see burning cars, masked figures waving metal pipes hammers hockey sticks, I can't really tell, it all happens so quickly, we're moving between the huge blocks of cement or whatever they are blocking the road with, chipboard over windows, smashed streetlamps, graffiti, rubbish; someone tries to jump in front of the car but he brakes and turns sharply, and there's a bang when someone takes off the side-view mirror with the precise, effective snap of a golf swing, cleanly severing it from the vehicle. I shriek and he turns the wheel again and steps on the accelerator, there's a scraping sound on the hood and then on the trunk lid, we've driven into something and I slam into the seat in front of me, the belt whips against my chest, and then we come to a halt.

"You OK back there?" he asks. "We need to—"

Something hard thuds against the windshield and a spiderweb of cracks shoots out from the center, circle after circle of broken ice. I cry out again and another rock comes flying, creating another, bigger solar system beside the first one. The guard yells *WHAT THE HELL* and a face appears in the window beside him, a woman's voice shouting *OUT OF THE CAR* through the glass, *OUT BEFORE WE BURN YOU ALIVE IN THERE, YOU BASTARD*, and the guard yells something back and I feel like I'm inside a tin can, I can see shadows moving all around us, kicks, thuds, rocks on metal, more voices, *GET OUT OF THE CAR, FOR FUCK'S SAKE,*

FUCKING PIG. I hear myself shouting *stop stop stop* and I struggle with the handle on my side, opening the door and tumbling out into the warm night, I'm on all fours on the tarmac, *stop stop*, I wail, *let me go.*

There are around ten of them, most younger than me, a few wearing masks and holding weapons. It's dark, but there is another burning car nearby, the flames casting a glow over us. I shout *just let me go home* and one of the masks asks *what the fuck were you doing in his car* and I don't even think, I just say *we were at the protest outside the airport.*

"So where's the rest of your group?" a hoarse male voice asks.

"They ran off, I think. The asshole guard chased them off."

Behind me the guard has been dragged out of the car. They're shouting at him, someone hitting the car with a metal rod. The guard sounds authoritative and angry and I hear a young man's voice reach a falsetto when he replies. They're frightened, I realize, they're frightened of the situation they've created, and there is nothing more dangerous than frightened people. I need to get out of here, but the nausea hits me again and I come close to throwing up. A man with a bare face comes over and points at me.

"You're Melissa, right?"

Short. Kind of chubby. Dreadlocks.

He smiles.

"You're the one who uploaded that film of me. Over five million views so far."

I shrug.

"Don't know what you're talking about."

"My mom's got cancer," he says. "This might be her last summer. She and my sister were meant to be hiking in the mountains, but now they're stuck in a refugee camp. In Sweden."

He comes a few steps closer, getting right up in my face.

"What was it you called me?" he hisses. "A prophet of doom?"

A chubby hand holds up a long, black, squirming snake, and an image flickers through my mind: Didrik, the eel. But no. It's a bike chain.

"Don't you think you owe me an apology, at the very least?"

I meet his eye. He really is short, I have to look down at him. Make my voice smooth, cold, lustrous.

"Since when have I owed a fucking thing to anyone?"

Dreadlocks waves his chain, letting it swing in the air between us.

"Fucking live with it."

Sharp cracks pierce holes in the night, and I hear someone cry out. The security guard is standing by his car, feet wide apart, one arm reaching up into the dark sky. *GET OUT OF HERE*, he shouts, *GET OUT OF HERE BEFORE I*, but then there is another bang and I see that his arm ends with something black and angular, that he has pulled out a pistol and the terrorists seem to be in two minds, though several have already scurried away like rats, and I see Dreadlocks glancing around before running off into the darkness and I hear them chanting *WHAT DO WE WANT? TO SAVE THE PLANET! WHAT DO WE WANT? TO SAVE THE PLANET!* and there is something euphoric about their cries, a sense of relief.

"You get lost too," the guard tells me. "You'll have to make your own way home."

His breathing is rapid, hunched over his car at a strange angle, almost as though he is in pain.

"Things got a bit . . ." I begin, but he just waves his hand.

"Get lost."

I can hear sirens, the whirring of a helicopter, voices that sound much too loud over megaphones.

"And try to find something to care about. Something other than yourself."

IT'S A TINY INSECT, LIKE A SMALL, YELLOWISH-BROWN BEETLE. I'VE googled it thousands of times, but actually seeing it with my own eyes still comes as such a gross shock that I practically shriek. It scuttles over the white sheet, straight as an arrow, without any hint of fear, like a child running down the sand to the sea. Becka is sleeping soundly with Snuggly pressed to her cheek, wearing the pink pajamas I bought for her yesterday, or was it the day before, they've all merged into one. The disgusting little creepy-crawly moves confidently, with no sense of urgency, toward her tiny foot, and I remember the bites Didrik showed me on her bottom. Maybe that's where it's going, again, for more blood? Or do they try to find a new spot every time? Maybe it's going for the back of her knee, her groin, her anus? Maybe it'll leave her alone tonight and aim for Didrik instead; he's lying naked on his back, snoring, his dick half-hard. Isn't it a bit weird to sleep like that, with a baby right by his side?

It crawls up onto her foot. The girl twitches in her sleep but stays in the same position, and the bedbug scuttles over her toes and the sole of her foot, toward her soft white calf. I can see the gap around the bottom of her pajamas, right by her ankle, and I watch the bug squeeze in beneath the fabric and disappear up her leg. It makes my stomach turn. I watch her calm, sleeping face and try to tell myself that it's not like it's going to kill her, every home used to have bedbugs back in the day, they were just a part of everyday life, something you had to live with, and people still wrote books and painted masterpieces and sparked revolutions. Then they started using hydrogen cyanide and DDT to get rid of them, but those things were banned and the bugs became resistant, they started spreading again during the 1990s, first through travel, then the heat. They die at temperatures of negative 1 degree, so in the past it was enough to just open the windows, but these days it never gets that cold.

Still, it's comforting somehow. The world might be going to shit but the bedbugs are still here. When everything else is chaos, the little creepy-crawly in Becka's pajamas might be the only normal thing left.

"Hi."

His voice is gravelly, almost as though it's still breaking. The kind of voice a man only ever uses when he has just woken up, when he's confused or in the panic-stricken ecstasy that washes over him just before orgasm. Didrik looks up at me through half-closed eyes, reflexively pulls the sheet over his naked crotch.

"Hi. There you are."

"Yeah."

He smiles softly, raises a lazy hand in greeting.

"I . . . thought you'd never come back."

I don't speak, just perch on the edge of the mattress. Once you've seen them, it's hard not to think that they might come scuttling toward you from all angles. My skin is crawling but I have to force myself to sit here, I need to do this, it's now or never.

"The night you showed up here, you said that all you wanted was to wake up beside me." I sound calm, composed, considered; the nausea has faded and been replaced by a strangely crisp sharpness.

"Well, I'm here. And you're awake."

Didrik nods and reaches out, places his hand on top of mine, links our fingers.

"But you said something else too." I clear my throat, swallow. "You said you were ashamed because you'd never been able to forget me."

The sun has risen above the rooftops, and I see its rays hit the balcony, bathing it in warm light. We should eat breakfast out there, him and me, coffee and croissants, the whole day ahead of us to fuck talk read drink be together, but that world is gone now, it's our Pompeii, our rain forest, our two-degree target.

"I need . . . I want you to know that I'm ashamed too. That I've been ashamed."

Didrik rubs his eyes, props himself up in bed, his hand still on mine.

"I'm ashamed for falling in love with you and for thinking that we'd ever actually be together. I'm ashamed for believing all your promises when you said your love wasn't just some lame midlife crisis, that you'd actually made up your mind, that you wanted a different kind of life and that you'd chosen to live it with me."

I feel my body start to tremble with anger and I look away, can't bear to see him, need to keep my head. Cool, calm, confident.

"I left Vitas and bought him out of the apartment, and then the pandemic came along and I had no money and no work but I still believed in you, sitting there in my super-expensive studio flat, waiting for you to call. I thought you were on your way, that you just needed to straighten things out with Carola, maybe go to a few sessions of couples therapy, then you'd be standing there in the hallway with your bags. But the days passed, the weeks, and do you know what the worst part was, Didrik? The worst part wasn't that you betrayed me, it was that you didn't even have the guts to tell me that you'd never been serious."

Becka moans in her sleep and rolls onto her back. She might be about to wake up, but I don't bother lowering my voice.

"I was at rock bottom, and you dumped me. And now you're back, acting like nothing has even happened."

He's starting to get that tautness around his mouth now.

"Nothing has happened? Nothing has *happened*? Look around you, for God's sake, do you think I'd . . . what the hell, don't you *get* it? We're on the verge of something mankind has never experienced before."

I shrug.

"Yeah? So why does everything feel so familiar?"

The thought has never crossed my mind before, but suddenly it all seems so clear, like a plane taking off, that moment when you look down and see the motorways and the buildings and the people like tiny little ants down below, and you realize how everything fits together and how small the world is.

"Because men like you always find an excuse. You used the pandemic as an excuse to stay with Carola, and now you're using the climate crisis as an excuse to come back to me. But the truth is that you just take whatever you want, you take, take, take, and it's people like me who have to give. But not this time."

Didrik sighs.

"Melissa, I don't know what you—"

"*My mom isn't allowed to eat meat.* People like you have convinced the government to take meat off the menu for environmental reasons, but then you sit here and wolf down steak like a fucking . . . fucking . . ."

"I don't know what your mom has to do—"

"Because I told her about you."

I can feel the tears streaming down my cheeks. I didn't realize I was crying, how long has that been going on?

"That's the part I'm most ashamed of. That I went out there to her awful fucking rest home and told Mom about you, showed her pictures of you and Vilja and Zacharias and said that you'd be my family, that she'd be a bonus grandma, and then after you dumped me she asked about them and I couldn't bring myself to tell her, I said that she must have imagined the whole thing because I was ashamed, I was so fucking ashamed that I couldn't even tell my therapist."

I wish I was holding my phone, not because I need to call anyone or check anything, just because it would feel so nice to have it in my hand, but it's charging.

"I know you remember what we had," I say calmly. "That I left . . . a mark on you. That you've saved me like a secret treasure somewhere. But I've changed. Everything has. And you're a closed chapter for me. You remind me of everything I don't want to be. Everything I just want to forget."

He looks like he is about to say something, but he holds his tongue and stares down at the bed instead. I focus on my breathing, go on:

"Pack your things and get out of here. You can't stay here anymore."

Didrik gives a quick nod.

"I understand, it's just . . . Wille hasn't been in touch, and I've been thinking about going to a hotel, but it doesn't seem like my account has . . ."

"You don't get it."

"No, no, I do, if it wasn't for Becka I could've . . . but if we could just stay another night or two, until . . ."

"No, Didrik. You don't get it. I mean you *can't* stay here any longer."

I point at Becka's foot, and it's crazy, because at that very moment two disgusting little bugs come crawling out of her pajama leg and scuttle across the white sheets, toward the head of the bed. They prefer to hang out by the head, I know that.

"This room is infested with bedbugs. They live in the bed and under the skirting boards and maybe even in the walls, no one really knows. And they come out and feed on you and Becka every night, that's why she has those bites."

Didrik stares down at Becka, at the sheets, at me.

"They're resistant to all poison," I continue. "The only thing that helps is a powder made from crushed algae that you sprinkle around the walls and the bed frame, it makes them dry out and die. But the whole thing takes a while, and in the meantime someone has to sleep in the room, luring them out so that they're exposed to it. That's why he's letting me stay here for free. As bait, basically."

He slowly scratches his leg. I know how he feels; once you know about them, your body suddenly starts itching all over.

"You were only meant to be here one night," I hurry to add. "I didn't even think. And then I didn't know what to say. But it's been too long now, you have to go."

"So by sleeping in here, we're essentially helping you pay the rent?"

I don't know what I was expecting—a furious outburst, a lecture about bedbugs being yet another consequence of global warming—but he just yawns.

"Perfect, then, I'm sure we can put up with it for a few weeks. We can do this, bedbugs are a first world problem. Was there anything else?"

When I fail to reply, he curls up beside Becka and pulls the sheet over both of them. Girls who say that dads are cute have never witnessed the combination of morning glory and a pair of pink pajamas, that's for sure. I'm sorry, but seriously. So creepy.

———————

I'm standing with my laptop beneath my arm, staring at the devastation. It's the same story all up and down the street. The windows are all broken, and someone—maybe even a group of people—has really gone berserk inside. My favorite café has been relatively lucky; several of the other places nearby have had their tables and chairs ripped out and smashed to pieces. Some seem to have been used as weapons or to build some sort of barricade, others just heaped up and burned. But at my place, it looks like they made do with ripping out everything behind the counter and breaking most of the glass. It seems to have happened while they were open, because the few remaining shelves are still full of sandwiches and sweet buns and muffins, and I can see a plate and a half-drunk latte on one of the tables.

I open the crooked, broken door and step into the chaos. The smell of destruction and rubbish hits me in the balmy morning heat. Didrik always used to say that we can get by fine without air-conditioning, that we're just used to having it on full blast everywhere, that it's a huge waste of energy and that if we just turned it off our bodies would quickly get used to the temperature, and maybe that's true, but I'll never get used to this stench, to how dirty everything smells the minute you let a little heat in, all yeasty and musty and organic. It's as though the barbarism has cast a shadow over the place, like using an outhouse and knowing that there is a disgusting pit of feces festering away only a millimeter from your ass.

I notice a movement in the gleaming chrome debris of the coffee machines behind the counter. A quiet whisper.

"Hello?"

No reply. Just a few days ago, I never would have dared, but right now it's as though I no longer care about anything. I move closer, jumping over a stinking gray pool of spilled milk, stepping on crunching shards of glass and china as I round the corner. It's the beggar, her children curled up like kittens beside her, and she looks up at me in terror, not moving a muscle.

"Hello?"

"Hello," she replies, gesturing to the café around her. "Broken."

The boy glances at me from behind his filthy black bangs, his fingers covered in crumbs, pearl sugar clinging to the downy hair on his upper lip. When I fail to react, he smacks his lips and licks his palm and smiles shyly. His sister is playing with the coffee beans, holding them in her cupped hands, throwing them up in the air and letting them fall to the floor with a laugh. I turn back to the mother and see that she is holding the sleeping baby in her arms. She has dragged the trolley full of junk inside, left it over in the corner beside the broken register. The place is cash-free, nevertheless someone seems to have really gone to town on that.

"Here," says the beggar, holding out a tray of ham-and-cheese sand-wiches. "Here. You eat."

"No," I say. "You go."

She says something in her language.

I point out to the street.

"You go."

The woman gives me a defiant stare and sits tall. She puts down the sandwiches and holds her child tight.

"Police?" she asks, a teasing note in her voice. "No, no police."

"The police come soon."

She sneers. "Stupid girl. No police come."

As I turn to make my way back to the door, I stumble over some-thing, a sign among all the junk on the floor. Cheerful, welcoming rounded letters: *WE ARE BLACK, WHITE, LATINX, ASIAN, MUSLIM, JEW-ISH, HINDU, BUDDHIST, CHRISTIAN, ATHEIST, GAY, LESBIAN, TRANS, AND STRAIGHT. IT WORKS REALLY WELL!*

I bend down and pick it up. The glass in the cheap frame is cracked, and I don't even think about what I'm doing, I just throw it at the floor with all my might, corner first. The glass comes loose with a crash and I pick it up again, start pulling the white frame apart. The pieces of wood are held together with tiny nails, and I slam it against the floor until I'm left holding a long white stick. I turn and move back over to the beggar, hitting the cupboard door just above her face. She reflexively raises her arm to protect herself, and I rap the floor beside her instead, hitting it again and again, harder this time, hitting the walls, the shelves, everything that is still intact and can still be broken with a deafening crash and a shattering sound. The woman shuffles away with her baby in her arms, and I step over her and smash the tray of sandwiches she held out to me earlier, and they're all quiet, all silent, huddled together; I think I can hear someone screaming but it's just me yelling *GO,* Vitas *GO* is standing in the garbage room saying *you whore, what are you looking at,* Didrik *GO* is panting *you can always take a morning-after pill, please, it feels so good,* Mom *GO* has received her benefits, and she uses them to buy jelly beans and gummy candies that she hands out to the neighbors *GO.*

I peer down into the cart, a few plastic bags and two empty cans inside. The beggar and her family are gone. The piece of frame has broken, and I'm clutching a stump of wood.

I catch a glimpse of something pinkish orange in one of the plastic bags and I lean forward and reach into the cart to fish it out, untie the simple knot.

A pill. It isn't tramadol, isn't Oxy or codeine, nothing I've ever seen before.

My heart is pounding. My stomach turns.

The feeling that something beautiful is about to happen.

I dig a pricey little bottle of ginger-and-guava juice out of the wreckage, wash it down.

There.

Yes.

Collapse to the floor in the shadows, in the aroma of coffee beans and spilled milk.

Right.

The numbness feels so good.

Right. There. Now.

Finally.

Right.

Cupcake.

A cool hand in my hair.

Cupcake?

———

The woman from the conference is wearing a white bathrobe, her blond hair damp. We're floating over the ruins of the city, through neighborhood after neighborhood of gutted cafés and restaurants, looted clothing stores, crossing between burned-out cars and stranded emergency vehicles, all while she blabbers away about the hot guy who runs the afternoon sessions. Her bathrobe transforms into a ball gown and she starts glittering and sparkling like a Disney princess with her beautiful red lips.

At the crossroads, the police have blocked the road with a couple of large shipping containers now daubed with graffiti, *CLIMATE JUSTICE NOW* and *NO PLANET B*, and there is only just enough room to squeeze past against the wall of the building. There are soldiers or something on the other side, men in camouflage and berets, and a beefy officer from the security services pats me down through my clothes before letting us go on, *what a hunk* she whispers loudly, *you should have a chat with him later, about you-know-what*, and we both laugh, pass another roadblock, and then we're in a square, crossing a wide avenue. It takes me a while to work out where we are, the city looks so different now, like it's been broken and divided and smashed to pieces; the streets and buildings are like strangers meeting at a party, pretending to know one another's names, nothing makes sense anymore but I look up at the sky and see the trees, my poor sun-bleached trees that never know when to blossom, and I suddenly know exactly where we are: in the park outside the department store.

We walk around the park. There's a stage here, I remember, there were always concerts and festivals before the pandemic, and whenever one sportsperson or another did well in some competition, they got to climb up onstage and receive people's applause, thousands of people packed into a small park without anyone deciding how many of them were allowed or how far apart they had to stand. It sounds like a dream.

There is another police checkpoint, and I say what she whispers for me to say before we make our way through a doorway, a small set of steps leading up to some sort of platform, I can make out a bright white light, speakers, a pop singer who had a hit song when I was younger, standing with an acoustic guitar, singing something calm and singer-songwriterish, trying to get the crowd to join in on the chorus, but other than a few shrill men's voices the response is pretty weak.

We huddle together by the side of the stage, hidden behind a wall but with a clear view out across the audience. There aren't many people in the park, and practically every other person looks like a police officer or a security guard of some kind. There's a helicopter hovering overhead, drowning out most of the sound, a few people waving Swedish flags, and all around the stage there are banners with smiley faces in blue and yellow, the words *FOSSIL FREE FUTURE* printed on them.

Once the singer is finished, a gospel choir takes to the stage, a group of Black women in loose, colorful dresses and long shawls, singing along with a backing track, all swaying backsides and clapping hands. I zone out a little and almost doze off as I'm standing there, I can't have gotten much more than two hours' sleep last night, and when I next look up, I see an old man. I think he was a party leader or a secretary of state, maybe both, back before I was born, he's the kind of old person people listen to, and he's holding the mic and strolling across the stage. He talks for a few minutes about *the importance of sticking together* and *difficult times, but Sweden is strong* and

I've seen with my own eyes how conflict can tear a country apart; his speech is at once boyish and statesmanlike, and it all sounds so true and nice.

"Rather than viewing this as a catastrophe, we should see it as an opportunity," he says. "For a green transformation that will forge a new future for Swedish businesses and Swedish jobs! Don't forget that the Chinese word for *crisis* means both danger and opportunity."

A woman with a walkie-talkie and a stressed look on her face comes over to me and starts asking questions. I can feel myself zoning out again and I glance over to my friend from the conference hotel. She suddenly seems so small, almost translucent, and she tiptoes over and takes my hand, and she's as light as air when she whispers *let's do this, cupcake*.

———

I take a few steps forward, and as I slowly make my way across the stage I remember waiting by the bridge. It was a morning in March, and the cold, clear rain was pouring down on me and my little black umbrella like I was in some romantic black-and-white Woody Allen film in Manhattan, clarinets playing in the background; he was coming to meet me, he'd bought two plane tickets to Thailand and we were going to run away from everything, make a decision about our future, and as I watched the rain transform the smooth, gray surface of the water into a simmering stew, I decided that one day it would be me who bought the plane tickets. One day, he would be proud to be my man. The minutes passed but I didn't turn around to see if he was there, it would only ruin the atmosphere if I turned around, a bit like that story from the Bible, with the woman who looks back over her shoulder and turns into salt. I just stood there watching the raindrops bounce and play in the water, thinking that they were like an audience, that they were eyes watching me. The new handbag I'd bought started to vibrate, and I took out my phone to read his message, but it was from the organizer of a panel I was supposed to be taking part in, she wrote that it had been canceled because of some virus and that they might be in touch again in a few weeks' time, and I could hardly believe they were serious, a virus, how ridiculous, I thought, I'd have to tell Didrik all about this, how absurd could things get, it's 104 degrees in the Arctic Circle, half a billion animals have just burned to death in Australia, and you're worried about a fucking *virus*? We would laugh about it and then we'd order champagne and watch Sweden's dark, endless forests disappear beneath us.

The sound system screeches and the audience looks up at me.

I don't have a problem, I say. *I can stop whenever I like.*

A small apartment to begin with, his kids every other week, a box beneath the bed, you could get cheap bunk beds online, and then we could fuck, talk, think, go to cafés to write, would it really be so impossible?

It's you people who have the problem. It's you people who can't stop.

I point at the besieged city.

You talk about community and solidarity and all that cutesy stuff, as though . . . I pause, like I'm searching for the right words, though I know exactly what I'm going to say *. . . as though there wasn't a war going on around us. A war between those of us trying to enjoy our lives as best we can and those who want to snatch everything away from us.*

It felt like I'd been waiting for an eternity in the rain that day when I eventually turned around and stared out at the damp, empty darkness; the street was deserted, no one but a middle-aged woman cycling toward me. She braked and stopped a couple feet away.

"You're Melissa," she said. I nodded, immediately knew who she was.

"Didrik told me this was where you were supposed to meet." She smiled stiffly. "He told me everything."

She stared at me with cold eyes.

"Whatever you thought you had, it's over now. There's no point waiting for him. You should go home."

"Where is he?" I heard myself ask.

"Back at our house. With Zack and Vilja. It looks like he's going to be working from home all spring, because of the virus. Me too."

She pulled a face.

"Which means we'll have time to . . . well, heal. To fix what you and he broke."

I took a step toward her. She looked so pathetic in her red cycle helmet and her crappy makeup that I felt an urge to put an arm around her, don't ask me why.

"Carola, I know it's . . ."

"*Don't touch me!*" she shouted, moving her bike. Her fat calves hit the pedals, and I tried to grab the rear rack but she lost her balance and fell toward me. The sudden, unexpected weight of her ungainly body and the smell of her damp functional clothing, then the wheel scraping against my leg. I tried to back away but instead I fell too, like a drunk in an old TV sketch; she was half-sprawled across her bike with me beneath her, and the edge of her helmet hit me in the face and I felt a searing pain flash through my teeth. The world exploded in agony and I screamed and raised a hand to my cheek.

"Oh my God, I'm sorry," said Carola, sounding shaken. She managed to get back onto her feet and carefully lifted the bike off me. "Sorry, Melissa. God, I'm so clumsy, I didn't mean to."

"It's OK," I muttered, getting up and brushing myself down, using my tongue to explore my mouth. None of my teeth seemed loose, it was just so fucking painful, as though I'd tried to bite through a wedding ring. "Probably serves me right."

We stood there in the rain by the bridge, her and me, and neither of us spoke for quite some time. I leaned back against the railing with my hand to my cheek, felt the pain slowly ebbing away.

"I'm going home now," she eventually said. "I just wanted to . . . I don't know. He doesn't know I cycled over here, but I felt sorry for you waiting for him."

"He wasn't going to let me know?" I asked, my lips fat like sausages.

"No. Maybe later."

"But isn't he even . . . sad?"

"Yeah, a bit. Though as luck would have it the airline will give him a full refund. They're canceling everything now anyway, all the hotels are closing, everything is shutting down."

She sighed and shook her head, pulling a frumpish, motherly expression that was probably supposed to convey some kind of shared *ha-ha-tell-me-about-it* understanding of just how stupid men can be.

"Forget about him," she continued. "You're young and beautiful, you can have whatever you want. Just not my husband. Or my kids. Try to be happy anyway."

She put an arm around my shoulder.

"Choose joy."

I can no longer see the audience, they're nothing but a gray mass, their outstretched phone screens like gleaming soap bubbles. I keep talking, hear my voice echo over the sound system, but I've run out of words. I want to say something else, there should be more, something about the morality of taking responsibility for your own life, about the duty to be happy against the odds, about Mom and the Christmas meal, but there he is, right at the very front of the crowd, like a column of light in the gray muddle, finally, he came at last, all the brokenness and hungriness in his eyes focuses on a point just beneath my navel and then floods downward, he's proud of me and his lips silently form my name, but that's not enough and I see that she, my friend from the conference hotel, is still standing by my side, smiling her fresh-from-the-shower smile, and I remember that I once dreamed of being a woman like her, independent, self-sufficient, free to sit and read and think and sip coffee without having to rush off for someone else's benefit, and I realize that that isn't enough either, it's no longer enough for me, she pokes the tip of her tongue between her teeth in her sweet, girlish way and I drop her hand and let her fade away like the jingling of a silver bell, and then the pain is gone for good.

———

He's crying when I get home, lying on the disgusting bug-infested bed and crying with his phone in one hand. I perch on the edge of the mattress and stroke his head (keeping a safe distance from his wound) saying all the usual things, that it'll be fine, that what we had was beautiful.

"I need to go back up there," he sobs. "He's disappeared again. I'm so tired, but I have to."

At first I don't know where he has to go or who has vanished, but it keeps coming out of him in long, hacking sobs. Carola called; it turns out Zack isn't in Hedemora after all, the whole thing was a lie.

"I don't know what kind of sick person would do something like this," he cries. "What's happening to us, you know?"

"Where's Becka?" I ask calmly, and he points to the roof terrace with a trembling finger.

The phone starts ringing and he picks up, seems to be talking to some sort of authority because he clears his throat and his voice becomes shrill and demanding; I leave him to it.

I pour myself a glass of wine and go out to water the plants on the terrace. The kid on the phone was right, they really are starting to look a bit sad. Becka is asleep on the sofa, and the evening sun is making the rooftops and church towers glow. I can hear sirens in the distance, the sound of breaking glass, hoarse voices yelling, but up here on my roof terrace the sunset is more beautiful than ever. In my naivete, I thought this magical summer was over, but it just keeps going and going.

A sip of rosé as reward.

I absentmindedly check my phone. The clip has had over two hundred thousand views in just a few hours, and someone has even added English subtitles. My phone is buzzing and pinging with notifications, messages, texts; calls come in from four different numbers just while I'm holding it, but I reject them all, don't have the energy.

A soft whimpering. I get up and walk over to the sofa with the glass in my hand, hush her gently.

ding-dong-ding-dong-ding-dong-ding-dong

The doorbell melts over me like a lump of garlic butter on a well-done entrecôte, *ontrecott*, and I feel neither shame nor fear, just relief. It's the guy from the security services, the hunky one with the sideburns, and he has brought two police officers with him.

"What was it you wanted to report?" he asks me, peering into the apartment.

"You deal with terror, right?"

He nods.

"And what counts as terror?"

Sideburns shrugs with a weary smile. "These days?"

I mutter a few words about the axe and the train and then point into the bedroom where Didrik is on the phone, hurrying back out to the terrace and closing the door behind me.

She whimpers again. Guess it's time to figure out that formula gunk. You mix the powder with liquid and then microwave it until it's lukewarm. I've seen him do it, how hard can it be? But what happens if she refuses to eat? What happens if she just keeps crying and screaming and I lose my mind and start shaking her, even though I'm not allowed?

Angry voices from the apartment. Didrik hissing, the police officers replying in authoritative tones, the sound sends a twinge through my gut.

Didrik shouts for me, starts yelling about Becka, about Zack, I bring up the clip and turn up the volume to drown him out.

All those people burning cars and looting shops and vandalizing our city, do you seriously think they care about the polar bears, or tuna, or the Siberian tundra?

An American TV company has uploaded it. I'm standing alone on the stage, my voice tense and weak, almost nervous, as though I'm walking a tightrope.

The only thing driving them is hate. Because we're eating wrong, traveling wrong, thinking wrong, loving wrong, dreaming wrong. The climate movement has become a death cult, a violence machine that wants to chase us back to the caves.

She has been napping for two hours, maybe I should wake her soon, if I'm going to get her back into some sort of routine? Or would she be happier if I let her wake up naturally? I honestly have no idea.

But that's where we're ultimately heading anyway. I'm not denying that everything is going to shit, that technology and grand promises can't save us.

I feel my stomach turn again. My wrist has started aching, too. Strange, I didn't feel it at all yesterday. Ten hours since I last took anything, the diarrhea is on its way. I pour myself another glass of rosé. I'm going to do it this time. I have to do it.

We're the last people. But my life is still my life, and they've declared war on my ability to live it the way I want. And the thing is, in war . . . in war you don't talk about solar panels or lab-grown meat, you defend yourself and put up a fight, you crush those fuckers and never apologize.

The noise inside has died down. They've gone.

I take out the picture from the ultrasound. The darkness, the gray sac, the white mark that was the heart. I kiss it and put it down on the sofa between Snuggly and Becka's sleeping head.

"You're going to help me," I whisper. "You're both going to help me. We just need to make it through the night."

Six gleaming military planes fly in formation over the city, their roar following half a second behind them as they cross the pink-flecked sky, and just as I reach up to crush them like mosquitoes, all the lights go out.

3

WE DON'T INHERIT THE EARTH

THEY CHOSE MY FATHER TO BE KING.

I had just learned to read, and the box was on the carpet behind the shabby brown corduroy sofa in my grandparents' basement, in a corner that smelled like damp and old darkness. A perfectly ordinary dusty, lead-gray box, dry and rough beneath my fingertips, a piece of paper with *ANDERS!* written in neat black marker in the plastic pocket on one side. Lift the lid of the box and it was full of black ring binders, the kind with stiff covers and metal prongs that nipped your fingers when you tried to open them, the kind that Grandpa might have brought home from the office. The folders themselves were stuffed with sheets of cardboard that had been trimmed and hole-punched by hand, labeled with stickers reading *ANDERS!* and the date. Granny had cut out newspaper articles and stuck everything to do with *ANDERS!* on those sheets of cardboard.

Two narrow, dirty windows up by the ceiling, at the same level as the ground outside, shaded by dog roses and a set of wooden steps. What little sun filtered through painted a rectangle, a grainy veil of light on the floor beside me as I traced a finger over the tall black-and-white guy with dark curls and a gap-toothed grin and a racket in his hand, standing beside boys who looked at least three feet shorter than him. The gap in his teeth eventually disappeared but the smile remained the same, year after year, appearing alongside framed certificates and bouquets of flowers, then cups and trophies and huge prize checks, the pictures got bigger and the articles longer, in the local papers at first, with ads for Karlskrona pizzerias and lighting shops and cut-rate jeans, then nationwide, with ads for package holidays and X-rated movie theaters and the Swedish Social Democratic Party; there were front pages and headlines and in-depth interviews and superstar portraits, with full-color shots instead of black-and-white. My dad's handsome smile was everywhere as the air stood still in the cluttered basement where I was curled up on the old corduroy sofa, trying to feel something, anything, for him, graying with age, lumpy with glue.

The folders were at the top of the box, resting on a muddle of newspaper clippings, Granny probably ran out of energy to keep gluing them down in the end. Most were scraps of paper filled with match reports and sports columns, but there were also more and more clippings from gossip magazines, articles about his life with Johanna and the kids, blurry images from airports and hotel bars, taken from a distance on sandy beaches, Dad with his film-star looks and his long, dark curls, Jakob and Karolina pale and shy in the background. And once I'd dug through the sediment, all the way to the bottom, I found an envelope almost the exact same shade of gray as the box itself; it would have been easy to miss it was even there. I pulled it out and opened it, found a center spread inside, slightly tattered in the middle where it had once been stapled into an evening paper. It was from the summer of 1986, the year Dad won the Australian Open and got pretty far in both the French Open and Wimbledon and was the favorite for the U.S. Open, too. I had no idea what any of those things were, just that people often mentioned them when they listed all the amazing, beautiful things Dad had done or been expected to do.

But I understood the article perfectly. It said *HELL FOR KING—SWEDEN HAS ITS SAY*. The paper had asked people to send in suggestions for who should be king, and there were a whole load of pictures of men who worked in politics or wrote for the papers or played music or were on TV. But right at the very top, there was Dad, lifting a tennis trophy. They had drawn a gold crown on his head, and the image text read: *The King of Tennis? (Image is a composite.)*

They had chosen my dad to be king, and though the article contained words that helped me understand that the poll was just a bit of fun, that people had only torn out the form and written a name on the dotted line and posted it off in order to be in with a chance of winning one of three air mattresses, that it wasn't even *possible* to pick a new king because we already had that grumpy guy in the suit, the one with a bunch of weird letters in his name, Carl XVI Gustaf, I realized that he had come first in the only competition that mattered.

My dad had once been celebrated by an entire country. By people who didn't know him, who might never have even met him or seen him anywhere other than on TV. Strangers. He had been Sweden's most respected, admired, and beloved man.

When I was a little older, maybe seven or eight, some people made a documentary about him. This was after we moved to Uppsala, and Mom said it was OK for them to interview me so long as she could sit in on it, behind the camera, out of shot. And when the reporter asked when I'd first realized how big a deal my dad was, I told her about the box in the basement. I'd told the story plenty of times before, the kind of cute thing adults love hearing from children. I told her that I hadn't understood a thing about the matches, the tournaments, the names, the figures, but that I'd eventually found a clipping that I did understand, the magazine spread in which they'd chosen my dad to be king.

"You must have been so proud," said the cute woman in the tight white jeans. I didn't know what she meant, so I just mumbled something in reply, and then she asked me to repeat her words, *I was so proud of him then*. I did as she said, mostly because I was so surprised.

Because it had never occurred to me that I should be proud. It had never crossed my mind that what I should feel was pride, or joy, as though my dad was something I should boast about, as though the love the Swedish people felt for him had somehow rubbed off on me.

The warm, tingling feeling I'd had in my chest as I sat on the old corduroy sofa and the light filtering in through the basement window faded as I worked my way through the stupid article was jealousy. I was still a kid, but I knew that if Dad was king then that should make me a prince, that was how fairy tales worked—kings and queens, princes and princesses. But I was just a little boy in piss-flecked underpants, one who hadn't brushed his teeth since the summer holiday began, who spent his time rummaging through boxes of old junk in the basement of a house on the outskirts of Karlskrona. I felt like I'd been duped, robbed. He was everything, but I was nothing.

And it wasn't my fault, I decided there on the floor in the half darkness. I came along too late, that was all. They had chosen my father to be king, but the fun had stopped long before I was born.

FRIDAY, AUGUST 29

THE WATER IS GRAY, WITH FLASHES OF SILVER. THE OLD MAN IS sitting naked beside me, still dripping wet, eating cold ravioli straight from the tin. He's hungry, wolfing it down, and a blob of the jellylike tomato sauce drips from the spoon and lands on his left shoulder. He doesn't seem bothered, just uses his stubbly chin to rub some of it off while the rest trickles down onto his chest.

The horizon is slowly growing pale in the dusk.

Martina rocks in the evening breeze.

"Suffering," I say.

Dad nods blankly.

"Human suffering," I quickly clarify. "It'd be way too much if I included animal suffering, that's been the normal state of life for domesticated animals since the agricultural revolution—did you know that the meat industry carries out two hundred million slaughters a day? That's a Holocaust every hour, that's suffering on a scale it's almost impossible to take in, it's . . ."

He isn't listening, he just sighs and looks out across the water.

"But if I focus on human suffering . . . Homo sapiens, to be specific, because we obviously wiped out all the other human-like species, under conditions we can only try to imagine. If we didn't manage to get them with clubs or rocks, we probably killed them through starvation, cold, driving the kids into the forests to be torn to pieces by wild animals once we'd raped their mothers—DNA tests have actually shown that we're partly descended from Neanderthals."

He raises a bushy gray eyebrow.

"Really?"

I nod.

"All to the same extent?"

"Nah . . . probably some more than others. In their genes."

He chuckles.

"That explains a lot."

"But suffering," I continue, "as documented since people actually started recording their lives. And I don't mean during the big catastrophes, stuff like the Black Death, the wars, the Spanish Inquisition, but everyday life, as a matter of course. Aches. Trauma. Constant hunger. Corporal punishment, slavery, a justice system in which torture and sadism are standard. Our history is the history of pain, we've lived with a degree of suffering that the average citizen of a first world country can no longer even imagine. Did you know, for example, that—"

"But I can imagine it," Dad says calmly. "Just ask Rafael Nadal. His whole career, terrible pain. His foot, wrist, shoulder, knee, everywhere. Playing under injections, five hours against Federer, pumped full of painkillers."

I nod eagerly.

"Exactly, and in the past that applied to *everyone*, not just sportsmen—people wore out their bodies in the mine or the forest or in childbirth, or they experienced serious violence as a result of war or crime or sexual assault, suffering broken bones that never healed, infected wounds, phantom pains from missing body parts, gonorrhea, genital warts, syphilis."

Dad cackles.

"Like I said, ask Rafa, heh heh."

Martina is anchored in a bay off an island called Nåttarö, as far south as you can get in Stockholm's archipelago. The heat is like a pressure cooker, and we're both naked, half-sprawled on either side of the cockpit, each with a can of lager and a can of ravioli. That's how it has to be, according to Dad: straight from the tin. No messing about with plates or glasses that need washing, not when it's *just us boys*.

Sitting here like this is almost unbearable. I take off my cap and wipe the sweat from my forehead.

"The history of suffering, basically. Because there's a very interesting question in there: were people unhappier in the past? If, for example, I'd eaten so much sugar that all my teeth eventually rotted, I would have been in constant, agonizing pain and that would've made me *sad*, it would've significantly lowered my quality of life. But when they opened Gustav Vasa's grave they discovered that he had terrible dental problems—inflammation, holes in his jaw; he must have been in agony for years. Does that mean the pain ruined his life? Or did he just accept it somehow, because most people in the sixteenth century were in the same boat and there was nothing they could do about it? Maybe he didn't even know the reason. Do you suffer less if everyone around you is suffering too? Do you suffer less if you don't know why?"

Dad sighs again and scratches his damp brow. A slimy gob of tomato sauce is still clinging to the hair around his left nipple, glistening in the fading sunlight.

"You know," he says, "Rafa has been in so much pain that he sometimes tries to psych out his opponents. Players usually pep each other up before a match, sharing training tips and that kind of thing, but not Rafa. So intense, that guy. Robin told me about this one time in Paris . . ." He launches into an anecdote I've heard a thousand times before, about Nadal trying to get a psychological advantage over Söderling by walking behind him from the changing rooms to center court. I eat the rest of the tasteless, rubbery ravioli and wash it down with a mouthful of lukewarm beer. I hate beer. If I have to drink alcohol, I'd much rather have a hard soda or a cider, but this is how he wants it: canned food and cans of beer, because it's *just us boys* out here.

The last week of summer is always our week. It started as a joke, it's so typical of him to make his constant excuses and half-assed conscience into a joke. When I was younger we sometimes had an obligatory week together in Monte Carlo, always during the last week of the school holiday, when he couldn't put it off or come up with any more excuses or tell Mom or Granny and Grandpa that he wanted to wait *until the good weather really arrived* before he had his week with me. Then he bought *Martina*, and for the past six or seven years we've come sailing, usually around Stockholm, and I remember that when I was a kid we used to joke about the whole weather thing, that it was typical that it'd be during this cold, blustery autumn week that *the good weather really arrived*, but now we're sitting here, sweating buckets. The water is a velvety seventy-seven degrees, and it's too hot to spend any time on deck during the day.

"You want another beer?" he asks. "I've got some Czech stuff, you said you'd been getting into Czech stuff, didn't you?"

"Could go for something to snack on, too," I say, pointing to the cabin. "There were some chips, weren't there?"

"We just had dinner."

"Yeah, but . . ."

I notice Dad glance over to me, to my round, sunburned body, the rolls around my waist, the flab on my chest, and I wish I had a towel.

"Have a cold potato," he says, looking away.

"A what?"

"A cold potato. If you're hungry, I mean. There are some left from lunch."

"But . . . I don't want a potato."

He laughs.

"You wanted chips, didn't you? Aren't they potato? With a load of added fat and sugar. Besides, we don't know when we'll next get to a shop. Better to use up the leftovers than open a new bag."

It usually happens much earlier than this. When I was younger, he would bring it up while we were still at the airport in Nice, something about how he could tell I must've had plenty of cinnamon buns at Granny's place that summer, or that we should go shopping for clothes because I seemed to have gone up a few sizes since he last saw me. But he's pulled himself together this year—or tried to, anyway. It's taken him two days. That's always something.

He knocks back the rest of his beer and burps loudly, putting his entire body into it. I see his stomach muscles tense, a bleating, bellowing sound that echoes across the empty bay. He smiles, pleased with himself, as though he's just passed a test of strength.

"What were you saying, buddy, suffering?"

I nod.

"We'll have to see, I'm not sure it'd work as a PhD thesis, maybe just a popular science book or even a series of books."

"Books?" he says. "Do people still read books?"

"I could imagine it working on TV, too. I'm thinking about reaching out to Netflix to see if they're interested—people like documentaries, and stuff about history is really popular right now."

He nods thoughtfully.

"So, what do you think?" I ask. "Could it be something?"

A heron takes off from the trees, flying low across the bay. The unnatural curve of its throat makes me think of someone with a neck injury, wearing one of those big braces made from plastic and steel that forces them to drift around with a kind of artificial dignity. It's so quiet that we can hear its rhythmic, slowly accelerating wingbeats. The calm surface of the water captures the sound, transmitting it, amplifying it.

"You're nineteen," Dads says.

He gets up and climbs onto the foredeck. Stands by the edge, one hand on the shroud and the other on his dick. I look away, there's a limit to how much *us boys* I can handle.

The light, rippling sound of piss as it breaks the mirror-still surface of the water.

"If you want to go to university, I'll support you," he continues, with a sigh of pleasure. "And if you need to retake any exams in order to get in, we can sort that out too."

"Jakob started a company," I say, trying to make my voice deep, calm, like his. "You helped him out with start-up capital, a car, an office, computers. Contacts."

"Jakob was different. Have I ever told you about the time he went to confirmation camp out on Värmdö? All the candy?"

"Yes."

Dad smiles at the memory.

"He took a whole load of candy out there with him, you kids were all the same, but after he'd been out there a week or so he called to say that he needed more, so I drove out there with a few bars of chocolate and a bag of licorice, I think that was it, and then . . ."

"Dad. I've. Heard. This. Before."

He leans forward slightly to avoid getting the last few drops on his toes. The movement makes the boat rock.

"You've had a new computer every year since you were what, five? Tablets and phones all the time, too. My God, I remember all those empty boxes scattered around the place. And you always got a new PlayStation as soon as a new model came out."

"I'm not talking about toys! I really want to make a go of this."

Dad shakes off his dick, wipes his hand on his bare thigh, and turns back to me.

"When I was your age," he says, his voice a drawl, "I was flying around the world. All alone, no coach, nothing. I moved to Monaco when I was twenty, no help from anyone. Sorted out all the paperwork, found myself an apartment, did everything."

He's still standing by the gunwale. There must be something about sportsmen and nudity, all those years of physicality, of showers, changing rooms, massages, hospitals. Face your enemies naked, celebrate naked, hate naked. Command respect, even though you're naked.

"Though I was never actually there, of course. I lived out of a backpack. In hotels." He smiles. "Or with different chicks, heh heh. The best years of my life, not that I knew it at the time."

The hair on his crotch is curly, grayish-black, his glans pale blue against his thigh.

"I think your mother spoiled you a bit much. Me too, of course," he hurries to add. "I'm not saying it was all Malin's fault. I have to take responsibility too, obviously, especially now, and . . . and this is something I've been thinking about for a while. That you need to get going. Do something for yourself."

He moves slowly over the deck, around the mast, pulls on one of the lines, pushes something to one side with his foot. Comes back to the cockpit and slumps down with a sigh.

"So I don't want to give you any more money. Like I said, supporting you through your studies is one thing, but if you're just going to go home and drift through life, then I'm not going to bankroll that. It's for your own good."

An encouraging smile. A strong, wiry hand on my knee.

"You see where I'm coming from, don't you, buddy? You're nineteen, and it's great that you have all these dreams and ideas—I had them too when I was your age—but there are just some things you have to do on your own. So, I'm cutting you off."

He says the last part in an American accent, that's kind of his thing, whenever he wants to emphasize something, or if he's half-joking, he switches to Hollywood English, a voice that makes him sound like he's trying to imitate Harrison Ford.

"I've never asked for charity," I hear myself say. "I've never come to you and begged. I mean, I'm living in the apartment, so all I'm really asking for is a bit of money so I can travel around and gather material, there are some incredible collections from the Middle Ages in Florence and Rome, and London too, of course."

"Right," says Dad, smacking his lips. "The apartment. I'm glad you brought that up. We need to talk about the apartment. Once we've gotten rid of the damn bedbugs, I'm planning to get in touch with a real estate agent I know."

The sky has started to darken, and the trees around the bay are now nothing but grayish-blue and black silhouettes. I see the first flash of a lighthouse in the distance.

"I'm sick of Stockholm. And the country's gone to the dogs, hasn't it? All the shootings, the gang violence, the uncontrolled immigration and a welfare state on its knees—despite the highest taxes on earth."

"That's the right-wing populist narrative."

He sighs.

"Nadja has been looking at a little vineyard outside Adelaide. We were down there this summer, after the TV thing. Incredibly beautiful place. She's going to paint, run courses. I can build my own court, give private lessons, people are willing to pay a fortune for that kind of thing—I'm a legend down there. Cycling, walking, fishing. Making wine. What do I have left, maybe fifteen good years? I want to make the most of them."

He smiles through the darkness, pale blue eyes shining, beautiful white teeth.

"You can take over *Martina*, if you promise to look after her. And we'll still have our boys' week, of course."

———

Dad has gone off to his cabin at the stern and I'm in mine at the bow, scrolling on my phone. Checking what Douglas and Toffe are up to, liking pictures, watching a funny clip of some lame guy with a baby, threatening people on a train with an axe. A few old bloopers, a couple of TikToks, a clip from a protest in town today. The dumb bimbo Dad has staying in our apartment was there, apparently, there's a video of her giving a speech. The sound is off, but she's really sexy in a kind of high school, unobtainable way, and I get turned on and automatically gravitate to the porn sites, my phone in my left hand while my right moves up and down, quickly on to the other pages with the slightly more hard-core videos, the ones I try to forget afterward, and my hand is moving faster and faster and I'm getting close, my left hand fumbles between clips and suddenly I feel the boat rocking. Softly, almost imperceptibly, but still. It's rocking.

I immediately stop what I'm doing and the boat does the same a few seconds later. I try again. Same thing. The minute I start masturbating even slightly rhythmically, it starts rocking in time with my hand.

Dad will wake up if I keep going. He'll think the anchor has come loose, that the boat is drifting; he'll get up and start pottering about on deck and then he'll work it out. *I'll be damned*, he'll say, *what do we have here, right then, top o' the morning, you little wanker*. I try to see the funny side of things and feel my dick trembling in my hand.

My first impulse is to go ashore, to find a bathroom somewhere and finish off there. But as the horniness fades, my mind clears. We're anchored in the middle of a bay. The only way to get ashore is in the little rubber dinghy, and how is that going to go?

Yeah, how is that going to go?

Isn't this my problem? That I'm always giving up before I've even tried?

I put my phone down, get onto my knees, and open the hatch. It's hazy, no stars, but in the light from the lantern I can see the rubber dinghy strapped to the guard wire. We've barely used it over the past few years, not since I was younger and we were sprawled on some rocks somewhere and Dad thought I should *go off and explore* while he got drunk with a bunch of admiring strangers. It would be easy enough to loosen the straps, lower the dinghy into the water, drop the two blue plastic oars into it, and then carefully climb down. Cut the moorings. Set off. Why have I never done that before?

Who's been stopping you, you fucking loser?

The voice in my head is cold, dry. Judgmental. I should go back to bed. I don't need to jerk off, not really. I feel more like eating something.

I crawl back into the forepeak, close the hatch, and slowly open the door into the main cabin, tiptoeing past the sofa and the dining table into the kitchen. I check the shelf beside the jar of instant coffee to see if there's any Nesquik, a few spoonfuls of chocolate powder straight from the tub usually does the trick, but Dad hasn't bought any this year, he probably thinks I'm too old for it. With deft hands I open the little wooden door to the pantry instead, carefully grip the edge of a packet of chips between my index finger and thumb to stop it from rustling.

Have a cold potato.

I drop the bag.

Have a cold potato, because if you can't even manage to row a little rubber dinghy, then you don't deserve any chips.

I can hear Dad's quiet snoring through the door. We used to sit up late together, watching TV shows or playing cards, he taught me how to read nautical charts one summer, to tell the difference between the different types of lighthouses and buoys; we talked about the long sailing trips we would take once I was older, to Croatia, the West Indies, or at least the outer archipelago, maybe even all the way out to Svenska Högarna on the eastern fringes.

But I'm older now and we aren't doing any of that. We just chat for a while before he goes back to his cabin to watch TV for an hour or two and then falls asleep.

It's because he resents you. You're a disappointment. No, worse. You bore him.

I grab the bag of chips again. Crispy Bacon & Sour Cream. I have a sudden inspiration and carefully open the fridge, take out a can of beer. Staropramen. Czech.

———

The water laps softly beneath me, a comforting, summery sound that seems to reverberate through my body. I'm naked in the dinghy, a cheap, basic model, more a toy than anything. The oars are loose in the oarlocks, but I keep going anyway, splashing and jolting my way forward. I remember seeing a nice rocky cape at the point where the bay opens out onto the sea, and I can just picture myself chilling there with my beer and my chips (and a bit of porn, too). Sweet. The kind of thing teenagers are supposed to do.

It was hot and stuffy in the boat, but out here on the water the breeze is cool, almost chilly. I was planning to put on some sweatpants and a T-shirt, but that would have ruined the spontaneity of it. I regret being in such a rush now. The plastic feels damp beneath me, and I have goose bumps on my arms. I try to keep my eyes fixed on *Martina* to avoid drifting off course, but she quickly fades to a ghost ship in the darkness, dimly lit by the lone anchor lamp.

I turn my head and try to make out the rocks. A faint shadow, still pretty far away. They looked closer in the daylight, is the bay really that big?

Water keeps sloshing into the dinghy, and I clamp my phone between my thighs to protect it. No funny business now, slow, steady movements, no splashing with the oars. Pull through the back, not the arms. Glide through the water. I'm freezing now, practically shivering, but with the cold comes a sense of pride, *none of you expected this*. The kid has gone out to sea in the buff in the middle of the night, and all so he can rub one out in peace. Crazy times.

When we weigh anchor in the morning, I'll point out the cape and tell Dad all about it. *I rowed out there last night, by the way, just sat on the rocks and chilled for a while, had a beer, you've gotta make the most of these summer nights, you know?* and he'll cackle and say *let me know next time, I'll join you*, and he even might take out a pack of cards or ask if I want to watch a TV show with him.

Or maybe he'll think I'm lying? I could leave the can and the empty bag of chips on the rocks, somewhere they'll be visible from the water? Point using my thumb, say *whoops, forgot to take my garbage with me last night*. Something like that, cocky. And then he'll ask what I mean and I'll be all, *oh, I just went ashore for a bit, hung out on the rocks over there, chilled*.

The dinghy scrapes against something hard beneath me. I turn around. A rugged gray rock has emerged from the darkness. Two more strokes, then I let go of the oars and twist around to grab it with my hand. It feels cold and rough beneath my fingers, and I fumble for a hold. There's a sharp edge sticking out, and I wrap my hand around it, get a good grip. I grab the beer and the chips and throw them up into darkness, then get onto my knees in the little dinghy, the rope in one hand. Suddenly it's as though there are two versions of me: one who hauls himself up onto solid ground with his right hand, planting a bare, nimble foot onto the rock and following it with a leap into the darkness, and another who feels the cheap piece-of-shit dinghy float backward the minute he pushes forward, who is briefly left hanging between the boat and the rock, like some ridiculous cartoon character, before the laws of gravity conspire with his pathetic core and back muscles and his hand is forced to let go and his upper body plunges into the water a split second before his legs flip the dinghy.

The water is an insult, a stale, dark jelly that floods my mouth and nose and throat. My feet are tangled somehow, and I panic for a moment before managing to struggle away from the dinghy and get my legs beneath me so that I can kick upward, I'm not even sure where the surface is in the darkness, everything is upside down, bubbles, shadows, evil dreams. I cough, splutter, gasp, flap my arms, and in the far, far distance I see the boat and the lantern, it looks like a lonely star above the mirror-still surface of the water, and I hear black horses galloping through my vocal cords as I roar *DADDY*.

SATURDAY, AUGUST 30

IT'S BEEN A HELL OF A SUMMER. I WAS ACTUALLY SUPPOSED TO start working once I finished school. Well, "working," Douglas and Toffe had taken over a restaurant down in the resort town of Båstad, and they asked last winter if I wanted to head down there with them. No dog work, obviously, they were quick to point that out, there were plenty of people desperate for shifts in the kitchen or waiting tables, Douglas would be in charge of them while Toffe looked after the financial side of things. I wouldn't really have to do anything, they promised, just talk to the guests, welcome people by the front door, hang out at the bar from time to time, mix drinks for fun. It didn't pay much, of course, but I'd get a bit of cash in hand, free food and parties, plus I could stay with them in the house they'd rented, a place with a sick yard where we could hang out during the day.

You'd be, like, our public face, said Douglas, and I knew exactly what they meant. Dad had taught me early on that it's nothing to be ashamed of, it's not ugly, you just have to take it as it is. His best anecdote is about the time he partied his way around Melbourne a few years after he retired from competitive tennis. He had free tickets to all the Australian Open matches, naturally, and a group of women came over and asked if he wanted to join them on a bachelorette party the next weekend.

Business girls, you know? Real broads, with the clothes and the bags and the shoes, the whole lot. They were having a party in a house on the coast, it had its own hard court and they wanted me to show up topless, surprise their friend, and play a bit of tennis—how d'you like these balls, heh heh.

Douglas said it would be enough for me to hang out at the restaurant for a few hours every night, that the important thing was that my name was everywhere, on all the press releases and photos and the VIP invites, *André*

Hell, youngest son of tennis legend Anders Hell, is a co-owner of Båstad's hottest new restaurant with his friends Douglas Merithz and Christoffer Petraeus.

I'd just started dating Malin at the time, and she was seriously pissed off, Dad always says with a huge grin. *Yeah, and they probably want you to strip too, don't they,* he mimics her shrill voice. *So I said no, of course.* At this point his expression changes and he looks serious, almost glum. *And missed out on all the fun. Champagne, splashing about in the pool—imagine being a single guy at a bachelorette, surrounded by a load of sexually starved upper-class MILFs who've had a few drinks. Why not make the most of it? You only live once, you know?*

As summer approached, Douglas started whining about there being too little "buzz" around the restaurant. Opening night was only two weeks away but there were still plenty of tables available, and though they'd sent out the invites to the VIP event and celebrity parties months ago, they hadn't had many replies, mostly from friends; the advertising agency bill was due soon, and they hadn't even started paying the rent on the property yet, plus there was the amazing house with the sick yard to pay for, the wages too, though people were only paid on an hourly basis.

I said I didn't have any more money. Douglas was quiet for a moment, and then he said *what about your old man, though?* and I mumbled something vague about accounts and funds and long-term investments I couldn't access, but he interrupted me, *no, no, I didn't mean it like that, I meant maybe your old man could come down? Bring a few friends? Show his face a bit? Or at least talk to a few of the papers?*

It took me three days to get hold of Dad. He was taking part in some TV show where a bunch of celebrities were cycling from coast to coast in Australia, and he was in the middle of the outback. Meeting some journalists in Alice Springs tomorrow! he wrote, 200km to go! Will get you a bit of PR! Followed by a sun and a smiling face and a tensed bicep.

A few days later, Mom's sister Nathalie got in touch to say that she was staying in a house in San Francisco, right in the center of town, a place with a patio and a garden—even its own little pool. I'd been to San Francisco a few times before, it was one of Mom's favorite cities, we always used to rent an Airbnb somewhere. One of Nathalie's friends from her modeling days had married a Silicon Valley millionaire and bought a house in Pacific Heights, and she was letting her borrow it while they went on a meditation retreat to Kathmandu.

Why don't you come over? she said. *It would be so nice.* I didn't have to spend the whole time with her, of course, *but you could use it as a base*, she said down the line, *for your . . . adventures?* Mom had probably told her I was gay at some point, she was convinced I was. It made no difference what I told her, how often I used her computer to watch porn without deleting the search history afterward, or how often I farted at the dinner table, she'd decided I was gay when I was just eight, when I not only refused to play tennis but soccer, hockey, and golf, too.

We could go to Alcatraz, said Nathalie. *Or drive down to Monterey and visit the aquarium.* I said no and reminded her that I was going to Båstad to work in a restaurant with a couple of friends. She was quiet for a few seconds, then asked if I'd seen what was online.

I never heard from Douglas and Toffe. Dad blamed it on the cycling and the heat, he'd been exhausted when he got to Alice Springs, and the TV crew hadn't even let him catch his breath or take a shower first, they just sprung the journalists on him, to capture the whole effect, the *reality feeling*, as they put it: a sweaty, exhausted tennis star, parched bush in the background. And to top it all, the sponsors had wanted him to have a beer in his hand during the interview. *And you know*, Dad laughed down the line, *it's just so easy to knock that back and ask for another. It was ice-cold, I mean seriously cold, and then they asked about that restaurant you were starting and I don't know what came over me.*

So Nathalie sent me the money and I caught a direct flight, and sure, as I sat in the taxi on my way into the city—an early morning in June, the air practically quivering above the expressway, the huge billboards, the plasticky smell of the car, a Starbucks coffee and a doughy, sickly sweet cinnamon roll in my hand, the glittering, dizzying feeling of The City as you reach the top of the hill and see the silver platter stretching out in front of you, the bridge to Oakland to the right, Golden Gate straight ahead, the gentle hills, the skyscrapers, the slender pyramid of the Transamerica building, the muddle of chalky white rooftops like a filthy snowdrift surrounded by gray, glittering water; San Francisco is so small and cute when you really think about it, it reminds me of Monte Carlo in that sense, though it's nowhere near as cramped—I thought that maybe everything would be OK after all.

The summer I was nineteen, I lived in San Francisco, I told my cinnamon bun. That wasn't something you could say about a loser, it could practically be the opening line of a halfway decent novel.

And the first few days *were* fine. I went for long walks up and down the hills, trying to get in shape, rewarding myself with an ice cream or a can of Coke in the blazing sun. Either that or I wandered around Chinatown, and if it got too hot I'd nip into an icy-cool café somewhere, or walk around one of the department stores. I took a load of pictures, too. Everywhere you turn in San Francisco it's like your eyes are telling you to grab your phone and take a photograph *now*, it makes no difference whether you're standing in a dingy alleyway in the red-light district in North Beach or at the top of Telegraph Hill, looking out across the city, it's like an artwork you can never get enough of—though later, when I wanted to upload the pictures, I wasn't happy with any of them. Nathalie and I watched TV together in the evenings, and we went out to eat a few times, but mostly we just ordered take-out pizza and Thai food and ate it on the terrace by the pool.

One evening, after I'd been there maybe two weeks, I was just about to go to bed when she shouted over and asked if I wanted to smoke with her. I went out into the little garden, where she was lying flat on a sunbed, staring up at the stars. There were a load of dead plants in reddish-brown terra-cotta pots out there, and the tang of marijuana mixed with the scent of dry earth and withered plants, which in turn mixed with the aroma of food and exhaust fumes and tarmac and rubbish and everything else given off by a hot, filthy city at night.

She sucked on the little joint and then passed it to me as she held her breath in that lame way some people do, lips pressed together.

"Only if you want some, that is."

I took a drag and held it in, felt the sweet, burned, almost moist smoke radiate across my face.

The summer I was nineteen, I lived in San Francisco.

"Your mum liked this kind of thing," she said with a soft smile. "She was here the summer before she met Anders, did you know that? Stayed on the other side of the bay, up in the mountains. It was because of the golf, just for the week, but she told me how magical it was."

"I remember something about a golf tournament," I said, "but she didn't mention anything about dope."

Nathalie laughed.

"Yeah, she got to know an American girl there. Neither of them made the cut, so they spent a whole afternoon smoking and looking out at the city together." She smiled and mimicked Mum as a young woman, making her voice light, naive, girlish: "*You could see the fog rolling in from the sea, lying in wait like a big gray pussycat! And then it slowly gobbled up Golden Gate Bridge and the buildings and sort of . . . swept over the mountains like an old woollen blanket, and then we were high and the city was gone. It felt like you could reach out and touch it, it was totally amaaazing!*"

Without looking at me, Nathalie held out her hand and I passed her the joint. She took a deep drag, her eyes on the stars. Breathed out a thin column of sweet, herbal dirt.

"She loved this. *If I could start over, I'd be a hippie in Haight-Ashbury,* that's what she always used to say. *Or a beatnik in North Beach. Or I'd study at Berkeley. I'd have a house up in the mountains with a balcony looking out to sea, and I'd sit there in the afternoon and get high and watch the fog rolling in, that would've been amaaazing!*"

She handed me the joint again and I took one toke, two, three. My head was full of treacle.

"Malin loved this," she repeated. "I went over there today, while you were out. I still had the address from one of her old letters, from back when we wrote letters, you know, she was always traveling to one place or another with the golf, but no matter where she went she wanted me to write to her. So I had the address, but the house is gone, the golf course is gone, there was a fire in the mountains last summer, or maybe it was the one before last, and the whole area is off-limits, a building site, there was a sign about some development but I couldn't see anyone there, it was just full of . . . shipping containers and fences and . . ."

I leaned forward to pass her the joint, but she didn't react, barely seemed to realize I was there.

"So I drove to a viewpoint and found a shady spot beneath a tree where I could sit and look out across the city. The plan was to try to see it as she did. I'd even bought some weed . . . and I sat there, waiting for the fog. I wanted to do what she'd done, you know . . . to get closer to her in some sense. Stupid, really. But I sat there anyway. And as the fog rolled in I would light the joint and get high and then Malin would somehow . . . in the fog she'd . . ."

She trailed off, her lips moving without a sound. I couldn't think of anything to say, so I took another drag and held my breath for as long as I could before I exhaled.

"But it never came," my aunt eventually said. "The sun shone all afternoon, a clear blue sky. Super hot, not a single cloud, no fucking fog, nothing. A couple of people turned up and had a picnic nearby, and I asked them about it as I was heading back to the car. *No more fog*, they said. *There's no more fog.*"

My head was spinning and I still couldn't think of anything to say, so I just held the joint out to her again. This time she took it, with a loud sniff.

"Malin really fucking cared about that kind of thing," she continued. "She loved getting out into nature and she loved golf, but I remember one time she told me how anxious she felt after watching some TV documentary about the drought here, how the golf courses use more water than all the hotels and restaurants and hospitals combined, how a single golf course in Palm Springs goes through as much water in a single day as an entire African village does in a decade, and there are over one hundred golf courses out there, it's completely insane, 122-degree heat and she . . ."

I saw the glowing tip of the joint in the darkness. It cast a faint glow over her face, tears glistening on her cheeks, and I tuned out for a while, grinning when I realized that I could actually choose the volume, as though my head was a computer and I could just turn down the sound, dim the lights, and sink into a soft, fuzzy slumber. My aunt's voice was like the chatter between tracks on the radio in an Uber, you have no idea who is talking or what they're saying or even which station you're listening to, that's all utterly irrelevant, and besides, you've almost reached your destination.

"André?"

Her voice cut through the frothed milk, making me jump.

"André? Are you listening to me? It got more frequent later on, when she was ill."

"Yeah. Much more frequent."

"Your mom was *really* worried, André. She talked about this, about everything we're going through right now. About how you'd cope. She used to say that there was an old Indian proverb that says, *We don't inherit the earth from our ancestors, we borrow it from our children.* I mean, the Amazon rain forests are being turned into a fucking savannah, and I don't mean a hundred years from now, but *right this moment*, it's happening *right now*, André, and—"

"That's a myth," I said.

It didn't even sound like my voice. It was a tired old man in a basement somewhere, talking in his sleep.

"What?"

"The proverb, or whatever you want to call it. Some American environmentalist made it up in the seventies. And then they came up with the whole Indian thing to make it sound better."

Nathalie studied me through half-open eyes.

"Is that true?"

I slowly got up from the lounge chair. I felt like I was a ghost in a film, one of those scenes where the person leaves their body behind, slumped in the chair while their blurry spirit rises up out of it. Either that or a zombie waking up in some apocalyptic movie and then staggering around the place, back from the dead. Everything started spinning and I braced myself against the wall.

"People think the Indians were so fucking nice, but they wiped out countless species when they got here. Giant tortoises, mammoths, carnivorous birds. Bears that weighed almost a ton. All of it gone. Thanks for the loan, you know?"

I wanted to say something else, but I needed to take a leak, so I just turned around and walked away. And when I got back from the bathroom, she had gone to bed.

———

The rock is so cold and hard beneath me that I've lost all feeling in my ass. It's so quiet you could hear a pin drop, so quiet that I can hear my own heart pounding like a sewing machine.

I still can't believe I'm actually alive. Everywhere I turned, the rocks were smooth, steep, and covered in slimy seaweed. The rubber dinghy had drifted off in the darkness, and my phone was gone too. I heaved myself up, slipped back down, plunged beneath the surface. Again. Again. Again. I shouted. I roared. Again. Again. Again. This went on for an eternity, several minutes at least; I honestly thought I was going to die, and I accepted that. I made a few last half-hearted attempts, reached up to the rocks with cold, stiff fingers, and kicked my legs, which were like spaghetti in the water, trying to haul my body up the rock. I felt the rough surface beneath my chest for a few split seconds before I slipped or was sucked back down into the void.

But now I'm sitting here, up where the rocks flatten out, about six feet above the surface of the water. I open my eyes, raise a shaking hand to my face. It looks like a shadow against the dark sky. I wave it, sense the movement in my joints. It's real. I'm here.

I try opening my mouth, moving my lips.

"Fuck."

All the salty water and shouting has left me with a sore throat, a husky voice. But it's me talking.

"Fuck a duck."

I'm naked, shivering despite the warm evening. My hair is plastered to my forehead, and I push it back from my eyes, feel my cold fingertips brush across my face.

I don't understand a thing, but somehow I must have managed to make it up here. I must have panicked, become desperate, discovered strengths I didn't realize I had.

I didn't die. I survived.

"Fuck a duck up the ass!"

I try to laugh but start coughing instead, then shaking with cold. I pull my legs in to my chest, use my hands to brace myself on the rock, get to my feet, swaying. I can see the lantern glowing in the distance. Dad.

I get down onto my knees, crawl slowly along the rocks. Something glitters in front of me, in a hollow beside one of the rocks. I shuffle down toward it, reach out. A can.

Staropramen.

I clamber back up onto the flat surface again, wrap my arms around my knees, fiddle with the can with trembling, aching fingers until I manage to hook a nail beneath the tab and crack it open. The hiss it makes sounds so alien, like an echo from another world. I pour the liquid into my mouth, feel it spill down my chin. My body is so cold that the beer actually feels warm on my skin. I hate the harsh, bitter taste, but I force myself to swallow, want my body to feel something else, anything. Drink, deep gulps, *it's just bread*, I tell myself, *beer is like drinking bread: energy, calories, warmth.*

Dad sitting with a beer in his hand under the hot Australian sun, a cap from his own clothing brand on his head, smiling his wrinkled wolf's smile at the TV cameras. *The kid and his restaurant, right, yeah . . . down in Båstad, wasn't it . . . right, right . . . ha ha, they're a couple of parasites from his school days, those two . . . a pair of fucking daddy'll-pay brats, ha ha.*

So is that where we'll find you this summer?

Dad rolls his eyes and smiles again. He has new teeth, big and white; he looks like an old-school Hollywood star in the evening light, holds up the sponsor's beer with the label to the camera.

Yeah, ha ha, yeah, sure, but only if the pizza joint across the street is full, that's the only reason I'd ever set foot in there with all those fucking coke whores. Thought I'd already found enough ass for the boy.

I flinch and look up. The rock feels rough beneath me. A bit of gravel has found its way between my butt cheeks and my balls have gone numb, my toes too. After several days of sweating on the boat, the cold feels absurd, unnatural, like getting toothpaste in your eye. What time is it? One? Two a.m.? It's late August, which means the sun won't be up for hours.

I can't stay here. I can't just sit here, waiting for dawn. I just can't.

I get up, shake my body, stamp my bare feet on the rock, paying no attention to the pain. I slap my arms against my sides to get my blood pumping, shout, groan, fill my lungs with air and bellow. Beer sloshes from the can, and I take a few more deep gulps before throwing it into the darkness with a howl. It hits the surface of the water with a pathetic, barely audible splash. I start groping the rocks around me for the bag of chips, but it's nowhere to be found.

A cool, damp wind is blowing from the east, and I'm now so cold that it feels like my guts have goose bumps.

Dad! I roar toward the boat again, coughing. My throat feels wounded, raw. Nothing.

I turn away from the bay, toward the open water. There must be something there, out on one of the islands, someone having a crayfish party or a late summer wedding, even a sleepless night in their cottage, I can't be the only person left in the world. I shout *hello* and feel my throat burn, and that's when it dawns on me.

It's strange I didn't see it before, it's been there the whole time.

Because there are houses out there, I know that, huge waterfront properties with little boathouses and jetties and saunas, the kind of people who buy houses in the archipelago love doing woodwork and DIY. I turn toward where Stockholm should be. Big cities emit so much light, and it floods outward, a glowing dome stretching up into space. This close to the city, it never gets fully dark. There's even a name for it: light pollution.

But it is. It's dark dark. All the lights are out. The sky isn't gray, as it should be; it's jet black, no nuance whatsoever. As though someone has draped a thick black veil over the world, and you can no longer see even its outline.

I close my eyes. Open them. Close them again. It makes no difference.

Hello, I shout again, weaker this time, more to prove that I really am still here.

Hello, I whisper. *Where did you all go?*

I stopped being afraid of the dark when I was twelve years old. It happened in Karlskrona, while I was at Granny and Grandpa's for fall break. This was after everything with Mom, and I snuck out one night, all alone, to wander around the quiet, dark neighborhood with her old electroclash in my headphones. The fear of the darkness, of ghosts and pedophiles, came on suddenly like a deadweight in my gut, and I started running, wanted to get away from it, running past the damp orchards and the bare hedges, over cobblestones, through a disgusting playground, convinced I could hear footsteps over the drum track in my ears. I reached the boatyard and tore across the gravel, the sailboats on their wooden cradles towering above me like standing stones. My breath formed clouds in the air, and I thought I could see someone moving between the hulls; none of the hiding places were good enough, there were no corners, no holes, no doors I could close.

The streetlamps cast their glow all around me, and the cold light and the dark shadows built a never-ending labyrinth of white boats and long gray keels beneath dark green tarps.

I panicked, grabbed a boarding ladder and stepped onto a wooden stool, hauled myself up. Before I knew it I was inside, beneath the tarp, in the cockpit. The strange, unfamiliar feeling of being inside a yacht that had been brought ashore. There was something stunted about it, handicapped, robbed of its water it becomes nothing but a cramped plastic hut. I crouched down and crept through to the cabin, sat in the stranger's boat, breathed in the scent of fabric, oil, gas, old adventures, and long-lost summer holidays, surrounded by dense, animal darkness.

And that was when I stopped being afraid. I realized that the darkness brought safety, because if I couldn't see anyone, then no one could see me, either. My hand groped the cushions. There was a toolbox, the owner of the boat must have been fixing something. A knife, a screwdriver, I don't remember which, something sharp, I gripped it in my hand. No one would be able to get close to me without me noticing them.

Slowly but surely I felt the knot loosen and the tension fade. I was the dangerous one. I was the one lurking in the darkness.

A small slit in the cushion. A small chink out of the wooden panel. Just for fun, to make sure the knife or the screwdriver or whatever it was actually worked, that it had *bite*.

A few more notches. Stabs. I pulled out the padding, hacked it to pieces. More tools: a saw, an axe. The dashboard. Cupboard doors. Kitchen implements and old cardboard boxes full of rice and pasta and muesli.

Mom's music pounding in my ears.

Need to pee. Need to shit. Who cares. No one can see me. No one knows.

Serves those motherfuckers right.

I fill my lungs with the crisp, raw sea air and scream into the blackness.

Scream.

Scream.

I turn around and glance back over to *Martina*. How far can it be? Five hundred feet? A thousand? Suddenly I feel neither cold nor tired.

It's time to stop being afraid, to stop feeling sorry for myself. I'll swim back, climb on board, and curl up in my warm, cozy sleeping bag.

In the darkness, no one can see me. In the darkness, they can't touch me. I'll find my cubbyhole in the darkness.

And once I'm there, I'll come up with a plan to kill him.

Just need to finish that wank first, I think, my hand automatically moving down to my crotch before I remember that my phone is gone and that it'll take forever out here in the cold, it's really just wasted time and the sky is already turning pale pink in the east.

━━━━━

They had chosen my father to be king and he lived in a kingdom by the Mediterranean, in a place where all the streets were named after princes and princesses. As we sped around in his red BMW, I saw signs for *rue Princesse Caroline, rue Princesse Florestine, rue Princesse Antoinette*, and just plain old *rue des Princes*. Up above, the mountain plunged down toward the beach and the buildings sat on shimmering white steps like pieces of Lego, so steep that it felt like the whole city was about to come toppling down on top of us. He parked the car in a garage that was as clean and sterile as a hospital, and as we took the elevator up to his apartment he smiled and said *eleven hundred square feet, buddy!* The air smelled strange, like bleach, and everything was gleaming and silver. *Plus three hundred twenty-five square feet of terrace looking out onto the water!* I didn't really know what a terrace was, never mind a square foot, but Dad seemed happy about it, so I smiled and said *cool beans* and one wall of the elevator was a huge mirror and I saw him look down at me with the expression of someone watching a cute animal try and fail to perform a trick.

His apartment had two dark bedrooms and a huge open-plan living room that was flooded with light from the panoramic windows, and I immediately ran over to check out the view. It was morning, and Monte Carlo was bathed in a pale haze, skyscrapers and a muddle of buildings and then a white sky above an expanse of white water and dazzlingly white yachts, everything in shades of white, stretching out to the clouded, barely visible horizon.

"It's man-made, the whole place," said Dad, ruffling my hair. "Do you see where they're building over there?" He pointed to an empty scrap of land in the harbor where the cranes loomed like a family of dinosaurs, the faint rumble of boring machines cutting through the noise of the traffic.

"There was a hotel that sprung a leak over there, the place was sinking into the sea, but they've laid some artificial land there now, to hold it back. They're in the process of building some fake islands out here too, they've run out of space, no room for people, just like in Dubai. Have you ever been there?"

I shook my head.

"Their new downtown and beach area are super nice, and they've got an indoor ski slope too, unbelievably cool! I usually borrow a friend's place whenever I'm over there, we'll have to fix it so you can come visit sometime!"

I stood by the railing, peering down at the beautiful boats in the harbor. There were young men in jeans and T-shirts on the foredecks, shouting to one another over the jetty.

"Are they your friends?" I asked.

He shook his head in surprise.

"I . . . no, not really. They're the ones who work on other people's boats. All registered in the Cayman Islands, the lot of them."

"So are we going to borrow a boat and sail out to the Key Man Island?"

"I don't know anyone who has one of those."

"Don't you know that man with the boat?"

"No, André," he said, ruffling my hair again. "I don't think I know anyone with a boat. They're only for the people with lots and lots of money."

I stared up at him, wide-eyed.

"Don't *you* have lots and lots of money?"

Dad laughed.

"Come on, buddy, let's see what we've got for lunch."

I followed him into the kitchen. It was pretty small, almost cramped, and I noticed that strange chemical smell again, as though someone had just been there to clean. He had a few slices of pizza left over from the night before, *you like pizza, don't you?* and he reheated them in the microwave. There was juice and milk too, and he had a beer. Dad put it all onto a big tray and told me to grab two simple white plates, *everything's from Ikea, you know, it's a matter of principle, I'm not the kind of person to buy something fancy just for the sake of it*, and we went out onto the terrace again. He'd pulled on a cap because of the sun.

"It was just like this when your mom and I met," he said after we had been eating pizza for a while and were looking out at the milky sea. "Did she ever tell you that?"

I shook my head.

"With the leftovers, I mean. You see, I was married to Jakob and Karolina's mom before that, you know that, don't you, to Johanna? But then I fell head over heels for Malin and I was living alone and she stayed over one night, you know, the way grown-ups do when they're in love, and in the morning she asked if there was anything to eat, because she wanted to . . . well, stay a bit longer. So I tiptoed out into the kitchen . . ."

Dad took a swig of his beer and nodded enthusiastically at his own story, as though to egg himself on.

". . . and, you see, I'd bought everything the day before, really nice bread and cheese and slices of ham, the kind of thing girls love, *but.*" He held up a warning finger. "But then I started worrying that it would look weird, like I'd *planned* for us to have a nice breakfast together, because, you know, girls don't like it when you plan too much, they want everything to be sort of spur-of-the-moment, spontaneous, a bit happy-go-lucky."

He grinned beneath the brim of his cap and put a hand on my shoulder. I was still wearing the denim jacket I'd had on the plane, summer had been over for weeks back home.

"You're eight now, it's time you learned about this kind of thing. Girls like considerate boys, don't get me wrong, but not in a wimpy way. They want you to be romantic but not fawning. Can you see the difference? Do you know what *romantic* means?"

I nodded eagerly as I chewed. I had a great vocabulary, my teachers had been telling me that since preschool.

"So I tiptoed out into the kitchen, like I said, and I grabbed the cheese, sliced half of it off, quick as hell, and threw it away, then I cut the bread in half and did the same thing again, straight in the garbage. I got rid of half the pack of ham and I poured out half the juice, the same with everything, so that when she came into the kitchen the place was total chaos, crumbs everywhere, and I was all *I think I can probably throw something together . . . give me a minute* and then I grabbed whatever was left from the mess, the amazing bread, the prosciutto, cheddar, jams, a whole load of gourmet produce, but it all looked like . . . leftovers."

I took another slice of pizza, my fifth, and he frowned but didn't say anything, wanted to remain in his story.

"I served your mom leftovers," he said quietly, almost sadly. "And afterward, she told me that was the moment when she fell in love."

"Was it here?"

"*Here?* No, no, buddy, we were in Stockholm, at my apartment there. I've still got it, it's got a roof terrace with a great view, a bit like this, we'll have to arrange it so you can come and stay sometime. That's where I live when I'm in Sweden, didn't you know that?"

Dad has an apartment in Stockholm. He has an apartment there. And I've never even been allowed to visit him.

It was as though we both paused and looked away, each struck by our own variation of shame—mine the result of humiliation, his of guilt.

It passed much faster for him. He took a swig of his beer and almost seemed to wash it away.

"I'm hardly ever there," he blurted out. "Almost never, actually. But you're always welcome."

He took off his cap and held it out to me. It was nice, a deep shade of blue, with a red-yellow-orange stripe and *SERGIO TACCHINI MONTE-CARLO* written in white letters beneath two crossed tennis rackets.

"Have you seen this? It's my tour cap, the one I wore when I won in Australia."

I took it, turned it over in my hands. The material was surprisingly soft, almost silky beneath my fingertips.

"Try it on!" he said.

It was like putting on a huge black hat. The edges came down over my eyes and ears, and he laughed and angled the brim so that he could see my face.

"See! You look super cool in it!"

I met his eye, the peak was obscuring everything else, and I felt like one of those horses wearing black eye patches.

"Do you want it? It's too big for you right now, but you can save it for when you're older!"

"Cool beans," I said, and his tanned face broke into another sad smile, like he was face-to-face with a charming but ultimately pointless animal, a dog that had swum out after a stick only to lose the stick and start whining and splashing around in circles; you think the dog is cute but more than anything you just want to go home.

"Well, now you know," he continued. "Your mom probably never told you, but I'm going to teach you all about this kind of thing. How to be a bit manly, a bit macho, no frills. Girls like boys who dare to be themselves."

He thought for a moment.

"But not in the bathroom, that's where they draw the line. Never forget that. No piss stains or skid marks, no stinky old towels. You *have* to keep the john clean, that's extremely important."

There was only one small piece of pizza left on the plate. Little more than a bit of crust with some dry cheese on it.

"What did you do with the food?" I asked.

"The food?"

"The stuff you threw away."

He frowned.

"Uh . . . I threw it away, in the garbage."

"But you're not supposed to throw food away."

Dad shrugged.

"No? Well, eat up, then."

I took the last piece. He sighed and looked out at the water.

"Have I ever told you about the time Jakob went to confirmation camp on Värmdö? He took a whole load of candy with him, but suddenly we started hearing from the other parents that their kids owed him money."

I took off the cap and lowered it to my knee, ran my fingers over the white letters, which bulged slightly from the fabric. *MONTE-CARLO*. The symmetry of the name, five letters and five letters. *MONTE-CARLO MONTE-CARLO MONTE-CARLO*. I tried it backward, *OLRAC-ETNOM OLRAC-ETNOM*.

"André?"

I tried mixing up the letters, creating new words, *CELAT-MONOR ONT-RECLOMA*, sometimes you could find real words in the old ones, sometimes there were puzzles like that beside the crossword in the newspaper, *CARL-MONTEO MARTEN-COOL*, but I couldn't come up with anything much.

"André?" Dad repeated. "Buddy?"

I looked up at him.

"Where will I live if Mom dies?"

The first thing I see is the pale blue sky, framed by the skylight hatch in my little cabin. My sleeping bag is damp with sweat, and I get onto my knees and push the hatch open using my wrists, then crawl out onto the deck. The sunlight bouncing off the waves is merciless, piercing, but there's a breeze, it's windy, the crests of the waves coming thick and fast farther out toward open water. Dad is messing about with something down in the cockpit, and without a word I move over to the very tip of the bow and feel the sun beating down on the back of my neck.

Then I dive into the water. I've never been much good at running or jumping or lifting, but I've always had a technically slick dive, ever since Grandpa taught me one summer in Karlskrona. I enjoy feeling the shock and fear of the first split second give way to comfort and calm, and I open my eyes and see the veils of white sunlight filtering down through the water. A few quick kicks and I break the surface, breathing, spluttering, pushing my hair back and swimming alongside the boat, rounding the stern and gripping the ladder. When I get to the top Dad smiles at me and holds out a plastic mug of hot coffee, and that's when I remember.

Oh, God.

I glance over to the white rock. It's only a stone's throw away, was it really so far to swim? Did I seriously stand over there and shout? My throat is still tender, and I can feel my fingers aching as I grip the ladder, the way they do after you've been really cold.

So fucking stupid.

"Morning, kiddo," says Dad, handing me the coffee cup and an old towel with some tennis thing on it. "Great weather again today. I thought we might head in to Sandhamn, should take about four hours, just in time for lunch. We could do with stocking up."

"We're out of chips."

He cackles.

"Have we had pirates on board?"

I nod.

"Real chip fiends. *Pirates of the Crispy Bacon and Sour Cream.*"

He lets out another cackle, so hard that his shoulders shake, then he ruffles my hair and says *buddy* and that calm, warm feeling spreads through my gut again.

I drink my coffee and pull on yesterday's boxers. Dad is at the helm with his old sailor's cap on. He heads us up into the wind and I raise the mainsail as he cheerfully shouts *two six HEAVE, two six HEAVE*, and I feel the strain in my back as I use my body weight to pull on the halyard, throwing myself to the deck over and over again, *two six HEEEEAVE, two six HEEEEAVE*. It gets tougher and tougher and my palms start stinging, and in the end I wind the halyard around the winch and crank it the last foot or so. *A little bit more* says Dad, looking up at the mast, another few sluggish turns of the winch and he nods *good* and gently steers us into the wind. The feeling of euphoria as everything goes quiet, as the sail stops flapping and starts to bulge, the slight creaking of the rigging as the breeze takes hold of *Martina* and we're gently, almost imperceptibly, sucked out to sea; the feeling of giving yourself over to the elements, like a leaf swirling in a storm, and I raise the anchor, same thing there, it's easy at first, heavy toward the end, as Dad steers us out into open water. The bay where we were just anchored is now calm and flat and empty, as though we were never even there, and we speed past the bare rocks where I sat and shivered in another world. It was right here, but now it's gone.

He didn't hear you shouting. Of course he didn't. He was listening to music on his headphones, he'd taken his sleeping pills. Dad would have helped you if he'd heard you shouting.

"There's a power outage," he says after a while, as we're tacking through the strait. "Might be a few hours before they manage to fix it."

He nods to a white sector light in the middle of the bay.

"Fingers crossed they do, otherwise things might get a bit hairy tonight. We'll have to stay in Sandhamn."

"Why is the power out?"

"Didn't you get the news flash?"

I shake my head. Last night was so stupid that I haven't even been able to think about the fact that—on top of everything else—I lost my phone, and now that it's morning it's like I've convinced myself it'll turn up again, unclear how. Either that or we'll stop off somewhere where I can get a new one. Something like that.

"Nah," I say. "Haven't had time to check."

"It's complete chaos in the city," says Dad. "With everyone escaping the fires in the north, plus all the refugees on top of that. And as though that wasn't enough, the climate freaks have started kicking off, protesting. The military's been called in. And now the power's out, apparently."

He leans forward with a sigh and trims the jib.

"Good thing we're out here, so we don't have to worry about it. When you're out in the boat it's like everything else just fades away."

"I read about a rich merchant who did the same thing," I tell him. "Back in the eighteenth century, when the Black Death was raging in Stockholm. They knew it was infectious, so he rented a ship and took his entire family on board. And then they just sailed around the Baltic until the plague had passed."

"The fourteenth century."

"What?"

Dad smiles, squinting.

"It was the fourteenth century. The Black Death, I mean. Even I know that."

"But there was a plague epidemic in the eighteenth century, too."

He frowns.

"Are you sure?"

I nod.

"Half the population of Stockholm died. Mass graves everywhere. Refugees. They painted white crosses on people's doors."

Dad shrugs.

"Never heard of it."

"Because most of the people who died were poor," I eagerly explain. "That's typical of the history of suffering: if it doesn't affect the upper class, it doesn't leave a mark. The people who lived in cramped, dirty conditions, close to rats—and who also had to bury the corpses—were the people who got sick and died. The ones who could afford to leave the cities and isolate in the countryside survived. The royals went into quarantine in Falun and introduced the death penalty for anyone who tried to make their way up there."

He clears his throat and spits into the waves.

"Sounds unlikely. That's just something you've read online."

"What's unlikely about it? Rich people have always run from catastrophe. The world has always been unfair."

Dad gives a thoughtful nod. Then he parts his buttocks and lets out a sleepy fart, slowly gets to his feet from his worn blue cushion, and waves a hand for me to take the helm, *aim for the red house over there*, he mutters, pointing to a cottage in the distance. I stand at the wheel, enjoying the feeling of the smooth wood in my hands, the vibrations from the water surging beneath us traveling through the rudder. He moves over to his usual spot on the foredeck and starts pissing with one hand on the shroud, his eyes locked up ahead, then he lets go and uses both hands to shake off his dick, swaying slightly but steadying himself with his feet.

Would he notice if I let go of the wheel? If I snuck up behind him? A quick shove, as hard as I can? But even if? And no life jacket? He'd probably just swim. Yeah. Won't work.

The moment passes and he turns around, wipes his hands on his ancient workout shorts. His body is still lithe, his balance perfect as he deftly makes his way back over the deck and down into the cockpit.

"I don't agree," he says calmly.

"But Dad, it's, like . . . established history," I say, slightly ashamed of his resistance to facts. "There are official documents from back then. Poems, songs. Plague cemeteries."

"No. I'm saying I don't *agree*. With the last part, about the world being unfair."

He has the same superior look on his face that he always gets whenever he has one of his little speeches lined up. He's so used to being the center of attention, to people listening to him. Ever since he was a child, he has been surrounded by sports journalists and sponsors and junior players, even just random filthy-rich old men buying an hour of his time on the court in an effort to improve their backhand. Everything he says is important, worth listening to and taking away as though it were treasure.

"You say that the rich managed to avoid the plague? Fine, but how did they get rich in the first place? They worked hard. They had ideas. They gave it their all."

"But back then it was all about inherited wealth and class differences and . . ."

He holds up a crooked index finger.

"You said he was a merchant, right? Who took his family out to sea to save them from illness? So you tell me, what did it take to become a successful merchant in the eighteenth century? *Taking risks*, that's what. You had wars disrupting your trade routes, storms sinking your ships—you had to put everything on the line. Isn't it reasonable that they enjoyed a better standard of living as a result? Had a better chance of survival? Was it really so *unfair*?"

"Just because some people were lucky enough to be born into the upper class—"

"Fall off a bit," he interrupts me, pointing to the luffing sail. "You're heading up too much."

"You said to aim for the red house."

"You need to fall off a bit. You've got to be able to adapt to the wind. Steer by the sails."

I bite my tongue and do as he says. He has the pleased glimmer in his eye that he sometimes gets when he's feeling clever. The boy who didn't even graduate from high school but still knew how to put a cheeky sports reporter in their place.

"I don't believe in luck, either," he says. "Luck is something you create for yourself. Have I ever told you about the exhibition match I played against Ivan Lendl?"

"Yes," I say quietly, but he just ignores me.

"It was in Tokyo. I flew in the night before, but somehow or other I'd managed to forget the bag with my shoes in it. My rackets were in the other bag, along with everything else apart from my shoes. We tried to sort it out, but we didn't stand a chance. Ordinary people just don't get this kind of thing, but the fact is that it's completely impossible to play if you don't have the exact things you're used to; socks might be a borderline case, but the wrong *shoes*?" Dad makes a face. "Mission impossible. Count me out."

I fix my eyes on the horizon as he continues. There are a few motorboats out here, a small turquoise-and-yellow sail that looks like a Windsurfer closer to shore, but we've only seen three other sailboats all morning. We're heading east, away from the city, and when I turn my head and look in that direction all I can see is clear blue sky and yellowing forest; it's hard to imagine that today is different from any other late summer's day. Surely there should be helicopters in the air, assault boats, corvettes, or whatever they're called out here in the archipelago? But there is no sign of any emergency, no protests or refugees, it's just another way-too-hot day, an unnatural, unhealthy heat only made bearable by the cool water.

"But it wasn't about the prize money or the ATP points, because it was just an exhibition match, like I said, so I turned to Lendl in the changing room and I said, *Listen, Ivan, I don't have my shoes so let's just go out there and have a good time, OK?* and he was all *shuuuure, Anduuuurs.*" Whenever Dad imitates Lendl, he always makes him sound like a vampire from some old horror film.

The breeze drops in the midday heat, and we've slowed to two or three knots. To the lee side of a rocky cape, we hit a windless patch and drift slowly through a sludge of blue-green algae, a disgusting mush that forms long veils on the still surface of the water. In the space of just a few generations, the Baltic Sea has become an overfertilized, stinking puddle. Once upon a time you could see right down to the seabed in most bays, visibility was at least thirty feet, but these days the water is murky, gray, dead.

"And then he steamrolls me! Bang, bang, 6–0, 6–0. I'm limping around in the kicks we managed to find at some sports clinic, late on every ball, and he completely humiliates me. The Japanese are so polite, so when even they start booing you, when they reach the point where they're letting you know just how much they despise you, when they practically expect you to commit suicide on the baseline . . . well, it's no fun at all being stuck out there on the court. My God, I was this close to blaming the old back and calling it a day, but it was a charity thing for the victims of an earthquake, so I just had to grit my teeth and get on with it."

We pass a red buoy, a green buoy, another red one. Dad loves this story. Sometimes it takes place in Vienna, sometimes Milan, and the charity is either for child leukemia or prostate cancer. He has it mixed up with a publicity stunt following Kobe 1995 today, everything has started to merge together for him, the years and the places but never the opponents. It's Ivan Lendl in every single version, and it's always his shoes.

"And in the changing room afterward, I go over to him and I say, *what happened, man?* Because in matches like that you usually win one set each and then go all in for the third, giving the people what they've paid for—*plus* I'd told him about my shoe problem. And do you know what he said?"

I nod and smile. It's a good story, one of his better ones.

"*Well, Anduuuurs, zat's juzt who I ammm . . .*"

He laughs, a loud, wrinkled, tanned, grinning laugh. And then he turns serious again.

"And my first thought was, *fuck me, that bastard*, but once I'd really retired and started following the kids instead, all the elite initiatives and junior programs and the kind of thing they want you involved in, well, I realized that Lendl is *exactly* the kind of person we're lacking in Sweden.

That goddamn winning mentality. There's too much lovey-dovey stuff and motivational crap and gender nonsense, when all that really matters in tennis is being *exactly* as good as you need to be on *exactly* the right balls. If you've got a guy who's six and a half feet tall and left-handed, he doesn't need some tennis academy to throw money at him; he needs a container full of balls and someone to tie him to the baseline until he's learned to serve like a fucking beast."

I'm not so keen on this part, and I look out to sea, at the sail, peer up at the wind indicator to see which way it's blowing.

"But that mindset is *completely* lacking back home these days. When I started out there were fourteen of us Swedes in the draw for the U.S. Open. Seriously, fourteen guys, plus the coaches—we had our own goddamn Swedish corner in the changing room. Sure, we've got Stefan and Mats, but I'm talking about the *breadth* of the field back then, the fact that there were so many good players at the same time—Micke Pernfors was ranked tenth in the world, and he didn't even make it onto the Davis Cup team! It was us and the Americans, the Spanish were nothing but a bunch of losers, you barely knew who they were. If you saw ESP beside someone's name, that was your sign to march out onto the court and flatten them. But these days you don't stand a chance if you're up against a Spaniard."

He makes a face, rolls his eyes.

"The only good people we've got these days are a couple of Ethiopian refugees, and that just confuses the other players. They think they're about to face a *Swede* and then a Negro comes out and—"

"Dad, for God's sake . . ."

"Fine, *sorry*, dark-skinned, African, whatever you want to call them, I'm not like that, you know me, André, I've *never* had a problem with anyone, but people think they've bought a ticket for the wrong court! And as for the girls . . . they're either bimbos or dykes, a few Blacks there, too—did you see that Williams sister jumping around like an ape, bickering with the judge? Those fucking—"

"Injustice," I say, trying to change the subject.

"What?"

"You were talking about injustice. About how it doesn't exist."

He frowned.

"Was I? Ah, I . . . there's just too much whining these days, that's what I mean."

Who's the one whining here? I think, though I don't say anything.

"People in this country need to get a grip. Stop thinking the state is going to step in and help you all the time. If I've got enough money to buy my freedom, to buy a boat and steer clear of all the shit, then that's something I've earned. I'm not going to apologize for having a winning mentality. I've fought for my successes. I've enjoyed them. I've had a great life."

The wind drops again, and the sail starts flapping. It's baking hot. The sea usually cools down at this time of year, it wasn't unusual for us to be wearing sweaters, hats, and thick socks in the past, but right now we're sweating even though we're half-naked.

"Bury me in Melbourne," Dad says, squinting up at the sun. "As quickly as you can. I don't know what crazy ideas Nadja might have—she's Russian Orthodox, and they're all about having an open casket and what have you, but don't let that happen. I want you to get me to Melbourne as fast as you can, throw a big party in Flinders Park, then take my ashes out to sea and scatter them by the Great Ocean Road."

He trims the jib slightly to stop the luffing, then continues with his back to me:

"I've already told Jakob. That's my one demand, buddy. *Just do it.*"

Suddenly, as though the thought of no longer being around is too much for him to bear, he gets up and goes down into the cabin, mutters something about how it can't be too early for a beer.

I watch his slender back disappear.

Something hard and heavy. The boat hook. No, the anchor. Maybe while he's asleep. And then make it look like we were sailing into the wind and there was some problem with one of the sails and suddenly we jibbed and the boom hit him in the head and cracked his skull. Or like he'd had a few beers and was going down to grab another when he tripped on the stairs and hit his head on the leg of the collapsible dining table. Though they'd probably see straight through that in no time at all, wouldn't they? They'd examine his body and check his head injury and then it'd be bye-bye.

Come up with something better.

A final between Federer and Nadal, we were back in the apartment, it was on the TV. Dad was pissed off because they hadn't sent him VIP tickets for Paris again that year, and I watched the two men dance across the red clay.

He's completely fucking impossible, Dad said. *Unbeatable, really. Agassi said the same thing, Roger's a total machine. Everyone has a weakness. McEnroe didn't like training, Connors and Edberg both had a poor forehand. Becker had an embarrassingly bad backhand, and he also had a tic that meant he'd point his tongue in whichever direction he was planning to serve. Once we'd worked that out, his serves weren't a problem. Björn didn't have a serve at all, and he was terrible at facing left-handers. Everyone has something.*

He pointed at the TV.

But not Federer. If anything, his thing is finding his opponents' weaknesses. Using them. Exploiting them.

I reached for the bag of chips.

What was your weakness, Dad?

He smiled and ruffled my hair.

You'll find out, buddy.

───────

Sailing into Sandhamn in *Martina* is always a bit of a high point. It's the closest thing to a community you can get in the Stockholm archipelago, and I remember the feeling I got as a child, spotting the big red and yellow wooden buildings in the distance, the tall white chapel, the lighthouse, the Swedish flag fluttering from the hotel, and behind it all the forest of masts crowded into the guest harbor. The feeling of having come home, of moor-ing and jumping ashore, the jetty so comforting and welcoming beneath my feet, the wooden planks warm from the sun; the pleasure of using a real toilet for the first time in a while as Dad sorts out the Wi-Fi with the harbormaster's office, then trudging up to the shop to buy something tasty. Farther up the hill among the old wooden houses there is usually a bakery selling freshly baked bread, buns, and croissants, a lush garden, a pool, a beautiful sandy beach, people who know Dad everywhere we turn, coming over to shake his hand or pat him on the shoulder—no face masks, no so-cial distancing, not even the summer when things were at their worst—or ask him if he wants to come down to the courts or to some party they're throwing, me standing off to one side, drinking a cold soda, as Dad smiles and says *no, no, I'm just taking it easy, we're having our annual boys' week.* One summer we went to the souvenir shop and Dad bought us match-ing zip-up hoodies with the words *SANDHAMN SWEDEN* printed on them, followed by the longitude and latitude, and we walked around the island wearing them. I wore mine all autumn and winter, even slept in it at night, until the cuffs started to fray. There are no cars, the signs are all old-fashioned; it's like arriving in a secret island village, a pocket in time, a place where everything has been at a standstill.

But not today.

As we round the cape, there are only a handful of boats in the guest harbor. The water in harbors is always a bit murky, but today it absolutely stinks in the quivering heat. There are no more than a few people out and about on the jetties, and over by the quay I notice that one of the bigger motorboats is at a strange angle, tipped sharply toward the starboard side, hanging like a fish from a rod with its bow line taut.

"Shit, the gas pump," says Dad, pointing to the pontoon jetty where we usually fill the tank on our way in or out. That's another part of the tradition: Dad throwing a couple of lines to a tanned teenager with crisp, hair-sprayed locks who then tosses the gas hose over. The people on the boats nearby always glance over, trying not to seem starstruck, and I jump down onto the jetty and buy ice cream from the convenience store while the pump does its thing. A nice, simple, wordless routine. But today the kiosk is nothing but a sooty wreck, the gas hut half gutted by flames, its broken windows like toothless, gaping mouths. The door is hanging from one hinge, and the pumps are either broken or overturned. In the midst of the chaos, one sign has survived and is flapping in the breeze. *NEED A BREAK? COFFEE + BUN 30 KRONOR!* it says in red-and-yellow text beside a picture of a paper cup of coffee and a big sweet bun covered in pearl sugar.

On the charred, broken wooden jetty beside it, someone has written *FUCKING LIVE WITH IT* in red spray paint.

I hear the spluttering of a motorboat approaching. A guy in a red-and-black life jacket and a cap with the guest harbor's logo on it deftly turns his rubber dinghy and slaloms between the buoys, heading straight toward us.

"Turn around!" he shouts, letting the engine run idle once he gets closer. "The harbor's closed."

"Closed?" Dad yells back. "But there's plenty of space!"

The guy shakes his head.

"All closed!"

"What, the whole of Sandhamn?"

"Decision from the harbormaster this morning."

Dad laughs.

"Come on, kid, you know . . ."

"Closed!" The guy practically screams the word, pointing at us with his entire hand like a soldier. "Turn around! You are *not* welcome here!"

Without waiting for a reply, he revs the engine, turns sharply, and speeds away with a roar. He's around my age, I realize. I wonder how hard it can be, whether he's nervous, whether it's fun, whether he feels tough, full of big-dick energy, or whether he's as frightened and powerless as I am. Would he dare? *Next time we stop to swim somewhere, I'll hurry while the old man is still in the water. The anchor, it's heavy, point at something to distract him and then just let it drop.*

"Fucking brat," Dad sighs, turning to me. "Can you sheet her home? I've got an idea."

————

Last night's power outage affected the entire greater Stockholm area, from Södertälje in the south to Uppsala in the north, and the grid is still down in much of the region, including the inner city and the archipelago. A small group of hooligans showed up in Sandhamn late yesterday evening. They just shouted and smashed windows and tagged a few walls at first, but then they went down to the guest harbor and started vandalizing the motor-boats. Before a few sailors chased them away, they managed to set the little gas hut on fire.

"It was a Norwegian," Kalderén tells us once we're sitting on his jetty. "The beefy type, ex-military, apparently. Everyone else froze to the spot in their boats, typical Swedes, but he and his crew grabbed some boat hooks and anchor chains, I'll be damned if one of them didn't have an axe too, and he started yelling in Norwegian and the little bastards ran off!"

There is no food or gas to be bought in Sandhamn, and given the chaos back in Stockholm it'll probably be a while before anyone comes out here, maybe even longer before the power comes back on.

"How did those idiots even manage to get here?" Dad asks out of curiosity. "Did they have a boat or something?"

Kalderén shrugs.

"People went out looking for them last night, but no one saw anything. In any case, they've closed the guest harbor now. A big fucking mess, the whole thing." He pokes at the embers with the sooty tongs. "But also kind of cool to experience. And we're sitting pretty out here."

"I think there should be a few cold beers left," says his wife, a sporty woman in a pair of tight Lycra pants, setting a cooler down on the jetty in front of us. "We were planning to have a barbecue for lunch anyway."

The Kalderén family have been friends of Dad's since their son came

up as a junior. Djursholm Tennis Club usually organizes a local tournament in late April, and Dad has gone out there to *do the celebrity thing* a
few times—that's what he told me as we rounded the cape and sailed into
the narrow bay on the other side of the island. *Claes is always saying I
should swing by next time I'm in Sandhamn. You know the type, always
brown-nosing.* Dad chuckled and reefed the jib. *But contacts are there to be
used, heh heh. It's that jetty, I think. The one to the left is the Gyllenhoffs'.*

So, here we are. Claes Kalderén has the peachy tan of a pale blond man
who can't really handle the sun but still doesn't bother to protect himself.
We got lucky, he said as he came lumbering down onto the jetty, ready to
chase us off as intruders. Most people have already headed home, but he
and Gunilla decided to stay put at the last minute. *We've started drawing
out the summer*, he said, sounding pleased with himself, catching the line
I threw to him. *Ever since the pandemic, it's been so easy to work from out
here.*

Dad and I are each sitting in a deck chair, beneath an umbrella. After
being anchored at sea for the past few nights, it's good to feel the sturdy,
warm planks beneath my feet, and Dad has already been for a swim and
washed his hair. The jetty is attached to a freshly painted boathouse, red
with white corner panels, and continues along the rocks to a small sauna, up
a staircase to a two-story house painted the same color. Kalderén inherited
it from his grandfather, he proudly tells us. "Everyone out here inherited.
No one could afford it otherwise."

Everything feels weirdly normal. Mrs. Kalderén is in their newly fitted
outdoor kitchen, slicing a few boiled potatoes from yesterday and mixing
them with olive oil, red onion, and capers while her husband turns two big
flap steaks over a velvety bed of coals. They're chatting about the food, he
says something appreciative about the quality of the meat she bought and
she asks him something about the recipe for the potato salad, and for a brief
moment my mind turns to Mom and Dad, to what things might have been
like if they hadn't divorced, if they'd stuck together, if Mom hadn't died.
Would they have lived like this, out in the archipelago, in a place with a

jetty, having vanilla conversations about nothing at all? Would they have wanted that?

I can make out another couple of equally idyllic houses around the Kalderéns' property, but I can't hear any voices, no clinking glasses or music, not even the spluttering of any motorboat engines. It's as though someone has pulled the plug on the world.

"We're sitting pretty," he says again a while later, raising a forkful of grilled meat to his mouth. "You're actually much less vulnerable out here, have you ever thought about that? If the toilet stops working, we've got the old outhouse. The cellar's full of jars and dried goods, the woodshed's full of logs—makes you feel like a real prepper! We were a bit worried about the kids, but Filip is at his girlfriend's place in Skåne and Evelina is in Marbella with her friends, so they've both escaped all the nonsense in town."

"It was worse with your mom," says Gunilla, her mouth hardening slightly. "She was up in the Dalarna forests with her seniors' association, on a painting trip to an old mine not far from the fires, it was sheer hell trying to get her out of there. The whole thing's been really tough on you, Claes honey."

"I had to make a few calls," he mutters and shrugs. "But we managed to get her transported out of there yesterday. Sometimes you just have to get a bit creative, you know?"

"Speaking of transport—how much does a beauty like that guzzle?" Dad asks, pointing to the motorboat moored beside *Martina*, an elegant white day cruiser that looks brand-new. "What is it, a Jeanneau?"

"Princess Flybridge, bought her a year or two back. She's a thirsty devil, three gallons a mile," Kalderén replies, rolling his eyes.

"Three gallons a mile?" I do the calculations in my head.

Three gallons per 1,800 yards. I try to make sense of the figures. *One gallon of gas every 600 yards.*

Dad smiles. "Come on, you know how much fuel these things use?"

"Yeah, but...that's..." I hesitate. "Coming out here from town must..."

"Twenty-five gallons, give or take." Kalderén nods proudly. "Yup, you feel like closing your eyes when you swipe the damn card. Though back home I drive an electric car, of course."

"You're a growing boy, take another piece," says Gunilla, holding out the plate of meat to me, neat grill markings seared into it.

"But how do you . . ." I shake my head and take the biggest piece, one with a quivering lump of fat on it.

Dad squirms uncomfortably beside me.

"Seems like the boy's become a tree hugger lately, Claes, heh heh."

"I just think a person's got to live, you know?" says the man. "Otherwise what's the point? Speeding across the water in one of those on a summer's day, with the kids and their friends on board, it's like . . . well, it's like flying."

"But do you actually *enjoy* it?" I hear my voice break into a falsetto and I swallow, try to make it deeper. "It's like stopping every two thousand feet to burn a gallon of gas. Do you really think that makes you *happy*? You said you bought it a year or two back, but are you really planning to . . . *keep* driving it? Just for fun?"

Gunilla pours more beer into Dad's glass.

"I think people should mind their own business," she says, giving me a cold smile. "This is our life."

I sprinkle some salt onto my meat and press the knife against the tender, juicy flesh. A ripple moves across the calm water.

"And this is mine," I say, immediately realizing how clichéd it sounds.

———

We spend the day with the Kalderéns. I have a nice hot shower using up the last warm water in the tank and take a long shit on their gleaming toilet. Dad checks the news—they have a power bank, so he can charge his phone; the internet seems to be down, but his satellite phone still works. Stockholm is complete chaos, with violent demonstrations in several places, widespread vandalism and looting in the shopping district, tens of thousands of people stranded at the train stations and airports and on the high-ways. The fires in northern and central Sweden have now claimed over nine hundred lives, and much of inner Lapland is burning out of control, the roads are inaccessible, the phone network is down, *reports from the area are deeply troubling.*

We walk down to the guest harbor in the afternoon. A quiet, threaten-ing atmosphere hangs over the deserted street. The broken glass has been swept into piles along the sides of the buildings and some of the spray paint has been scrubbed away, but on the board showing the timetables for the boats into town, the words *CLIMATE JUSTICE* still glow in red. The grocery store is closed, planks of wood and sheets of cardboard over the windows and doors. A dozen large motorboats and around the same number of smaller boats are still moored in the harbor, but I can see only a handful of sailboats. The air smells stale and rancid, and people are moving slowly in the heat, almost hunched over, chatting in small groups, glancing back when they hear footsteps approaching. *Hell*, I hear someone say, *look, there's Anders Hell.*

By the harbormaster's office, a broad-shouldered man in a navy blue captain's hat is fiddling with a walkie-talkie. Dad goes over to talk to him, flashing his celebrity smile, laughing and patting the man on the shoulder, but all he gets is a cold look in return. He turns around and comes back.

"No food, no fuel," he says glumly. "Anyone who had anything left in the tank has already gone." He ruffles my hair. "We'll have to buy some chips in the next place, kiddo. Fortunately the wind's forecast to pick up this evening, so we can move on in the morning."

"Why are the boats still here if there's nothing to buy?"

He glances over to me.

"Because there's nothing to buy, buddy. They've got nothing left in the tank. They can't get home."

A herd of children in orange life jackets row between the boats in a rubber dinghy, laughing and chattering. One of the boys says *look, it's him*, and points. Dad smiles and waves.

"Cute kids. Do you remember splashing about like that?"

I'm on the verge of telling him that that never happened, or not like that, anyway—I was always alone in the dinghy, never had anyone to play with—but it would only sound whiny, and Dad doesn't like it when I whine, so I just nod.

"What happened to it, by the way?"

"What?"

"The dinghy." Dad squints over to the children, waves again. "Last night, you didn't bring it back."

I stare at him.

"No . . . no, it flipped and floated away, I had to swim."

He makes a face.

"Tough luck. Shame everything's closed, otherwise we could have bought a new one. Handy to have."

Dad waves one last time and turns around.

"So . . ." I hesitate, two steps behind him. "So . . . you heard me, last night?"

He doesn't reply, doesn't wait, just keeps walking, glancing up at a weather vane to see which way the wind is blowing.

———

We're back at the Kalderéns' place again that evening, up on their veranda this time. There are reports that it might be a full week before the power is back in the archipelago, and Claes is no longer quite so chipper. He did the rounds with the neighbors earlier, on the hunt for gas, but most people have already left the island and those that are still here are in the same situation, either that or they've sold whatever they had to one of the motorboats down in the harbor. There was a family whose son had diabetes and needed to get to a hospital, so someone gave all their reserves to them, and then there were a couple of government officials who'd come out to Sandhamn to kick off the autumn season; they needed to get back to Stockholm, citing national security, and then a few businessmen who were willing to pay handsomely turned up, and with that all the gas was gone.

"Gyllenhoff next door isn't home, but I bet he has an extra jerrican in the boathouse," says Gunilla, setting another few candles on the table.

"Locked," Kalderén replies. He squirts ketchup onto his hot dog, which, judging by the taste of mine, has been at the bottom of the freezer for years. "I checked."

"But surely you could break in?" says Dad. "If it's an emergency, I mean."

"Then we'd be just like that madman in Dalarna, have you seen the clip?" His wife smiles. "Dirty Dennis or whatever his name is."

"No one's going to break in anywhere," Kalderén snaps. "It's not even up for discussion. That's how trouble starts. When I was stationed in Kenya, that's exactly how the chaos began, one group started a rumor about the other stealing or murdering or raping, and then people wanted to take revenge and do the same, and just two days later they'd started tossing kids into burning churches."

"How's Filip getting on, by the way?" Dad sounds so breezy. "Has he made any progress with his forehand?"

"He's got a wild card for the qualifying tournament for the Stockholm Open," says Kalderén. "Assuming it actually happens. Things look so bleak for his generation. First he had an entire year ruined by the pandemic and now all this crap."

"But you learn a lot outside of the matches. When Jakob was fourteen or fifteen he went to a tennis camp out on Värmdö, and the tennis was really by the by, but my God the kid developed some skills."

I eat my third hot dog with a few salty crackers, then get up and head into the house. The toilet is dark, but Gunilla has lit candles in there, too, and it feels cozy to shit in the dark. Their voices seep in through the door:

. . . and after they'd been there two weeks one of the other mothers called Johanna, furious because her son owed Jakob money. It turned out he'd sold all the candy I gave him and used the money to buy the other kids' candy. He kept going like that, buying and selling, buying and selling . . .

Claes Kalderén asks something I can't catch.

No, says Dad, *but apparently he'd convinced one of the camp counselors to go and buy more, and then he sold that too!*

When I attempt to flush the toilet, there isn't any water. I try the tap instead. Nothing. Outside, Dad delivers his punch line.

And by the time we picked him up two weeks later, Jakob was the candy store and the bank and the enforcement officer combined! I thought maybe his friends would, well, you know, when I showed up, it's not uncommon for . . . a few autographs, signing a racket or . . . but the kids were all WHO THE HELL ARE YOU?

The Kalderéns are still laughing when I come back out.

"There's no water," I say.

They look up at me in surprise.

"It usually . . ." Claes begins.

"It's off between ten and seven," Gunilla quickly butts in. "We might not have mentioned that?"

"But that's not for a few hours?"

"We usually fill a container in the evening, so we can brush our teeth and that kind of thing, right, Claes?"

"I was planning to do it after dinner," he mutters.

"We've got a bit of fresh water left in the boat," says Dad. "André, can you scoot down there and grab some?"

Gunilla flashes him a smile.

"Otherwise we've probably got some bottled mineral water. The boy doesn't have to—"

"André doesn't mind."

I nod and head down the stairs. They're narrow, built into the steep rocks. There wasn't a breath of air earlier, but the wind has now picked up and I can see whitecaps on the waves as they roll in to the jetty, I have to put all my weight onto the bow line to bring the boat close enough for me to climb on board. *Martina* is rocking, straining so hard against her moorings that I need to grip the stays as I make my way down into the cockpit.

At first, all I see is a shadow, a movement from the corner of one eye. Around a hundred and fifty feet away, on the other side of the narrow bay, by the dark house. The Gyllenhoffs' place. I wouldn't have been able to see it from the jetty, only from this angle, from the cockpit.

I freeze, feel a tingling in my gut, as though someone has hung an iron from my testicles and tied my anus in a tight knot.

I slowly back up, away from the cockpit, over the deck, kicking off my sneakers to dampen the sound. Keep my eyes fixed on the other side of the bay, on the hidden corner between the fishing hut and the rocks, which may well only be visible from the spot where I was just standing. I jump down as quietly as I can, tiptoe along the jetty and up the stairs.

. . . I actually brought it up with him this spring, "listen," I said, "how do you think this summer is going to look on your résumé ten years from now?" His original plan was to start some new restaurant in Båstad with a couple of friends, leeching off my name like usual . . .

I pause behind a lilac bush. The candles are flickering on the veranda, their faint glow filtering through the leaves to where I'm standing in the shadows.

. . . so he decided to go to San Francisco to stay with Malin's crazy sister, who does nothing but take drugs and feel sorry for herself, but then there were all those wildfires, and he had to come home again . . .

Claes Kalderén's hoarse laugh echoes over the rocks.

. . . but then, of course, he had nowhere to live, so he had to go down to Karlskrona to spend the rest of the summer with my folks. They're really getting on in years, you know, so he was supposed to paint a fence for them, but that was a nonstarter too, it's just so goddamn . . .

Dad lowers his voice.

. . . what can you do if your kid's a loser, you know? Like, what's in it for me?

I don't even think, I just turn around and head back down the steps. Out onto the jetty. I loosen the bow lines and jump up onto the boat as it starts drifting out into the bay. *Martina* tilts and sways as she swings around, and before long the bow is pointing straight at the house on the other side.

They're hard to see in the darkness, but I can tell from their movements that they've spotted me now. They start whispering. One of them wants something, another protests.

The boat comes to a halt, right in the middle of the bay, the stern still moored to the buoy on the Kalderéns' side. I grab another rope and use it to lengthen the stern line, drift another fifty or a hundred feet toward the Gyllenhoffs' jetty. Bump it gently with the bow, not too hard; I've done this so many times before, Dad always wants to move the boat so that it has the best spot in the harbor.

I go down to the cabin, to the compartment beside the nautical charts, dig out the flashlight, and head back up. Run over to the bow and shine it straight at them.

"Hello?"

There are four of them. Two men and two women, I think at first, but one of the long-haired ones turns out to be a guy. Ripped jeans, wind-breakers, sneakers. A couple of backpacks.

One of them, a tall strawberry blond with cropped hair and a long beard, steps into the flashlight beam and holds up two empty hands.

"We don't want any trouble," he says. "It was stupid, the whole thing."

The woman moves forward and stands beside him. She has a woollen hat on her head, a Palestinian scarf around her neck.

"We tried to turn ourselves in," she adds. "We called the coast guard, but they never pick up."

"What are your plans?" I ask, surprised by how calm I sound.

The guy with the cropped hair takes another step forward. Now that he can see I'm not some beefy Norwegian, just a teenager, at least five years younger than him, he seems to stand taller.

"Honestly, we just want to get out of here."

We don't say much more after that. I toss them the bow line and he holds on to *Martina* while the others climb on board. They smell like smoke and dirt. No one introduces themselves, they just sit down in the cockpit, huddled together as though they were still hiding behind the fishing hut.

I'm too weak. Too scared, too lame.

Someone else will have to do it for me.

"Do you know how to sail?" I ask the guy with the cropped hair, and he nods.

"A bit."

One of them loosens the stern line from the buoy while I tell two of the others how to unfurl the jib. I'm at the helm, and I feel the wind take hold of the boat. We glide out of the bay, silently, quickly, toward open water. One of them, I don't know which, starts whistling the *Star Wars* theme.

"To Stockholm?" asks the tall one, looking west, where the last few rays of sunlight are fading behind the forest.

I shake my head and pull on my cap.

"To sea."

SUNDAY, AUGUST 31

THE APARTMENT WAS ENORMOUS, MUCH BIGGER THAN THE ONE IN Monaco, and the view from the roof terrace was much more interesting. You might not be able to see the sea from it, but it was cool to be able to look out at all the church towers and skyscrapers, completely different from Mom's little terraced house in Uppsala. Not that I went out there much, I spent most of my time in my room. Dad had bought three or four different gaming consoles and saved his card details in them for me, which meant I was free to download whatever I wanted to play. Margit lived there too those first few years, and she made sure I did my homework in the evenings. She tried to take me to museums or to her place in the country on the weekends, but by the time I got to high school she was gone and I mostly just gamed in my room. Before that, back when I lived with Mom, I'd been the kind of kid who read a lot of books, usually the classics, by Jules Verne and Mark Twain, *Robinson Crusoe*, *Treasure Island*. In the living room there, we had a big encyclopedia that Mom had found at a flea market, she thought it looked so nice, and I used to flick through that in the evenings. But in the penthouse apartment, everything was different. Books had never been important to Dad.

The fridge was always stocked with ready meals, and a company turned up to clean every Friday. Dad came and went. He would be home for weeks on end sometimes, sitting out on the terrace or chilling in front of the TV in the living room. Some days he wanted to talk about my *studies*, for us to look into private schools in the United States or exchange programs in Australia or New Zealand, *somewhere warm, you could do with a bit of sun, buddy*. He occasionally tried to help me with my homework, but he was terrible at everything other than English, and whenever he tried to explain anything—the difference between Judaism and Islam, how to calculate interest and percentages, what the word *philosophy* meant—he would get nervous and start telling me about something exciting that had happened to him a long time ago instead, though it always sounded like he was talking about someone else. Either that or he would plan trips that we'd take together one day, to Dubai or Singapore or Miami, white tigers, Latinas in G-string bikinis, business class.

Other times he was gone for weeks and weeks. Jakob lived out in the suburbs, but he came by to check that everything was OK, filling the freezer with yet more colorful frozen dinners. As his gaze hovered somewhere just above my face, he would ask whether I didn't want to come out and stay with him and Hanna and the kids for the weekend, whether he should stay over for a few nights, but I always said that I was planning to hang out with my friends and then he nodded and grinned and nodded to the bar cabinet and said he could see why I wanted the place to myself, *I remember what it was like at your age*, and then he left.

When the virus hit, everything got much lonelier. School went online for a while, and even once it opened up again I started staying home more and more, listening to podcasts, bingeing on TV shows, mostly fantasy or historical things about pirates and Vikings. I handed in assignments and took exams when I had to, mostly to make sure I passed; I'd always found school easy and largely got by. Dad was sometimes home, sometimes not, and the apartment was so big that I often wasn't sure which was the case.

One morning in spring, I came out into the kitchen in nothing but my boxers and a T-shirt and saw a girl scribbling away in a notebook at the dining table. Women had occasionally slept over since Margit left, but they usually tiptoed from his bedroom to the hallway, a few crumpled pieces of clothing in hand, faces streaked with yesterday's makeup, accompanied by the sweet scent of perfume and old alcohol; they almost never just *sat* at the table like that. And she didn't look like the rest of them, either: sober and bare-faced, wearing dark green outdoor clothing. Her long dark hair was braided, and when she spotted me she seemed surprised, but then she gave me a warm smile and put down her fountain pen and said *oh, I didn't realize anyone was home.*

"Come here," she said, pointing to a folder on the table in front of her. "What do you think?"

I took a few steps forward, still hovering at a safe distance, and saw that it was full of pictures of trees, bushes, fruit, something that looked like a climbing plant.

"What do you think would look good?"

Her name was Jennie and she was a garden consultant. She had just started working for a company that had really *blossomed*—she smiled again—now that people were staying in Sweden rather than going on holiday abroad, people wanted to make improvements to their homes. Dad had made an appointment with her, but then he'd gotten bored and left her to it, typical him; he'd had an idea that the roof terrace could be like a lush jungle with all sorts of beautiful orchids and magnolias, mango trees, an olive grove, maybe even a babbling waterfall, but Jennie had explained that some of those things might be more realistic than others and then he had lost interest and told her she had free rein to do what she liked and gone back to bed.

"But what do you think?" she asked again, flicking through her folder. "We could have a few dwarf palms in pots, and I think an orange tree could work, in the corner that gets the most sun. Do you cook a lot, you and your dad? We could grow thyme and rosemary, or other herbs if you want them."

"Dog roses," I said without even pausing to think. "I like the smell of those in summer."

She nodded approvingly.

"Dog roses are nice. And you can pick the hips and make ketchup. Or sweet chili. Is it OK if I grab a coffee?"

I'd never seen anyone move with such confidence at Dad's place before. The cleaners always worked silently, music in their ears and eyes on the floor or the wall; the handymen who came around to replace the appliances in the kitchen or renovate one of the bathrooms were the exact opposite, staring at everything, pausing in front of the photographs and souvenirs and the racket on the shelf by his trophy from Australia, *that's the one I used in the last set, the one I hit the match point with*, he always said as they pressed their noses to the glass. But not her. She rummaged through the pantry for a jar of coffee, and as the machine bubbled she wandered around the room, picking things up, peering into the fridge, opening drawers, and flicking through the mail on the table in the hallway as though it was the most natural thing on earth.

"Your dad told me to make myself at home," she said when she noticed me staring at her. "It's important I get a sense of who lives here if I'm going to find the right style."

She laughed and winked.

"But I'm also nosy. Is it true he was a tennis pro? Like Björn Borg or something?"

Whenever anyone who doesn't know much about tennis finds out that my dad is Anders Hell, they almost always confuse him with someone else. No, he's not Björn Borg, Borg won way more titles and was around a few years before Dad broke through, in the seventies, they only ever met a couple of times. No, he's not Mats Wilander, who had a two-handed backhand and was funny and wrote poetry. No, he's not Stefan Edberg, who lived off his volley and was boring and made pasta ads.

"Dad was the other one," I explained. "He was only good for two or three years, but he won lots during that time."

"So what was your dad known for?" she asked, pouring coffee into her own thermos. "Like, what was his thing?"

I considered her question.

"I guess tennis is a gentleman's sport and he was . . . more of the coarse type. Or that's how people saw him, anyway—as not so gracious. Because of the accent, maybe. He's from Karlskrona, in Blekinge, have you ever been there?"

She shook her head and laughed.

"No, I've been almost everywhere but there."

Jennie came back a few weeks later with a van full of plants, and I helped her carry them out to the terrace. She lugged bags of soil up there, connected a watering system, brought in a carpenter to build a trellis; the days got hotter, and sometimes she made her coffee and sat down in the kitchen for a while. Dad showed his face from time to time, said *hello, welcome*, but she wasn't the kind of girl he bothered to say much more than *hello, welcome* to, and he just murmured at her sketches and then went out.

She was new to the gardening business, she told me. She had moved to Africa after graduating from high school, first living with her boyfriend in Nairobi and then traveling around Kenya, Tanzania, Uganda.

"Then I met some people who worked in agricultural aid and they needed someone who spoke Swahili, so I became their local fixer and traveled around with them, and then I started working on a few projects myself, mostly with small-scale farmers growing sustainable crops."

The way she told it made it sound so simple: she was twenty-three and had already lived through four break-ins, three robberies, two attempted rapes, and a plane crash. She had climbed Kilimanjaro and walked the Inca trail to Machu Picchu, spent last Christmas alone in a hut on a Malaysian island, celebrating with a bottle of beer and two bananas.

"I only got this job because I started blabbering about working on large-scale agriculture projects near the equator," she said with a laugh. She often laughed. "Though I really just handed out money to coffee growers and tried to convince them not to sell their kids as slaves to the tobacco companies."

She started coming over for a few hours every week, loosening and watering the soil, planting seeds and bulbs, her smooth, round face focused beneath her sun hat. Her body was big, tough, muscular, and after working for several hours she often smelled strongly of sweat.

"What about you?" she asked me one day. "What are you going to do with your life? When are you going to go off and explore the world?"

I shrugged.

"Once it opens up again, maybe. After the pandemic. Or after school, in any case. I might study abroad. Dad'll give me the money, but he says I need a plan first."

"Or maybe you don't," said Jennie, pointing to the city below us with a muddy finger. "The world's right there, you just need to get out into it."

"Maybe . . ." I hesitated, slightly ashamed. "If I had someone to travel with, but I don't really know many people here."

"You don't need friends either," she said, getting up and brushing the dirt from her knees. "You'll find them along the way."

―――

The sun hasn't risen yet, but on the horizon the dawn is already painting the sky and the dying sea pink. I'm alone on a rock, just like I was almost exactly twenty-four hours ago. Yesterday the horizon was hidden behind wooded landmasses, pines and firs, rocks and houses. Today I'm on the very edge of the archipelago, and the only things interrupting my view are a few bare rocks and skerries shimmering in the calm air. The surface of the water is smooth and milky, reflecting the grayish-white sky and the light, pink-tinged clouds that will soon burn off.

The Baltic Sea is dying, that's a scientific fact. Around forty thousand square miles of seabed are already completely deoxygenated. Another fact is that it's amazingly beautiful. And that I'm young, healthy, strong, and full of life.

If I could just be happy, I think for the billionth time. *Happy just to exist. To sit here, like this, alone in the late summer dawn at the edge of the archipelago. And be grateful.*

The rock where I'm sitting is on the northern fringe of the cluster of flat, mostly bare islands known as Stora Nassa. The cool thing about traveling through the archipelago from the inside out is that you get to see the effects of land uplift in reverse. First the bigger islands, the forests, the buildings, the clumps of reeds, and the rocky knolls. Then, gradually, everything gets sparser, flatter, thinner; from larger landforms to fragments, galaxies of scattered grains of sand. And even farther out, windswept rocks that barely rise above the surface of the waves. And then nothing.

They must have seen it happen. A few of them, the ones who lived by the sea for generations, watching over time as the water slowly retreated and unfamiliar rocks emerged, the seabed gradually became visible, the places where their ancestors had caught salmon and cod and brown trout transforming into muddy pools where nothing but eels thrived. The change must have been frightening for many of them, these people who cursed the sorcery, the witchcraft, the gods for stealing the sea from them.

But others saw opportunity. The smart ones made sure they owned the coastline, through transactions, conquest, and marriage. Coastal meadows that grew larger, grazing pastures that swelled, skerries and outcrops that merged into islands on which you could build harbors, because once the big lagoons and waterways were cut off, new meeting places and fairways emerged, spits of land and isthmuses where you could force ships and merchants to pay tolls on their way to or from the rich, half-mythical cities on the other side of the water, and around these tollbooths they built locks and their very own cities that leeched off the foreign cities' wealth, trying to emulate their iron power. They saw the transformation and took charge of nature and of other people, making themselves into masters and the world their slaves.

Because the truth is that it's mankind's ability to adapt that brings the most suffering. If we were any other species, we would have just died out and that would be that. But we're burning down the rain forest to grow soybeans, forcing child slaves into cobalt mines so that we can have ever cheaper batteries in our electric cars, crowding into our garbage dump communities in the absurd quest for more life.

It's a brilliant thought, one I should write down, but the words vanish the minute they cross my mind and the first rays of sunlight break over the horizon.

I've made it out to the very edge of the archipelago, past dark islands where they still don't have any electricity, using nothing but a battery-powered GPS and the glow of the lighthouses, which, as luck would have it, run on solar power. The four activists—that's what they call themselves—were frightened, freezing, and badly dressed, and I took care of them, let them steer while I made sandwiches, coffee, mixed up some blueberry soup from an old package of powder I found. They're all asleep now, the tall one and the girl in Dad's cabin, the others in mine, and I've moored us to a flat, barren rock in the clear, empty dawn. I should be exhausted but I feel weirdly awake, a jubilant sense of freedom and triumph and adventure swirling through my fuzzy brain.

If I could just be happy. Because this is probably the coolest thing I've ever done.

The youngest of the four, the long-haired one I thought was a girl, is the first to wake. He climbs out of the hatch and peers around, blinking, before joining me on the rock with a surprisingly agile leap from the bow. I've made a thermos of coffee and taken out a pack of crispbread, and the kid—he's probably older than me, but somehow he feels younger—munches eagerly.

"I didn't know it could look like this," he says. "It's so beautiful."

The sea is still calm, now a shade of iron gray with hints of silver and blue, tinged with yellow and violet on the horizon, a cool, soft breeze disturbing the surface. For the first time in a long while, I feel like I could do with a jacket and a hat.

"I've never been this far out before," he continues. "I thought there'd be more people, jetties and Jet Skis and luxury cruise liners everywhere, but there's nothing. Jack shit."

"It's the wilderness, somehow," I agree. "Desolate. The water out here used to freeze, can you imagine all this covered in snow and ice? Like a big, flat, white desert."

"Ice?" The guy seems confused. "What, out at sea?"

"I've seen pictures. People used to come out here in big groups, mile after mile across the bays, around the islands. Some of them used to bring sails, carrying them on their shoulders, a bit like going windsurfing. Either that or they rode ice yachts, it looks incredible."

He frowns.

"When was this?"

I shrug.

"I don't know. A hundred years ago. Fifty. Before we were born, anyway."

"Does it make you angry?"

"What?"

A sudden gust makes the boat rock. The wind is supposed to pick up today, south-southwest.

The guy pushes his long hair back from his face.

"That there won't be any more ice," he says. "That we'll never get to experience it. Or our kids. It'll be like something out of a fairy tale. Like Atlantis, or the manatee, the dodo, the Tasmanian wolf. Gone for good."

"No," I reply, looking out to sea. "Not angry. Mostly sad."

A gull screeches in the distance, softly at first, then louder.

"OK, maybe a bit angry," I admit after a moment. "You know that feeling of wanting to punish someone?"

One by one they emerge from the boat and sit down around me, alternating between crouching and pulling their knees in to their chests, as though I were a campfire. That's how they work, I realize, they're the kind of people who sit in circles and listen to one another, like a Communist terror cell or a religious sect or a gang of role-playing eleven-year-olds.

I explain that we have barely any fresh water left on board, or gas, or food for that matter, and that we'll run out of power at some point during the day. Then I ask about their backpacks and they start squirming. In one of them, they've got nothing but spray paint, a lighter, and a couple of cheap knives. They're part of some network, apparently, coded messages in an online forum, different groups planning to *cause maximum chaos* in Stockholm, but by the time they decided to join in—*I still wasn't sure, right up to the last minute*, says the tall one, *I've always kind of struggled to see sabotage as the solution, I guess I'm just too fucking middle-class*—the other targets had all been taken, though no one had even considered the archipelago. The fact that it's full of luxury restaurants, flashy houses, gas-guzzling motorboats: the playground of the extreme, segregated superclass. And all of it unguarded, far removed from the police cars and barriers, places where even helicopters struggle to land.

"So what did you do?"

The girl is on her feet, standing away from us in the sunshine, doing some sort of salutation with her hands clasped beneath her chin.

"Do?"

I sigh.

"*Maximum chaos*, you said. So what did you do?"

They squirm again, one of them grins, they whisper to one another. In the end, it's the tall one who speaks.

"Once we got to Sandhamn we broke a few windows in a cottage and took some booze from a bar cabinet. Then we snuck out and stole gas from an outboard motor and we went down to the guest harbor and did some tagging and torched the jetty with the gas pumps on it. We were planning to do more, but . . ."

"A huge fucking Norwegian," the little one mutters. "With a goddamn harpoon or something."

"It's called a boat hook," I say, still looking out to sea. The sun is already clear of the horizon.

The spluttering of an engine cuts through the sound of the wind and the waves. I glance over to the girl, who is still busy with her sun salutation, and just above her shoulder, I see it: the gleaming mahogany boat cruising toward the skerry where we're sitting, waiting for something to happen.

———

He wanted to show me his city, the place where we once lived together, even though I no longer remembered it, and we took the sterile-smelling elevator down to the street and stepped out into the heat and the noise. I gripped his hand, bare-chested construction workers in caps, row after row of looming high-rises lined up like children in a school photo, women walking quickly and with purpose, heels clicking.

We came to a small beach with a plastic jungle gym I wanted to check out; the sand was rough and grainy, *like cat litter*, Dad laughed and smiled, and somewhere, deep down, I recognized the smell of the salty gray sea and the beach and the exhaust fumes from the road just behind us.

"We used to come down here," he said. "It was just me and the Filipino nannies, maybe the odd day trader. Sometimes there were so many other kids that there was barely room for you—you'd only just started walking—so I took you up to the club and rented a clay court so you could run around a bit. Kick the balls, climb the umpire's chair."

"Were we together a lot?"

He nodded.

"A few times, at least. I spent more time with you than Jakob; I was still playing back then, so it could be months between visits."

Dad looked sad, and he dug the toe of his sneaker into the cat litter sand.

"It got easier once he was a bit older, because we could talk on the phone. At first, anyway, but then it got harder again."

"Why?"

He ran a hand through his hair.

"Because Johanna taught him to say that he missed me." He put on a nasal woman's voice, baby talk. "*Tell Daddy you miss him. Tell Daddy you want him to come home.* That was all I heard, nonstop. Alone in some hotel in the U.S., with the entire hard court season left to play. *Miss Daddy. Daddy home.*"

We moved on, to a restaurant by the quay, and I thought about how strange it was that no one had spoken to Dad. Whenever we were in Sweden people were always coming over, grabbing hold of him, grabbing hold of me, wanting pictures and autographs, but here it was like he was just anyone else. The girls wore short jackets and tight jeans, and the men were older, with bulging stomachs that hung over their belts; the waiters had gray faces, black shirts, and red ties. A huge man in a loose black suit pushed past us while he talked agitatedly, with a strong accent, on his phone. *Things have changed, people still don't understand.*

Dad smiled.

"Iranians. There are tons of them here now. And Russians. It's not like it was in James Bond's day."

I ordered an ice cream and a Coke, Dad a beer, and we sat quietly as the sun slowly dipped behind the rooftops. Two well-dressed men with thinning hair were talking loudly about *distressed assets*. The fatty in the suit was wolfing down French fries, chewing with his mouth open. A blond woman in a bloodred leather jacket sat with an untouched glass of champagne in front of her. She looked bored, like she was waiting for someone she had no interest in meeting.

"How tall are you?" Dad asked out of the blue.

"Tall?"

"Yeah. And your weight too, if you know it."

"I'm the same height as Adam," I said helpfully. "We were friends in swim school."

He fixed his eyes on me over the top of his beer.

"And how tall is . . . Adam?"

I came close to saying that he was the same height as me, but I knew that wasn't the kind of answer Dad wanted.

"We were the tallest in our class," I said. "And when we went to the deep end we could always touch the floor the longest."

His eyes softened, and I caught a hint of pride.

"Exactly. I knew it. You're big for your age."

He leaned toward me over the table, suddenly eager.

"I'm going to talk to Malin, because it's actually *incredibly* important to make the most of these years. I was a big kid too, and that's one of the reasons I was so dominant as a junior. If you're lucky you'll hit puberty early too, do you know whether, have you . . ." He gave me a hesitant look. "I mean . . . well, whether you've noticed you . . . at night, or . . ."

The man in the suit pushed past our table with his phone clamped beneath his double chin, *there's thousands of you, they don't care . . . private jet and everything.*

"Because, you know, I only ever played tennis," Dad continued, in a different tone. "But lots of the others also played soccer, hockey, handball. And looking back now, I can see that it would've been smart to get more all-around training in, it would've helped avoid injuries going forward, but I was all about tennis tennis tennis, and it went so goddamn well in those years because I was stronger and taller and could steamroll my opponents, they used to stare at me when I stepped out onto the court—one kid actually started blubbering in a final."

He smiled sadly at the memory.

"But then, when I was thirteen or fourteen, they finally caught up with me and it all got much harder—though I still beat them. My coach arranged for me to play against boys who were two years older than me; they didn't start whining over harsh decisions from the umpire, and if they slipped on the clay and grazed their knees, they just got . . . quiet."

He leaned back in his chair, his face closed and indifferent, his mouth a thin line, hollow-eyed, something dark and cold and lonely about his gaze, a kind of creepy pantomime, but then he turned into my usual dad again.

"And I realized that if I wanted to beat them, I couldn't afford to do anything else—no friends, no class trips, no parties. By the time I turned fourteen I'd already missed hundreds of days of school, and what had once been just a bit of fun had turned into all sorts of sacrifices and demands and opponents who just kept getting bigger and older and tougher, and it was never as fun again."

Darkness had fallen over the harbor. The waves rolled in against the breakwater, the foam shimmering in the dusky light slowly getting lower and lower in his glass. The boats were dark and empty, uniformed guards on the jetties.

He sipped his beer and sighed.

"You know, I just had to forget everything, all the things that're normal at that age. I was eighteen the first time I got drunk, and I'd had to plan it months in advance—during a two-week break from competition, otherwise it had too much of an impact on my form. Imagine growing up like that. It's not right, really."

The blond girl had been joined by two others who looked almost identical to her, and they were laughing and smiling in the sunset. Dad glanced over to them and gave me a wry smile.

"I'll fix you up with some girls like that once you're older," he said, beckoning to a waiter who looked older than Grandpa. I'd never seen someone so old working in a restaurant before.

"Nope, the tennis was never quite as fun again," he continued as the old man poured him another beer. "But I still beat them."

———

It's a Pettersson. I've seen boats like this before, Dad always points them out. There's virtually nothing like this in Karlskrona, but you occasionally see them in Stockholm and Sandhamn. A beautiful, slender wooden boat, sleek and elegant, built for cruising across the water in the capital. Some of them are on show in museums, there are entire books written about this exact type of boat. Dad used to look them up online, but he never got any further than that; he always said he'd buy one once he was older, but then he got old and had different plans.

The engine dies down and the Pettersson glides the last thirty or so feet toward us. It's well tended, the mahogany gleaming and shining like caramel, a crisp new Swedish flag fluttering from the stern, the dark blue and bright yellow almost unnaturally sharp against the deep luster of the wood. The driver, who lithely steps up on deck, is a big, slightly overweight man in his fifties. He has the beginnings of a bald patch, and his cheeks are hidden behind several weeks' worth of graying stubble. A broad grin, a simple gray T-shirt and denim shorts; only his brand-new deck shoes and Breitling watch give him away.

He deftly moors the boat midships on our port side, and I drop a few fenders and help him clamber up onto *Martina*.

"What weather we've got at last," he says, using both hands to gesture to the wide, open sea as though it were something majestic, divine. "Hard not to feel happy, despite all the nonsense."

"Everything's much simpler out at sea," I agree. "All the rest just disappears."

Holding out a warm, smooth hand, he introduces himself as Sverker. He's a pediatrician and the boat is usually moored in Dalarö, but there were a few hooligans wreaking havoc there last night, so he decided to get away.

"She was my grandmother's," he explains with pride. "A wedding present from my grandfather. Already had a few years on her then, of course, but he renamed her after my granny, look." He points to the bow, where *Tekla* is written in looping white letters on the glossy brown wood.

"Meticulously tended for over a hundred years—you know, a classic like this can basically keep going forever if you look after her properly, that's why I cleared off last night." He smiles. "*Under cover of darkness*, as they'd say in the adventure books I used to read."

Sverker studies *Martina*, me, the little group on the rock.

"It's my dad's boat," I blurt out. "My dad's and mine, I mean, we own it together. I'm just out with a few friends."

He smiles warmly. "Aha, and where's your dad, then?"

"He stayed behind, in Sandhamn."

I see his eyes scanning the boat, the rigging, the moorings, the knots.

"Well, you seem to be managing just fine on your own. It's not easy to find a natural harbor out here, so you must be an experienced skipper."

I find myself straightening my cap, and Sverker glances approvingly at the crossed tennis rackets.

"You play?"

"Nah, but my dad does. He got it down there, in Monaco."

Sverker seems to relax a little. He's not going to ask any more questions, he isn't the type to ask questions, to want to seem impressed. His smile is the only thing that changes, becoming a little broader.

"How long are you out for, then?"

"Just today," I say. "Hardly ever dare come out this far, but the wind was perfect. And you?"

"I'm stocked up for a week. Probably just as well if this chaos is going to continue. You've got everything you need on a boat, you know?" He gestures discreetly to the right pocket of his shorts, where he has shoved a roll of toilet paper. "Other than a shitter, maybe. I'm just nipping ashore, then I'll leave you and your friends in peace."

"We'll probably be here a while," I say. "Take your time."

He gives me an amiable thump on the shoulder. His hand is heavy, there's power in that arm.

"Thanks, kid. So hard to find any shelter out here, I was happy when I spotted a buddy to moor onto."

Sverker gives an ironic salute and then saunters over to the bow, putting his weight on the bow line to make the boat swing in toward the rocks and then making a neat, confident leap, moving with surprising suppleness for such a big body. The group on the rocks claps and whistles, and he bows as he walks past them, muttering what must have been a joke—they laugh, in any case—before confidently continuing over the uneven ground toward a small clump of trees.

I'm still standing on deck, looking down into the Pettersson. The bright blue cover, the solid stern, the narrow, elegant bow. *They used to say that Pettersson was responsible for the birth rate going up,* Dad always liked to add, one of his favorite jokes. *The forepeak is so cramped you can barely have two people sleeping in there without making a baby. Talk about a banging boat, ha ha.*

I hesitate for a few seconds. Close my eyes. Take a deep breath through my nose and smell the hot, sun-baked veneer.

I open my eyes and glance over to the rocks. The little guy with the long hair is staring back at me. I give him a slow nod.

It all happens so quickly, so easily. They move fast, without a sound, the girl whispering to her boyfriend to help her on board, swearing softly when she slips and almost falls into the water, the others shushing her. The little guy is last, loosening the lines on *Martina* without even needing to be told; he's learning. The bow drifts out from the rocks, and he holds it back for a few seconds as he skips forward and jumps on board; the others help him up and then we're fifteen, thirty feet away, out at sea, the Pettersson following us like our own little floating pontoon, bobbing and slapping against the fenders, a cozy creaking sound as the waves rock the old wooden hull against the moorings.

"Look!" the girl shouts, her voice both terrified and triumphant. We all glance back toward the skerry and see Sverker come running from between the trees, naked below his gray T-shirt, dick swinging. He roars something inaudible and darts across the rocks, but we're sixty feet away, a hundred, he pauses by the water's edge, his entire body tensing into an arc, he clearly wants to dive in and swim after us, but we're already a hundred and fifty feet away, two hundred, he shouts again and the girl yells *FUCKING LIVE WITH IT FUCKING LIVE WITH IT*, laughing nervously as one of the boys moves over to the guard wire and pisses into the water in Sverker's direction. Some of the piss hits the Pettersson, and he howls like a wolf with his fist raised in the air, and then the others start shouting and laughing too, roaring *FUCKING LIVE WITH IT FUCKING LIVE WITH IT FUCKING LIVE WITH IT FUCKING LIVE WITH IT* as though they are at a hockey game.

I turn away from it all, away from the furious, bellowing man on the skerry and the kids shouting back at him, and I fix my eyes up ahead. There's something about the sense of freedom that spreads through me, through the soft, light movements that slowly unfurl the jib, the gentle vibrations from the rudder that carry through the hull and the wheel into my hands; the boat is alive, forcing water slowly beneath it, but still manageable.

Towing the Pettersson alongside *Martina* means it keeps pitching and bumping against the hull, and I tell them what to do: loosen the motorboat's lines and take them back to the stern. The little guy and the girl do as I say, they carry the lines like they're out walking an unusually expensive dog, and the Pettersson glides smoothly down the side of *Martina* and tucks neatly in behind us like a dinghy. I let out about thirty feet of line and then secure it tightly. Nice. It acts like a real brake, of course, making everything jolting and disharmonious, but it'll be fine for a few miles.

Nautical miles, I correct myself, feeling rather than seeing the wind fill the sail. *We're at sea now, buddy.*

———

The sun is high in the sky as *Martina* glides into the harbor in Björkskär, south of Stora Nassa, with the outboard motor running. To the east the sea opens out like a big blue film screen, and to the west the land is nothing but a dark, brooding shadow. I've never been here before, Dad doesn't like coming this far out, but once while we were in Sandhamn I read a brochure about the islands, full of beautiful photographs of a small fishing village, a jetty stretching along the rocks, a barbecue spot, the harbormaster's picturesque red cottage and cute patch of lawn, a tiny island paradise in the middle of nowhere.

"Three sailboats," the little guy with the long hair whispers, he's keeping watch from the bow. "Two motorboats. Not many people."

The minute we come into view, he and the girl get to work. They're great, giving an improvised performance in which they let their tension and nerves spill over into their roles, shouting to each other with panic in their voices, echoing over the calm surface of the water, and I see two men with bare chests—one in a white cap, the other more hipsterish, with a red woollen beanie and huge tattoos—look up from their boat.

"Help! Please, help!" I shout, pleased to hear my voice break into a falsetto. I deliberately mess up the landing, coming in so fast that we almost plow straight into the jetty. I put it in reverse and rev the engine, turning too sharply so that the Pettersson almost hits the stern of one of the other boats, fumbling with a line and throwing it into the water, trying again, managing to reach the hipster guy, who stares at me and the others with concern, then the Pettersson, which we're still towing behind us, and without asking any questions he secures the line and bears off the boat, helps the girl down onto the jetty. She lets herself fall heavily, helplessly, like a newborn calf. She found a change of clothes inside the motorboat, a pink life jacket over an oversize white T-shirt that hangs down over her hips, flip-flops, and the effect is funny and pathetic and confusing.

"Dad," she begins, "my dad has . . ." She leaves them hanging, in the hipster's bare arms, shaking with tears.

"We found her in the strait on the other side," I say, pointing across the island. "Her and the boat, we had to tow her over."

"What happened?"

A few children have appeared in the cockpit of one of the other boats, curious blond heads in orange life jackets, and a mother—theirs?—who was lying on a towel on the jetty, doing a crossword, has stood up. She comes over and wraps her arms around the girl. White Cap Guy—her husband?—is also there, and a small group soon forms around us.

"Where's your dad?" the crossword lady asks.

The girl starts to say something, but her words are drowned out by sobs. My God, we told her to act like she was in shock, but she seems completely traumatized.

"Have they done something to you?" The woman stares straight at me, at the little guy at the bow, at *Martina.* "Have these boys *done* something?"

She shakes her head, her face pressed up against Red Beanie's hairy chest.

"There was some sort of gang out there, apparently," I say, pointing across the island again. "They showed up last night when everyone was asleep and started burning and breaking things. Her dad tried to chase them away, but they took him with them."

"I went to find help . . ." the girl begins, ". . . but the damn engine."

"Seems like there's something wrong with the nonreturn valve." I have no idea what I'm talking about, but we decided that there's probably something with that name. "The boat was just drifting around, so we towed her over here."

"We tried to call the coast guard," says the little guy with the long hair, managing to sound both frightened and self-important. "And the police. And . . . my mom and dad, they're back in town, but it's impossible to get through."

The adults exchange a glance.

"It must be the same gang who were in Sandhamn," says the woman. "The ones who burned down the gas hut. They were talking about it on the radio."

"I don't know," the girl sobs. "It was so dark. Dad said if I stayed perfectly still they might leave us alone, but then they started shouting for everyone to come out, and when one of the mothers tried to get them to calm down they set fire to her boat, even though there were little kids on board, and . . ."

The woman puts an arm around her and pulls her into a hug. Another, younger mother has come running, and they all drop to the jetty, a warm heap of comforting femininity, leaving Red Beanie standing empty-handed, unsure of what to do.

"Andreas?" says White Cap. "Can you get online?"

He glumly shakes his head.

"No signal since yesterday. Everything still seems to be down."

"Damn it." He fixes his eyes on me. "Hey, kid, where was she when you found her?"

"Some way north of Horssten. I marked it on the chart."

A gruff, appreciative glimmer in his eye.

"Nice work."

Everything happens very quickly now. The men and the boys gather on the jetty, the girl tells her story again, I point out the spot, and the little guy with the long hair backs me up with a suitably vague line about seeing smoke rising above one of the islands off Horssten ("though maybe someone had just lit a fire, or maybe it was a cloud or something"). They grab their boat hooks and axes and hammers, and one of the boys, a little Black kid with curly hair, runs off and pulls up a loose plank of wood by one of the old fishing huts. He waves it threateningly, a nail still sticking out of one end; this is all an adventure to him, something is finally happening, something to tell the grandkids one day.

"Hold on, Andreas," says the mother, now in tears herself. She is still hugging the girl, they've moved over into the shade and draped a red-and-white towel over her and brought her water and cookies and poured a cup of coffee. "Isn't it better to wait for the police? Think of your back."

"No one is coming," he says, struggling into his life jacket and attaching a sheath knife to one of the straps with the determined movements of a seasoned commando. "We're on our own now, and I'm not going to let those damn cowards think they can scare us."

They get into the faster of the two motorboats and set off. I thought they would tell me to follow them and show the way, I'd prepared an argument to get out of it, but no one says a word to me. Maybe I look too pathetic, too weak, too fat. I go over to the little guy with the long hair, still sitting at the bow. The whole thing has taken no more than ten minutes, and we watch the men and the boys disappear into the distance. He starts whistling the theme from *Star Wars* again as he knocks on the window of the forepeak. The two other guys down below knock eagerly in reply.

———

Half an hour later, we're leaving the island. Behind us, columns of smoke spiral up into the clear blue sky.

When the two older guys emerged from the boat, dressed in black and with their faces covered, jumping down onto the sun-baked jetty as they shouted *WHAT DO WE WANT? TO SAVE THE PLANET!*, the people left behind, the mothers and their young children, got such a shock that they just dropped everything and ran. We ransacked their boats for anything we could use—food, water, fuel—as the girl sat on the jetty pouring gas from a jerrican into empty soda bottles, tearing out pages from the crossword book and shoving them into the necks of the bottles. There was something almost hypnotic about how focused she seemed, the way she sat on the woman's towel and slurped her coffee as she prepared her Molotov cocktails. We grabbed the gas canisters from all the boats and lowered them into the bottom of the Pettersson, then we unmoored *Martina* and drifted out from the jetty as the tall guy lit the Molotov cocktails and tossed them into the other boats. He only missed once, and they went up one after another, the flames licking their way over the jetty and down the mooring lines, up into the grass and the fishing huts as we loosened the Pettersson and used a paddle to push it over toward the jetty and the fire as we quickly reversed out of the harbor. *Shit shit shit* shouted the little guy with the long hair, and I revved the engine to get away faster and then there was a *WHHHOOOOOFFFF* as everything became one great big flaming inferno and everyone started shouting and cheering and splintered wood rained down on us. A burning plank of wood from the Pettersson hit the little guy on the shoulder and he mewed like a kitten in pain, it was complete chaos and I stood up in the cockpit and roared into the air, everyone else joined in, even the little guy, everyone but the girl, who sat quietly as though transfixed, staring back at the burning island, the trees, the houses, everything was ablaze and I saw her thin lips mouth the words *fucking live with it.*

I'm now down in the cabin, studying the nautical charts.

"Where are we?" asks the guy with the long hair. He's busy rubbing some sort of cortisone cream into his arm, that was all we could find, a tub of something Dad bought for mosquito bites.

The rest of the gang has crowded into the cockpit. One of them has opened a bottle of champagne, and we've got chips, beer, candy; we've got steaks and red wine and a load of canned goods, we've got fresh water and gas, we've got everything we need.

"Here," I say, pointing to the expanse of blue water at the very edge of the archipelago. "Here somewhere."

"Where are we going?" he asks, almost shyly. "Back?"

I shake my head.

"To sea."

"But . . . aren't we almost done now? We've . . . I mean, surely now they should realize that . . . you know, that it's time to take the climate crisis seriously?"

I laugh, realize I don't recognize my own laugh, it sounds tinny and flat, like the canned laughter from some old TV comedy.

"Seriously? Take the climate crisis *seriously*? People who spend their life savings on motorboats that guzzle three gallons of gas per nautical mile will never understand. There's no point even trying to convince them. That's not what we need to make them realize."

"So what is?"

The boat rocks and the guy reaches up to his shoulder, grimaces in pain. The ointment doesn't work, of course, and I hope someone remembered to grab the first aid kit from one of the boats we looted, because I don't think he'll be much use going forward otherwise.

I put the charts away and take a beer from the fridge. Not one of the ones we stole, one of Dad's. A Czech lager.

"We need to teach them that the worst thing isn't what nature is going to do to us, it's what we're going to do to each other."

———

Once I started high school, I was a bit less lonely. I started hanging out with some of the boys from my class, and though they all came from money, none of them lived anywhere as big or as cool as me, plus Dad was almost never home, so even though I still wasn't quite part of the gang, Douglas and Toffe started bringing their friends over on the weekends, emptying the bar cabinet. I didn't really know how to talk to people, so at first I tried knocking back the booze, but that only made me throw up, so I switched to weed, someone always had weed, and I would sit at the edge of the party, smoking, and after a while I just went numb.

She turned up again one morning, among all the empty bottles and overflowing ashtrays and take-out boxes, drinking coffee from her usual mug, sitting in her usual seat at the kitchen table, as though she had never left.

"You should probably clean up a little," she said when I emerged in my boxers. How did she always manage to surprise me when I was wearing nothing but my boxers? "I can help."

She was there to check on the plants, she told me as we tidied. The cleaners did all the basic things, like watering and removing any dead leaves, but when the plants needed pruning or cutting back or repotting, she had to be there. She was no longer an employee, she explained, she was now free-lancing as a *landscape engineer*. We both laughed at the title, and I asked *is that a bit like a hygiene technician?* and she smiled and said *more like a car care specialist*. We seemed to share the same sense of humor, as though we'd both worked out what the world was really all about.

I pulled on one of Dad's tracksuits and followed her out onto the terrace, it was cold that spring. There was some broken glass in one of the pots, the wooden deck sticky from spilled hard soda. We quickly tidied things up a little, mostly her, and then she pulled a pair of gloves from a canvas bag and lovingly set out her tools on the wooden bench. Small scissors and spades and rakes, bags of seeds, long wooden skewers, something that looked like a miniature axe. And then she planted a rhododendron and fussed over the orange tree and the dog roses and the other plants as she asked me how school was going and whether I'd decided what I wanted to do later, whether I was reading anything or just spent all my time playing video games. I answered her questions like I always did: evasively at first, then increasingly self-pityingly the longer the interrogation went on. It was easy for people like her to have opinions on my intellectual ambitions, *but a steady stream of income doesn't necessarily imply a corresponding stream of deep thoughts, and in my experience it often comes hand in hand with superficiality and banality*, I snapped, and she just smiled and said *well, that was certainly deep*.

She pulled a book with a red cover from her bag, *In Cold Blood— Sweden and Covid*. It had just come out, and according to the blurb on the back the author was critical of the many mistakes the Swedish government had made, both during the initial rapid spread of the virus and in failing to distribute the vaccine effectively enough.

"I finished it on the way over," she said. "Read it, we can talk about it sometime."

A few weeks later she was back. This time, somehow, I had known she was coming and I'd spent several hours cleaning and tidying so that the place would be nice when she sat down with her coffee in the kitchen. I didn't really know why, it's not like she was my mom, she was just another gig worker Dad had paid to come in, so why did I care what she thought? I pulled on a new navy blue tracksuit and went out to the terrace, it was warmer that day and she was over by the rosemary, picking off a few dead sprigs.

"Did you read it?" she asked without looking up.

I cleared my throat and said that I had, but that I didn't like its tone. How could it be such a tragedy that a few thousand old people in rest homes—badly run rest homes, but still—had died of flu a few months or a year or two, at most, before they would've croaked anyway? All while my generation of teenagers had been forced to sit alone in front of their computer screens, becoming lonelier, fatter, and receiving a poorer education?

Plus, I said, leaning back against Dad's comfortable old souvenir cushion from the Seoul Olympics, it was actually quite shocking that they were suddenly willing to throw so much borrowed money at society because of an illness that kills less than 1 percent of the population while also claiming they couldn't possibly find the money for measures to counter climate change that would save 100 percent of future generations. Did she know that just a tenth of the money splurged on Covid-19 stimulus measures would have been enough to keep global warming below two degrees? A tenth!

She slowly got up from the planter and brushed the soil from the knees of her dark green trousers.

"How do you know that?" she asked.

"I saw it online," I said.

"Yeah, but how do you *know*?" She smiled. "What impact are the methane gases in Siberia going to have, or the fires in the Amazon? How much does it cost to build solar or wind power and how quickly can these measures be implemented and what are we supposed to eat or drive or live in in the meantime? How do you even come up with a figure?"

I shrugged.

"I guess you've got to trust the people who know about this kind of thing. The experts."

She went inside to get her coffee and then sat down beside me on the sofa. Close up, she smelled like sun, earth, a slight hint of sweat and old clothes.

"OK, let me put it like this: Have you even seen any changes to the climate? With your own eyes, I mean."

"It's getting hotter in the summer, more really hot days. And worse winters, not as much snow or ice."

Jennie shook her head.

"You're seventeen, it's statistically impossible for you to have lived through enough summers and winters to have seen any change. What you're saying is based on comparison with average temperatures, which were calculated long before you were born. What you *know* is that it's hot in the summer and slushy in the winter, but what you *don't* know is whether that's normal or not—and by the way, people have always complained about the weather."

I thought for a moment.

"I know that when I was born the southern peak of Kebnekaise was Sweden's highest point, that it had been that way since at least the Ice Age, and that during my lifetime the glacier has melted so much that it's no longer the highest point."

She sighed.

"André, have you ever been up Kebnekaise?"

"No, but Dad says that he and I are—"

"Exactly," she interrupted me. "It's the same thing again, you don't *know*. You've never seen it with your own eyes."

We sat quietly on the sofa, looking out across the city. The sun had disappeared behind a cloud, and a cold wind was blowing up from the shadows down below. A bird hopped around in the orange tree, and I thought about building a nesting box and putting it up somewhere, either that or hanging one of those feeders or balls of food so they had something to eat, that would be cute, though the real question was whether Dad would like it or find it annoying, in all likelihood he probably wouldn't even notice it. I held my tongue and assumed she would say something to smooth things over, something nice to make everything feel good again, that's what our teachers always did at school, the female ones, anyway. They always wrapped their criticism in something soft and warm: *It's clear that you understand the principle, at the very least, I just want you to explain your thinking. What I'm really saying is that I think you can do better.*

After sitting in silence for a while, she emptied the last of her coffee into one of the pots and then went over to her bag.

"You don't know anything, André. You just sit up here feeling sorry for yourself, convinced that you've outwitted the world." She took out another three books and put them down beside me on the sofa. "Read these till next time."

===

A red lighthouse stares down at us from a rocky height. The island is surprisingly big, densely wooded, and I can make out a number of buildings on the other side of the hill. Over in the bird sanctuary, the gulls are screeching. The place doesn't *feel* alien, it's like coming home to a cozy little islet; it's only when you let your eyes pan outward, taking in the wide-open space all around us, that you really feel it, it's like being in a Tolkien book, somewhere that feels completely natural yet still tinged with a sense of incomprehensibility, vastness.

The group of islands, Svenska Högarna, is the most easterly point in the Stockholm archipelago. Beyond them is nothing but the open horizon, behind us the mainland is nothing but a brooding gray dream.

This is where Sweden ends.

The islands have come up as a target destination year after year in our summer sailing trips. Sometimes Dad would say it was too windy, other times too still, and sometimes the wind would be absolutely perfect, only blowing in the wrong direction.

For the first time, I realize that he didn't dare come out here. Dad never wanted to go on an adventure. He wanted to moor up in Sandhamn and have people admire him—either that or flit between the guest harbors on Möja, Grinda, and Finnhamn. More than anything, he wanted to get through the week with as little effort as possible. And it's only now, as I slowly, with the foresail taken in, cut past sunken rocks on the port side, the crew dead silent, just the girl at the bow, shouting out the course to me, that I realize I've always wanted to come here.

I'm wearing swimming trunks in the blazing sun as we break the mirror-still surface of the water and glide into the shallow, narrow basin. *It's hard to moor up out there*, Dad always said when he could no longer blame the wind; he usually relied on GPS and the plotter he'd downloaded onto his tablet, we never used the nautical charts. But I'd grabbed an old book from the Pettersson before we sank it, full of detailed sketches explaining how to approach the tricky harbor, and I'm sitting with it like a treasure map on my knee. *Stockholm Archipelago Routes and Harbours*, it must be from at least the fifties, maybe earlier, but it's perfect for making our way through the labyrinthine channel. As soon as we're parallel to a large rock on the port side, we need to yaw sharply to starboard. The water is no deeper than six feet anywhere around here, and the kids are staring at the sharp rocks all around us, turning to me like I'm some sort of wizard, and for the first time ever I'm no longer ashamed of my body, I let my stomach hang out, stop caring about my nipples and the fact that my dick looks tiny in these tight swimming trunks.

"Should we . . ." the tall guy whispers, taking out his mask. I nod and whistle the theme to *Star Wars*.

"There's no one here," the girl whispers from the bow. "I don't see any boats."

She's right. The minimal jetty is empty, as is the little bay for smaller motorboats. Three or four empty buoys bob in our gentle swell, and the heat is like a cast-iron lid over the calm surface of the water. A listless, sleepy feeling has crept up on me, and I realize that I haven't slept much over the past two days.

We secure the boat. The girl and the two older guys jump ashore with chips and some boxed red wine, the tall one is puffing on a cigar he found somewhere, and the others laugh when he starts coughing. The little guy with the long hair is still sitting in the cockpit, his eyes closed in the sun, his arm bandaged. The swelling is worse now, apparently; he has both a burn and a nasty wound, should really see a doctor.

Fuck it, this will all be over soon anyway.

I don't really want to leave *Martina*, but it doesn't feel right just to sit here and wait for what needs to happen. When I was younger, I used to love visiting new places, hopping ashore onto an unfamiliar rock and exploring the beaches, the bays, the brush, and the boulders. But not today. Possibly because it's not the unknown I'm looking for now.

Once the others have disappeared, I jump down onto the little jetty and set off. Svenska Högarna isn't like the other islets in the area. Rather than being smooth and flat, there are crevices and slight elevations everywhere, ravines and boulders, a network of jetties and walkways set up to allow any visitors to comfortably make their way across the rocks.

I pass an old churchyard flanked by low stone walls in the middle of the island, a parched patch of grass where, according to the information board, the old lighthouse keepers and their families are buried, but the cemetery could be older than that, the island has been inhabited since the fifteenth century, an era when I imagine it often must have been cut off from the world for weeks, possibly even months at a time, by storms, ice, or lack of wind.

I keep walking. According to *Stockholm Archipelago Routes and Harbours* there should be crowberries, heather, sea pearlwort, and *Rubus aureolus* out here, but all I can see are dead plants, withered leaves, soil the color of ash. Orchids once grew in the archipelago, I've seen pictures of a species known as Adam and Eve, a purple flower growing alongside a creamy white one like some miracle of nature, an innocent dream of paradise on earth, but now they're all gone, swamped by the juniper bushes, eaten by invasive snails, by white-tailed deer and wild boar.

Everything will disappear, all the plants and animals and fish and birds, the whole world is completely fucking screwed. I sit down on the stone wall and cry at the misery of it all, the sea levels are going to rise, the forests will burn, the arctic ice will melt. There is no end to it, because there is nothing but endings. My whole life will be one long goodbye to the future that was stolen from me years ago, and I stagger up from the wall and lie flat out in the cemetery, staring up at the dead blue sky as I doze off.

———

fucking kids

The voice is gruff, full of hatred. The ground hard beneath me. Slightly cooler.

My body is aching, I sit up with a groan. Evening light over the bushes and the stone wall; I must have been asleep for hours.

The voice again:

the fat one, with the cap

I curl up, huddle against the stone wall, shivering in the shade. The footsteps draw closer, pass on the other side.

the house up there

The sound of sturdy soles on gravel.

the lighthouse keeper

I hold my breath, make myself smaller, try to melt into the rocks, instinctively taking cover while another part of my brain watches everything

from above: the ridiculous sight of a tall, fat teenager in a snug pair of swimming trunks, lying low against an old stone wall like an enormous bug.

I hear the footsteps fade, moving upward, away, toward the center of
the island. Crawl in the other direction, back toward the harbor. Shallow
breathing, buttocks tense. I crouch down behind a bush and see two men
and two boys trudging off toward the lighthouse keeper's cottage. One of
the men is the guy with the red woollen beanie, the other one is big and
stocky, with denim shorts and a bald spot that catches the light. I creep
along the walkways in the other direction, down toward the little guest
harbor, see *Martina*'s mast sticking up above the rocks. Catch a glimpse
of the motorboat from Björkskär. Leave the walkway and scramble up the
rock to get a better view.

White Cap is sitting in *Martina*'s cockpit with two teenage boys, and
they're all peering anxiously in the direction the others just walked. There
is no sign of the little guy with the long hair.

I crawl another couple inches but can't see any other people or any
other boats, and I feel a rush of fear in my groin.

He isn't here.

He's not coming.

I shuffle back down, head the same way I just came, past the cemetery,
a wide arc to the left, smooth, warm stones beneath my feet, the sound of
voices up by the red lighthouse keeper's cottage but I don't even glance in
that direction, feel strangely calm, no real use in getting scared, it's not like
there's anywhere to run.

The girl's voice, shrill and angry.

ow! you bastard

Her boyfriend, the tall one, his voice trembling and full of cracks.

hey, could you

A hint of fear in her anger now.

ow! fucking idiot, what the hell

Sverker. Sonorous, ordinary. A polished, veneered voice, so used to giving orders that he doesn't even bother to raise it.

stupid brats, you should have thought before you

I creep past the voices and climb the hill behind the sleek rusty-red steel of the lighthouse. From the base of it, I can look down on the little house. Considering it's on an isolated, windswept lump of rock in the middle of the sea, the lighthouse keeper's cottage looks so normal it's almost surreal: a square of dead lawn in front of the freshly painted red facade, dotted with colorful plastic toys. A swing set, a few terra-cotta pots. They're crammed on the bench by the peeling white table, the two guys and the girl, with Sverker, Red Beanie, and two of the teenage boys standing in a semicircle around them, as though they've been caught red-handed stealing apples or flicking cigarette butts into the flower beds.

the fat one?

The boy who grabbed the plank of wood, the little one with the dark skin, his voice shrill and hard.

The girl mumbles something in reply. The tall one with the beard fills in.

all his fault, we said we wanted to go home but he forced us to come out here, complete fucking nutcase

The beautiful reddish-orange lighthouse looms above me like a stubby red finger. They'll search it, of course, though maybe there's some way I can defend myself in there, a door I can lock from the inside.

I smell metal and paint as I cut around the structure to the door. For a split second, I'm completely visible from the yard, and though I know it's pointless I try to tiptoe through the gravel. It's like I can see myself again, an awkward, half-naked boy attempting to play cowboys and Indians, of course they can see me, they can obviously see me, the door swings open without a sound and I'm in the darkness, no lock on the inside, a spiral staircase leading upward. I creep up one step, two steps at a time.

And then I'm at the top, a glass cage and a platform that opens out onto the sky and the sea, an empty, endless horizon. Nowhere to hide, nowhere to lock myself in, from the top of a lighthouse at the end of the world there's nothing to do but admire the view. I can see the boats down in the little harbor, I can see the cemetery, I can see the yard right below and feel an urge to wave at Sverker just as he turns his head and squints up at me, meeting my eye.

He waves back, says something to the others, points up at me with a look of satisfaction.

there

I walk around the platform and look west, toward the archipelago, a faint shadow, a sad memory, the mainland should be out there somewhere but maybe it's nothing but a myth, it feels like I've been out here all my life, in the open, naked; a flat, dead wilderness pierced by the relentless, freakish sun.

But there it is, the boat, like a scalpel cutting across the calm surface of the water, coming straight toward me. If I hold my breath and really listen, I can hear the roar of its engine. A dazzling white Princess Flybridge, heading for the edge of the earth.

———

During the last year of high school, Jennie came up to the apartment every few weeks, sometimes to work in the garden but often just to hang out with me, play some video games or watch TV or drink coffee. She even helped me with my schoolwork from time to time. I'd always found languages and social studies—history in particular—easy, but I was hopelessly behind in math, chemistry, and physics, and she patiently plodded through them with me, helping me to understand, hour after hour at the kitchen table, she seemed to have all the time in the world. When I asked if she didn't have anywhere better to be, she just shrugged, *not much business these days*. She would occasionally say something vague about friends and a boyfriend, but it was obvious she wanted to keep that part of her life at a distance.

Sometimes she brought books with her, dog-eared volumes from secondhand shops or borrowed from one of her grandmothers. When Jennie talked about her family—which she almost never did—she often hinted at some sort of inheritance, bookshelves, paintings, old pianos, surnames uttered with the same reverence Dad used to talk about McEnroe, Borg, and Năstase. The books were usually about history and politics, difficult and horrible subjects, about starvation and death, the Troubles in Northern Ireland, the camps in Siberia (and how they were linked to the Putin regime today), lynchings in the United States (and how they were linked to Trump and everything that had happened after him), about the Holocaust, the extermination of the Comanche people, the extermination of the last Aboriginal Tasmanians, the Uyghur genocide. I flicked through them and we talked about how easy it was to avert our eyes from evil, fear, and darkness, but most of all from our responsibility to see the world as it is.

"You need to understand," she said. "We need more people who understand."

Sometimes, if he was home, Dad would come out and say hello with a wry smile, but he never said anything about the books. It was his fault I was behind, I realized; he had never supported the side of me that loved reading and thinking and debating. Mom was always the one who encouraged my curiosity, who let me spend hours flicking through the encyclopedia at home. I managed to turn things around at school, got my grades right up. I felt a certain pride in disagreeing with my teachers, in questioning their lazy teaching methods and their Wikipedia knowledge. Whenever we were taught about climate change, it was always in the context of understanding the greenhouse effect and the impact of carbon dioxide, they wanted us to believe in renewable energy and planting trees, describing the benefits of biodiesel and quietly reeling off the number of square miles of sea ice that had already been lost, the number of inches by which sea levels had risen, the number of people whose ways of life would disappear.

But there was never any mention of the catastrophe, the real catastrophe. Nothing that would prepare the students who were lazily taking notes for life in a state of constant, chaotic flight from the fall of civilization. Nothing about suffering.

It was a warm winter's day, and I was sitting on the terrace in the sun while Jennie tended to the dog roses and talked about her farmers in Africa, about the sense of hope and the will to survive that could be found there, even among families who had been living on the same garbage dump in Lagos for generations, as far back as anyone could remember, if you asked where they were from they said *here*.

"The key thing is not to let yourself get depressed," she said. "To become brooding and passive. That's what they want, for you to give up—or worse, become a self-pitying downer. A killjoy. Promise me that, André, that you won't use the end of the world as an excuse to wimp out."

She went away that spring, and I partied with the boys from my class, with Douglas and Toffe and the others. We were about to graduate, and though I was neither cool nor handsome, they let me tag along. We'd started planning for our nightclub in Båstad. Jennie had made me more confident, better at talking to people—especially girls. Sometimes, when we talked, she gave me tips about compliments they liked to hear, not the kind of thing Dad had taught me, about throwing away food or shoving socks into your boxers or always making sure to pay for everything.

One night in May, there was a knock at the door. She was standing outside, tired, thin, dressed in varying filthy shades of dark green, gray, and brown. She had just got back from Zimbabwe, she told me, had been traveling around at random, staying in youth hostels; her old backpack was covered in dried-on food and dirt.

"Can I crash here?" she mumbled. "Things are a bit of a mess."

The bed in Dad's room was made up, so I told her to take her things in there and get freshened up, then we sat down in the kitchen like we always did, in the same chairs as usual. She helped herself to a bottle of wine from the cupboard, opening it and pouring two big glasses. She was wearing Dad's big white bathrobe that smelled like his deodorant, and I was supposed to be going to a party at someone's place in the country but I realized I would rather be there with her, the bright summer evening gleaming in the stainless steel on the fridge. It was just Jennie and me, like always.

"I climbed Mount Kilimanjaro. There's no snow left at the top," she said, pouring more wine. "It melted. When I was there seven years ago, there was still some snow at the very top, but now it's all gone."

She reached for my hand and took it in hers. I flinched; she never usually touched me.

"And then I wanted to see the Victoria Falls, but they're gone too, did you know that? The drought has gone on for so long that there's no water left. It was the world's biggest waterfall, you could hear it rumbling like thunder for miles, but first it turned into a pathetic little trickle and now there's nothing there at all, it's so fucking sad."

She pulled out a carton of cigarettes and lit one. I'd never seen her smoke before, and as she exhaled I said that Dad would rather people didn't smoke inside.

Jennie smiled and poured more wine.

"Your old man probably doesn't care if it's me."

We sat quietly for a moment. I wasn't thinking about anything in particular.

"He pays me to come and see you, to help with your schoolwork and that kind of thing. You know that, right?"

I nodded but still asked how long.

She shrugged.

"Since the beginning. Because you're so fucking lonely. Because he feels sorry for you."

In the faint glow of her cigarette, I saw tears glittering in her eyes.

"He even asked if I'd spend the night a few times, but I didn't want to do that because it's not right, André, it's not fucking fair to you, it shouldn't have to be like this."

She shrugged again.

"But this time I really don't have anywhere else to go. I've never been so broke in all my life."

There is a certain kind of shame, I discovered as a small child, that doesn't come from something you've *done* but from who you *are*. It's the shame of not being invited to a birthday party even though everyone else you know is going, or the shame of being invited even though you don't know anyone, because their parents are the kind of people who want to be responsible and caring, and while you hold out the gift-wrapped Lego set you brought with you, you hear someone whisper *his mom's in the hospital*. It's the shame of spending the summer holiday alone with your grand-parents, knowing that there are kids your age playing in the houses and yards and on the rocks and beaches while you're busy rummaging through a box of old newspaper clippings from forty years ago, articles written by sports journalists about the father you only see for one week a year.

And it was the shame of being the person who followed Jennie into Dad's bedroom and sat down on the edge of the bed as she undressed. I'd never seen a real live naked woman before, and though she was bigger and flatter and hairier than the ones I'd seen in porn videos, she was also more beautiful somehow, because I could hear her breathing, I could smell the tobacco and wine and earth and dirt. And I realized that what separates sex from jerking off to porn, what makes sex sex, is the shame of being seen, the shame of your dick being too small, your body too ugly, your breath too disgusting; the shame of being imperfect, of the fumbling as I unhooked her bra (she had to help me in the end), as I took out a condom and couldn't work out which way to roll it, as I lost my erection and she pulled me down onto the bed beside her and said *forget about it* and we kissed and she did something weird with her tongue and I tried to do the same and her saliva tasted sharp and then we just lay there naked and didn't do anything at all and I was ashamed, I was so ashamed of everything.

And in the darkness she reached for my limp dick and said *what the hell, André, let's do this*, and I finally realized that real arousal stems from the depths of our shame, not from the lips and tits and pussies on-screen, everything wiggling and jiggling; it comes from those quiet, gelatinous mo-ments, when you're so ashamed that you come back out on the other side and your shame becomes a kind of freedom, a comfort, a place where you have nothing left to lose. Being naked with someone else is so embarrassing that you may as well just fuck and get it over with, and she tugged at me with deft, callused fingers, reaching down to my crotch, gripping my balls like I was a weed or a dead plant to pull out, roots and all, and I felt a sudden calm as I rolled over and got on top of her and let her coax me inside, it was surprisingly warm and wet and not especially nice, but my entire crotch still started tingling after just a few seconds and I remembered the first time I ever jerked off, how it felt like I was pissing myself, I'd wondered how the hell you were supposed to do it with a girl, it must be super awkward to piss yourself while you're inside a girl, and I realized it was in that awkward feeling that it was hiding, that everything was hiding, the fear and pleasure and grief and deep shame of being human, and she stroked my back and whispered *there there*.

Dad came home from Australia a week later, and he'd only been back at the apartment for a few nights when he came out onto the terrace one morning, his graying hair standing on end and red streaks around his eyes. He pulled up his T-shirt and turned around and hissed *can you see something here?* Anticimex came around the very next day and announced that his entire bedroom was full of bedbugs, that even if we threw away the bed (which was new and had cost a fortune), they were behind the skirting board and in the cracks on the walls and in the wallpaper; the only documented method for getting rid of them was spraying a powder around the room and then sleeping in the bed for a month.

"We'll have to bring in a tenant for the summer," said Dad, scratching his armpit with a grimace. "I'll see whether I can find someone who needs a place to stay. Did you let Jennie sleep in there? With all her stuff?"

I nodded.

"That explains it. All those filthy third world countries she's been to, my God. If that scabby whore ever sets foot in here again, I'll . . ."

He trailed off when he saw the look on my face and put a hand on my shoulder.

"Sorry. Didn't mean to overdo it." He switched to his Hollywood voice. "That came out wrong, heh heh. You go to San Francisco, I'll find someone to stay here. We'll be laughing about this a few years from now. It'll be a funny story, like the time I forgot my shoes when I was playing against Lendl, have I ever told you that one?"

———

The day after we smoked weed together, I found my aunt sitting at the kitchen table, fresh out of the shower and with her hair combed back, a huge mug of coffee in her hand. She had left an old Lonely Planet guide that looked like it must be at least ten years old beside my bowl.

"I found this," she chirped. "A lot of it will have changed, but it's full of great tips about museums and libraries and historical walks and other things to do."

I looked down at the book, weighed it in my hand. The cover image was of a gaudy, newly painted cable car, the kind I'd seen the tourists waiting for down on Market Street. I picked a page at random. Color pictures of the TransAm building, the hairpin bends on Lombard Street, Chinatown. The Golden Gate Bridge peeping out from behind white tufts of cloud.

I opened the box of cereal, some sort of mint chocolate puffs I'd found, I never got tired of walking up and down the aisles in American supermarkets, exploring the synthetic, sugar-packed junk food. I filled the bowl almost to the brim and then added milk, enjoyed the popping sound.

"Why do you treat me like a child?" I asked quietly, pushing the book back across the table.

Nathalie sighed.

"You're nineteen. You don't have a job, you're not studying; you have a whole summer to yourself in San Francisco, and I just thought maybe it would be good for you to . . . I don't know, *move forward* somehow? Rather than just wandering around, eating and drinking all day? The world isn't going to bend over backward for you just because your name is André Hell. How do you think this summer is going to look on your résumé ten years from now?"

I almost started laughing.

"Anything else Dad asked you to pass on?"

She looked offended.

"Anders? I don't think I've spoken to him in years."

"I've never heard you say anything like *résumé* before. Never."

Her pale lips tensed and she got up, grabbed the book, and dangled it in front of me.

"Here. Out."

So, I tried. I wandered around Haight-Ashbury, I took the subway to Berkeley and walked up and down Telegraph Hill. I went to Chinatown and North Beach and into a bookstore called City Lights, listed in the guidebook as an *intellectual hot spot* and the *epicenter of beat literature*; I'd been past its pretty facade several times but had never felt like going in.

The air-conditioning seemed to be broken and the place stunk of musty old books. It struck me that it had been several years since I was last in a bookshop, I usually just ordered everything I needed for school online, either that or downloaded it. A guy with a gray ponytail was standing behind the counter, beside a punk girl with a ring in her nose who glared at me. The shop was like a library, with shelves for every subject you could imagine. *U.S. Politics*, *Anthropology*, *Cinema*, *Latinx Literature*. I went upstairs and saw *History*, *Environment*, *Cultural Studies*, and then I came to a small side room without any windows, where the shelf simply read *Suffering*.

I paused in front of it. A book about the Ethiopian famine in the 1980s, a baby with flies in its eyes on the cover. Beside it was a book about the plague in the fourteenth century, an image of Hieronymus Bosch. The deadly famine in Ukraine under Stalin. The labor camps in Siberia. The brutality of the Japanese soldiers during World War II, the Nanjing massacre, the death march from Bataan.

"That's new," the punk girl muttered as she walked past with a cart of books. "Since last winter, suffering's had its very own shelf."

"Why?"

"More and more research is being done into forgotten or hidden atrocities"—I'd never heard the word *atrocity* before and had to look it up later—"that have come to light as we've become increasingly aware of what people are capable of."

"OK, but shouldn't it just come under . . . history?"

"We've got a shelf for *Religion*, but what does a Jewish millionaire in the States today have in common with a Jewish sex worker in Palestine two thousand years ago?"

She pushed the books onto the shelves with loud, robotic movements.

"But why . . . why right now?"

She pulled a face.

"Have you seen the state of the world?"

She wandered off with her cart, leaving me alone in front of the books. The Tiananmen Square massacre. The Uyghur genocide. Half a shelf on the Vietnam War.

I pulled out a title about Germany in 1945, bombed ruins and sooty, emaciated boy soldiers on the cover. It seemed interesting, I'd always liked reading about the Second World War, and I took it over to a dusty but comfy-looking armchair. I wanted to read about Hitler in the bunker, that clip of him whining about all the traitors and cowards and the unfairness of the world is so funny, but the book seemed to be more about the civilian population, women who'd been raped and other horrible things. After skim reading a few pages and then flicking through the rest of it, I put the book down, disappointed, and I thought about how you could depict that moment, the instant when you realize it's all over. When the last sliver of hope trickles out of you like diarrhea after a questionable kebab pizza.

Being a loser. Most stories about losers focus on how they became winners, blockheads who win the princess and half the kingdom. Either that or they *first* become winners and *then* losers—Hitler comes out of nowhere and conquers Europe, becoming the most powerful man on earth, bringing an entire continent to its knees, but he still ends up like a rat in a heap of smoking ruins.

But what about someone who's just a loser? From start to finish, someone who doesn't stand a chance, who's helpless, pointless. Because that's how it is for most people, why doesn't anyone ever write about them?

Suffering, that's what life consists of. Different degrees and different types, sure, but everything ultimately boils down to suffering.

It started thundering the next day.

I'd heard of dry lightning before, the strange phenomenon of flashes without any rain, in a landscape so dry that any rain that does fall evaporates before it hits the ground. But actually seeing the night sky illuminated by strobes of light, the way the heavens to the east, above Berkeley and Oakland and the suburbs farther inland, sparked like a severed cable, that was something else.

The forest fires in Washington, Oregon, and Northern California had been burning since April. The drought in the ground there never really eased up these days, they explained, and the spruce bark beetle had started spreading through the bigger forests, killing trees and making them even more susceptible to fire. Everyone was afraid of the dry lightning, that it would come closer to the coast, to the big cities, the expressways, places that were home to more than a few thousand people.

And I started to understand what exactly Jennie had meant. That there is a difference between reading about the end of the world and actually seeing it with your own eyes. Watching a kingdom, drunk on sugar and youth culture and hippie nostalgia and reality TV and porno dreams and Hollywood lies, shrivel up and fall apart; it's like watching Alexandria and Constantinople and Rome and Athens all crumble to ash. Rising poverty. The annual migration inland, as the unemployment and homelessness and hopelessness on the West Coast spread like poison through a society that hadn't yet recovered from the pandemic. And on top of that, the forest fires that began earlier and ended later each year, meaning that a period that had once stretched from June to September now spanned April to November. Some parts of California were now more or less uninhabitable, there were places the insurance companies refused to cover, with homeowners unable to renew their existing policies, and I knew enough to understand that once the money starts leaving a place, the people follow.

The lightning had struck on the northeast slope of Mount Diablo, around thirty miles east of San Francisco, in the suburb of Contra Costa. It looked like a beautiful place on TV, with stunning views from long walking trails, desolate though it was so close to civilization. The fire initially covered an area of roughly a thousand acres, then five thousand. The unit of measurement meant nothing to me, but there were hundreds of firefighters battling the blaze, and several thousand inhabitants of a small community called Blackhawk were told to gather in the parking lot outside a supermarket to await evacuation.

Then the wind picked up, a hot, dry wind unlike anything I'd ever experienced before, I imagined that must be what a desert wind felt like. The lightning also started again, and the wind turned and pushed the fires on Mount Diablo toward the coast, toward the golf clubs and luxury hotels; schools burned to the ground and the fire jumped over Interstate 680 and merged with a number of smaller fires in another nature reserve, Las Trampas Regional Wilderness Park. There was a large lake there, the Upper San Leandro Reservoir, and plenty of people thought it would stop the westward spread, but the lake had dried up and the fire simply skirted around it and jumped over it and reached the next park and the next golf course, and before long I started to notice people on the streets around me, people from places like Danville, San Ramon, Alamo, and Walnut Creek, they lived out of their cars or pitched their tents down on the beach, the shops and cafés gave them water and food and there was free candy and ice cream for the kids everywhere, they were all healthy, curious, and playful, like American kids always are, but the adults had glazed, empty eyes, scrolling in confusion on their phones.

And then there was the ash, the powdery ash that fell over San Francisco, a fine layer of grayish-black dust on every street, every car, every rooftop, the green lawns that were no longer being watered but were sprayed green instead. And the sky, a golden-brown haze that turned orange when the sun was high in the sky, the same color as morning piss.

I wandered through the dawn haze one day, the air thick and difficult to breathe. Most people were wearing face masks, a habit that had clung on since the pandemic. Rather than my usual amble to North Beach and

City Lights, I went north, to the strip of beach leading to the Golden Gate Bridge. It was like people were transfixed, staring over to Marin County on the other side. The forests were burning up there, they were burning inland, a huge new blaze had started to spread around the city of Vacaville, up in Napa and Petaluma and Mendocino, in the vineyards, the ancient forests, in Yosemite, the skiers' paradise of Tahoe; the state was in flames right out to the desert.

And we stood there, at the tip of a peninsula in the richest country on earth, and watched the world burn. The Golden Gate Bridge looked majestic against the sepia-tinged permadusk, and I saw people taking pictures, selfies, groupies. Someone was selling hot dogs. Another was hawking T-shirts and postcards and face coverings with the skyline of the city against a golden-brown haze.

I stayed there for quite some time, not to see the smoke or the poisoned air but the people around me. They were witnessing the end of civilization, but they didn't scream, they didn't start a revolution, they didn't smash any windows or burn any cars, they didn't storm the TV companies' propaganda machines or execute any politicians or fossil-fuel capitalists or the lobbyists who, thanks to half a century of denial, lies, and corruption, had led them to that point.

The summer I was nineteen, I lived in San Francisco and I saw people taking pictures of the end of the world.

I thought about the fact that the fires had started on Mount Diablo, the devil's mountain. I thought about my surname, *Hell*. It's an old name that emerged during the eighteenth century, and it probably meant either "light" or "luck" at one point in time, but people usually just think of the English meaning, cracking jokes about it. When I was younger I used to imagine hell as a place where the guilty were dealt their punishment and finally had to repay their debts, but the older I get, the more I realize that it's really just a comforting myth of justice, because there won't be any punishment, no score settling; judgment day is mankind's collective lie, because time keeps marching on even as everything ends.

———

"What a bunch of crap, eh?" Dad says with a laugh. "People get up to such crazy stuff. I heard them talking on the radio about a couple of Sámi who've occupied a hotel up in Lapland. They've dragged their reindeer down there with them and are demanding to talk to the government, did you ever hear anything like it? A bunch of damn Laps!"

The others stare at him in silence. Dusk has started to fall, and I'm crammed onto the garden bench beside the other activists. Dad must have braced himself with a few glasses of Kalderén's best whiskey, because he is being unusually loud and cheerful. He thumped Red Beanie on the shoulder earlier, and he almost looked like he wanted to give Sverker a hug when the man recognized him. *I saw you in the Davis Cup final, Munich 1985, it was the decisive match*, the pediatrician said slightly stiffly, and Dad corrected him, *no, that was Stefan, I'd lost to Becker in the match before*, he grinned his wolf's grin and continued, *though it was kiiind of deliberate, because it was always so fun to mess with Stefan, he got so stressed when it all hinged on him*.

He is now leaning back against the wall of the cottage, squinting in the evening sun, radiating a kind of triumph at the fact that he finally made it all the way out here, *even if it was a bit unexpected, heh heh, had to break into a fishing hut to find some juice, it's wild how much these engines guzzle up*.

"And have you seen the clip someone uploaded earlier? Some preschool teacher has taken over an entire camp and started making speeches to the Swedish people?! Totally crazy." Dad smacks his lips and chuckles to himself. "A little preschool teacher! With a huge goddamn dog."

"*Tekla*," says Sverker, his tone cold.

Dad's face is blank. "Tekla?"

"My boat. Inherited from my grandmother. Meticulously tended for over a hundred years."

Dad gives a solemn nod. "Yeah, I'll be damned. Those boats are fantastic. Incredibly bad luck with the accident. But like I said, the main thing is that no one got hurt. Everything else can be replaced." He shrugs and puts on his American accent. "It's just money."

"Accident?" says Red Beanie.

"Well, whatever you want to call it. Everything is insured and the youngsters have said they're sorry, so surely you gentlemen just need to write down your addresses and phone numbers and we'll stay in touch, work something out."

"My kids were chased away." Red Beanie's voice breaks. "My wife ran for her life with our baby in her arms. While these . . . *youngsters* shouted and laughed and set fire to all our things." He points at me with a trembling finger. "And that piece of shit, he was the worst."

"Like I said," Dad repeats calmly, "André is very sorry that things got out of hand." He nods at his own words. "Really, it's terrible, what a day we've all had."

He crouches down, never looks more like a former sports star than he does when he's crouching down, something sporty about the balancing act between his thighs and his glutes, no dignity whatsoever, like someone taking a shit. He runs a hand through the dead grass and looks up at the other men.

"But I think we need to put things into perspective. There's chaos everywhere, soldiers on the streets, a national state of emergency. It's hardly surprising the kids flipped out a little."

Dad stands tall again, lets out a sigh.

"And that means we adults need to set a good example. Show them that the rules are the rules. This is Sweden, after all."

Sverker and Red Beanie look at each other, at the two teenage boys, at the small, dark-skinned kid. Then they nod wearily.

"Fine," Sverker mutters. "Go, before it gets dark. We can sort everything out once we're back in town."

"Excellent." Dad smiles. "Come on, then, we can all fit in the motor-boat." The activists get up, move toward him, not looking at each other.

"And we'll leave the police out of this, of course," he adds as though in passing, his tone neutral.

The scene turns to ice.

High above us, the lighthouse looms like a prehistoric predator, a reminder of where we are, farthest out, farthest away. Alone.

"Weren't you just talking about rules?" says Sverker, his voice flat, smooth, hard.

Dad shrugs, ignores the question, and keeps walking, trying to pretend he didn't hear him.

Red Beanie puts a firm, slender hand on my shoulder.

"This guy needs to be punished."

Dad turns around, makes a face, and rolls his eyes, as though he has just heard something incredibly embarrassing, like when he wanted to challenge a bad decision on the court, anyone could see that ball was in.

"To be *punished*? What, ten lashes? Chop his little finger off? Do we live in Saudi Arabia now, heh heh?" He shakes his head. "The boy has apologized. Do you really think this needs to go on his record? All because a few boats got knocked about a bit? Come on."

He keeps walking with his head held high, making his way back toward the little harbor. The hand lets go of my shoulder, I'm free.

"But I haven't," I say.

It's the first time I've opened my mouth since Dad arrived, and it has the effect I was hoping for. Everyone freezes. The Black boy looks up at the adults, at me, like he is following a tennis match, his mouth a thin line of tense expectation.

"I'm really not sorry for destroying your pathetic little fuck boat," I say to Sverker, turning to Red Beanie. "Or for teaching your spoiled brats a lesson. Those boats you like to show off with could have paid for clean water, vaccines, solar panels, food parcels for starving families in Yemen. You deserve all the shit you get, all of you who turn your back on the suffering in the world."

Sverker is staring at me. I smile.

"Just think of all the history in a boat like that. It was so fucking awesome watching it burn. Shame you didn't get to see it. Sorry. I should've filmed it."

Something happens below his thinning hair, beneath all the layers of education and career and family and friends; it's the memory of all those long winter hours spent sanding and scraping, of summer days and splashing children and clear blue skies and the scent of varnish, it's the story of a boat that represented something more, a story with an ending he knows he'll have to live with for the rest of his life, and I see his fists clench and lower and his eyes darken, and I steel myself. Finally.

But the doctor just takes a deep breath and shakes his head.

Whispers:

"Get out of here. I hope I never have to see you again."

Red Beanie shouts something, the teenage boys shout something, but I don't hear a thing. All I know is that I've failed again, that my plan to provoke an outburst, a show of violence that would force Dad to step in and protect me, was naive and stupid and embarrassing, of course it was, just like the rest of my life has been one long line of embarrassing failed attempts to be something other than the loser I am, and I turn around and trudge after Dad and the others.

I hear footsteps behind me, it's the little Black boy waving his plank of wood, shouting *just go home, you chicken, go home, go home to your mommy, you fat pig* and maybe it's because of the disappointment that my plan didn't work out, or maybe it's because he said the word *mommy*, maybe it's everything, but I turn around and fold my arms and say *shut your mouth, you fucking monkey.*

and he shouts something

swings the plank of wood toward me like a tennis racket and I take a step back, stumble, fall to my knees the adults start shouting, I see Red Beanie running toward us

stop Alex stop Alex stop

the boy raises the plank again, his face twisted in anger

and Dad's hand is on my arm, trying to pull me up

and the sickening, dull thud of wood on flesh and bone

and time that seems to slow to a crawl when I see Dad lying on the narrow walkway, the blood, the hole in his head

the boy is still holding the plank

the nail at the very end

fuckfuckfuck Alex

fuck Anders what happened it wasn't

Sverker is by his side, his hands on Dad's head, a clinical, gloomy gaze

fuck this needs stitches Jesus if the nail went in then I don't know if he

and Dad's eyes open and he looks at me and mumbles

out of here

and I don't know what that means, whether it's me who should leave, or him, or both of us, but I manage to pull him up with his arm around my neck and I yell *just leave us alone! fuck off!* and we limp away together, leave the others behind.

My dad and me.

———

"Does it hurt?" I ask.

Dad mumbles something in reply, stumbles, almost falls. I look down at the wound on his temple. The blood isn't seeping out, it's sort of pumping in small squirts, and his face is pale.

"They hit me," he mumbles.

"Yeah, God, they fucking hit you. Stay with me, Dad."

We stagger down a walkway, around a rock, another walkway. Past the little cemetery. We can see *Martina*'s mast now.

He got hit on the head while he was trying to protect me. We escaped together.

His body is heavy on mine, his breathing shallow, the blood sticky on my bare shoulder.

We escaped together, but we were at the very edge of the archipelago and there was no one to help us and he was dying.

A few more rocks, then the little harbor. I can see from the corner of my eye that there are still people on *Martina*, but the motorboat is just beyond it, Kalderén's Princess Flybridge. Good. I've never driven a boat like that before.

He was dying and I tried to pull him on board but I was too weak.

Voices behind us, the others have gathered, they're going to try to save him, hurry now.

I lead him over to the motorboat, feel a slight twinge of sadness when I recognize Dad's neat mooring, two half hitches.

But I was too weak and he was too out of it. And then he fell into the water and drowned.

He can't hear me, reaches for the bow pulpit, groans, pulls it toward him, fumbles, tries to crawl over.

He fell into the water and drowned. And I couldn't help him because I'm too fat and clumsy and weak.

I grab his belt as he is mid-step, hold him back. The boat swings out and he is left with one foot on the bow and the other on the jetty. Yet again, I'm reminded of a cartoon character hanging horizontally in the air, just like when I tried to get onto those rocks. Dad whimpers, practically doing the splits, and as I feel him lose his balance I let go of his belt.

I let him fall.

I come *this* close to calling for help, the impulse is so strong, and that might actually have been a smart move; if anyone starts asking questions later I can always say I tried, that I really did all I could. But there's a risk that Sverker and the others will come to the rescue.

Then it strikes me that I can say anything I like, I can claim that I shouted, cried for help. What are they going to say, that I'm lying? Why would I do that? Everyone saw what happened.

So I stand quietly, leaning down to watch his arms flail in the water. I see his jerky, silent movements, hands searching for grip on the smooth rock, the bow of the boat hitting his shoulder, his blood mixing with the seawater, his white eyes, the black water, the damp gray locks of hair clinging to his head.

"I'm too fat and clumsy and weak," I whisper. "Zat's juzt who I ammm."

Dad had given Granny and Grandpa some money to renovate and extend their house, which meant that what was once my bedroom was now part of a guest wing with its own kitchen. *It's good*, they said, *because this way we can rent it out and bring in a bit of extra money.* I could always sleep in the basement if I wanted to, they told me, the old corduroy sofa was still there. Slightly worse for wear, of course, but perfectly comfortable for sleeping.

I had flown home from San Francisco earlier than planned—the smoke from the fires made it impossible to spend any time outdoors, so I changed my ticket—and since Dad had someone else staying in the apartment, helping to get rid of the bedbugs, I had nowhere else to go except the old, now rebuilt, house in Karlskrona.

It was warm and I didn't know anyone else in town. I borrowed Grandpa's bike and rode to the center, ate ice cream and burgers, walked along the waterfront, occasionally went to a swimming spot nearby to sunbathe. Grandpa was incredibly fit for an eighty-year-old, and he nagged me to go out fishing with him a few early mornings. You could catch cod, pike, and perch there not so long ago, and eels, of course, but we didn't land a single thing. There were no fish left in any of the bays or clumps of reeds, everywhere was empty, dead, the only sound from Grandpa's old outboard motor. I thought about trying something new, windsurfing looked fun, or maybe learning the front crawl, but the weeks passed and I started reading some of the books I'd brought home from City Lights. Jennie had gone back to Africa, and I wrote to her on the various chats I knew she used, but she never replied.

The summer I was nineteen, I lived in my grandparents' basement in Blekinge and life was nothing.

Since I didn't seem to have much to do, Granny discreetly suggested that I might like to paint their fence for them. It would probably take a week or so, but maybe I could fit it in? I wasn't used to doing DIY, but the idea of painting the fence was appealing, there was something so concrete and definite and Tom Sawyerish about it, so Grandpa and I went to buy brushes and rollers and paint, we planned and measured, the sun kept shining, perfect painting weather.

Grab some gloves from the garage so you don't get all messy, Grandpa told me once everything was ready. So I went inside, it was full of old junk, tools, nuts and bolts, an old bike, life jackets, a broken outboard motor, an ancient TV, and several long, slim boxes of film slides no one would ever look at again; the almost humiliating inability of old age to get rid of worthless junk.

And then I spotted the box. *ANDERS!* written in black Magic Marker. I'd forgotten it even existed. It must have been ten years since I last opened it.

Without thinking, I took out one of the ring binders, flicked through the clippings, traced a finger over the golden era of Swedish tennis triumphs. I hadn't been able to read the British tabloids in the past, but now I smiled at the clever headlines. If Dad had had a good week, they wrote things like *Swedish Ace Delivers . . . The Week from Hell*; if he served well it was *The Serve from Hell*, if an opponent faced him in the quarters or the semis or the final, *Welcome to Hell*, and if his opponent won it was *Back from the Brink of Hell*. The scent of old newspaper, glue, ink.

And then I spotted a red plastic folder I didn't remember. I pulled it out, leafed through the sheets of paper. Printouts of emails.

Emails didn't exist in the 1980s. Dad's career was over before the internet was even a thing.

I sat down on the floor to read. The sender was info@kryc.nu, the recipient teamhell_official@gmail.com. The emails began politely enough, but the tone quickly became unpleasant.

They were from Karlskrona Royal Navy Yachting Club, the boat club not far from Granny and Grandpa's place. One of their CCTV cameras had caught a young boy breaking into the club's premises late one night in October, and with the help of IT experts they had managed to produce such a sharp image (attached) that you could clearly see the logo on his cap. Using the cap and other distinctive features, they had eventually come to the conclusion that the boy in the image was none other than André Hell, who they knew visited the city during the school holidays—the local press had written about Anders Hell's parents and children several times, highlighting their links to the city.

We tried unsuccessfully to reach you both over the phone and through your agent, and are therefore now attempting email, the club wrote. *The reason we are keen to establish contact is that a boat was vandalized that same night, and we have reason to believe that André was responsible.*

Dad had replied, evasively at first; he was incredibly busy but promised to get back to them shortly. He hadn't, of course, and the boat club had sent more emails, to which he eventually responded—dismissively: *Find it very hard to believe that it's André in the picture, those caps are everywhere.* Then, when the club supplied more evidence, he became increasingly arrogant: *It could be absolutely anyone. I find it incredibly hard to believe that André could have done what you're claiming and find it rather strange that you're wasting so much time on such an insignificant matter.*

But then, once he could no longer worm his way out of it and the boat club threatened to hand over the evidence to the police, Dad's tone changed.

André is extremely fragile, he wrote. *His mother just died. You have to feel sorry for the boy.*

Karlskrona Royal Navy Yachting Club demanded a sum that was probably higher than the boat was worth. Dad requested their account number.

All I ask in return is that you keep André out of this. No police, no contact with his school or social services. Just leave him in peace.

The boat club pointed out that in addition to the money, the owner also wanted to meet the boy who had vandalized his beautiful boat.

Just leave him alone. He shouldn't have to deal with you.

The boat club thought it would be good for a boy of André's age to face up to the consequences of his actions.

What is it you don't get? Enough with this nonsense. I've told you, forget about André, otherwise I'll take this up with my lawyers and then you can KISS YOUR PETTY FUCKING CASH GOODBYE.

This time, the boat club didn't reply.

The last email was sent a few months later. Dad apologized for losing his temper and wrote that the money should now have been paid, along with a small bonus. He would print out their correspondence and keep a copy in a suitable safe place in case the matter ever came up again. The email was strange and incoherent, full of irrelevant information and links to various child and youth psychology forums; I guessed he must have written it while drunk.

Finally, wrote Dad, *I'd like to say THANKS for being so discreet and helpful. André is sensitive, he's insecure, he's nothing like I was. He's called André because Agassi was my last competitive match. He beat me in straight sets and I sometimes wonder if that's why the kid's such a loser, because I named him after a loss, after the moment when it was all over.*

He continued:

He's my love child, all I have left of Malin. I'm embarrassed of my son, but I'll never stop protecting him. Never.

———

"This is where he lived," says Dad, his voice weak and quivering like jelly.

We're speeding over the water in our borrowed Princess Flybridge. He is lying on the big white sofa behind the steering wheel, damp, bloody, his face ghostly white.

We've passed Sandhamn, heading for town, and darkness is quickly falling around us in the powerless August night, but the boat has GPS and radar and cameras that mean it could get back to central Stockholm on autopilot. Still, I'm standing here at the wheel in Claes Kalderén's old shorts and T-shirt. It's the first time I've ever driven a motorboat, or at least one that can go as fast as this, and it's a powerful feeling: the wind in my hair, the roaring engines cutting through the waves, the raised bridge. If I could just work out how to turn the stereo on, I'd try to make it play some Wagner.

"Who?"

Dad doesn't reply, he just sighs, closes his eyes, whimpers.

He's not going to survive, I think.

He has to survive.

He can't survive.

Then:

Maybe it doesn't even matter anymore. What mattered was to show him that I could.

"Who?" I ask again.

"Who what?"

"Who lived here?"

"Borg. Out here on Ingarö."

I peer over to the dark shadows, the screen, the nautical chart. Ingarö isn't here, Dad is wrong, he rarely gets anything wrong about the archipelago, can find his way everywhere, and I'm about to point out his mistake when I decide that enough is enough. I don't have anything left to prove. Let the man be old. Let him die. Let me forget. Let me forgive.

Let me stop being ashamed of the person I became.

"Have you ever been there?"

"Yeah," Dad wheezes. "Yeah, of course. When he turned fifty, big party."

"What's he like, then?"

He doesn't reply, just rolls over onto his side, his breathing shallow. He takes blood thinners, I know that. Is that good or bad?

"Dad," I say, a little louder this time, suddenly afraid. What am I going to tell Jakob and Karolina? Nadja? The police, the hospital, the media?

"Yeah?"

"What's he like?"

"Who?"

"Björn Borg, obviously."

His voice is a whisper:

"No idea."

I see lights flickering to the west. Just one at first, then an entire cluster of them. The power is back on the islands. Up ahead, above Stockholm, a bright dome has formed in the dark sky.

Light pollution. An environmental catastrophe we still don't fully understand.

"But you said you'd met him."

"Who?"

A cold wind cuts through the silence. A few drops of rain hit my face. It's been so long since that last happened that the unfamiliar sensation makes me jump.

I pull on my cap, straighten it.

There.

"Who?" he asks again.

"Come on, Dad. Björn Borg."

"Yeah, met." He sighs, groans slightly, breathing more heavily now. "But you don't just *talk* to Björn."

"No?"

"Nah."

Everyone You Meet

THE FIRST TIME I NOTICED THAT THE GROWN-UPS WERE afraid of the weather was the summer Zack learned to read. It was super hot even before the semester ended, we had to take sunscreen and water bottles to school every day, the teachers opened the windows during class, and Mom stocked the freezer with ice cream. And a few weeks later, while we were renting a house on Gotland, I heard Dad having a serious conversation with Mom about something he'd read online. I don't remember exactly what he said, but two words jumped out.

Emergency slaughter.

Two horrible words, crammed together. Slaughter is when you kill an animal to eat it, and emergency is when you need help, so what was *emergency slaughter*? I imagined a cute little cow with an axe in its neck, standing beside a big red button, and then Mom saw I was upset and started explaining what Dad meant, but I didn't want to know, didn't want to hear about all the animals that had to die just because it was so nice and warm and sunny.

Because it was nice, I remember that. I learned to swim really well that summer, right out to the raft and back again without any trouble; I learned to dive from the jetty, and at night I left the windows wide open so I could hear the birdsong and smell the garden, and every morning we sat beneath the apple tree and ate long breakfasts with strawberries and milk and Dad's homemade bread. It stayed warm until late in the evening, and I ran barefoot through the dry grass in my pajamas as the sun dipped like a big red orange.

Then we went home, and just a few days before school started again Dad decided we should do something fun together for the last night of our holiday, so we went down to the sea, just him and me and Zack. There was a little scrap of sand where we sat sometimes, by the jogging track, and Dad lit a fire by the water's edge and took out a bag of marshmallows and a knife, said *let's toast some marshmallows, we used to do this all the time when I was your age.* He told me to go among the trees to collect some long branches, and he showed me how to whittle them into skewers. We gathered more twigs, bark, and dry leaves, and he built a kind of pyramid and then lit it from the bottom with a match, and we watched as the flames took hold and it started to burn.

Technically there's a fire ban, he said, sounding kind of ashamed, *but we're so close to the water I don't think anything can happen.*

Zack was reading Harry Potter on the sand. Mom and Dad were so proud that he wasn't stumbling his way through some easy baby book full of pictures, that he'd gone straight to reading big, fat books that were practically for adults. We were having a nice time in the evening sun, the flames crackling and popping, and Dad let me try a cold marshmallow while we waited for the fire to be ready. But then the wind started blowing from the sea, a warm, dry wind that whipped up the waves and played with the fire and sent sparks flying into the air, and suddenly I spotted some smoke a couple feet away, in the grass above the beach. Dad shouted *shit* and ran over and started stamping and jumping on the flames, *grab the thermos*, he yelled, we had a thermos of hot chocolate and I unscrewed the lid and poured it onto the burning grass, but it felt like it was just a tiny splash and Dad tore it out of my hand and ran down to the water, filled it up, and came back to the fire, which was now at least twice the size, almost like it was chasing itself over the grass, *shit shit shit it's the fucking drought*, Dad shouted, trying to stamp it out again.

Before I knew it I was on my knees in the water, gathering up armfuls of seaweed. The water was murky and smelled kind of gross after months of hot weather, there were black-and-white lumps of duck shit floating on the surface, and beneath that there was seaweed and seagrass that was brown and yellow and green, like Zack's snot when he was a baby, and I grabbed as much of that sloppy mess as I could and then got to my feet and ran up the beach and dumped it all on top of the fire. The wet slime covered the burning grass, making it hiss, and a thick column of smoke rose up into the air. I couldn't see any more flames, but Dad kept stamping all around it, and the fire died out. He stared at me in confusion and yelled *keep going, for God's sake* and then rushed down to the water to get more seaweed. I did as he said, kept going up and down to the murky water with armful after armful of disgusting, filthy seaweed, stamping over and over again, and before long there was nothing but smoke and sticky seagrass and duck shit on the ground.

The fire we'd built for the marshmallows was still burning, and I noticed that Zack was staring into the flames. He had put down his book and was sitting on the sand, looking into the flames with his old man's smile, and I wanted to yell at him for being such a useless, worthless brat, but Dad gave me a stern glance and sat down beside him, hugged his shoulder, and said *you OK, buddy? You weren't scared, were you?*

"Do you know why horses run the wrong way when there's a fire?"

Zack gave us both an amused look, like he was telling us some kind of funny riddle.

"It's because before they were tame they lived in the wild, and they only survived the fires if they ran through them to the other side, where everything was already burned!"

Dad dug out a marshmallow, stabbed it with his stick, and held it in the flames.

"Let's toast," he said wearily. "Let's toast these and then we'll go home."

"But," Zack continued, "that means if there's a fire in a stable it's really hard to save the horses because they keep escaping and running back into the flames."

Dad looked at me, at my filthy tank top and wet pants.

"You'll have to wash those when you get home. And not a word to your mother."

"Why not?"

With his free hand, he speared another marshmallow and handed the stick to Zack, showed him how to hold it close to the heat.

"Why not?" I asked again.

Dad sighed.

"This goddamn weather," he said, his voice thick. "It's crazy. It makes me so sad that you two have to grow up like this, that it's only going to get worse every year. In the paper today, they said this was the hottest summer on record, but it's still colder than every summer you and Zack will live through going forward."

He turned the stick so that his marshmallow was evenly toasted.

"You'll miss all this, one day," said Dad. "You'll miss the time when you could live like this, when everything was so simple."

"It doesn't feel simple," I said.

We didn't say much more after that. Zack dropped his marsh-mallow into the ash and started crying his eyes out, but Dad comforted him and gave him his. My little brother and I ate marsh-mallows until our stomachs were bulging with the gooey, sugary mess, and then we poured water onto what was left of the fire and went home, and I told Mom I'd tripped and fallen.

MY FAVORITE VINTAGE SHOP HAS A PAIR OF RED BOOTS THAT look like Bianca's Docs, only more of a retro style, kind of slim fitting at the top, like cowboy boots. They've also got one of those American varsity jackets, green leather with white letters, and there's a little yellow baguette bag too, with a silver buckle; I'll have to go and have a look as soon as we get home, I get so stressed that they have all this stuff in while I'm stuck here in a fucking line that I almost feel like crying. It's just like when I was younger and Ghetto Girlz released new merch at six p.m. It was *first come, first serve* but Dad was still at work and Mom was putting Zack to bed and no one seemed to get that the merch was about to sell out, and when Dad eventually came home he said that he had no intention of buying any goddamn hoodies before I'd cleaned my room, you could hear that he'd been drinking and Mom slammed the door and I crawled around on the floor by my bed, crying and picking up socks and underpants and tissues and old shopping bags and candy wrappers, and when Dad eventually nodded with that grumpy look of his and said that my room was *acceptable* I started screaming that it was *first come, first serve* and he said *it's* first come, first served, *as in you'll be served first, surely you know that, what the hell do they teach you in school,* and I said please please please please, I'll do anything, I'll clean cook look after Zack put the laundry away hang out with you and watch documentaries about Greta Thunberg and the climate if you'll just get this for me, if I can just have one, and he finally sat down in front of the computer with his credit card in his hand and one of those heavy, weary, almost *damp* sighs of unhappiness, and I brought up the Ghetto Girlz website with shaking hands and clicked on merch and it was all gone.

All gone.

Everything I want always disappears. Everything I love gets taken by someone else.

If you want something, you've just got to grab it. No hesitation. No waiting.

There are still a load of people ahead of me in the line, waiting to get to the bottles of water on the wooden table. I turn around and peer back over to the platform. Nothing. Still, Dad is wearing a purple Lacoste T-shirt that practically glows through the dirty, sweaty, whiny crowd, plus they've got Becka's bright red diaper bag; I'm sure I'll be able to find them. Most people are just taking their bottles and moving on, but some are asking a bunch of questions the kid at the front can't answer, either that or they're complaining, moaning about the buses trains food parcels doctors who should be here but aren't; almost my turn now, I wonder how many bottles you're allowed to take, some people are taking three or four, their arms full, but there aren't very many left on the table now, I'm sure they must have more somewhere. An old woman who stinks of rotten flowers and piss comes over to the line and stares at me with sad eyes. *I'm about to pass out*, she whispers, *I'm going to pass out if I don't get something to drink, I haven't had anything to drink since yesterday*. She's leaning on a golf club and looks like she might collapse at any moment, sweat and makeup running down her wrinkled face. I tell her she'll just have to get in line like everyone else, but I can hear from my voice that it's not going to work, she just stands there with her golf club, staring at me, her sad eyes streaked with gloopy mascara, her trembling lip and old-lady perfume and piss stench and one of those cute little Mulberry bags—it's so sweet when old women have Mulberry bags—so I let her cut in front of me and the line is slowly lurching forward, there'll only be ten people ahead of me soon. I glance back over to the platform, it's even more crowded now but there are still no trains, there'll probably never be any trains because nothing works anymore. I scroll through my feed again. Adeline is in Miami, Stella is in Portugal, Bianca is at their place down in Skåne and she's dyed her hair black and had it cut into one of those short pixie styles, it looks totally insane and I zoom in on the picture to try to come up with something positive to say, something nice to write, but it's actually impossible to think of anything that doesn't sound totally fake, so in the end I just like it and then I look up and see that I'm at the front of the line and the table is empty.

"Water," I say to the boy.

"All gone," he says, pointing to the old woman, who is hobbling away quickly with her golf club. "She got the last two."

I stare down at the table, at him, at the table again.

"But you must have more bottles somewhere, right?"

"Nope."

"But . . . what about in the shop?"

"Do you see any shops that're open?"

I glance over to the old woman again, just as she disappears—moving amazingly fast now—into the crowd of people pushing toward the station. Her pink Mulberry catches the light in a final farewell, and then she's gone. I turn back to the boy and he meets my gaze with his calm blue eyes.

"Seriously, what the fuck?" I say.

"Yeah." He smiles. "What the fuck."

Then we just sort of stand there, looking at each other. He's maybe fifteen or sixteen, with thick dirty-blond hair parted in the middle and a light fuzz on his upper lip and cheeks. He looks like he has a wad of tobacco under his lip, and he's wearing what seems to be a blue-and-white team shirt under his hi-vis vest. Slim, angular shoulders; he looks like the kind of person who works out all the time but will always be a little scrawny.

"You here on your own?" he asks. I even like his accent. Most people up here annoy me the minute they open their mouths, but he's got a kind of singsong voice and it doesn't sound lame at all, just nice.

"Nah, I'm with my parents. And my sister, but she's only a baby." I should probably say something about Zack too, but why? It's not like he's here. I think about Lana Del Rey and then I think about how I shouted at him, shouted and said horrible things until his feet started bleeding, and now he's missing and Mom and Dad just keep arguing. The total chaos of yesterday sinks in, making me feel sick, like when you've eaten too much popcorn and chips and cheese puffs at a sleepover. I'm ashamed of everything, I wish I was someone else standing in front of this cute, awkward country boy with his big, kind smile and his dimples that are so sweet I have to stop myself from reaching out to touch them with my fingertips.

"I've got my own water, if you're thirsty," he says, holding out a blue plastic water bottle. I take it and gulp down a few warm mouthfuls. The bottle feels rough beneath my fingers, and I look down at it once I've finished. There is a big strip of white tape with the word *PUMA* written on it in black letters, and I glance up at him and frown and give him a questioning smile and he blushes.

"So, there was this guy on the team who started calling me Puma because I was the only one who had those shoes, and then everyone else on the team started doing it too, and so did my friends at school, and now that's what everyone calls me. My real name's Rob, though." The way he kind of trips over his words is so cute. "But my mom's the only one who ever actually calls me that. Robert, I mean, not Rob. I doubt anyone's ever going to call me anything but Puma, except maybe if I have a wife one day."

"I'm Vilja," I say. "Stupid name, I know."

"Are you from Stockholm?"

I nod.

"You on your way back home, then?"

I shrug.

"Maybe. I guess so. Not sure. You?"

"We were meant to be playing a match against Lima, but it got called off because of the fires, so our coach sent us out here as volunteers, to help people."

"Fun?"

"Not really. Everyone seems totally crazy."

He holds out the bottle again, and I'm just about to take another sip when a blaring siren scatters the people still crowding in front of the train station, and we both turn toward the sound as an ambulance glides quickly through the throng. I see an old man in one of those power wheelchairs or

whatever they're called roll out of the way in panic, and I find myself thinking about the old woman with the golf club, whether she'll be run over or
whether she'll be OK. I half hope she'll be fine, there was something kind
of cool about the way she counted the bottles and got into the exact right
place in line so that she'd get some but I wouldn't.

The ambulance comes to a halt when it reaches the table where we're
standing. The window rolls down and a man in uniform peers out.

"You're Vilja, right?"

Zack, I think, *they've found him*. I turn to the platform, looking for
Mom and Dad, but I can't see either of them and the fear is like an icy snake
slipping inside my top and down toward my gut. "Is he alive?" I whisper,
and the guy in the ambulance looks tense.

"He's going to be admitted. We've been trying to reach his relatives, do
you know whether he has any other family nearby?"

"I . . . other family?"

"Yeah. He's your granddad, isn't he? We tried to find you at the campsite."

Everything grinds to a halt. Granddad?

"We're taking him to the hospital now, in any case." The paramedic guy
sounds stressed. "If you're going to come with us, now's your chance. Otherwise, get in touch if you think of anyone else who should be informed . . .
who should know, I mean . . . that he . . . that Martin doesn't have long left."

"Is that your granddad?" asks Puma.

I squirm.

"Kind of, I don't know . . ."

"You don't know if he's your granddad?"

The paramedic says something else and then rolls up the window and
pulls away. I watch the ambulance drive off and I think about being in the
countryside when I was younger, the dogs I used to walk, taking them
down to the lake, the old man who drove us around yesterday in the heat
and the smoke, the way he told me and Mom everything would be OK, he
never got lost, he knew the roads, the fires were nothing to worry about

and Dad had probably just taken a wrong turn, and I feel the tears rolling down my cheeks.

"Vilja?" Puma asks softly, taking my hand. "Is everything OK?"

I shake my head.

"No," I say. "Nothing's OK."

"Shouldn't you go with him, then?"

The ambulance turns off onto the main road and disappears behind the buildings.

"Come on. I've got a moped over there, I'll take you."

"But . . . we're meant to be getting the train to Stockholm."

"There aren't any trains, and even if there are they're going to be packed, you can just send a message to say you went to the hospital. Come on, let's get out of here. You should be with your granddad."

"But . . . don't you need to stay here?"

Puma shrugs.

"No more water, nothing else to do. Plus our coach said we should look after anyone who needed help."

Those dimples again, my God. I wonder what I must look like. I left my eyelash curlers at the house, and it's probably burned to the ground by now. Typical.

"So I want to help you. If you'll let me."

His eyes are bluish green like the sea, and they're looking at me like I'm the most important person on earth.

His moped is a few blocks away, a nearly new blue-and-silver Peugeot. Going to the hospital with Martin! I write to Mom, followed by a heart and a sad face, then I put my phone away, along with all my worries about Zack and Mom and Dad and Becka, my sadness over Martin, and my anxiety about all the horrible things that happened yesterday. I tighten the back-pack and climb on behind him, hesitantly wrapping my arms around his waist, my cheek resting against his slim, hard back. *Hold on*, he says, and we set off. After being sweaty for about a thousand years, the breeze in my hair feels amazing, and we leave the chaos and the broken, weary people behind us and then it's just him and me and this is my life, it's all mine, and it has finally begun.

———

The hospital is small, much smaller than the hospitals in Stockholm, I think. I've only ever been to the hospital once, right after Becka was born, but it was huge, like a small town, with several tall buildings and an inner courtyard with restaurants and shops and underground tunnels; you could get a fancy coffee there, you could buy flowers and candy, and they even had great Wi-Fi. This is more like an old school building or something, and it's total chaos, people sitting and lying beside an ambulance with a broken windshield, some of them in ripped clothes, bandages on their hands. A kid is screaming for its mother, and there are a bunch of journalists with cameras, shouting questions. We're not technically allowed inside, but we sneak past a police officer busy arguing with an old man, past the people running down the corridors inside. One of Puma's teammates' moms is a nurse here, and she comes down and takes us to a reception desk where we jump the line—there are long lines for everything—and I have to sign some sheet of paper and then we get into an elevator and come out onto a ward that smells disgusting and chemical; I know it's just some sort of disinfectant or spray, but to me it's the stench of fear and illness and death. There are people in beds everywhere, most of them old. One person's face is covered in blood, and I shriek when I see it. Another is an old woman who is naked from the waist up, her tits hanging loose like deflated balloons. We turn off to the right and into a room and there he is.

There he is.

Martin looks so small and thin under the tangle of ugly tubes coming out of his mouth and nose, some of them taped to his cheeks. Damp locks of sweaty hair are clinging to his bald spot, and he has grayish-black stubble. His eyes are closed, his mouth half-open in a horrible grimace, and I remember last Christmas when Bianca had a girls' night and started imitating what guys look like when they orgasm (as though she would know) and we practically died laughing, Emelie laughed so hard that she got chips all over the sofa, and I snort at the memory, at the fact that that's exactly how he looks, stupid, empty, soulless, and then I feel ashamed and get upset.

"Hi, Martin," I say, swallowing my tears. "Hi. It's me, it's Vilja."

He doesn't react, his creased eyelids don't even twitch, nothing.

"I'm here now. I'm with you."

Nothing.

"Are . . . your mom and dad coming too?" Puma asks quietly. He's standing beside me by the bed. It's a small room, but there are two other old people in here. Both seem to be unconscious, hooked up to various machines. There are bags of clear liquid on stands beside them, tubes going into their arms, screens full of numbers.

"Nah," I say. "Nah, I don't think so."

He nods.

"Do you want to tell me what happened?"

I think about us standing by the road yesterday, me and Mom and Becka, after Dad ran off without a word about where he was going. Becka was screaming and coughing, Mom fumbling with her phone and sobbing behind her face mask. The heat, the smoke. You see dogs tied up outside the supermarket sometimes, lying down with their butts in the air and their heads on the ground, watching everyone going in and out through half-closed eyes. There's something so tragic about them, I don't know how anyone could do that to their dog, but that was exactly how Mom looked: lonely, abandoned, pathetic. I remember that we heard the horn first, that we turned as he came around the bend in his big old car, that the air was shimmering and quivering above the hot tarmac. The relief when he pulled over, when we recognized him through the dirty windows, when we shoved our bags into the trunk, which was full of old tools and plastic bags and smelled like gasoline and rubber. And then getting into the car, the air inside. There wasn't any AC, obviously, but the car blocked out most of the smoke, you could actually take a deep breath without it making your lungs burn. Putting Becka down on the backseat, cleaning her face with wet wipes, kissing her watery eyes, feeling the fear start to loosen its grip; we could almost laugh at the crazy situation when the old man muttered that his car wasn't roadworthy, *they said it put out too many fumes when it was idling. What do you reckon, is that it for the climate now? Have I ruined everything for us?* And we sat in the shade with the engine running for almost an hour, no, I don't know how long it was, I think I dozed off. Mom was in the back with Becka, I was up front beside him, he had that scarf tied around his face and he kept saying that everything would be fine, everything would work out, that Dad (he said *Dad*, not Didrik) would be back any minute now, but Mom tried calling him, I tried calling him, he was gone, he'd left us.

Why don't we have a look around, the old man eventually said, sounding almost cheerful as he put the car in gear and pulled out onto the road. *Are you old enough, by the way?*

I froze a little then, it was a weird question. Old enough? For what, you know?

To take your driving test. My girl spent an entire summer practicing on these roads, must've been back in '91.

I told him I was only fourteen but that I was going to take my moped test soon, and then he started pointing at signs and asking if I knew what they meant, main road, right of way, which direction to check first, how to indicate before I turned, the rules if the road was slippery or wet or even just dark. And he didn't get angry when I didn't know the answers and he didn't ask any questions that were too hard or start using all sorts of difficult words like *circular intersection* or *safety margins* or *gyratory*, he talked normally, and when he noticed that I'd stopped responding he stopped asking questions and then we just sort of sat there, driving around in silence. Becka had started crying again, and the smoke was billowing over the forest like a silent black thundercloud.

"He saved us," I tell Puma. "My parents were all, like, confused, and he turned up in his car and took care of us."

He nods and seems to be about to ask me something else when the door opens.

"Are you the grandkids?"

The woman is an immigrant with ugly glasses and a crumpled bluish-green coat, and she stares down at a sheet of paper and then at Martin and then at nothing and then at the screen and then at Puma, who points at me.

"Just her."

She sighs.

"Are your parents here?"

I shake my head. She sighs again and looks around for a chair, but there aren't any, so she sort of perches on the edge of Martin's bed and takes off her glasses and rubs her eye.

"OK, so, as you know, Martin suffered smoke inhalation, irritating his airways and causing what we call chemical pneumonitis." She rolls her *R*s like Arabic speakers often do, *irrrritating his airrrways.* "He had some trouble with his breathing last night, which means he can't get enough oxygen, so we brought him here."

"Is he going to be OK?"

It's Puma who asks, his voice tense but calm, he's holding my hand. God, I really need to pee.

"That's a really good question," says a girl in the doorway, I hadn't noticed her until now. She's around twenty, wearing a hospital uniform, blond highlights in her hair, and she smiles stiffly. "A *really good* question," she repeats. It's obvious this is something she has practiced. "I just *wish* we had a good *answer* for you."

"It's good that you're here," the other woman tells me, a slight hint of warmth in her voice. "Good. Visiting hours, they're usually limited, but things now . . ." She waves a fat finger in the air. ". . . not normal."

She gets up with a sigh and moves over to the sink to wash her hands.

"DNR"—*dee enn rrrrrr*—she mumbles to the younger woman, who gives a slight nod. "See you later," she says to me and Puma, stifling a yawn, and then they both turn and leave.

———

I want him to stay, but I still tell him he can go at least five times, it makes no difference to me. He doesn't go. We both know that if he goes, we'll never see each other again, that this stuffy room is all we have, the old men in their beds, the beeping machines, the stench of death.

They wheel the other two people away, and then it's just us and Martin. We talk about bands we like and video games we play and what we got up to during the summer holidays. He seems to be the type of guy who just plays soccer and hangs out with his friends at home over the summer, and I tell him that I'm supposed to be going to Thailand on, like, Monday and he says that his parents are always talking about going there, he's never been himself but he did go to Greece once when he was little, and it was so hot they could hardly even walk on the beach, the sand burned their feet through their shoes.

There is a black plastic bag on the floor beneath the bed, and we peer inside. It's full of gross clothes that stink of old man and smoke, the gray windbreaker and the scarf Martin showed me, an ice hockey team he's been supporting since he was a boy. Puma takes out the scarf and whispers *look, he's a Leksand fan, that's so fucking cool* and then sets it down beside the dying man in the bed. I don't know whether that's even allowed, but it looks so nice with LEKSANDS IF in big white letters against the blue.

He asks what living in Stockholm is like, and I say that it's probably just like living here, though there's all this pressure to get good grades before starting high school, and in the summer tons of bands play there and I like looking in the shops, the best vintage shop I've ever been to was in the East Village in Manhattan when I went there with Dad, the owners were these super-grumpy people, Chinese or something, but they had the sickest clothes, kind of hood only cooler, and he asks what *hood* means and I struggle to explain, the people who live in the projects on the fringes of the city who shoot each other and make hip-hop, they're hood, and I mention a couple of tracks that he seems to recognize even though he's never heard of hood music before, and as we talk about all this normal stuff I realize that I want to curl up in his arms and kiss his hair and stroke his dimples with my fingertips. I want to be alone with him on an empty dance floor as the lights flash red green and yellow, spinning around and around like a disco ball; I'd like to swim with him in a lake on a summer's day, then lie down on a jetty and tell him all my deepest, darkest secrets, or maybe just spend all evening laughing at YouTube clips in Mickey D's, anything really, anything other than sitting on the floor in a drab hospital room, and after an hour or two I get up and go over to the bed and say for what must be the tenth time that it really is OK if he wants to go, but then Martin opens his eyes and whispers *Vilja*.

It happens so suddenly that I almost scream. I put my hand on his, which feels strangely small and soft beneath my fingers. *Martin*, I whisper, leaning over him. *You're in the hospital. Everything is going to be OK, I promise.*

His eyes seem watery, blurry, like he's looking up at me through a dirty window, but I can see that glimmer, the soft spark, that tells me he's still in there.

"The fire."

I nod.

"Yes, Martin, there was a fire and you saved us, me and Becka and Mom and Dad."

He nods and gives me a weak smile, with only half his face.

"Good."

His hand stirs, I feel his fingers gently gripping my wrist. His thin lips move, but no sound comes out. There is some kind of white gunk at both corners of his mouth. A rattling sound.

"Martin? What is it?"

"The dogs."

His smile grows and he traces a finger over my hand. I don't understand.

"Will you look after the dogs?"

I don't know why, but I nod. No, I do, of course I do, because it's another boring rainy day and Mom has made lemonade and put on a movie, Zack has just learned to crawl, and Ella comes over with a big black dog on a leash and we go down to the water together. There's a tall, quiet old man walking alongside us and he says that we're clever for taking such good care of Ajax, real experts, real pros, that's what we are, and we stand on the shore throwing a stick for Ajax, who swims out to fetch it, he never gets bored and neither do we, he swims back with the stick over and over again, dropping it at our feet and then panting, his big red tongue lolling out of his mouth. The old man sits down on the bench and looks out at the jetty and the lake, he doesn't seem to care that it's raining, the drops like pinpricks on the calm surface of the water, that special, almost earthy scent of summer rain, and I meet his eye and before I have time to reply it's as though Martin abandons his own face and his eyes suddenly look as big as marbles and his breathing sounds weird and then he closes his eyes and is making that horrible expression again, his mouth open.

"Hello?" I say. "Martin?"

Right then, I feel Puma's breath on me. He has crept over and put his long, slim arm around my shoulders, and it's like all my birthdays and Christmases have come at once as I get to sort of roll into his arms and press my face to his T-shirt and he gently strokes my hair, but then the sad feeling comes creeping back up on me and I turn to the bed and see that Martin's breathing is uneven, like he's gasping for air.

One of the machines starts beeping, an LED flashing, and in TV shows this is when the people in white coats come running with carts and equipment and someone shouts *CLEAR*, but none of that happens. The machine just keeps beeping, the LED flashing, and Martin's skin slowly changes color, getting paler and paler, like crinkled old paper, *should I go and get someone?* Puma whispers, but I just shake my head and grip his hand as hard as I can, *it's OK, I can run and get someone*, and I lean in to his body and say *don't go don't go don't go* and his lips change from pale pink to purplish blue and I say *Martin* and reach out and touch his old face. There must have been someone who loved him, someone who would have wanted to be with him, someone who wasn't a fucking dog; I refuse to believe that it should be me standing here now, where are all his kids and grandkids and siblings and friends, even the random old men he used to play chess with, or whatever it is they do?

But it's just me, me and Puma, and I pull back from his forehead. Puma takes my hand and then he grabs the hockey scarf and puts it in Martin's cool palm and we place our warm hands on top. The old man suddenly takes a deep, rasping breath, his bony chest rising and falling. *He's alive* Puma groans, *look, he's alive*, but his body seems to settle in the bed, I feel his hand twitch through the ratty fabric and then it relaxes and Martin's whole body is suddenly weirdly calm.

"I'll go and get someone," Puma says again, turning to the doorway. "This is crazy, he's dying." But I keep hold of his hand.

"No one is coming." I can feel the tears running down my cheeks, which is strange because I'm not at all sad. "Don't you get it? No one is coming."

His eyes dart over the screens, that guy impulse to always try to understand how technical stuff works; he wants to decode the numbers and the charts, wants the display to speak a language he understands. I turn back to Martin and see the light from outside filtering in through the filthy windows. The purplish, pale blue color makes his lips look horrible, and his skin slowly grows cooler beneath my fingers.

"Have you ever seen anything like this before?" he whispers.

"What?"

"Someone dying."

I think about when Mom's dad died, how they put his body in a room beside the hospital. I was so young at the time, Mom and Dad were there, Dad carried Zack in his arms and Mom pointed at Grandpa, who was just lying there peacefully in his black suit and white shirt, they had lit candles and combed his hair and the priest told Mom I was a good girl, I seemed so *grounded*, and Mom put her hand on Grandpa's forehead and said *touch him if you want, we get so cold when we die*, but I didn't want to and then at the funeral they played the Beatles.

I shake my head.

"No, nothing like this. You?"

He shakes his head and bites his lower lip and I realize that he's about to start crying. I haven't seen a boy my age cry since I was little, and I reach up and stroke his hair and whisper *shhh, it's OK, it's going to be fine, there's no need to worry.*

And then we just stand there with our hands on Martin's, watching the life drain from his face. It's like we're both looking out across a precipice, a foreign continent, a natural disaster on a scale no one could have ever imagined, and I think that going through something like this must bring people together in a way that can't ever be broken, a shared experience no one can take away from us, *we stood there and held each other the first time we saw a person die*, and in a world full of lies nothing can be more real than that.

Puma clears his throat and starts singing, in a low, trembling voice:

oh L-I-F, hear the north stand sing
oh L-I-F, the blue and white kings

There are tears streaming down his cheeks, and his hand grips the scarf.

oh L-I-F, the pride of the town
it's Leksand's turn to lift the cup
and Mora's going down

I've never seen a guy my own age do anything like this before, and it's as though my heart, my lungs, all my internal organs melt as he slowly sings the team song, over and over again, so focused, like a priest giving Mass or one of those things they have in Islam, a minaret, it's so beautiful, so dignified. I think about Mom, who spends her evenings on the computer, sorting photographs into albums that she never actually finishes, and Dad, sitting at the other end of the sofa, staring at pictures some influencer has uploaded, turning his phone screen-down if I sit beside him. But this is how it feels, I know, I finally know how it feels.

━━━━━━

His body is cold and stiff when Puma realizes he can call the mom he knows from his soccer team. She and two others show up not long later, and they look angry and tired when they find out we've been alone with Martin all this time. *This shit isn't how it's supposed to be*, they say, *what a goddamn mess, imagine if the papers find out, this is Sweden, isn't it*, but I say that we won't tell anyone, that it was me who talked our way onto the ward, that it was a good thing he didn't have to die alone, and then they tell us to leave and say that someone might be in touch with our parents *once everything has calmed down*.

We leave the hospital late that afternoon. I really need to track down Mom and Dad, I've been so sick of them and their bickering, maybe that's one of the reasons I left without asking this morning, but my phone is dead, and when we get back to the train station they aren't there. There's almost no one there, just a few groups of sad-looking people, most of them old, and they don't look like they're waiting for anything in particular. A police officer is talking to an old woman who seems upset and keeps pointing at his car. Puma asks someone, who tells him that service on the line has been suspended after problems with several trains getting stuck in the heat. I feel a sudden, suffocating panic. *Have they left without me? Why didn't they come to the hospital to get me?*

I hop down from the moped and stand outside the station building, at a complete loss. There are a few plastic bags and an old sleeping bag on the ground. My head is spinning, the heat unbearable, and I brace myself against the wall.

"Are you OK?" he asks.

I nod.

"Yeah. Probably just . . . need something to eat, that's all. And to charge my phone."

"Come home with me," says Puma. "We'll work something out."

He drives me through the small town on the back of his moped. There are more people around now, wandering along the roads, sitting on sidewalks, a tense, stressful, frantic atmosphere everywhere; broken shop windows, a gas station that looks like someone has tried to set it alight. The bushes around it are black and sooty and there is a burned-out car, nothing but a rusty shell left. Puma's drab house is tucked among a bunch of others that all look exactly the same, with big, flat lawns and stupid little trees in the gardens.

"Everything's new around here," he explains. "Mom and Dad don't like fixing up old houses."

He parks the moped and we go through to the kitchen and he boils water as I plug in my phone. Fifty-seven missed calls and at least twenty messages, most of them from Mom, nothing from Dad. As I start skimming through them, I can't work out why she seems to have completely lost her shit, it's like she thinks I've been raped and buried under a pile of bricks or something, but then I see the message I sent that morning, Going to the hospital with Martin! and I realize that it's highlighted a weird red color and that it says *Not Delivered* underneath. I shout *fuckfuckfuck* and immediately dial her number. It rings and rings but no one picks up, so I try Dad instead, but his phone is completely dead, and in the end I call Granny, who picks up on the first ring and starts crying when she hears my voice. I try to calm her down and tell her that I just went to the hospital, then I give her Puma's address, which I find on a postcard on the fridge.

Once I've hung up, I see that he is busy mixing powder into a bowl of noodles, staring at me.

"I only really like the chicken flavor," I say, trying to sound like I'm being kind of sarcastic.

"Who was that?"

"My granny."

"Your granny? As in . . . your granny and granddad, same side of the family?" He looks at me like I've just said something stupid.

"Yeah."

"And she's . . . cool that he just died?"

I try to come up with something smart to say, but it's impossible with him staring at me like that, looking so disappointed and accusing.

"I mean, she and Granddad weren't close. They were divorced, you know?"

"Ah, got it."

My God, I'm a terrible liar.

"Or, uh . . . he was more a kind of bonus granddad, really."

He looks suspicious. He's smarter than I thought.

When you lie, you shouldn't explain so goddamn much. If someone is telling the truth they don't feel the need to explain everything, they just take it for granted that people will believe them.

"So you weren't really his granddaughter?"

I mumble something and pour myself a glass of water. He is standing by the sink in the dull, dusty kitchen, and he looks almost mocking somehow, as though I've just done something embarrassing. Then he glances out of the window and smiles, and I follow his eye out.

A cute brunette has just parked her bike by the gate and is cutting across the lawn. Blue denim shorts, a dark blue shirt with the sleeves rolled up—it looks weird in the heat, prompts vague associations with some sort of lame uniform.

"That's just Linnea," Puma blurts out without looking at me. "My girl-friend, I mean. She likes the chicken flavor too."

She marches straight up to the door, enters the code, and steps inside, and he goes over to the hallway with a smile that tears my heart to pieces and then I hear The Kiss and their soft whispering and this must be what it feels like to die, this must be what it's like to drown in a sea of earthworms and feel them slowly squirm into your mouth and fill your body with their slithering, sticky grossness.

They come into the kitchen hand in hand, and she's good, I have to give her that, only the slightest hint of dark hatred in her blue eyes.

"This is Vilja," he says. "Who I texted about."

Texted about?

"I've heard everything. God, how horrible." She turns to Puma. "But it's great you were there for support. What a hero." She stands on tiptoe and kisses him on the ear, grabs his hand in such a way that it seems to accidentally brush her upper body.

Eat earthworms. Chew them, big fat lumps beneath your tongue, between your teeth, down the hatch, like a cold, wet dough of squirming, writhing shit.

"Linnea has been a hero today too," says Puma, clearing his throat. "She's in the Scouts, they've been handing out fruit and sandwiches."

"We were down in Borlänge," she says humbly. "On the trains. Some of those people are so *vulnerable* right now. I just hope we made a bit of difference."

"Of course you did." He gives her a stupid grin. "No one can do everything, but everyone can do something."

"It's crazy, isn't it, Vilma?" she says to me. "With the fires and everything. That they've just forgotten about the two-degree target and accepted that we're past the tipping point, that it'll be our generation that has to deal with all this."

"Seriously," I say, though I have no idea what the hell she's talking about. Two-degree what, tipping what? "Totally crazy."

She flashes me a compassionate smile with her angel eyes and then takes a seat at the table, putting her phone screen-down. The case is baby pink, with looping letters that say *Everyone YOU meet is struggling with something YOU have no idea about . . . Be kind. Always . . .* and it's so cringe that I would laugh if it weren't all so awful.

"So . . . so you're in the Scouts?"

She rolls her eyes.

"It's more like a bunch of friends I've been hanging out with since we

were Cubs. We go camping sometimes, build shelters. In the winter we sometimes go skiing and bivouacking in the mountains, it's actually really cool."

I try to remember what I know about the Scouts. Isn't it some religious
thing, or does it have something to do with the army? When I googled *pedophiles* once, there was a whole load of stuff about the Scouts, and I feel an
urge to ask Linnea whether it's really so fun to be stuck in a fucking snowdrift with a bunch of fascist pedos, but I force back the question the same
way you swallow a bit of vomit before it reaches your mouth. She pushes
her hair back from her forehead and ties it up, her elbows so high that it
really emphasizes her breasts in her tight shirt, and her brace-filled mouth
cracks into a grin.

"Do you do much in your free time, Vilma?"

I shake my head.

"Used to do athletics, but it was really boring."

I eat my noodles as they talk about their friends and their plans for
some beach party they're going to tonight. They're both sitting with their
phones, reading news flashes to each other, chaos in Stockholm and trains at
a standstill, dead children; he has his hand on her thigh. Earthworms. Chew
and swallow. Chew and swallow.

Mom calls, hysterical, and I give her directions to the house and then
say goodbye and go out to wait in the yard, sitting in the shade by the
wall and thinking about nothing at all. Before long I hear her shout and
then I see her coming down the road, a lone mother moving almost jerkily,
as though she's struggling to walk, and everything from yesterday comes
rushing back to me: Mom and Dad's argument, Zack disappearing in the
back of a stranger's car, Becka screaming and red-eyed. I peer back inside
and see Puma and Linnea making out in the kitchen. She looks straight at
me over his shoulder and smiles coldly. Her hand is on his back, and she
clenches it into a fist and extends her middle finger. I turn around and run
across the yard, through the gate, and over to Mom, who cries out when she
sees me, her eyes old and dry with sadness. I throw myself into her arms
and start crying too, we just stand there among the boring little houses on

the outskirts of Rättvik and cry like two dying swans. I'm crying as though my chest might crack open and send my heart tumbling out onto the red-hot tarmac in a slimy, warm mush, and I whimper *get me out of here Mom please get me out of here now.*

━━━━

A big dog lumbers along the water's edge. From a distance it looks black and shaggy, but as it gets closer I see the white patch on its chest and the rusty red spots on its paws. I always wanted a dog exactly like that when I was younger, and Mom and Dad sometimes talked about getting a poo-dle or a Chihuahua, but I would interrupt them and announce that what I wanted was a *teddy dog.* They laughed and thought I was cute with my constant nagging for a *teddy dog,* and that Christmas I got a cuddly Saint Bernard toy and we never really came to a decision about whether to get a real dog or not, they thought Zack might be allergic and Dad read some-thing about how pets have a *deeply unnecessary carbon footprint,* and then they gave us a little sister instead.

We're sitting outside our cabin. It's smaller than the one we were in last night, and we have to share it with a family from Mora, but Mom doesn't seem to care, she's just staring down at her phone as though she might get a call from God at any moment. Zack is still missing, Dad has taken Becka and caught a train to Stockholm, and she and Dad, she explains with a trembling voice, *are going through a bit of a rough patch right now.* She has shouted at me, alternated between shouting and crying, because I disappeared ("so incredibly selfish of you"), because I didn't get in touch ("so *unbelievably* selfish of you"), because I'm back, and because everything has gone to shit.

They've been handing out little yellow polystyrene boxes containing a slice of gross white Scout bread, a hard-boiled Scout egg, a slimy bit of Scout ham, a Scout banana, and a carton of lukewarm Scout juice, and I have no appetite whatsoever but Mom forces me to eat every last crumb of the bread and then we sit at our table, a few cabins over from where we sat this morning, and glare at each other. It's a super-hot evening with zero breeze, and I'd like to go for a swim in the lake, but I don't have a swimsuit and I also don't know where I could get changed, because there are hour-long lines for all the toilets. Dad and Becka should have been back in Stockholm for ages by now, but he still hasn't been in touch.

"At least it's pretty here," Mom says in a flat voice, looking out across the lake. "I've got to give them that, it's a nice place for a campsite."

Her phone starts ringing, making it buzz and vibrate on the wooden table, and she jumps and throws herself over it as though she were disarming a nuclear bomb, but the life drains from her eyes when she sees the display. *Pernilla*, she mumbles to me, hunching up with her knees pulled in to her chest and her hair hanging over her face. The conversation only lasts a minute or two, but she manages to start crying again, she says *no* and then *no, nothing*, then her friend starts telling her something, and it seems like it must be bad news because Mom whispers *what the hell . . . seriously, what the hell* and then there's all the usual stuff about speaking later and no, she's sure everything will work out soon and Christ, imagine being in this mess and then her words cut through me as she says *at least Vilja is here now, thank God, at least the two of us are together.*

It's almost like she has been sedated once she hangs up, staring down at the worn wooden planks.

"She's going to look up a few things and call back . . . She said there's been all sorts of problems with the trains to Stockholm, trains standing still in the heat. Several children have been taken to the hospital, two of them died outside of Östersund. There are . . . power cuts too, and Pernilla says no one knows how to . . . So Dad might not have even made it back to Stockholm with Becka." She shakes her head. "Honestly, this is so much fucking worse than the pandemic, nothing works anymore, absolutely *nothing* works in this stupid fucking country, and . . ." Her voice becomes gravelly and she hits the table a few times with one hand as she presses the other to her eyes and sobs *shit shit shit.*

I really wish there was something I could give her—a glass of wine, a cheeky *no, I shouldn't* cigarette like I saw her smoke at Midsummer, put on some random episode of *The Simpsons* so we can laugh together—but I don't have anything, just me, so I go around and hug her and she crieswhisperssings *oh, my big girl, Vilja-vanilla, Mommy's big girl* like she used to when I was little, and then we just sort of sit there, sobbing, until it gets too much, and then we check our phones instead.

After a while I feel something soft against my knee, and I look down and see the dog. It's incredibly cute with fine markings on its snout, black and brown with a perfectly symmetrical white band running down its forehead, widening into a teardrop shape around its black nose. He nudges me again, his long pink tongue hanging out, pleading eyes fixed on me. Without thinking about what I'm doing, I take the disgusting slice of ham from the food package and dangle it in front of him. He barks and sits upright with his paws by his mouth—it's so cute when dogs have been trained properly—and I drop the piece of ham and his jaws snap open, snatching it from the air with a soft growl.

"It was one like this I wanted, wasn't it?" I ask Mom.

"You wanted a Saint Bernard," she says, giving the dog an indifferent glance. "That does look a bit like one. Where's its owner? It's not right that it's begging people for food."

We look around, but no one seems to have lost a dog. Most people are either in their cabins or in one of the tents on the meadow down by the shore. Mom's phone starts ringing again, and she picks it up and says *Pernilla?* and then she tenses.

Her eyes widen. She sits up, her back as straight as an arrow.

"Yes? Yes, that's me. Hello? This is Carola, who am I speaking to?"

A calm, slightly croaky man's voice tells her something. She closes her eyes, nods, *yes, he has longish brown hair, Zack, Zacharias, von der Esch, have you . . .* The voice continues in the same calm tone as Mom drops to her knees, bracing herself with one hand in the gravel. Her back is shaking, and I crouch down and put an arm around her. The dog pushes his snout into my armpit and I put my other arm around his fluffy head.

"Östra Silvberg, is that . . . OK, so it's not far from Hedemora? But how did he . . . Did they see the car, was it a white Toyota?"

The call lasts another minute or so, and she gets me to write down a phone number on my mobile, the name Claes Kall-something, and then she sobs *thank you* over and over again and hangs up and keeps crying into my shoulder, because Zack is safe, someone has spotted him in the forest an hour or two south of here, in a place called Östra Silvberg. It sounds nice, a couple of retirees who were there to paint near some old mine had seen him, or maybe it was in the parking lot when a car dropped him off, the details are kind of hazy but there seems to be a boy who looks just like Zack there, in any case; we're supposed to call back in the morning, if we can, the phone lines are really bad.

"We'll just have to cross our fingers," Mom sniffs. "We'll just have to hope that it's true. Imagine if it is him, he's always liked mines."

"So the guy who just called, had he spoken to Zack?"

"No, not exactly, but he'd spoken to his mom, who's there on a painting trip, she thought she'd seen a boy."

"How did he get your number?"

She wipes some tears and snot from her face.

"I guess he'd seen my post on Facebook."

I think for a moment.

"And the people in the car . . . why would they drive out into the forest and dump him there?"

"I guess they were lost, it's chaos on the country lanes, the man who called said it's almost impossible to get around down there unless you have an all-terrain vehicle."

"But the people who took Zack just had an ordinary car."

Mom gets a sad look in her eye.

"This is all we have right now, Vilja. The only clue. Why don't you want to let me hope?"

The dog rubs against my legs.

"I . . . was just wondering."

Her sad eyes harden.

"It would have been much easier for your father and me to look for Zack if you hadn't pulled your little disappearing act earlier, so it would be nice if you tried to help instead of being so *obnoxious*."

Shame makes my cheeks burn, and I nod and sink into her arms and we whisper that everything is going to be OK, that we'll call back tomorrow, and I try to feel relieved, to feel like Mom is in control now, the way it should be.

An older couple is walking down the gravel path toward us, chatting and sipping from coffee cups. I briefly wonder if the dog belongs to them, but he doesn't get up from the ground by our table.

"There's coffee over there," I say, trying to sound enthusiastic. "And I don't think there's a line, do you want me to get you one?"

"Coffee?" Mom dries her tired red eyes and gives me a blank look. "How do you know?"

I point to the couple.

"They're drinking coffee."

"But they could have brought it with them?"

"They've got identical paper cups, the kind you get from a takeout, only cheaper. The kind you get at the gas station. Otherwise they'd probably have camping mugs or something. Plus, who walks around with their own coffee cup? People only walk around with coffee if they've just been somewhere to get it."

Mom frowns.

"And what about there not being a line?"

I hesitate.

"That's more because . . . because they look so happy. People who've had to stand in line for ages always look grumpy, but those two look like they just marched right up and got their coffee. Plus, they're the only people walking around. There'd be more people coming back the same way if it was busy."

She gives me a slight smile. God, it's nice to see her look kind of happy for a change.

"Can you see whether they've got any fresh croissants from here?"

I smile back.

"Nah, but I bet they've got pains au chocolat."

"Well, then. You'd better hurry."

She ruffles my hair and stares down at her phone again. She's checking for updates on the trains to Stockholm now, and her smile disappears. I was just about to ask whether she wanted her latte with oat or soy milk, but the moment has passed, so I just trudge off in the opposite direction from the old people. I hear soft, padding footsteps and light panting behind me and I think *Ajax, I'll call you Ajax.*

———

There isn't a line at the wooden table where a couple of volunteers are busy pumping coffee from airpots, and they do actually have both normal milk and oat milk—there's even a box of sugar cubes. The camp stretches out beyond the cabins around me, neat rows of big green military tents, a few smaller tents, blues and reds and oranges, tents people brought themselves or that have been donated by locals.

I fill my pocket with sugar cubes and ask for two cups of coffee—I don't actually drink coffee, but this is probably a good time to start—and have just turned around when I hear the scream. It comes from one of the cabins, a red building, slightly bigger than the others, I guess it must be a meeting space or office of some kind. The scream cuts through the late summer dusk like a rusty Scout knife, and I pause, Ajax whimpering and darting around my feet. It's coming from a child, and it isn't the usual evening tears; it's a brutal, shrill roar of anxiety and despair. An image of Becka flickers by, but it can't be, of course it's not, I take a few steps toward the building and see a couple come out with a howling baby. They're around Mom and Dad's age, the man tall and thin, in a faded T-shirt with some old rock star and the colors of the American flag on the front, a bandage around his hand. The woman's face is dogged and hard, and she moves slowly, like something inside her has switched off.

On the steps beside them, I see two volunteers in hi-vis vests, a man and a woman, talking in that efficient, sympathetic, but impersonal way that grown-ups do when they can't help you. They sound like the woman from the hospital, *D-N-RRRRR*, what does that even mean? I move closer and hear the man, *the only solution is to take him to Borlänge*, the woman, *unless you can find someone who is breastfeeding and willing to pump for you*, and the father, shrill and angry, *it's insane that you're completely unprepared for babies needing formula, this fucking country, how the hell can everything be so badly planned?* You can tell that this is something he has said at least a hundred times today—not that it has helped—over and over again like a mantra, a defense, all he has left. *Borlänge*, says the man. His thick blond beard is braided, like he's an actor in some Viking show or one of those LARPers pretending it's the Middle Ages. His volunteer friend has curly, henna-dyed hair, *Borlänge, I know they have some there*, and the mother robotically says *but* how *is Wilmer supposed to get to Borlänge?* and the volunteer woman says *there might be a transport in the morning* and the mother seems to kind of shrink back into herself and starts crying so hard that she's shaking, and then the baby starts screaming again and the man says *this fucking country*.

"Do you need formula?" I ask.

The four of them stare at me. I take off my backpack, open the zip, and pull out a box, a big one, probably around thirty ounces, with a happy little baby on the front. I hold it out to them.

"Here."

It's the father who steps forward, the mother practically collapses behind him, shouting something confused that sounds almost angry. The father is right in front of me, long arms, two strong hands gripping the box, I can see flecks of blood through the bandage on one of them, on his knuckles, on the back of his hand, and his mouth asks *what do you want for this?* but his eyes are predator's eyes, telling me that it makes no difference what I want because this isn't a negotiation, the thing I'm holding is already his, so I say *nothing, just take it*, and he nods and stutters something grateful and then snatches the box from me and he and the mother and the baby hurry back into the cabin where I guess they must have water and a hot plate.

Braid Beard gives his colleague a jumpy look and then turns to me and the big dog by my feet.

"Where the hell . . . I, how come you had that?"

Because my parents are fucking useless, I think. *Because I don't trust them to take care of my sister, because they can't cope in this chaos.*

"Gotta go," I say. "My coffee's getting cold."

The male volunteer steps forward and I see that someone has scribbled *STAFF* in Magic Marker on his yellow vest, that he has a laminated badge of some kind with a stamp and numbers on it and the words *EMERGENCY TEAM*.

"Where did you get hold of that box?" he asks, looking down at my backpack. He seems kind but firm, a friendly authority in the way he approaches me, and I imagine him sending busloads of babies here and there, directing people to pitch tents, make food, hand out water; it's people like him who are in control here, I can see a gray streak in his beard in the dusky light, if you've got a man over forty with no visible disabilities and the ability to speak Swedish without an accent, he's virtually guaranteed to be the one in charge, no matter where you are. Always remember that.

"I just graduated high school," I say hesitantly. "Early childhood education. I was out on work placement. That box was all I managed to grab, things were really crazy."

He gives me a blank stare, and I come so close to giving in to the reflex to keep explaining, to say something about a pre-K group or maybe even a hospital somewhere, a fire, an escape, but I stop myself, remember that I shouldn't explain too much.

"How old are you?"

"Eighteen." This time my answer sounds flat, uninterested, better.

"Where are you staying?"

"Over there," I say, pointing vaguely in the direction I came from. "In one of the tents. Me and my boyfriend." I smile. "And Ajax, obviously."

He nods.

"With things as they are, we'd really like everyone with experience of . . ."

"My coffee's getting cold," I say again. "Seriously."

I turn around and head back.

"How much does a big dog like that eat?" I hear him ask behind me. "We've got a few sacks of kibble. It's meant for the rescue dogs, but I'm sure we can work something out."

I don't answer, just keep walking. This fucking country.

———————

I'm struggling to sleep in the stuffy cabin we're sharing with the family from Mora—they were arguing earlier, now they're snoring—so I go outside. It's a warm, clear night and I walk down to the lake. The dog finds me and lowers his big fuzzy head to my lap while I check my phone. I've got all the usual DMs from Bianca and Stella, with hearts and emojis that are crying or angry, and I quickly write that my brother is still missing but that he might have been found and that we're staying in a shitty campsite and that everything sucks but I've met a super-cute boy, I pause for a moment, then delete *boy* and type *dog*, take a picture of Ajax, and send it with some hearts.

Lotte from my old class has just turned fifteen and her dad has bought her one of those LSV things, like a mini jeep with white leather seats. She has it parked by the beach and she's leaning back against it, one of her heels on the wheel, looking up at the sky as the sun makes the body and the water and her lip gloss glitter like she's in some TV show. *My little monster*, that's the caption, with a bunch of flames and hearts. I keep scrolling, see that my vintage shop has got some nearly new Michael Kors pieces in, sunglasses and bags; I have a few bags already, but none like that amazing little black clutch with the silver bits on it, that would go so well with my thick black belt from Gina Tricot, maybe even a pair of black Docs, or oxblood. I see that Dad's influencer girl has uploaded a picture of a glass of milk and a computer, boasting about writing a book, and I like the post but then take back the like because it feels like I'm betraying Mom. I go back to the clothes and start putting together a wardrobe, we're going to Thailand on Monday and I need a new swimsuit because my old one has probably gone up in flames.

I scroll through my messages again. Bianca and Stella think that Ajax is the cutest dog they've ever seen, *OMG!!!* heart heart, and I heart their hearts and then take a picture of the empty black lake and the starry sky and the blinking lights on the other side, blue and white from the emergency vehicles, flickering yellow and red from the forest fires, upload it.

I pat the dog on his pretty head, scratch him under the chin, stroke his soft, smooth ears. You can train those dogs, Stella writes, her parents have always had dogs, check whether it knows how to sit or shake your hand. I put my phone down and give it a try, say *give me your paw*, and he immediately sits down with his front paw in the air, it's so cute. I say *roll over* and he lies down in the sand and rolls over twice, then jumps up and shakes himself off. I think for a minute and then say *bark*, but nothing happens, he just keeps panting and drooling like usual. *Go on, bark!* but nothing happens. I take out my phone and google dog commands, but it's too boring, I realize how tired I am, almost dozing off. I would much rather sleep out here than in the cabin, but that would only make Mom worry again, so I check Instagram instead, all the usual people have liked my picture, I keep scrolling and then go back to my DMs and:

A message request. From someone I don't know.

I click accept.

PumaRob07

My heart starts pounding. The message is a single line.

I see what you see.

No pictures, no hearts, just that one line, and I want to cry out with happiness, partly because he looked me up but mostly because he's so damn cool. I write a quick reply but delete it before I have time to hit send, put my phone down. No. Wait. I stare out at the lake for fifteen minutes before I check it again.

Are you OK?

How did you find me? I write.

1.35. Not bad.

It takes me a second or two to remember the high jump, it must be three years ago now. Athletics, that was all he had to go on, but it was enough. I want to ask how long it took him to find me—I'm basically impossible to google given that my name is also a Swedish verb—but he gets in there first.

Three hours. Man, you guys have so many clubs down there.

I have a quick look at his profile. It's mostly soccer stuff, boats, trees, burgers, clips from what looks like a soccer stadium, the billboards seem to be from Spain or somewhere, guys always like soccer teams with either Barcelona or Madrid in the name, so I guess it must be there. And then there's one of her. Only one, but God, it's hard to see: on a beach with the sun behind her, that sweet smile and a mischievous look in her eye. No braces, and her hair is longer, so it must've been taken before the summer. *Linnea_bp_forever* is tagged in the photo, and she has left three hearts in the comments, of course she has. *They've been together for ages*, my emotions roar, and I feel a stab of pain before my brain coldly calculates that *that isn't necessarily a problem, it could actually be part of the solution.*

He writes:

Don't get why you said he was your granddad.

I reply right away:

Don't get why you didn't say you had a girlfriend.

He is quick:

Didn't say I DIDN'T.

I think.

Nah. But this complicates things.

I've given him a chance here. What he writes now will decide what happens next. I've given him an open goal to smash the ball into. He can act like he doesn't understand, play dumb or insensitive, send a laughing emoji and pretend it doesn't mean A SINGLE THING that he spent all evening trawling through every junior athletics event in Stockholm until he found my name in the only district championship I ever competed in, then did an image search and tracked me down. There are thousands of ways he could shoot this thing down before it even begins, nip it in the bud.

But he replies:

How long are you staying?

I smile in the darkness.

As long as it takes.

The green dot showing that he is online disappears. He's pulling back, putting more distance between us again. Sure. Guys don't like feeling trapped, I'll give him some space.

I sit there for another hour, just to be on the safe side, then I get up. Ajax shakes himself off, sending soil and sand flying into the air around him. We take a few steps up the slope toward the cabins, and it's like everything catches up with me: knowing that Mom will be lying on the floor with her phone, that she might have started crying again, I've noticed that she always cries when I'm not around.

Right then, I hear a whooshing, hissing sound behind me, like the water boiling over when you make pasta. I turn around and see the sparks flying over the lake in the distance, probably around half a mile away, it's hard to tell in the dark. Ajax whimpers and cowers behind my legs as I try to make sense of what I'm seeing. It's like someone is standing over there with a huge blowtorch, spraying fire over Lake Siljan, and it reminds me of something I've only ever seen once before, on TV when I was younger. It was a soccer match and Dad got angry because it spoiled the game, *damn those hooligans, they should play with empty stands.*

A flare.

One of those fireworks people throw onto the field during soccer matches.

And it lights up the entire universe.

FRIDAY, AUGUST 29

THE CAR FROM THE RESCUE SERVICE IS RED AND YELLOW, AND I'M sure it was probably clean and fresh a couple of weeks ago, but now it's filthy, with broken headlights, a large crack in the windshield, and deep gashes down one side. Still, I love how it feels to drive it along the forest roads, to see the smoking, wounded nature race by outside, the bumpy track vibrating through the steering wheel and into my hands. I haven't quite got the hang of reversing yet, managing to coordinate my eyes and the wheels with all the mirrors, remembering to check what I've just learned is called the *blind spot* and kind of feeling the back of the car swing out behind me. That sort of thing takes practice, but there's no time for that now. Besides, all the grown-ups—especially the men—have incredibly low expectations of my driving skills, despite the fact that I immediately stepped forward when they asked if anyone had a driver's license during the morning meeting. No one expects an eighteen-year-old schoolgirl to be able to handle a vehicle in this fire-ravaged terrain, and they grinned when I initially struggled to start the engine and then drove straight into a tree. *I can't drive stick*, I told them. I'm not really sure what a stick is, but that's what people always say when they're bad at driving. *Too used to Daddy's new car, right? With its rearview cameras and parking sensors and all that stuff?* Braid Beard said softly, and I nodded, close to tears. They showed me how the clutch works, how to change gear, and then I could drive. Forward, anyway.

But I do manage to reverse onto the gravel outside the daycare center in Skålmo, a low white building at what was once the edge of the forest. Emil and I get out with our Ikea bags, and Ajax jumps down from his spot on the backseat and anxiously sniffs the air. The playground is a total wreck, with a couple of melted gray lumps of what I guess must have been plastic toys, a charred jungle gym, and the ruins of a swing set straining into the sky, its empty black chains rattling in the breeze. But other than a sooty facade and a few windows that have cracked in the heat, the center itself has survived. The authorities have barred the door with a piece of plastic tape, and for some reason Emil pulls it down before he takes out the fire axe and starts hacking at the frame with his left hand. It's slow going with only one hand, but after ten minutes or so he manages to make a big enough hole to push the end of a crowbar in, and he presses it using his left shoulder until we hear a crack and the whole lock comes loose. The doors are linked up to the alarm system in some places, but out here the electricity has been off for so long that the backup battery is dead. We walk straight into the dark hallway where the kids' clothes are still hanging in a row, name tags above each hook. Ajax pads in ahead of us. He doesn't seem frightened of places like this, despite all the darkness and dirt. Maybe to him the smell of young kids is also the smell of warmth and comfort, of food and family.

We brought flashlights with us, but the daylight filtering in through the broken windows is enough. There are a few small bottles and tubes of sunscreen lotion and spray on the shelves, left by conscientious parents, and Emil swipes them into his bag without a word. I go through to the changing room and fill my bag with diapers, plastic sheets, and wet wipes, plus a few large pump bottles of skin lotion for children. I also find an unopened box of plastic gloves.

"What do we need from here?" I hear Emil half shout, and I follow his voice through a playroom where the shelves and the floor are covered in a fine layer of ash, into a kitchen where the tiny chairs are set out around low, round tables. He has opened a cupboard, and I point to the boxes of oats, gruel, powdered porridge, and a few smaller tubs of lactose-free stuff for kids with milk allergies. Last of all we grab the first aid kit and the hand sanitizer, and on our way out Emil takes a few packages of coffee and cookies from the small pantry.

I give Ajax a cookie and he jumps up into the backseat and we set off for the next place on the map. Emil hums along with old rock songs and picks his nose with his good hand when he thinks I'm not looking. He grew up in the forests around here, and he starts telling me about a summer house his uncle had, by one of the lakes a bit farther north, he and his friends used to hang out there and get drunk and use the sauna and sit around the fire and play guitar; he wonders whether it's still standing or whether it's been wiped out along with everything else, and he tries to suggest a "quick detour" up there to check, but the road is closed and we have more important things to do than go off on nostalgia trips to the middle of nowhere.

If it wasn't for his hand, he'd be driving, he tells me for the third time today. I know he doesn't want to talk about how he hurt it, he seems to have fractured it somehow, keeps grimacing in pain and taking care only to lift and carry things with his left hand. *It was when Wilmer was screaming*, he said when I first asked about it, sounding embarrassed. *We found a woman who could breastfeed him, so he'd have a bit of milk at the very least. But then her boyfriend showed up, and things got a bit . . .* He shook his head. *People are animals.*

He manages a group of schools, a former head teacher. That's the arrangement, Braid Beard told us, that's what we should say if anyone asks. He's with an intern from a pre-K, out to collect ("feel free to say *requisition*") equipment and supplies from a few of the daycare centers, for use by the ad hoc childcare groups that have formed at the temporary assembly point in Rättvik ("don't say *camp*," Braid Beard emphasized, "*camp* sounds too negative, we don't have those in Sweden"). The key thing is that it's Emil who breaks down the doors, so that it's defensible, legally speaking, just in case ("otherwise people might think we're looting").

Today is our first day out on the road. We spent yesterday and the day before organizing childcare in the camp, working with a couple of retired teachers (Spanish and woodwork) who were evacuated from their summer house, a few outdoor education teachers on a walking holiday in the mountains, and a bored girl who worked as an activity leader at a holiday resort in Rhodes last summer, all under the leadership of a jumpy child psychologist the Civil Contingencies Agency sent up from Falun, who has to go outside and panic-smoke a cigarette during every meeting. There are some ordinary kindergarten staff too, several were bused in with the children they look after when the wind turned suddenly and the fires surrounded Mora, but a few of them are suffering from smoke inhalation and shock, and they're more concerned about looking after their own little flock than anything. The same is true of most of the parents who have offered to help as volunteers. The mothers are selfish and just want resources for their own kids—they want doctors, psychologists, crisis support workers, and PTSD assessments. The dads are less demanding, they mostly just want to palm their kids off on someone who can play with them and get them to stop whining in the heat, keep them entertained while they grab a few hours' sleep or wait to get through to their insurance companies or just sit in the shade outside their cabins, tents, or empty ski facilities, staring down at their phones and hoping for help.

There are already around a thousand people in the camp, with more arriving all the time, from Malung, Sveg, a few all the way from Östersund. Farther south, the expressways are jammed because of everyone trying to make it to the cities. Uppsala and Stockholm have barred all entry and Gothenburg has sent the 42nd Home Guard Battalion to set up an assembly point by Lake Vänern outside Karlstad, hoping to prevent both Swedes and Norwegians from overrunning the urban areas. On top of all that, six new fires sprung up in Västmanland, to the south of us, yesterday, in the forests around Hedemora and Norberg. Several people who tried to make their way down to Stockholm in their own cars have been forced to turn back by the emergency services, and there are now heavy fines for anyone leaving the main roads in the area without good reason, hindering the work to put out the fires.

"We're stuck here, in other words," Braid Beard announced with a dry laugh that morning. "Stranded, you might say. And right now we're short of everything, including the essentials. So you'll have to let the parents know that they need to supply their own diapers if they want their kids to be supervised during the day."

"But where are we supposed to get hold of diapers?" asked one mother. "The shops are all closed."

"You'll just have to make fabric diapers somehow, and wash them."

"How?" asked the Spanish teacher. "The laundry facilities are already limited as it is."

"The makeshift childcare facilities here at the assembly point are vital for families," said the child psychologist, glancing up from her folder with a stressed look on her face. "Routine is key for creating a sense of normality. If we exclude any children, it could easily lead to anxiety."

I raised my hand.

"Couldn't we just go out to all the preschools and take what we need? In the places affected by the fires, I mean, where everyone has already left."

Braid Beard stared at me.

"Take what we need?"

"Yeah." I shrugged. "It's an emergency, isn't it? And tons of the people here are from those areas anyway, so we'd really just be bringing their own stuff back. It all evens out, doesn't it?"

The grown-ups—I think of them as the grown-ups—started talking over one another, about what is *reasonable in an emergency* and *the importance of maintaining law and order* and *attending to the children's needs*. One of the retirees thought that we should *learn from the pandemic* and someone else said *you remember what it was like after the 2004 tsunami, don't you, when everything just ground to a halt rather than someone stepping in and FIXING things*, and in the end Emil wearily said that as an employee of the local authority, he could shoulder that responsibility and make sure it was done *in an orderly fashion*, but that someone else would have to drive.

Our next stop is farther north, closer to the mountains, a community the fire ripped through three days ago. We drive past a small town center, a supermarket and a lone gas station, the whole place empty and abandoned.

The green preschool building has survived unscathed, the sandbox in the yard outside littered with colorful plastic buckets and spades, small trucks and toy cars; there's even a swing set and an old white rowboat with flaking paint. The fire engines are still here, along with a huge van belonging to the Home Guard. Everything is dirty and gross and there are hoses and pipes everywhere, the ground still smoking in the distance, like a dense, billowing haze. I stop the car and hear Ajax whimper. The air here scares him, and with the engine turned off the AC disappears too, and the horrible smell of smoke starts seeping in. Emil seems unsure, but I grab my face mask and pull it up over my nose.

"Quick as hell," I say, and we jump out.

"Hey, you two, what are you up to?" A sooty black glove points at us. The man is big, wearing sturdy boots and the green uniform of the Home Guard, a bushy gray beard sticking out from beneath his face mask. "It's not safe to stop here."

"Rescue service," I say. "We're here to requisition supplies. For the assembly point, for childcare."

His forehead creases above his mask.

"On whose orders?"

"I work for the local government," Emil says with authority. "Chief education officer. It's our unit."

The Home Guard man glares down at us. A lock of damp gray hair has escaped from beneath his helmet and is clinging to his temple.

"Sounds weird. That you can just show up and help yourselves." He shakes his head. "You'll need a permit."

I make my voice weak and helpless.

"We've got a bunch of babies down in Rättvik, hundreds of them. They need food, diapers, medicine; we're short on everything. Do we really need to go back and get a *permit*?"

He grins and looks down at the axe in Emil's hand.

"And you're going to get in using *that*, are you?"

The chief education officer squirms.

"Uh, there must be a spare key somewhere, but . . ."

Without another word, the Home Guard man turns around and trudges over to the building. He opens the gate and makes his way to the door as he fiddles with a metal tool on his belt. I hear a deep sigh, followed by a loud bang, and the door swings open.

"So, welcome, or whatever you're meant to say," he snorts, turning to leave.

We don't find much in the kitchen or the changing room, nothing but a megapack of toilet paper, two packs of diapers, a bit of formula, and a box of sugar cubes—the staff must have taken the rest with them when they were evacuated. But as we go through the main room, full of toys and cushions and picture books and plastic tubs of crayons and colored pencils and craft supplies, Emil points to something and whistles through the mask.

"Look. That's a Gibson."

There is a guitar on the wall, a red one, hanging from a hook by its leather strap. He trails his fingers over the strings, soft, metallic tones in a broken chord. I remember singing at the piano as a child, how time would run away from me as I thought about nothing at all. *Needs tuning* he mumbles, taking it down from the wall, turning the little knobs at the end, humming to himself and turning them a bit more as his bandaged right hand awkwardly plucks the strings.

"It probably hasn't been used in years, look," he says, running a finger through the thick layer of dust on the top. "Nice guitars like this go bad if you don't play them regularly."

He lifts the leather strap over his head, hangs it around his neck, and plays a chord, sings something sad-sounding about cars and women called *baby* in an American accent. It sounds like proper dad music, but I like the way his voice becomes all silky and smooth when he sings, it's like looking at a cute photo of someone before they got old and ugly. He laughs and takes off the guitar, then stands holding it for a few seconds before he mutters something about how *no one ever plays it anyway*, and then he glances at me like he's looking for permission, I don't know why, and we head back outside. The man in green is still standing by our car, stroking Ajax in the hot sun.

"Nice dog."

"He's a Saint Bernard," I say.

His eyes smile at me.

"You don't know what kind of dog you've got?"

I shrug.

"I found him."

"Her."

"What?"

The Home Guard man shakes his head and points over to the supermarket.

"The window's broken over there."

Emil gives him a blank look as he quickly throws the guitar into the trunk with everything else.

"The window?"

The man sighs.

"We're leaving tonight, and then the place'll be completely unguarded. It'll probably be cleared out within the week. You were from Rättvik, weren't you?"

I think for a moment. Ajax is panting in the heat, her long pink tongue practically dragging in the dust.

"Bread," I say. "Sugar, flour, cereal. Cans."

The Home Guard man looks down at our Ikea bags.

"Four of those, full. No cash. No tobacco." His eyes smile over the top of his mask. "And that there, she's a bitch. A Bernese mountain dog. They cost a pretty penny, dogs like that. Always wanted one."

I hesitate for a second, then remember Zack. I nod, bend down to Ajax, and kiss the warm fur on her forehead before I give the man the leash. I feel a slight tug, like when Martin died, only slightly different.

"What the hell," Emil mutters, trudging over to the supermarket. "Fucking live with it."

===========

They usually gather on the beach in the evening, the guys from Stockholm, a group of mountain bikers who waited too long to head home from some camp in the forest, I know one of them a bit from school. They've been hanging around with a couple of cool, slightly older guys—the outdoorsy type—who are both pretty hot and speak English with cute accents, Dutch or Belgian, I think, and they seem to be gay. It'd be cool if they were gay, it's really in to have gay friends right now. There are a few random little boys no one really knows, too. Boys who pretend to be here on their own even though everyone knows they're actually with their families. There aren't as many girls, I guess their parents don't want to let them out in the evening, just two losers who are constantly by themselves, playing cards and giggling at everything the Dutch/Belgians say, a downer of a girl who wears too much makeup and complains that her tent stinks of farts, two sisters from Uppsala—the older one is always trying to make her little sister go away, and the younger one is always nagging her big sister to go back with her because she doesn't want to walk on her own in the dark, they do nothing but argue—and me. They meet by the swimming area, by the jetty and the sand and the place for lighting fires, three logs around a grill propped on top of a few rocks. Fires aren't actually allowed, but the mountain biking guys always have a few bits of wood and a lighter, and the Dutch/Belgians are usually messing about with something the others think is weed, the downer girl hovers around them in the hopes of a quick drag, and the family boys bring a few bags of chips and cheese puffs that they pass around and the fire crackles and the little sister wants to go home, and a few hours go by.

Back in our cabin, Mom just spends all her time on her phone. She has joined some Facebook group full of people who are angry with the authorities and think the media is *hushing things up*, they want to set up a people's court to try anyone who was wrong about the fires for *crimes against humanity*. Something about Dad pops up every now and then, and she always just scrolls straight past it or puts her phone down and goes out to see if she can *help with anything*, but after five minutes she's back again, staring down at the screen, and by the time she has to spell out Zacharias von der Esch for the fourth or forty-fourth time, she inevitably starts crying.

Because he's nowhere. The thing about him being at the mine was wrong, either that or a misunderstanding. Mom spent days on the phone but she never got through, and when that Claes Kall guy eventually called back he said that he'd now had it confirmed that there was a boy in the area, that they had to *be persistent*, and Mom managed to cry her way into arranging a vehicle to Östra Silvberg, a forestry entrepreneur from Hedemora drove down there in his off-roader this morning and rescued all the old people, but there was no sign of Zack, never had been, and when she called Claes Kall he obviously didn't pick up, and when she wrote in a thread about what an evil fucking psychopath he is, the admin deleted her post and warned her she would be kicked out of the group if she continued, and then she called Dad instead, but his phone is still off.

She has contacted virtually every single authority in Sweden: police stations, search and rescue leaders, hospitals, and volunteer organizations; she's even been in touch with the Swedish embassy in Norway. Using the letters I remembered, we managed to find out that the car was a rental, a white Toyota with the license plate LDR384, but it's impossible to get hold of anyone who can tell us exactly who rented that particular car, it might have been stolen, and there are so many missing people right now, so many people wandering around in the mountains and the nature reserves that are still burning, that my little brother is just another lost kid among many, and he has also been placed in the category *Believed to have left disaster zone*, which means he is no longer a priority.

She knows I've been helping to look after the little kids during the day, and this morning, before the latest with Zack, she hugged me and said she was proud that I understood how important it was for *everyone to try to do their part*, and then she sobbed at what a good big sister I'd always been to Becka, Zack too, of course, even though I was so young then, but none of that is true, I've never looked after my siblings, not in the way I should

have—when they told me we would be getting a little sister my first reaction was to ask Mom if she could have an abortion—and then I started
crying a bit too.

When I got back tonight she wanted to talk about *next steps*, about how
we're going to get home to Stockholm, about Dad and Becka and the latest
news about Zack (the latest news is always that there is no news) and whether
we should try to find ourselves a tent so that we can get away from the cabin
and the crazy family from Mora, neither of us can stand them any longer. I
listened to her for a while and then said I was going down to the beach and
she hugged me and mumbled *Vilja-vanilla* into my hair before I left.

I'm now sitting on the nice side, between the card-playing girls and the
family boys, directly opposite the Dutch/Belgians and the mountain-biking
gang, who are laughing and shouting like always. I chat a little with one of
the guys and listen to the downer girl saying that she's smoked some weed
and feels *fuzzy*, talking about her difficult mother who has just been treated
for cancer ("we were meant to be hiking in the mountains to celebrate") and
has all sorts of weird stomach issues now that she can't eat her special fiber
porridge. Other than that, I don't do much. I'm not here to hang out with
any of them, I'm just waiting.

Tracking down Puma—even adding him—is out of the question, I know
that, *Linnea_bp_forever* would notice right away. Unless she's as dumb as a
box of rocks she probably watches his accounts like a hawk. He isn't handing out water by the station anymore, I've already checked there, and since
yesterday they don't even want us to leave the camp without good reason,
it risks *causing tensions in the community*, apparently; one of the locals got
annoyed that people have been sleeping in the cemetery outside the church,
leaving shitty toilet paper in the bushes.

But there's a footpath from the campsite into town, and I've seen people on it, coming and going, and the jetty and the barbecue area are in a kind
of no-man's-land between the two.

We've been texting back and forth a little. No real messages, just pictures. He wrote Good morning with a heart and a picture of his face in pro-

file, a smoky sky in the background, and I replied with a heart and a video of me hugging Ajax. I don't know where he is or what he's up to, but the flare he lit wasn't so far away. A few hundred feet, no more than that. Which means he was hanging out by the beach, somewhere nearby. Which means he could come down here, if he wanted to.

I nod and murmur at the downer girl's story about her mom's operation and chemotherapy and how fucking ugly wigs are as I squint out into the darkness. I spotted what looked like a group of people in the distance yesterday, heard the growl of a moped, saw the glow of a cigarette. Voices.

Whenever he shows up, we'll sit down together by the fire and I'll tell him about all the crazy things I've been up to. Pretending to have an education, to be a grown-up, to have a driver's license, and all to give myself a chance of getting out of here. I don't know what I was thinking. Maybe I thought he'd be on the side of the road somewhere, handing out bottles of water or playing soccer, I don't know. But instead I've just been driving around with an old head teacher, breaking into a bunch of preschools. *It's totally crazy*, I'll say, *what your emotions can do to you*. And then we'll sit in silence, staring into the flames with a bunch of strangers around us, and we'll feel the same thing we felt at the hospital: the sense of sitting on a precipice, that anything goes.

I notice it from the others' reactions first, from the guys sitting opposite me. The way they sort of contract like jellyfish, spreading their knees, straightening their backs, puffing their chests out. Their voices get slightly quieter, or maybe it's that they become a little deeper, less cackling and giggly, more like Men Discussing Important Things.

They don't stare, don't even glance over. It's more like their energy focuses in my direction. Or rather: on a point above my shoulder. I try to switch off my body and resist the urge to turn around, to lean in to the downer girl and her mom's cancer instead. Let him come.

Linnea taps me on the shoulder.

"Hi," she says, squeezing in beside me on the log. I barely recognize her in her makeup and false lashes, a nice black skirt, hair loose.

"What's up? I thought I might find you here. We used to come down here when I was a kid." She smiles. "My parents were really into outdoor stuff. They made us go skiing or skating or cycling or walking every weekend. Sandwiches and hot chocolate." She pronounces it like a child, *choclit*, and I can't tell whether it's her accent or whether she's just putting it on.

"Is that why you joined the Scouts?" I ask.

"The opposite, actually. Mom and Dad just wanted to, like, *look* at nature, but the Scouts want to *use* it. Building shelters, tree houses. Cooking food, real food, no fucking hot dogs."

She sighs and throws a pinecone into the fire.

"I learned how to build a proper fire when I was eight. Me and my troop. You make a pile of rocks and clay on the bottom, then maybe a bit of moss or grass or saplings, then more rocks, and you light the fire on top. That way you can boil water and cook food on it, and once you're done you just bury the ashes and take everything away and throw the rocks back into the forest and no one can tell you've even been there with a fire burning all week."

"Is that true?"

Linnea nods.

"Building a fire yourself, cooking for yourself, doing the washing up yourself in a gross muddy puddle. Everything by yourself. Learning by doing, that's what they call it. You had to look after yourself, rather than leeching off other people."

She slowly turns to me.

"What you've been doing is so fucking disrespectful, Vilja."

I hold her eye, not flinching, not batting an eyelid. It's not like I can put the feeling into words, after all. What am I supposed to say, *sorry*? For something I don't even regret?

"I didn't know he had a girlfriend," I say, feeling like an idiot.

"But you do now, don't you?" She grins. "So what are you doing on his profile? What the hell are you even doing here?"

"Looking after the kids."

"Wow, so sweet of you."

She gets up and moves around the fire, over to the mountain biker guys. She whispers something and giggles and they mutter and laugh and shuffle along so that she can sit down between the Dutch/Belgians. She's great at dialing up that cooing, girlish side of herself when she feels like it. I've never been any good at that.

Right then, the downer girl clears her throat and leans toward the fire, as though she wants everyone's attention. She probably realizes that Linnea has just stolen the show.

"Everyone shut up, because I'm going to recite a poem," she says solemnly, and the guys grin nervously because they've been through this kind of thing before, girls who think they can sing or play guitar or tell stories, and then it's always just cringe, but she kind of sits tall and stares into the flames with a mysterious smile and begins in a loud, ringing voice:

been a long while
since I've sat down here
and looked out across the streets

One of the little boys is still talking to his friend, ignoring her, but Linnea shushes him, whispers *it's lovely.*

a wave of
European dusk
slides jacks under the city
and drifts away through me
while the poison acts

It's incredible, the way she does it, the way the mountain-biking gang become like insects buzzing around a lamp, their eyes fixed on her lips. The Dutch/Belgians can't understand a word she's saying, but even they look spellbound. Linnea is rocking back and forth like she's in a trance. The little sister yawns loudly.

even if everything comes to an end
it won't turn away its gaze

The downer girl keeps going, though it's like she's not quite present, deep in the embers and the ash. She recites the poem like an actor, like a priest, the words rolling like a funeral procession across the sand, out onto the calm surface of the lake, where they become a burning ship that drifts away into the darkness.

railway stations and rain
were great powers in my life

A soft breeze embraces us as we sit around the fire. Warm, with only a slight hint of smoke. It's the longing, the estrangement, the disorientation, the cruelty of being forced to grow up in an era where one crisis follows another, yet somehow we're still supposed to get used to all these lost dreams and lost hope and a lost future, a nightmare that never ends, a life that never begins, and I realize that one of the younger boys beside me is shaking with tears.

I came up to myself
I put an arm around my shoulder
with a feeling that we
had waited long enough

She gives an introverted smile, pushes back a lock of hair from her forehead.

that I had the very key
to the mystery

Everyone waits for her to go on, but she doesn't speak. She just smiles shyly and looks up at the Dutch/Belgians.

"Now I can take some weed!" she says in slightly shaky English, and everyone laughs, the spell broken. Someone claps, but most people just keep talking or staring down at their phones as though nothing has happened, as though we're ashamed that we were so obsessed with a stupid poem that didn't even rhyme. The downer girl sucks on the joint and Linnea perches on one of the Dutch/Belgians' laps, taking a long drag when it comes around to her, holding the smoke in. I don't know how she dares, Dad has always said that I'm not allowed to take drugs from strangers, but I guess that's probably just what people do out here in the sticks.

Voices in the distance. Figures coming closer along the beach path. Linnea glances over, slightly hesitantly, something searching in her eyes.

And then I hear a scream. A loud, piercing scream that bursts the bubble around the fire, a scream that is soon followed by several more. The men in the distance start running and Linnea screams again, alternates between screaming and crying, stumbling, sobbing, words like *you bastard* and *groped me* and *oh fuck* and the guys back away from her with their hands in the air, the Dutch/Belgians are staring at her in confusion, but the others have reached us now, Puma and two other boys, plus an older man with gray hair who looks like he must be someone's dad.

They run over to Linnea and push back the group around her. The mountain biker guys initially puff themselves up, but they quickly pull back, and in the scrappy argument that follows it seems like someone tried to put their hand up her skirt, and when the Dutch/Belgians try to deny it in stuttering English the dad sniffs the air with a disgusted face, the sweet scent of weed still lingering, and that's when Puma spots me. A quiet, confused glance, his mouth looks like it's about to say something, his face like it's being torn in two. Followed by resignation.

The sisters are already heading back to the camp, and the angry dad orders the mountain biker guys to fetch buckets of water from the lake and put out the fire. The Dutch/Belgians sneak away. And in the middle of everything, Linnea just sits on her log, opposite me. Leaning forward, like she's still listening to the beautiful poem, like she wants to hear another.

"How early did you say you had to get up to look after the kids tomorrow?" She smiles. "Maybe you should go to bed soon?"

I don't speak, just stare into the fire. It hisses as the guys pour water onto it, and the billowing smoke blows straight toward me, but I keep staring. At the small black pools that form around the steaming lumps of coal, at the damp, swampy ash, at death.

"At a jamboree once, there were a couple of guys who pissed on the fire," she says. "The smell was so gross, I can't even describe it. I could smell it on my clothes for weeks afterward."

Linnea makes a face at the memory.

"But it went away in the end, Vilja."

She smooths her hair and gets up from the log. Puma comes over and puts his arm around her, and they walk off together without another word. I watch them go, and when Puma shouts something to one of the other guys down by the lake, she turns around and gives me one of those Scout greetings, three fingers to her forehead, her little finger and thumb forming a ring, her smile as cold as steel. God, I hate her.

SATURDAY, AUGUST 30

THE TANK IS ONLY HALF-FULL, BUT ALL THE SPARE GAS IS RESERVED for the emergency vehicles and the helicopters and for transporting patients. *See if you can find any while you're on the road*, Braid Beard told us, and Emil muttered, *what, is there someone handing out gas on the road?* but I had already jumped into the driver's seat. It feels good to get away, because the mood in the camp is super glum now; the Home Guard troops have been turning people back when they try to leave on foot, the stench of the overflowing porta-potties spreads quickly in the heat, and then there's the smoke, which just keeps getting worse and worse. *We've also received reports of drug taking and sexual assault down by the beach*, said one of the leaders, a chief physician ("but professor is also fine") on holiday in the area who has increasingly started taking charge. He sounded concerned. *This kind of thing can easily spiral out of control, and we also know how quickly it can lead to tensions between the assembly point and the surrounding community.*

Emil isn't as chatty as he was yesterday. He seems tired, and mostly just stares out the window. Supplies are running low in the camp. The last of the yellow polystyrene trays was handed out ages ago, and for breakfast we're down to a single piece of dry bread per adult. Personally, I'm happier on the road than I am at the campsite. Getting away for a while, even if it's just for a few hours, gives me a chance to forget all the crap. Mom's scrolling through Facebook threads, the downer girl's self-pitying, Puma's glance, at once disappointed and sympathetic. All of it. And Thailand, too. We were supposed to be staying in a house with a pool by the sea, and I'd get to ride in a tuk-tuk. I've never been in one before, but Bianca spent the winter in Thailand once and she said that they're a bit like a moped with a carriage at the front, like a taxi, and you sit there and bounce along the bumpy little roads, past garbage and markets and luxury hotels, the unfamiliar scents of food and palm trees and sea and dirt; Bianca told me she met a whole bunch of people there, and they drove between pools and beaches, that a happy little Thai man took them wherever they wanted to go for almost no money at all.

I roll down the window in an attempt to feel the breeze in my hair, but the smoke is unbearable now, like a big, nasty hand slapping me with a fist of ash instead.

"I can't do this anymore," Emil says, his voice flat, as though he's talking to himself or thinking aloud. "This isn't me. I wasn't prepared for any of this, you know?"

I know that this is my cue to say something nice about how he's doing a great job, how he's a rock, someone everyone listens to, but I've actually been finding him kind of annoying lately, and I don't have the energy to comfort him.

"Did you only just realize that?" I ask instead.

"What do you mean?"

"You've worked in schools all your life, you're an educated person. You must have known things would be more or less this bad during your lifetime, so how can you not be prepared?"

He makes a face and cradles his hand and looks out the window for a long time, so long that I think he must have dozed off, but then I hear him mumble *I thought someone else would come along and take charge. Someone who would make sure there was some sort of order, none of this fucking chaos.*

We drive for a long time, to a place called Lima, so far away it's practically in Norway. There is a river running through the small community, and the sooty signs—the ones still left on the fire-damaged buildings—are all advertising canoeing trips and beaver safaris and wilderness adventures. The river is the only reason anyone would want to live out here, and I think it must be peaceful to spend your life somewhere like this, watching the water flow south, the ice forming and melting and forming again, the floes drifting away, the autumn leaves, the dead animals, the junk.

"Look how low the water is," Emil mutters, pointing at the rocks and the gravel visible in the middle of the riverbed. It's muddy and gross at the edges, the surface of the water oily, and it smells weird. They're using planes to take water from all the lakes now, you hear them more than you see them, those big Canadian water bombers that snatch up fifteen hundred gallons in a single swoop, emptying it onto the burning forests, but I guess the water originally comes from up there in the mountains, and just like everywhere else the dying glaciers will slowly mean falling water levels, not all at once but through record year after record year, little by little, until one day it's all gone and the people left here will look out at the dead black clay as it slowly turns to sand, and then they'll leave too and all that will be left will be ruins and crap and no one will remember the lives that were once lived here.

You're thinking like Dad now. Pessimism, the end of the world, all that stuff. You're seeing the world through his eyes.

So I try to see it through mine. How we'll come up with some plan to end the droughts. To stop the ice caps from melting. To put the fires out and suck up the smoke and store it in a mountain somewhere. There must be a way. This can't be how it ends, with us staggering through a broken nightmare like drugged-up child soldiers for a generation or three before just dying out. We can invent things. Work together. Survive. It'll be awful, it'll be difficult, but we're not just going to go under.

We drive past a soccer field with banners for pizzerias and plumbers, and then Emil points and says *there*. We get out of the car outside a sweet little preschool with a garden, just above the river. There's a tall, sturdy-looking fence around it, of course, but still: the kids have views across the water, and they've painted the fence in nice colors, red, blue, yellow, and pink. Back in Stockholm you'd probably have to wait years to get your kids into a preschool in such a great location, I remember Mom and Dad sighing as they went around the residential areas looking for a place for Becka.

Emil hacks at the door and we work together to push the crowbar into the gap, force it open, and head inside. There is a bit of fire damage to the ceiling and in one of the bigger rooms, but the kitchen and the bathroom are both fine. There isn't much left, just diapers and a few jars of food that we feel like we have to grab, almost as though we both know that this part is mostly for our own sakes. And then we're back in the yard with our Ikea bags, looking over at the rest of the community.

"Well," Emil says stiffly, "I guess we might as well take a look around."

We leave the car where it is and walk slowly through the small village, stepping over the rubble and the junk in the road, the rusty skeleton of a bicycle, the wreck of some kind of digger or forestry machine, grayish-black puddles with a sharp chemical smell, a charred, shapeless lump of black plastic and broken glass that it takes me a few seconds to recognize as a wide-screen TV that someone must have given up trying to take with them. People left here in a hurry. We pass a red wooden cottage promising *CRAFTS* and *WAFFLES WITH JAM AND*, a disused gas station, four new-looking houses, and a fence with a wooden sign hanging from a rope, the words *YOUR NEXT ADVENTURE STARTS HERE* above pictures of canoes, bears, and blazing campfires.

There is a small supermarket with signs announcing that it also serves as the local pharmacy and liquor store and bookmaker, and we cross the gravel parking lot and pause to look around. The white wood is dirty and could do with a fresh lick of paint in a few places, but other than that the building doesn't seem to have been damaged at all. It's in such good shape it's almost shameful, a few sooty marks, of course, but the windows are intact and the signs look like they've been painted recently—there are even a few banners advertising hot dogs and ice cream, like we could just march up the steps and go inside and ask for a cone of chocolate, strawberry, and raspberry licorice, sit down at the white plastic table in the sun, and listen to Zack's nonstop babbling about space or extinct mammals as Dad messes with his phone and Mom nags Zack to eat up before it melts.

Emil rings the bell on the door, I'm not sure why, and we hear the sound cut through the shadows inside. I glance around, take in the gravel parking lot, the little road along the river, but everything is calm, quiet, covered in ash.

"They should have some pharmacy stuff here," I say, pointing to the sign.

He nods.

"Right, then," he mutters. "That's what you say if anyone asks." He smashes the window above the door with an axe. The sound of breaking glass cuts through the silence.

═════════

The shop is so well stocked that we briefly discuss going back to get the car, but eventually decide not to take any more than we can carry in the Ikea bags. Emil's is heavy, and he makes a face as the straps cut into his bad hand. I lug mine behind me and remember walking like this with Zack when we left the summer house, his nonstop whining about his foot, going on and on about completely random stuff. I try to remember that day, what exactly did he say? Something about losing a tooth?

And what about me, what did I say? The last time I spoke to my brother.

Memory is like a big sack of shit: you can dump it in a corner and pretend you'll get used to it, tell yourself that the smell isn't so bad, but eventually you open it and peer inside and it's even worse than you could have imagined.

I told him that if he didn't stop whining about his foot really fucking soon we wouldn't make it to the buses in time, that we'd leave without him, and when he told Mom and Dad what I'd said I said *shut up, you retard, I did not*.

I swallow my shame, think about how I left Mom the slice of bread and ham that I'd saved for Ajax this morning, that was nice of me. I'm still dragging my Ikea bag and I hear Emil's hissing breath and look up ahead. There are two women in yellow-and-blue vests, and as we get closer we see that they say *VOLUNTARY RESOURCE GROUP* on them. One of the women has short red hair and looks a bit like the home economics teacher I had in sixth grade. The other is younger, barrel-shaped, with long blond hair and a blue cap. They have a wheelbarrow full of what looks like gardening tools, a spade, a rake, hedging shears, and work gloves, and they're both wearing rubber boots; they look like they've been busy weeding the gardens in a residential area.

"Hi there," says the redhead, giving us a warm smile. "We were just wondering if you were the ones who'd come from the rescue service." She points back to our car, which is still parked outside the preschool no more than a few hundred feet away. "So we thought we'd check what you were up to."

"We're just about to move on," says Emil, as though the woman were some sort of meter maid. "We're taking this stuff back to Rättvik."

Her smile grows. She points down at the Ikea bags.

"And what is *this stuff*, exactly?"

He shrugs and keeps walking, past them.

"Our things, aren't they?"

The woman pulls a mobile phone from the pocket of her trousers. No, phones don't work right now, it's one of those walkie-talkies.

"Because the thing is, I just spoke to my son." She points to where we've just come from. "He was over by the shop, and he said that there were two people inside. Looting."

"We're from the rescue service. I work for the local authority," Emil continues, his voice flat. "I'm the chief education officer. We're requisitioning supplies, it's . . ."

The big blond woman, the one who hasn't said a word yet, has already grabbed a shovel from the wheelbarrow, and she takes a few steps forward as she swings it through the air, both hands on the shaft, like a baseball bat. It all happens so slowly: Emil hears her footsteps, manages to glance back and see it coming, but he's awkward with his bandaged right hand and the heavy bag, and maybe it's something else too, a sense of weariness; the lack of food and water over the past few days has left his movements sluggish, like a sleepwalker, and the blade hits him square on his right shoulder, making him stumble and cry out and drop the bag to the dirty ground with a wet crunch.

The blonde grunts unhappily and stands over him with the spade raised. *She was aiming for his head*, I think in amazement. *For the back of his neck.*

The redhead trudges over and bends down over him and sniffs the air. It looks ridiculous, like she's pretending to be a dog. I miss Ajax, should never have given her up.

"Vodka," she says. "Or is it whiskey? Did you just grab spirits, or did you find space for a few bottles of vino too?"

There was a locked door behind the till in the supermarket, and I watched from the corner of my eye as Emil forced it open, muttering something about checking what was in there, whether they had any gas or anything like that. You can order booze to supermarkets in the countryside, I know that, I've seen Dad do it a few times, for some Midsummer party somewhere.

Emil is now sitting motionless on the ground, his arm at a really weird angle below the shoulder she hit, his lips moving in a quiet whimper. The redhead pokes at his bag with her toe, nudging out cigarettes, multipacks of snus tobacco, and, from the very bottom, a few glugging bottles. She rolls them beneath the sole of her boot, chuckles.

"Auch . . . en . . . to . . . shan," she reads from a label. "Our Steffan got one of these when he turned fifty. Nice stuff you lot drink down in Rättvik."

She waves, and I see two guys walking along the road toward us. They're around my age, maybe a little older, in shorts and T-shirts. Three more appear from the red cabin with the *CRAFTS* sign, like the community has just stirred to life around us.

"You can take the booze," I blurt out. "Take the booze and the tobacco and everything else. We'll leave now and never come back."

But the redhead shakes her head. For the first time, she looks angry.

"You don't get it, do you? You're going to put everything back where you found it. We're going to report you to the police, and you're going to have to pay fines and compensation for any damage."

She picks up my Ikea bag in one hand, without batting an eyelid—there must be muscles in there somewhere—and throws it into their wheelbarrow.

"This isn't Stockholm; we won't have any anarchy here," she goes on. "We want law and order. No criminal gangs snooping around, snatching whatever they want."

"We don't want people like you," the blonde adds, the first time she has opened her mouth. She is standing with the shovel over her shoulder, and she looks down at Emil with a bored expression, as though she were a gardener and he were the last bush she needed to prune before her coffee break. Her voice is flat, completely tuneless. "We don't want any anarchy."

"But we're from the assembly point in Rättvik," I say. "It's the authorities who organized it. The rescue service and that kind of thing."

"And we're from the local government, Malung-Sälen," says the red-head, pointing to her vest. "Voluntary resource group. Civil defense. And you have no right to come up here and loot private property."

"No anarchy," the blonde repeats. She is starting to seem more annoying than dangerous.

Emil has shuffled back with his injured shoulder and is glaring up at the two women, his face a mask of pain, cheeks streaked with tears. The others have reached us now, and I stand beside him as they form a ring around us. They're mostly middle-aged women and teenage boys, a few of the older ones wearing vests with *VOLUNTARY RESOURCE GROUP* on them too. The men are probably out fighting the fires somewhere, either that or helping with evacuations or clearing wrecked cars; these are the people who've been left behind to guard what little hasn't already burned down or been destroyed. There is a sharp smell coming from Emil's bag, a pool of liquid seeping into the ugly brown earth.

The big blonde points at me with the sharp end of her shovel.

"We don't want people like you," she says. There is something stiff about her, absent. Her eyes don't move when she speaks, like she's an alien in her own body.

The circle gets tighter, denser, there must be ten, fifteen people standing around me and Emil now. One of the boys is holding a rusty mudguard from a bike, another has the oar from a rowboat, which he keeps drumming softly against the ground. It's the same height as him.

I calmly look around.

"We're from Rättvik. There are hundreds of children in need of medication there."

I point to my Ikea bag in the wheelbarrow.

"We've taken painkillers, cortisone cream. Rehydration solution. Bandages. Some of the children have inflamed eyes because of the smoke, so we've taken some eyedrops, too."

Emil opens his mouth to say something. I know it's not going to be anything good, so I quickly go on.

"I'm going to keep the medication and that kind of thing; you can do whatever you want with the rest."

I turn to the blond woman and try to get through to the person inside.

"And you're going to put that stupid shovel down and let us leave, OK?"

The redhead sighs and takes a step closer.

"Even if you do have medical needs down in Rättvik, that doesn't mean you can come up here and loot our supermarket."

Her breath smells like sour milk, like when Becka throws up. I lean forward, into the scent.

"Look at me. I look like a fourteen-year-old girl. I have to show ID to buy energy drinks. If Rättvik was on a looting spree, do you seriously think they'd send a nursery school teacher?"

"You broke into our supermarket," one of the other women shouts. "You took things. What do you call that?"

I wait a few seconds. Let things come together.

"My granddad died of Covid," I say slowly, giving myself time to make things up as I go. "In the spring, months after the vaccine was approved. He was seventy-five and had an irregular heartbeat, and he used to call up to ask when he could have his jab every single day, but no one could ever tell him because no one knew what the plan was or who was in charge or who to prioritize, there were different rules in different regions, and then the bosses vaccinated themselves and the celebrities got a VIP lane and the king got his, but for everyone else it dragged on and on and no one really knew why and no one could make up their mind and then my granddad got sick and died."

I turn to the redhead and smile.

"This isn't looting, it's a coordination of resources. The children need medicine, and if the medicine is locked in a shop somewhere, it's not doing any good. The state will step in and pay for everything later."

"The state?"

"Yeah, or society, whatever. All of us." I shrug. "We're in this shit together."

They pull Emil to his feet and the big blond woman actually decides to be nice, helping him walk the short distance back to the car. One of the teenage boys is wearing a *New York* cap, and he pushes the wheelbarrow with my Ikea bag in it for me, asks if I have a boyfriend back in Stockholm. I tell him that we could really do with some gas, to make it home.

It's only once I'm back behind the wheel that I finally start shaking. Emil is sitting quietly, whimpering, his hand on his shoulder, but once they've all stepped away from the car he unbuttons his trousers, gives me a sly smile, and pulls a pack of cigarettes out of his underpants.

"Shame about the booze, but at least I managed to grab these," he whispers, sounding pleased with himself. "We're completely out of cigarettes in the camp. Good to have."

I take one and he lights it for me. It's only the second time I've ever smoked, and I try not to cough like a loser, to take light, shallow breaths, only inhaling small puffs of smoke at a time. The filthy taste fills my mouth and makes my lungs burn. It reminds me of the day we drove around and around and then I think about Martin and I almost start crying and then I realize that I'm not shaking anymore, I'm not scared, everything is OK.

Someone knocks on the window. It's the teenage boy again, the one with the cap that says *New York* even though he's probably never been there. He triumphantly holds up a can of gas. I roll down the window.

"On us," he says, throwing it in to me. "Because of the whole shovel thing. My aunt's not totally with it."

He peers around and then leans into the car door.

"You can have these too, from me," he says shyly, holding out a pair of sunglasses. I take them, try them on, look up at him through a sooty film, and then study myself in the rearview mirror. Fear surges through my body like diarrhea, settling like a hard lump in my gut.

I don't speak, frozen to the spot.

"They look great on you. You can have them," he says again. "But I want a kiss in return."

I lean out through the window and give him a quick kiss with my lips closed, hoping like hell that the cigarette makes me taste like shit. And then I start the engine and pull away.

———

It wasn't meant to be like this. When I first lied about my age and then talked them into letting me drive this car, I imagined . . . I don't know what, but it wasn't this. He was supposed to be handing out bottles of water somewhere, and I would cruise by and roll down the window. I might not even say anything, just teasingly raise one eyebrow, and he'd drop everything and jump in beside me and then we'd drive into the middle of the forest somewhere, find a magical little lake that looked like something from one of the fairy-tale books Granny used to read to me when I was little, and I'd be wearing a super-hot bikini and there'd be water lilies and that kind of thing.

Or maybe he'd be at a beach party somewhere, with her and her lame Scout friends, and I'd pull up in my red-and-yellow car and at first they'd all wonder who that badass Stockholm girl was, the guys would just stand and stare and the girls would glare with jealousy. I'd feel all gangsta and

hood and the car stereo would be pumping and time would come to a
standstill when I opened the door and got out and swaggered over the sand
toward him in a pair of black Rebecca Björnsdotter sandals and said *you're
my baby now.*

But the car stereo doesn't have Bluetooth, it only takes CDs, and it's
as tired and dirty as I am. I barely had the energy to help Emil out of the
passenger seat and guide him over to the medical cabin, never mind get
back into the car and drive out here, slamming on the brakes outside the
dull new-construction house with its dead, grayish-brown lawn, so flat it
could be a tennis court. There is no sense of triumph left in any of this, no
adventure, nothing but hunger and nausea and bad breath.

They're sitting on a sofa in the shade by the side of the house, both
on their phones, each with an empty bowl in front of them, a few noodles
clinging to the bottom. There are some cans of soda bobbing in a red plastic bucket on the floor, and I've been driving without AC for two hours
straight, I don't even stop to think, I just bend down and grab a Fanta Exotic. There might have been ice in the bucket at one point in time, but the
water is now the temperature of lukewarm piss; I don't care, I just open the
can and let it run down my throat like a fizzing, sweet miracle.

"Nice sunglasses," Linnea says without batting an eyelid. "New?"

"Nah, vintage," I reply, taking another sip. "Ivana Helsinki Special Edition. Try them on."

"Vilja." Puma seems anxious, his eyes darting from her to me. "What
are you doing here? Are you OK?"

"Try them." I hold the sunglasses out to Linnea, who grins and puts
them on.

I stare at her.

"Can you walk back and forth?"

"Vilja?" Puma says again.

I swallow it back. Don't start crying now. Fuck. Don't start crying.

"Linnea, please get up and walk back and forth."

She frowns but does as I say, gets up from the sofa and takes a few skipping steps across the lawn. I move back slightly, walk around her so that I can see her from different angles, searching for the right one.

Maybe?

"Pull your hair back."

"Seriously, Vilja, that's enough," Puma sighs. "What the hell are you—"

"It's OK," Linnea interrupts him. She gives me a stern look and tucks her thick, dark hair behind her ears. "Like this?"

I stare at her like a crazy person.

"No. In a ponytail."

Linnea gathers her hair in her hand and pulls it up.

"This?"

A shabby chic mother around thirty-five, preggo, hair messily tied up, she walks quickly toward me and Mom and Becka and Zack, talking angrily, rapidly, wearing a pair of big retro sunglasses, black frames with fake white and red gems that catch the light, they're super nice and I glance over to Dad, wonder whether he recognizes them too, and then I turn to the car and see the license plate and think Lana Del Rey.

I sway slightly, sit down on the grass. It feels like I'm about to pass out, the only thing I've eaten today is half a bread roll. Linnea takes out another can, cracks it open, and passes it to me. I take a few deep gulps, swallow a burp. My hair is a mess and I'm wearing a sweaty old T-shirt, my legs are hairy, and I'm crying like a pig, but there are limits.

———

All three of us are sitting up front, I'm not sure why. No, I am, it's obvious, one of them has to sit up here and help me keep an eye on the road, and it'd be super awkward if it was just me and him, or me and her, so they're both squeezed onto the passenger seat beside me, Linnea on his lap. She makes it look so elegant, like she weighs nothing at all. I think she must be subtly supporting herself against the door to make herself lighter, and on any other day I'd feel like crying with jealousy, but right now I don't even care.

Puma knows a few of the boys in Lima, of course he does, they travel around the area playing matches against one another practically every weekend, he's been to their field plenty of times before but doesn't know his way around the community itself. Still, he's quick on his phone. He has some sort of special plan that gives him superfast internet even when the connection is crappy. I don't know how he does it, but it turns out he knows a goalie in Lima and he goes through his profile and stories and checks the people who have left comments and likes, then he makes a fake account and starts adding them, he borrows Linnea's phone and uses it to make more profiles, sits there with both phones and starts fake chat threads where the fake profiles are bickering with each other, and he tags other people and eventually a few others start joining in, he adds them and swipes through their stories and checks who they hang out with and starts tagging them in the fake discussion between the fake accounts, and after only an hour he knows exactly which guys around our age could have been in Lima today.

"Puma is so good at this kind of thing," Linnea says proudly from his lap.

Yeah, sweetie, I've noticed. The thought just drifts by, all the excitement I felt earlier has ebbed away and now all I want is for them to find the New York cap guy for me.

I'm driving through the late summer evening, the air humming with the sound of the water bombers. There are roadblocks in several places, but the people manning them are all stressed guys who don't look any older than us, and they just wave us through when they see the red and yellow paintwork. I've fantasized about driving through the countryside with him so many times, but now that we're actually here all I want is to get back to the camp and be with Mom, because whatever is waiting for us in Lima is going to be horrible and scary.

"Was it him?" Puma asks, holding out his phone. A picture of a guy standing on ice, holding up a dead fish to the camera. I shake my head. "Or him?" In front of the Eiffel Tower. "Him?" Grinning, with a burger. "Him?" Expressionless on a sofa, sitting beside his mother.

I shake my head and Puma swears under his breath.

"None of them. Wait, hang on," I say. "Let me see the last one again."

The boy on the sofa is blond, slim, his face says nothing to me. But his mother. Long blond hair. Pale, doughy skin. And those eyes. That stiffness, like she's not quite there.

"Her," I say quietly. "She was the one with the shovel. His aunt."

The sky has started to darken by the time we reach the little gravel track that leads into the forest, down a slope, and through a clearing and then we're there: outside a shabby red house with a wild, overgrown yard that stretches down toward the river, rows of more or less rust-eaten cars, some propped up on bricks where their wheels are missing, a broken stroller, a couple of bicycles, and what looks like an old wood-fired stove. There are no lights on inside. The power has been down for the past few days in this part of Dalarna.

I turn off the engine and we get out of the car. We don't really have a plan—should we go straight up to the house and knock, or would it be better to take a look around the property first? I hear Puma hiss something about *fucking hillbillies* and see a gnarled tree in silhouette against the deep-blue sky, shadows like huge ice floes, but as we come closer the shapes peel apart and I see a fridge or possibly a freezer on a pallet. I was afraid of the dark when I was younger, but now I'm mostly just pissed that I can't see anything.

"Listen," Linnea whispers. "Once it's too dark to see anything, it's better just to listen."

We're standing several feet apart in the overgrown garbage dump of a yard. I hold my breath, see the others as dark shadows, and a memory of an Easter trip to Skåne years and years ago comes back to me. Dad wanted to take us to see some boulders on a hill above the sea, a bunch of old kings had dragged them up there and stood them on end at some point in the past, but Mom got distracted by a load of art galleries along the way and then we got lost and they started arguing, and by the time we'd parked the car and walked up the narrow path to the hill it was dark and Dad had stepped in a cow pie, but the boulders loomed tall in the dusk, several feet apart,

silent, brooding, like watchmen from the dawn of time, and for weeks afterward I lay awake at night thinking about those rocks just standing there
in the darkness. It was so hard to imagine that they'd always been there,
that they'd been there for several thousand years, and suddenly I wonder
whether they're still there now. They should be, but for how much longer,
before all the floods, erosion, and fires, or before the Gulf Stream flips out
and there's another ice age? It feels impossible to imagine them standing
there forever, surely nothing can last forever, or can it?

The wind, the rippling water in the river. A motor, somewhere in the
distance.

And as though from below: a soft, gravelly, scraping sound. From beneath us. Under the ground.

"A root cellar," I say.

We look all around. The wrecked cars. The stroller. A few trees. To the
right of the fridge, there is a small hump in the ground, and Linnea and I
both start creeping toward it over the dry, rustling grass as though we've
just had the same thought. I climb up onto it. Nothing, just dusty earth.
And the stench of something rotten, musty, dead.

"There," Linnea whispers. She has tiptoed around the hump and is
pointing to something right beneath me.

I head back down and stand beside her. In the gray gloom, a dark hole
opens up like a cave. A set of stone steps leads downward, and without
thinking about what I'm doing I make my way down them, three or four
steps into the void, using my hand to feel the way. A wooden door with a
cool, rough metal handle. The scraping sound is louder now.

For the first time, I feel afraid. Zack is probably tied up in there.
Chopped to pieces. Raped. Tortured. Or maybe he's just dead, stuffed into
a black plastic garbage bag. Horrible images from children's books, gingerbread houses and cages made from twigs and branches, a troll forcing him
to eat soup through the bars with a long wooden spoon.

I take a couple of deep breaths. Feel Linnea's hand on top of mine, her
fingers firmly gripping the handle.

"Move," she hisses, opening the door and slipping past me into the darkness without a sound.

The first thing I notice is the cool air. After being in the sticky, suffocating heat for so long, the chill in the basement is almost unpleasantly sharp. I can smell earth and clay, old potatoes, plus a hint of something sweeter, like apples. And beneath it all: dirt, rust, age.

I follow Linnea inside, and the first thing I see, up ahead, where a softly flickering light illuminates the darkness, are the tubes of toothpaste. They're in a small suitcase, the carry-on kind, lying open on the filthy floor. Beneath the red-and-blue logos I can see a couple of packs of condoms and some bottles of shampoo and conditioner, perfume and deodorant, and, in the other half of the case, small white boxes that I realize must be medication. There is a pile of toiletry bags to one side, makeup bags, plastic bags, a Louis Vuitton handbag.

Linnea leans toward the light, and I can tell from her back that she has relaxed a little. She beckons me closer. I take a cautious step forward and see the inner room open up. More suitcases, one with cell phones in it, another with tablets and computers, a third full of snus and cigarettes. There are shelves up against the walls, holding what look like old jam jars and cans. Some of them have been cleared and are full of bottles of spirits and wine, lined up beside a few jerricans. And next to them: china, glasses, a few paintings, and more handbags. Over in the corner there are two golf bags full of clubs, plus a large pile of something shapeless and plasticky, covered in fabric in shades of gray and black. The buckle of a seat belt catches the light, and I feel a jolt when I realize that they're child car seats.

He is sitting in the middle of the room, in a threadbare old armchair, his face half turned away from us, looking down at the floor. I can make out a pile of headphones in the black sports bag by his side, all different colors and brands. He's wearing a pair of zebra-print Bose QuietComforts, smiling to himself and nodding softly as he rummages through the bag. Those headphones are supposed to be noise isolating, but he has the music turned up so loud that it's seeping out. On the floor to one side of the armchair there is a candlestick, the kind people light at Christmas, giving the room a warm, cozy glow.

I feel a hand on my shoulder. Puma. He gives me a questioning look, mouths *is it him?* and I nod.

Everything happens very quickly after that, and it's only after a few deep breaths that I manage to process the shout and the thud and the flailing arms into some sort of coherent sequence of events and I work out more or less what must have happened when they marched over and tipped the armchair with him in it, Linnea stamping on his fingers before he had time to react, making him cry out. He instinctively rolled onto his stomach to crawl away, but Puma climbed on top of him and pushed his head down into the dirt, tore the headphones off at one side, and then leaned in and whispered *shut the fuck up, we just want to talk to you.*

I don't think, just take a few steps forward, around the sobbing, hissing, crawling heap of guys on the floor, grabbing a golf club from the bag. I've only ever played minigolf before, and this club is much heavier, the lump of metal feels like it weighs several tons. I slam it into the floor a few inches from the guy's terrified face and then lean against the handle, looking down at him. I don't feel any hatred or fear, the whole thing just seems gross and lame.

"You gave me these today," I say, holding out the sunglasses. "They're really unusual."

I crouch down, my knee practically brushing his shoulder.

"But I saw a similar pair a few days ago. On a woman. And now I want to know where she is."

"I found them."

His voice is squeaky, like it's still in the process of breaking.

I sigh.

"What do you mean, you found them? A pair of vintage glasses were just lying in the woods?"

"Someone left them in the restroom. At a gas station."

For a split second I feel a wave of relief wash over me. A gas station, a concrete location, CCTV cameras, mobile phone masts, cash registers, I'll be able to find him, it's all going to be OK, I've done it, and then I see the guy flinch and shout as something hits his face. I look up. Linnea is holding one of the candles, angling it so that the melted wax is dripping down onto his skin, into his hair, his eyes. The guy howls again and pulls his hand free to try to wipe it away, whining as more wax drips into his hair and onto his neck. I give Linnea a weary glance and she shrugs and straightens the candle again, making it stop.

"You're lying," she says coldly. "You stole them. Just like you stole everything else in here. Tell us where you got them and we'll leave."

The guy mumbles something inaudible, and I ask him to repeat himself.

"The cars," he whimpers. "I just take stuff from the cars."

"What cars?"

"The people trying to escape, who get stuck somewhere. In traffic or . . . if they've crashed or run out of juice or something. And then they just leave the cars and clear off. Sometimes they're not even locked."

I glance up at Linnea, who nods.

"It was a white Toyota," I say. "A family with kids. The trunk was full of stuff."

New York Cap, that's how I still think of him even though he isn't even wearing the hat anymore, squirms.

"Johannisholm," he eventually tells us. "By the campsite. There were a few cars there, they'd been heading back toward Rättvik but the emergency services redirected them to Karlstad."

"So why did they stop?"

"Trees," he says. "Some trees fell across the road."

"Did you see any kids?"

"I didn't see anything," he blurts out. "There was no one around by the time I got there, the car wasn't even locked."

More wax, dripping onto his throat, his cheek. She seems to be aiming for his ear, and he howls and tosses his head, but Puma holds him down. I can't take any more of this, and I motion for her to stop.

"You were hiding," Linnea says calmly once he has stopped shouting. "That's what you do. You hide and you wait to see whether they'll abandon their cars, and then you creep over. Nod if I'm right."

He nods slowly, tears streaming down his face.

"Go on."

"His wheel got stuck. They were scared of the smoke, even though the fires were miles away, so they continued on foot. Two adults and some little boys."

"How many?"

He closes his eyes, possibly because of the pain, possibly to help him focus.

"Two. Or three. It all happened so fast, they ran off in different directions. It wasn't even locked."

I try to keep my breathing calm.

"Different directions?"

"One of the kids ran into the trees, away from the road. They shouted after him for a bit, but then they left."

"What were they shouting?" I'm so eager I almost start stuttering. "What were they doing? What did they say?"

The guy shakes his head and turns his face toward the floor, as though to protect it.

"I can't remember," he mutters. "The usual."

Linnea holds up the candle again and he starts yelling that he doesn't know any more before the wax even starts dripping, shouting that he doesn't know anything, *please stop*, so we stop and Puma gets up and the guy crawls over to the corner and sits with his head in his hands, rubbing the angry red skin on his throat.

"Take whatever you want, just go," he whispers. "Please just go. There are a load of pills that'll get you high over there. And I saw a case in one of those handbags, full of earrings and necklaces and that kind of thing."

Puma peers around at the shelves, at the floor. Bends down and lifts something heavy, holds it up in the light. A chain saw.

"Johannisholm," he says, the first time he has spoken since he told the guy to shut up. "Did you say Johannisholm, by the campsite?"

The guy nods.

"It's nice there," Puma continues, looking down at the chain saw, gently stroking the chain. "But it's not exactly the wilderness. How could the trees just fall down over the road?"

New York Cap looks up at us with numb red eyes.

"My aunt," he says to me. "The one with the shovel, you know? She got a brain injury three years ago, but the government stopped her benefits. So my cousin and I, we thought . . ."

"Got it," I mumble.

He gives me an apologetic look. "When you know there are people from Stockholm driving around the place, breaking into people's cabins and stealing their quad bikes, you think it doesn't really matter, you know? Having a look around a car that might not even be locked."

I bend down and take a pack of cigarettes from the bag of stolen goods, mostly to avoid meeting his eye. Then we grab the gas and the pills and some of the alcohol, leaving the rest of it where it is.

———

It's pitch-black by the time we get to Johannisholm. I can only just make out the sign reading *ÖSTBJÖRKA 9*, and I realize that they didn't make it very far at all. Everything looks just how he described it: the fallen trees and the cars and the bags that have been pulled out, junk, clothes, plastic bags, a bloody sweater. I leave the car engine running, the headlights pointing at the fallen trees, and run over to the Toyota in tears, a sticker from the rental firm in the window, LDR384 on the license plate. I shout and tear open the back door as though what, as though there might still be someone inside? What the hell is wrong with me? My hands grope the seat and the footwell and the floor beneath the driver's seat and I find something made from glass, a bottle, no, a jar, something hard rattling inside. I crawl back out and slump down on the ground with the jar, Zack's milk tooth and a gold coin, and I whisper *you were here you were here you were here* and then I sit there for a long time before I feel them beside me, both of them, they say that it's OK, that everything is going to work out, everything is going to be fine because he's out here somewhere, and I grab the pack of cigarettes and lean back against the cool metal and light one for each of us and then I sit between them, smoking and coughing into the darkness, Linnea has opened a bottle and I take a few swigs, no one says another word, this is what Thailand would have been like.

SUNDAY, AUGUST 31

"IT WAS YOUR IDEA," MOM MUTTERS, SIPPING HER INSTANT COF-
fee in the dawn light.

"Was it?"

She nods.

"A great idea. We weren't sure how we'd be able to afford it at first, but
Didrik sold some shares from his last job. We'd been planning to save them
for you and Zack and Becka once you were older, but then we decided that
you only live once."

We're sitting in the shade outside the cabin. It's already too hot to be inside, and Mom is telling me about how she and Dad went online and found an
amazing little island off the west coast of Thailand, not Phuket or Phi Phi or
anywhere like that, they're all full of Russians and pedophiles, no, somewhere
really cool, with white sand and shallow water, a Swedish school that Zack
and I could attend. The bungalow had its own pool and a terrace looking out
to sea, black wooden furniture, a market nearby where we could buy exotic
fruit, mangoes and passion fruit and bananas, plus plenty of cozy little places
along the road selling cheap Thai food. This was right after Becka was born,
Dad had a few days off work and they were both crazy from the lack of sleep,
and when they found the house on some website they thought, let's just go.

"But it was originally your idea," she says again, stroking my hair.
"Don't you remember?"

I shake my head and try to remember, but it feels like I've been driving
around the countryside, looting preschools and breathing in smoke, full of
unrequited love for Puma my entire life.

"It was ages ago, after your dad and I had been arguing and whatnot.
You noticed that I was sometimes a bit sad in the evenings, and you came
over to me on the sofa one evening when I was feeling sad."

Mom smiles at the memory and pushes back a lock of dirty hair from her forehead. She hasn't dyed it since before Midsummer, and it's starting to look awful and gray again.

"You said that maybe we should all go away together. Somewhere warm. Just stay there and have a nice time. Start over."

The Dutch/Belgians are walking up from the lake, and they give me a cheery wave. Mom frowns suspiciously, but she doesn't say anything. She just sighs, clenches her fists, seems to be composing herself.

"I didn't want to say anything, but your dad and Becka have been staying with that . . . girl. The police went over to her apartment to arrest him the day before last, but Becka is still there, apparently. I spent all day yesterday trying to . . . sort things out, but unless I can prove that she's being mistreated there, social services say they have *insufficient resources*"—she angrily makes air quotes using her left hand—"to do anything."

"So Becka is . . ."

Mom nods doggedly.

"With that woman."

The camp has started to wake up around us. A father and his two sons trudge over to the place where we can pick up food parcels; a mother and her daughter, who looks about eleven, carry their bags over to the building, where there is already a line for the washing machines. There's a weary, hopeless atmosphere to the whole place now. Anyone who was too ill to stay has already been transferred, and the ones who kicked up a fuss and started making demands found other ways to leave, which means that the only people left are those of us who have nothing better to do than sit around and wait for something to happen. I'm thinking about Zack, spent all night trying to work out whether to tell Mom about the Toyota, but I know that she'll just want to go out into the forest to look for him, that she won't be able to handle it, and besides, we're not even allowed to leave the camp anymore, they announced that yesterday, after *several reports of suspected theft and vandalism, as well as incidents involving violence or threats of violence.*

A news team is busy making its way around the camp. There were two TV crews here yesterday, too. A dusty child is crying in the gravel, and as though on cue the team starts filming. Blond children camping in hopelessness and misery is world news, the images of us will shape a generation.

Or maybe they won't, Dad's voice says inside me. *Because things are only going to get worse, and one day you'll look back at this summer and you'll long for it.*

Mom puts her cup down.

"When Didrik and I were . . . having our little crisis, what hurt most was the idea that . . ." Her voice wavers, and she looks down at the ground. "Of you and Zack. That someone else would end up looking after you. I could survive without him, but the idea of that damn woman becoming some sort of . . . bloody . . . bonus mother to you . . ."

"Mom," I say, putting my hand on hers. "Please, Mom."

"And . . . when . . . when he came back to me, I told myself, OK, we can try, but no more kids, I'm not going to have any more children with this man . . . never, ever, ever, that part of our lives is over . . . but then little Becka . . . well, she came along . . . and now . . . I don't know if I . . ."

Her lips are wet with tears and mucus, and she wipes it away with jerky, stressed movements, but it just keeps on coming.

"We need to go home," I say.

She nods.

"But we can't, because Zack is somewhere," I continue.

She shakes her head.

"So that's why we're staying here."

Mom nods again, wipes her face, tries to compose herself.

"Yes. We have to stay here. You and me. Oh, Vilja-vanilla."

She picks up her cup again, drinks slowly. We have enough powder for two small cups of coffee a day, but there's often a long line for hot water.

"And the worst part is that I feel like I'm neglecting you," she says quietly. "That I'm just letting you drift along. It's so selfish. I mean, you're going through this too."

I sit down right beside her and we look out across the lake. I never thought it would be possible to hate such a beautiful view, but right now this feels like the most disgusting place on earth.

"What time is it?"

I check my phone. "Seven thirty."

She laughs. A rattling, sniffing sound.

"What?"

"This time tomorrow we were supposed to be on our way. The plane leaves at seven thirty. Extra legroom and everything. Choose joy."

———

The swimming area is on the edge of the campsite, near the barbecue spot. It's my shift on the lifeguard team this morning, me and the grumpy girl who worked in Rhodes, plus the two retired teachers. We're sitting at the far end of the beach, where the water is shallow a long way out, and the little kids are splashing around (and shitting and pissing, though no one has the energy to care) in front of us. There's a jetty that must be about sixty feet long slightly farther down the beach, and out in the lake there is a raft that the older kids—some of them around my age—swim out to sometimes.

The smoke has cleared a bit, and the air no longer makes my throat sting quite so much. They say that some of the fires have died down or burned out, and the sky is clear for the first time in at least a week. Maybe that's why there are so many people here today, families and teenagers from the camp, families from the local community, with blankets and cookies and lemonade. The kids from the camp play with the local kids, who have brought plastic toys and small rubber boats. Three little girls are busy burying a fourth in the sand, a few older boys with a white ball—and a portable speaker that's pumping out some nice bass—are talking about putting up a net and trying to get a beach volleyball game going, and a big group are doing cannonballs from the jetty and swimming out to the raft. I'm keeping an eye on the little ones playing by the water's edge. We're not technically supposed to bring them down here, but the child psychologist gave us permission providing they wear their inflatable armbands at all times and providing we stick to the shallows, *water and play will bring a sense of normality*, apparently. We have an Ikea bag full of beach toys, buckets and shovels and rakes that we've collected over the past few days; we have a plastic bag of different sunscreens and caps and sunglasses, we have everything.

Emil and his wife, the woman who never speaks, are sitting farther up the slope with their young son, the one who wouldn't stop screaming. The boy seems OK now, babbling away on a blanket beneath an umbrella they've found somewhere, but his father is pale and seems kind of hollow, hunched over in his underpants with the red guitar in his arms, his bandaged hand moving over the strings, humming to himself. After yesterday— I said as little as possible about what happened—the doctor decided that he needed some time off, that he needed *a bit of distance*.

He lowers the guitar to the sand and lies back beside the stroller. I see that he has a filthy bandage on his shoulder and collarbone, that there is already sand inside. He squeezes his eyes shut in the sun, lights a cigarette, and blows the smoke straight up into the air, like a chimney. His wife moves closer to the baby, holding out a squeaky toy, a pink-and-orange thing that sounds like a cat or a mouse. It feels vaguely familiar somehow, didn't Becka have one just like that?

I've been here too long, I think. *Everything has started to merge together.*

A little boy runs out onto the jetty with a big inflatable toy in the shape of a hot dog and bun. I watch him go, see his slender, bony shoulders moving like chicken wings beneath his thin skin. Even that feels familiar, making me think about the way Zack used to run around with his stupid blow-up dolphin, how he would sit on the jetty with it for hours, talking to it, after he watched some documentary that claimed that dolphins could talk to people.

One of the little kids has fallen over in the water, and I help her up and straighten her armbands. The grumpy Rhodes girl is busy peeling oranges, not even trying to hide the fact that she has scoffed four segments herself. The leaders have decided that any fresh fruit should go to the children, and we volunteers are under strict orders not to eat their rations. I'm just about to say something to her when I see the boy with the hot-dog inflatable paddling out toward the raft, and I think about Zack again, about how his foot started bleeding that day, how we started arguing, and how he snitched to Mom and Dad and I said, *shut up, you retard, I did not.*

Something in me freezes, like a phone about to run out of battery, the screen lagging for a few seconds before everything goes black.

I did not.

The boy has almost reached the raft. Six or seven guys I recognize from the mountain-biking crew have just hauled themselves up onto it, playing some kind of king of the hill–style game where they keep shoving each other into the water. They want people to notice their tanned cyclists' bodies, shouting and laughing and splashing so loudly that you can hear them all over the lake. The boy is younger than them, and he tries to clamber up onto the raft.

I didn't say we would leave him if he couldn't walk any farther. I said that he'd have to go back to the summer house. And then he lied about it and that's why I called him a retard.

Because I didn't say that at all.

One of the biker boys has grabbed another from behind. It almost looks dirty, the way they keep bumping and grinding and tugging on each other's swim trunks, trying to knock each other over, and then a third one climbs up and tries to push them both off. They spin 180 degrees and sort of lose their balance on the wet planks, the tangle of elbows and knees and stamping, slipping feet tipping slowly into the water, and the light catches the brown hot dog and the yellow bun and the thick line of ketchup faded to pink by the sun.

It's as though I'm removed from the chaos, from the mother who starts screaming, the inflatable floating back up to the surface, empty and light and almost carefree in the gentle breeze, heading off to new adventures.

The cycling boys are still messing around by the raft, they don't realize anything has happened, but more of the adults get up and start shouting and a bearded father dives in from the jetty and swims toward the spot where the little boy disappeared. I just look down at my preschool kids and make sure they get out of the water to eat their orange segments, that's the only responsibility I'm planning to shoulder today.

The water around the jetty empties out and two fathers carry the lifeless body onto the sand, the chief physician—professor is also fine—has been called, and he starts doing what I assume must be some kind of CPR, I can't see anything, the grown-ups are standing in a circle around the boy. The cycling guys are sitting quietly several feet away, and they look frightened. After a few minutes the circle breaks up and the voices become a little less tense, a sense of relief spreads across the beach and I see the mother walking away with her arm around a slender back with shoulder blades like chicken wings. The cycling boys smile cautiously and then grin at one another, but the bearded father marches over to them and yells *you'd better not even think about coming down here again.*

One of the guys says something I don't hear and the chief physician professor hurries over and says *just a knee in the forehead, could've happened anywhere, just an accident* and the father starts shouting again, *you'd better steer clear of our lake,* and the chief physician professor raises his voice slightly and says *communal swimming areas are actually* but the bearded father has already turned around and marched off in the same direction as the mother and the chicken wings, he holds up the hot-dog inflatable and shouts *fucking tent people, stay away from us* and

one of the cycling boys shouts something back

and everything seems to grind to a halt

and the bearded father turns around, several other men from Rättvik have done the same, and I see that more people have gathered in the distance, a few motorcycles gleaming in the sun, the cycling boys exchange nervous glances and then someone else shouts something and a pair of feet stumble in the sand, there's a shove, a clenched fist, the sound of a bottle breaking and

I meet Rhodes's eye and we get up and shepherd the little kids in front of us, away from the beach, away from the shouting and the swearing and the grown-ups' angry voices. It's slow going as they toddle forward, awkward in their bulky armbands; we try to make them walk in line, two and two, hand in hand, and I find myself wishing I was a child again, I want someone to take care of me instead of me taking care of others. We give up trying to keep the kids in line and start moving as fast as we can, I count them as I half run, there should be twenty of them and there are, I realize that I've started crying, people come rushing toward us from the tents and the cabins, heading down to the beach, the entire camp seems to sense what is about to happen.

We reach the fenced-off play area we've been using as the preschool and Braid Beard is waiting for us there, thank God. I blurt out something about a fight on the beach, but he stops me and snatches my walkie-talkie and the Ikea bag full of stuff.

"Carola was here," he snaps. "She wanted to talk to you."

I know it's pointless, but I still can't resist the urge to act confused. I've done so much lying these past few days that it's hard just to stop.

"Carola?"

He nods.

"Your mother. She came over because she wanted to see what you'd been doing all week, she said she was proud you were volunteering with us because you've never taken care of a child in your life."

Rhodes glares at me with her big, stupid cow's eyes.

"You're fourteen, in middle school. You don't even have a moped license. I don't know why you lied and right now I don't have time to care."

I drop to my knees in front of the children and start letting the air out of their armbands, one by one.

"But now it makes sense why there's been so much chaos whenever you went requisitioning," Braid Beard continues stiffly. "Total disaster on our part to let you out on the roads. We shouldn't have given a child that kind of responsibility."

I can still hear shouting and screaming from down on the beach, the sound of engines and police cars, and I find myself thinking that there's probably something ironic about this situation, but I don't have the energy to work out what, I feel light-headed from not eating properly in days, so I just turn around and head back to the cabin.

Mom is standing outside, talking to the mother from Mora, and she gives me a nervous smile as I approach, *is everything OK sweetie, they're saying there's a fight down on the beach?*

"Where have we looked?"

Mom's eyes dart from me to the Mora mother, down to the beach.

"Zack," I hiss. "Where have we checked?"

She seems confused at first, but then she starts blabbering, *a nationwide alert, we've spoken to the police in Mora Leksand Malung Karlstad Stockholm Gothenburg, all the hospitals and churches too, of course, and with the emergency services, several times a day, with everyone he knows back home and in his class, and I think Didrik tried to put out an alert with, what's it called, Interpol, but*

I grab her arm.

"Pack. We need to go."

She looks like she is about to say something, but then she just nods and follows me inside. We shove our few possessions into the Spider-Man backpack, she grabs her handbag, and then we set off, past the table where we sat on the first evening, past the downer girl who is drowsily peering out of her tent, past the two sisters from Uppsala who are busy heating food on a camping stove, past the bench where they usually leave the hot water for coffee and past the cabin where we slept with Becka and Dad, past the place where the now-empty medical tent is still pitched, the kids have started playing in there sometimes, the tent where I saw Martin beneath an oxygen mask and an orange blanket and knew he wasn't going to survive, that he had sacrificed himself for me.

The sound of the engine grows louder, and I see that a police car has pulled into the campsite. Two officers are leading one of the mountain-biking crew up from the beach, his forehead bleeding heavily, dripping down his throat and back and leaving big black stains on the dry ground, the sun has disappeared behind one of the dark clouds that have gathered overhead. The bearded father and a few others are walking behind the police officers, I recognize the gray-haired man who was there when they put out the fire a couple of nights ago, and the chief physician professor is running between them, trying to say something. Emil is bringing up the rear, still wearing nothing but his underpants, the guitar hanging from its black strap. Nothing but men everywhere, men who are fighting and men who are trying to keep the peace. A ring has formed around the police cars, and the group of reporters is filming the scene with a real sense of solemnity, as though this were a royal wedding or a moon landing.

"We've had enough of these hoodlums," says the gray-haired man, projecting his voice. "They've been doing drugs and groping our girls, looting our summer houses and local shops, and they very nearly just drowned a little boy in the lake. We won't put up with this anymore."

The police officers say something and then Braid Beard steps into the circle and says something about how *they're just children* and *split the time*, but the gray-haired man doesn't even look at him.

"We want you out of here. This camp is illegal."

"We'll take him in for questioning," one of the police officers says, sounding bored, "but you'll have to work out the rest of it among yourselves, we don't have time to keep the peace here."

I glance over to the road, where more people have gathered. Teenagers and old people, more motorcycles, it looks like a protest of some kind, another few photographers, a white bus with the Swedish National Radio logo on the side. There are honking horns, someone chanting *out with the riffraff*. More voices join in and the roar grows louder, *OUT WITH THE TRASH!*

The chief physician professor approaches the police officers and points to the crowd, his thin lips moving stiffly. They listen in silence and then shake their heads.

"You'll have to sort that out yourselves. We're all Swedes here, aren't we?" says the other officer, shoving the cycling guy into the backseat.

"Look." Braid Beard points, sounding relieved. "The Home Guard are here, at least."

As the police car pulls away, the large green van moves slowly, majestically, through the crowd, parking beside the table of airpots. People gather around it, expectation in the air. Something is about to happen, like a water balloon finally bursting. Maybe they've come to get us, to bring more food; we might get some clean clothes at the very least, a rumor passed through the camp earlier, about a shipment of clothes from Norway.

The door opens and Ajax leaps out, shaking her fluffy blackbrown-white coat and barking when she spots me. She tries to run over, but the leash stops her. The big bearded man climbs out after her and gives the crowd a cheery nod, raises his hand to a few faces he recognizes. I can see the disappointment in people's eyes. It's just him, no one else; there are no food parcels, no tickets home, just the same old Home Guard man as ever.

He leans into the cab and pulls out a white megaphone, presses a button. It screeches, he smiles, clears his throat.

"*Attention, everyone.*" His voice echoes over the campsite. "*This is what we're going to do: those of you staying at this temporary assembly point need to keep your distance from the community. That means no going to the beach, no walking around, no going up to the church. You need to stay here.*"

A dark murmur passes through the crowd. People exchange glances, a few shake their heads. The man clears his throat and wipes the sweat from his forehead.

"*Water use is also far too high. Showers will now be accessible between eighteen hundred and twenty hundred hours only. And as for washing up and the like . . .*"

But that is as far as he gets before it starts raining gravel. Small lumps of rock hitting the ground in front of his boots, dropping from the sky one after another. I look around and see the two sisters from Uppsala. They're standing close together, bending down for more pebbles. Braid Beard is on his way over to them to tell them to stop, but the gravel just keeps on coming, a few young boys have joined in too, throwing it at his feet and legs at first, then higher up. It clatters against the metal body of the van and the Home Guard man holds the megaphone up to his face to protect himself. The grown-ups are shouting over one another and I see the downer girl trudge over to the table of airpots, the kind with handles on the lids, and as she unfolds one and bends down to ready herself I have a sudden flashback to my athletics days: a couple of girls practicing shot put, or maybe they were learning to throw the discus, putting their entire body into the movement. The downer girl swings the thermos of coffee across the gravel, and there is a dull thud as it hits his upper body, making him sway and drop to his knees, where he peers up at the kids with a look that seems more angry than afraid.

And then Emil steps forward, still barefoot, still wearing nothing but his underpants. He holds up his arms against the pebbles, moves in front of the Home Guard man to protect him. No, he takes the guitar off and holds it at the very end of the neck, swings it down on the back of the Home Guard man's head with all his might, the sound of breaking wood and

Braid Beard shouts and

the crowd has started surging in from the edge of the campsite, a few on motorcycles, black helmets and leather jackets and

the Dutch/Belgians are fighting with a couple of the boys who were at the barbecue area and

Mom's hand is in mine and her voice is whispering *don't look don't look* and

Ajax trots between the bodies, her leash trailing behind her, over to me, rubbing against my legs, I remember saying *roll over* and *give me your paw* and then I remember that I googled other commands, I try to recall them, scroll through the page in my mind, things like *stay* and *out* and *find*, then I grab the chain around her neck and bend down and hiss *speak*

and she barks, she barks so loudly that it echoes, booms, barks so loudly that her entire body starts trembling: a rough, cutting sound that makes people pause and instinctively pull away. I see the chief physician professor shrink back and lower a hand to his crotch, but Ajax just keeps barking. I can feel the quivering muscles in her powerful neck and I force back the sense of panic, the primal fear, force back the urge to let go of her leash and run away and instead keep shouting *speak speak speak* as I lead her through the muddle of people turning running creeping away, over to the Home Guard man, who is lying on his front, a growing pool of blood around his head, splinters of wood and pieces of metal and strings all around him

and I bend down and pick up the megaphone, a red button, I press it.

"*This is what we're going to do,*" I say. No one is listening, Ajax still growling and barking. I pat her head and whisper *quiet* and she growls softly and stops. My God, what a pro.

"*This is what we're going to do,*" I repeat. "*We're going to empty the camp today. Everyone has to leave. No more tents, no more stuff. We're going to pack up and leave. Today.*"

They glower up at me in confusion, pointing, whispering. Braid Beard is shaking his head, Mom looks terrified, Rhodes grins and says *and go where?* and some of the others are shouting the same thing, *and go where?* and one of the Rättvik locals, a guy on a motorcycle, says *all the roads are closed, so where are you going to go?* but I just stare at him and raise the megaphone again and point to their town.

"We're coming to stay with you. We're going to sleep on your sofas. We're going to use your showers and toilets, and if we have to save water then we'll all do it together; we're going to eat your food, and once the food runs out we'll find more together. We're going to take care of our kids together, and if we run into any problems, we'll figure them out together."

Someone laughs, someone else swears, but I stay where I am with Ajax, trying to stop myself from shaking. On the ground in front of me, the Home Guard man's breathing is heavy, wheezing.

"You think this is hard, but it's going to get so much worse and more horrible and crazier every year, with fires and storms and pandemics and flooding and refugees and chaos and hell, and you can't even cope with a few days of this?"

But they aren't listening any longer, they're screaming at each other, the bearded father and the chief physician professor and Braid Beard and the motorcycle guy and all the others, and I'm just a fourteen-year-old drifting through the universe, a fourteen-year-old whose parents are in crisis, a fourteen-year-old who fell for the wrong guy, an embarrassing loser, and I try to look at them, to make sense of their faces, I should tell them that I've been rotting away in this worthless shitty camp for a week now and enough is fucking enough, I should tell them that my sister disappeared, my brother, my dad, a man I pretended was my granddad, and then I start thinking about Martin when he died and everything that has happened since and the days press down on me like some kind of gross, fatty whipped cream and I smell chicken-flavor noodles and realize that I'm about to pass out from hunger and a slim white hand reaches out and takes the megaphone from me.

"ATTENTION!" Linnea shouts.

She's wearing her ugly blue uniform again, a little scarf, her hair in neat braids, and her voice is soft but firm, used to giving orders. Behind her I can see ten, twenty, thirty other young people and grown-ups in the same uniforms, all lined up in a row.

"WE'RE FROM RÄTTVIK'S SCOUT TROOP, AND WE'D LIKE EVERYONE TO GATHER HERE IN TWO HOURS TO GET OR-

GANIZED, TAKE DOWN THE CAMP, AND DIVVY UP BEDS, WE ASK EVERYONE TO . . ."

She keeps talking but I don't have the energy to listen; the door of the big green van is still open and I tear off the backpack and climb up into the front seat. Ajax jumps in after me and I glance over to Mom, who looks completely nonplussed, but she still makes her way over, running on auto-pilot. The key is in the ignition, and I'm convinced that someone will try to stop me, that someone will see what I'm doing and say *what the hell do you think you're playing at?* but nothing happens and Mom makes her way around the van and gets into the passenger seat without a word, her bag in her arms, and I start the engine and put the van in gear and we pull away, away, I see Emil standing alone down by the shore, the bandage on his shoulder has come loose and the wound has started bleeding again, he's staring out at the dark water, his back shaking, the wind has picked up and big, dark clouds have begun racing across the sky, it looks like he's crying or laughing, maybe both, but more than anything he looks free.

We turn off, toward the road, out of the campsite. The people outside have started to split up, and those that are left move out of the way as the huge van approaches. It's so much more powerful than the car, and I feel bigger, stronger, clumsier and really hope that I won't have to do any re-versing. We sail out onto the road we walked along the morning we were supposed to go to the station and catch a train home and Mom and Dad got into a fight, that's nothing but a hazy memory now, something that hap-pened when I was still a child.

I glance up at the rearview mirror to see the campsite disappear behind us, to see the sign reading *SILJANBADET CAMPSITE—DALARNA'S RIVIERA*, and I smile to myself, notice a blue moped following us. I have to brake for an old man in a wheelchair, and the moped slaloms between streetlamps, up onto the pavement, past me and around, coming to a halt right in front of us, in the middle of the road, and I slam on the brakes and get out.

There is no one at the station today, there haven't been any trains for almost a week now, the one Dad and Becka got on might have been the last. Puma takes off his helmet and I try to remember where the table with the water bottles was, whether it was here or closer to the road. I decide that it was right here, that I was standing in this exact spot when we met for the first time, and he says *wait* and I shake my head and he moans *let me come with you* and I shake my head again.

"Stay here," I say. "Help her. She needs you more."

His fingers brush the handlebars on his moped, and I get right up close to him and whisper *but look me up later, Robert* into his ear, and he doesn't speak, doesn't nod, just wraps his arms around me and my lips move along his cheek and jaw to his mouth. It's a moment that contains cute kittens and trips to New York, student parties and hungover pizzas, money cars jobs, first apartments, first babies and first divorces, first gray hairs; it contains everything you might find in a shitty, pathetic, miserable little life in which every day without him is a day wasted.

"I can't," he whimpers into my hair. "I can't, Vilja, I can't do this, it's you, it's only you."

I kiss him again, one last time. Sorry Linnea, sorry God, sorry world.

And then I whisper:

"Fucking live with it."

A stack of wood, an anthill. The sign is yellow, with a red frame, the letters black and angular. I remember wondering whether it was a real road sign, the kind you need to memorize to pass your written test, but the image is of a child running after a ball and an old woman with a stick and a blazing sun, and the sign itself reads *WILD CHILDREN AND SENIORS AT PLAY*.

I'm grateful for the silence. I thought Mom would ask a bunch of questions, about everything that happened in the camp and about the dog and the boy and where we're going and why, but it's as though she has retreated into herself. Ajax has her head in her lap and she is stroking her with one hand, fiddling with her phone with the other, like she can't manage anything else. All my energy is going into staying awake and driving the van and not getting my hopes up. That's my real problem, that I'm constantly disappointed.

Still, I have to break the silence eventually. I say, *he was always so scared of Hansel and Gretel, he hated that story more than anything else but he kept asking for it anyway, and the worst part wasn't the witch or the gingerbread house, it was that Hansel and Gretel were led away and then got lost in the woods, and for years he kept scraps of paper plastic beads crumbs of bread in his pockets so that he could leave a trail if he ever needed to, that was how I worked it out, that he'd try to make his way home.*

Mom says *what, who are you talking about* just as the first raindrop hits the window.

The area around the cabins is deserted, no sign of anyone. All we can hear is the soft rustling of the trees in the wind and the rain. The neighbors' house we used to play in, the trampoline we borrowed from some old woman, the upside-down rowboat, the tree where Dad started building a tree house but then gave up. It's all still here, the same as ever and yet different somehow.

The car is still parked outside the house. We get out of the van and Mom walks over to the door, tries the handle, and cries out when it opens.

"We locked it." Her voice is trembling. "I locked it, I know I did."

"He knew where the spare key was," I say. "Dad showed him."

She shouts *Zack* and runs inside. I follow her in. His Harry Potter book is open in the kitchen, the Monopoly board neatly packed away in its box beside it. The whole place smells musty and disgusting, like garbage and piss and shit; there are empty bottles of mineral water, cans and jars all neatly lined up on the countertop, and you can see the order in which he has been living: first the pineapple and the halved pears, then the jam, then the sweet corn and the pickled gherkins, the pesto and the black olives, and last of all the chopped tomatoes, sardines, and mayonnaise, which I know he hates.

Ajax lumbers around the house, seemingly stressed out by all the new smells. She quickly comes back to me and rubs up against my legs with a soft growl. Mom shouts *Zack* again, and I hear her stomping around upstairs, but I know he isn't here, I got here too late, I wasn't quick enough. I check the cupboards and see that everything edible is gone; you can't live here without water or electricity.

She comes back down and my heart breaks when I see that she's holding his blanket, his old summer house blanket with Pippi Longstocking on it, a hand-me-down from me after I refused to sleep under something so babyish. She clutches it, holds it to her face, sobs *please God please God*, and I leave her to it for a few seconds, let her get the worst of it out of her system before I say *Mom, give me the blanket.*

She hands it over without a word, and I press it to my nose and smell my little brother: his unwashed hair and the sweaty scent that has started to come from his pits, the faint stench of pee.

And then I hold it down to Ajax and whisper *search*.

There's a hint of autumn in the air as I walk down to the lake behind the dog. The rain is coming down harder now, and it suddenly feels chilly. A shiver passes down my spine and I'm a little girl again, walking beside Ella with her red raincoat and those stupid rosettes in her hair, trying to seem cool because she has a big black dog on a leash, but I don't care because the dog is the cutest thing I've ever seen and we walk down to the water together and right there, at the very end of the jetty, I see a pale, skinny back. Mom cries out and runs past me, she looks so old when she runs, lumbering, staggering, she shouts again as she reaches the jetty, the boards are wet and slippery because of the rain and she stumbles after just a few feet, for a split second I think she's about to fall into the water like someone from a silly YouTube clip, but she just drops to her knees and shouts again, still crawling forward.

Ajax wants to keep going, wants to follow the scent all the way over, but I tug on her lead and then slump down on the old bench, the one where he always used to sit and look out at the water. I give them a moment alone out there on the jetty. Being a mother means getting torn up in a way that never quite stops bleeding, it means breaking over and over again. There are certain words that only a mother can ever say, tears that only a mother can cry.

So I just sort of sit here, thinking that maybe the old man is still beside me somehow, that maybe we're here together. I close my eyes and try to feel him, the rustling of the trees, the roar of the raindrops hitting the surface of the lake, the scent of rain.

MONDAY, SEPTEMBER 1

THE NIGHT IS NEVER-ENDING. THE RAIN IS TORRENTIAL AND WE'RE traveling through time, past screeching machines, smoking swarms of wasps, through a howling, cold emptiness. People shout for us to stop, holding their babies in the air as though they're trying to make an offering to some merciless god. Police officers and soldiers wave us past with tired, angry, dejected faces. In some of the places that were on fire, the scorched earth is now drenched, sending spirals of thin white mist into the sky above the forests.

Zack and Ajax are asleep in one corner of the cab. We're listening to the radio. There have been more shootings in Gothenburg, likely gang related. In Blekinge, a place called Ronneby has been overtaken by a group of migrants from Syria and Iraq.

We drive through deserted towns. We pass barricades, find routes around fallen trees and abandoned cars. We drive down dark forest roads, through hazy clearings, through puddles that must be at least a foot deep. We take turns driving the heavy vehicle. While I drive, she scrolls on her phone; while Mom drives, I sleep. She stops to get food somewhere, and when I wake she has a plastic bag of bananas and sausage sandwiches, and she has also filled the tank a little. I don't ask how she managed it, just wolf down a sandwich and drift off again.

More news comes through. The heavy rainfall over Scandinavia has extinguished many of the fires and stopped the spread of the ones that are still burning, but the flash floods have also caused a huge amount of damage. There are multiple road closures, houses that have collapsed; several people drowned in their basements while they were trying to save their possessions, and in Kristianstad seventeen people in a rest home died because they couldn't be evacuated quickly enough as the ground floor filled with water. Around a thousand Swedes are feared missing or dead after the fires, and the damage is estimated to be worth hundreds of billions of kronor. On social media, people have started debating whether there should be green conditions to the compensation payments, requiring any houses that are rebuilt to be fitted with solar panels. Another debate is focused on the illegal immigrants left homeless as a result of the disaster, and the fact that they won't receive any government support or be offered free medical attention if they suffered smoke inhalation. An author and award-winning cultural commentator gives an interview: *The scientists have differing views, of course*, he mutters, *but the most extreme doom-mongers think the climate will be two to three degrees warmer in a hundred years' time, something I highly doubt. And even if they're right, I honestly see no reason to get hysterical about it. The climate debate has become too emotional and judgmental.*

There are reports that the former tennis star Anders Hell has died following an accident, and someone has set off a car bomb in Malmö. Mom smiles to herself.

"This reminds me of your dad," she says. "We got stuck in Åre one Christmas, and Didrik somehow managed to find us a huge car and drove us down to Mom's."

"Was I there?"

"Yeah, you were there. It was you and me and Dad. He drove all night through the snow."

"Sounds cozy."

She shakes her head, a sad look on her face.

"Actually, no," she sighs. "We argued a lot and were angry with each other. Sometimes I think that might have been when we . . . first ran into trouble. That it was when all the bad things started."

"What were you arguing about?"

"I honestly can't remember. Just something."

═══

She's short, much smaller than I imagined, and nowhere near as cute as in her pictures. Her face is round, with perfect skin, and her eyes are big and beautiful, but without all the makeup she actually looks pretty ordinary.

Ajax comes over, sniffing and wagging her tail in the grand entrance hall. She strokes her neck, nails painted baby pink.

"Come in."

I've never been in an apartment like this before, the kind of place where a rich person might live in a TV show, several huge living rooms and a massive kitchen opening out onto a rain-drenched terrace. The door is ajar, and the cool, fresh air smells like greenery.

"She's in here," says the girl, walking over to a smaller room without any windows, full of old leather furniture and a wide-screen TV. "In our girl cave. She's still asleep."

On the double bed, my sister is sleeping in a pair of pink pajamas, her face pressed against a pillow, arms and legs outstretched. Something inside me seems to click, and though it feels crazy to lie down on someone else's bed, I crawl up onto the soft mattress and rub my face against her belly, breathe in the sour tang of milk and puke from Snuggly, mixing with the scent of her clean pajamas. Time seems to jolt and come to a halt.

"She's been OK. Cried a little at first, but she's been eating and sleeping fine."

The girl yawns.

"They're not really that interesting at this age, are they? They just eat and poop and sleep. Doesn't really seem that appealing, honestly."

"Was that why you didn't want him?"

"Who?"

"Dad."

She frowns at the question I can hardly believe I just asked.

"Nah. Or maybe. A combination of things. I guess he didn't really want me either."

A few seconds pass. She seems to be thinking. I rub my face against the pink pajamas and breathe in her smell.

"If we're being perfectly honest, it was more you I wanted," she eventually says. "I saw pictures of you and Zack and wanted the two of you. Baking buns, painting eggs at Easter. Picking you up and dropping you off. Going shopping together. It would've been perfect, being a kind of extra mom to you. I would've loved that."

I nod.

"Me too, I think. Though the other way around."

"Maybe we can stay in touch?"

"I don't think Mom would like that. But sure, maybe. Sometime."

I get down from the bed and take the sunglasses out of my pocket.

"You can have these. As thanks for looking after my sister."

She smiles.

"Ivana Helsinki. I've already got a pair."

"I know, that's how I recognized them."

I walk back over to Ajax. Kiss her softly on the head, pick up her leash and hand it to Melissa.

"You can have her too, she's really nice. A Bernese mountain dog. I can't take her home."

She gives me a sleepy smile.

"Super cute. What's her name?"

I shrug.

"Just make something up."

We say goodbye, and I lift Becka from the bed. She sighs against my shoulder, the sweet scent of sleep and formula on her breath.

"Let's go," I whisper, grabbing the red diaper bag and heading back through the kitchen, toward the door. I hear Melissa making her way out onto the terrace, can hear from her chirping voice that she is filming herself with the dog. *Cupcake and I are going for a walk on our roof terrace. Look, Cupcake, we've got dog roses and lemons and mangoes and all sorts of things, you can pee on them if you want, it'll probably do them good.*

"Let's go."

———

It's almost too easy, I think as I drive through the puddles. The roadblocks have been taken down, though lots of windows are still broken. Either that or they're boarded up with sheets of wood.

No one is going to believe that everything worked out this easily in the end.

It's morning, and I'm driving my mom and siblings down the motorway, past the wrecked cars that are glittering after the rain, past a burned-out gas station and a McDonald's covered in graffiti. The road up ahead is deserted and we're running on empty, but if you're wondering whether this story really is true, whether it isn't all just make-believe and lies and crazy fantasies, scroll through your social media feeds and ask yourselves just how realistic the world seems.

My head is fuzzy, I'm sick of driving. The sun is shining straight into my eyes, and I think *if you say this sounds improbable, I'll tell you to look out the window and describe what you see.*

Becka whimpers in Mom's arms. Zack is sitting with his forehead to the window, staring out at the landscape racing by. In his hand, he is clutching the jar containing his tooth and the gold coin, treasure from a lost world.

If you say you don't believe my happy ending, I'll say that it's neither happy nor an ending.

Because there are no endings. Even if I stop telling my story, it'll still go on.

Never believe that it's over. Never believe you've made it home.

None of you will ever make it home.

"Do you know what I hate most?" the blond guy in the suit asks as he absentmindedly checks the price tag on a dark jacket.

His friend shakes his head.

"Getting full."

The duty-free shop has a long rail of shirts, the majority of them white and pale blue. There are a couple of suits, too, plus the usual jeans and T-shirts, most of them that kind of preppy V-neck style I don't really like. A few summer dresses and blouses, shorts and underwear. Nothing in Becka's size, but Melissa had packed the diaper bag full of clean, fresh clothes.

"We were in Tuscany over Midsummer, me and Hanna and the kids. Eating dinner in an Italian restaurant, and everything tasted so damn good. Red wine and pasta and seafood and entrecôte, the whole lot."

The guy says entrecôte like the typical vulgar upper-class Swede, *ontraycoat*, and I have to resist the urge to correct him, stop it, that's Dad's thing, not mine.

"And then they bring out tiramisu, and you have, like, *one* goddamn spoonful and you're all ufffff. It was *deee*licious, but I just couldn't manage it."

I grab some boxers, panties, socks, and T-shirts, some jeans and blouses and short-sleeved shirts, enough to *keep us going for a few days*, as Mom put it.

"And the same thing happened the next week, too," the guy in the suit continues. "Hanna and I flew to Sydney for her friend's wedding. The day before: best barbecue I've ever had. Chicken and sausages and completely insane racks of lamb."

He shakes his head and rolls his eyes at his friend, who seems a little absent, just looking at things on the racks.

"And last weekend we were out at Henrik and Lisa's place in Djursholm for a crayfish party. I tried to save myself, but they had all these damn dips and sauces and pies and cheeses, and you know how it is, you just want to try everything, but then the chocolate cake came out and I practically ate till I puked."

I head over to the register. The blond idiot in the suit is ahead of me, holding two black suits, two white shirts, and two white ties.

"This should be OK, right?" he says to his friend, a teenager, I realize, only a few years older than me, tall and fat.

"But do people wear white ties at funerals?" the boy asks stiffly.

"Sure, if you're a close relative."

"That only applies in Sweden," the salesgirl says as she bags their things. The blond smiles.

"Then we'll make our own rules. The old man would've liked that."

"Where are you going?" the salesgirl asks.

"Melbourne," he replies, tapping his card on the reader. "Winter there right now, nice and cool, it's going to be great!"

"Yeah, after the temperatures we've been having here," says the salesgirl. "The hottest June, July, and August on record, apparently."

The fat boy shakes his head.

"That perspective is all wrong. This past summer wasn't the hottest; it's the coldest we'll ever live through going forward."

The salesgirl is quiet for a moment, clears her throat.

"Yeah, I . . . that's kind of horrible to think about."

The blond man smiles and puts a hand on the younger guy's shoulder.

"Totally agree, better we don't bother, bro. Karolina's waiting for us in the lounge. We've got time for a drink, to toast Dad. He would've liked that, too."

They walk away, and I pay for our clothes and then make my way over to the gate. Dad has just arrived, short of breath in one of the plastic chairs, Becka on his lap.

"Were you in prison, Dad?" Zack asks quietly, looking up at the bandage around his head.

"No, no, sweetie, they just wanted to talk to me, they were from the chat police. And then I got to stay somewhere a bit like a hotel."

"Chat police?!"

Dad nods. "Yeah, they were all chat, chat, chat."

"So instead of a rule book they had a dictionary!"

"And instead of pistols, they had cough drops!"

"And . . ." Zack's face lights up in triumph, he must have come up with something really good now. ". . . and if there's a robber, the police have, like, a speech bubble, and they catch them in a lasso of chat, chat, chat!"

Mom pulls the passports from her purse and then starts scrolling on her phone.

They call our flight at the gate, and we get in line again. What I love about airports is the feeling of stepping into a bubble, like you're already in the new place even though you're still at home. I remember when we flew to Florida once, during winter break, people at the airport were wearing shorts and T-shirts even though there was snow and slush outside; some were already wearing sandals, a bottle of sunscreen sticking out of a pocket. I remember how fascinated I was by the idea of being in two worlds at once, mid-leap, in a buzz of expectation and longing and Adventure.

Finally, I think. *Life can finally begin.*

I take Becka in my arms and go first, Mom behind me with our passports, Dad holding Zack's hand. I turn around and study my family, Mom smiling softly when she sees Dad messing about with Zack, Dad glancing up at me with a dumb look on his face. I whisper *is everything OK?* and he says *yup, Vilja-vanilla, I'm just so happy, I can't remember when I was last this happy, everything is perfect right now.*

There is another security check, and I try to take Becka through the scanner or whatever it's called, but a man in a blue uniform stops me, says we have to go through one by one, even babies, those are the new rules. A woman in an identical uniform drifts over and smiles tenderly; *I'll take her through the metal detector*, she says, *that's how we do it these days, come on, little one* and then she holds out a small polka-dot rabbit and smiles as though paradise were awaiting.

Mom and Dad are about to say something, we've already been through so much, we can't take any more, but they keep quiet. The rules are there for a reason, after all; this is Sweden.

Becka reaches for the rabbit and I press my face to her cheek, *it'll be OK, sweetie, everything will be OK*, I whisper, *dontworrydontworrydontworry*, and then I hand my sister to the stranger.

ABOUT THE AUTHOR

Jens Liljestrand (b. 1974) is a critically acclaimed journalist and writer who made his debut in 2003 with the reportage book *Made in Pride*. He has been a critic for the newspapers *Sydsvenskan* and *Dagens Nyheter* and was a long-serving editor of the culture section of *Expressen*.

His biography of Vilhelm Moberg, *The Man in the Woods* (*Mannen i skogen*, 2018), was a bestseller in his native Sweden and was nominated for the prestigious August Prize.

His latest novel, *Even If Everything Ends*, was originally published by Albert Bonniers Förlag in September 2021 to great critical acclaim.